"You're barking up the wrong tree," voice bouncing off filthy walls as he moves closer. "She won't open that door."

I smile at the voice, non-muffled without the door between us, and glance at Jeremy to see if he understands the man's comment. His face surprises me. Tense, his back leaving the wall, his posture stiff as he straightens. I have forgotten that he knows Simon, that they have bitched countless times over the package of pills that he delivers monthly.

Simon pauses, a hitch in his step, when he is ten feet away, his eyes warily recognizing Jeremy. "Oh. Hey, man."

The druggie's gaze jumps left, and stares me up and down, his eyes taking their time. "What—delivery boy bring you to see the freak show?" he cackles. "I've got stuff a lot more exciting in my place. If you want…" He steps closer, smiling, and I see Jeremy's fists clench.

I smile brightly, using the young innocent smile, the one that my clients love, the one that dissolves all tension and puts them all at ease. He moves closer and I jump into action, bringing my knee up quickly, into the soft flesh between his sweatpanted legs, the hard impact causing his eyes to tightly close, his torso doubling over as all air leaves his chest in one brittle exhale. He wheezes and I bring my forearm up, under his chin, and press hard, pushing him back against the wall, my four-inch heels putting us at eye level with each other. "Hi Simon," I drawl, watching his eyes jump to mine, a hesitant recognition of my voice in their red-rimmed depths. "Welcome to the freak show."

DO NOT DISTURB

A DEANNA MADDEN NOVEL

A. R. TORRE

REDHOOK

www.redhookbooks.com

Redhook Books/Orbit
Hachette Book Group
1290 Avenue of the Americas
New York, NY 10104
www.HachetteBookGroup.com

Printed in the United States of America

RRD-C

First edition: April 2015

10 9 8 7 6 5 4 3 2 1

Redhook is an imprint of Orbit, a division of Hachette Book Group.
The Redhook name and logo are trademarks of Hachette Book Group, Inc.

The Hachette Speakers Bureau provides a wide range of authors for speaking events. To find out more, go to www.hachettespeakersbureau.com or call (866) 376-6591.

The publisher is not responsible for websites (or their content) that are not owned by the publisher.

Library of Congress Cataloging-in-Publication Data

Torre, A. R.
   Do not disturb / A R. Torre.—First edition.
      pages ; cm.—(A Deanna Madden novel)
      Summary: "Too much of a good thing can kill you... I broke the rules. I left, I killed, I loved it. But it was for a good cause, so that should count for something, right? But it wasn't enough. I'm afraid it will never be enough. Now that taste of freedom, of normalcy, calls to me. But so does the blood."—Provided by publisher.
      ISBN 978-0-316-40445-7 (softcover)—ISBN 978-1-4789-8661-4 (audio book)—ISBN 978-0-316-40444-0 (ebook) 1. Serial murderers—Fiction. 2. Psychological fiction. I. Title.
   PS3620.O5887D6 2015
   813'.6—dc23
                                                            2014043667

To Dad.
Thank you for always being proud of me; you are the best father
a girl could ever wish for. I am so lucky to have you.

DO
NOT
DISTURB

IN MARATHON, FLORIDA, on mile two of the old Seven Mile Bridge, there is a tree. It has grown out of a crack on the pavement, starting out as a weed, then a stalk, and is now a teenage pine, standing five feet tall, with branches that extend out the width of a car. It squats on a barren strip of concrete that is the old bridge, pavement stretching for miles in both directions before dead-ending into air, sections of the bridge destroyed—years ago—in an attempt to forbid human weight to ever rest upon it again. Now the island of hot asphalt is home only to birds, rain, salt air, and this tree. It is an impossibility, this pine, growing in such an inhospitable place. No dirt or nutrients to pull from, stiff, unyielding concrete surrounding its roots. Yet it has grown. From a weed to a tree, its roots have pushed aside concrete, fed on nothing yet thrived regardless, surviving hurricanes, tornados, and droughts, springing branches and needles with uncontained gusto.

I saw the tree when I was fifteen, my head resting against a warm window, headphones on, music drowning out the incessant sounds of Summer and Trent. Our family had flown to Miami, then rented an SUV and driven down to Key West. The tree had caught my attention, my eyes sticking to it as the vehicle swept alongside it, our tires on the new bridge, my view interrupted seconds later as my father drove on. At the time, the tree fascinated me.

Now, it terrifies me.

It makes me realize that no matter how much I may starve my desires, may shield myself from triggers and pitfalls...*it* can survive. The blackness in my mind can live, can grow into something too big to control.

PART I

"Kiss me. Now."

CHAPTER 1

I REMEMBER FIRST-DATE jitters. My first date was with a boy named Josie. His name should have been the first tip-off. The second should have been his excellent sense of style, movie selection (*Hairspray*), and his propensity to wave his hands in the air excitedly when describing the latest season of *America's Next Top Model*. But I was fifteen, naïve, and spent the entire dinner tongue-tied and nervous, clasping and unclasping my hands underneath the Ruby Tuesday table while wondering what I'd do with my hands when he kissed me at the end of the date.

He didn't kiss me. There was an awkward handshake before I fled inside my home, the rest of the night spent bawling into my pillow while I dissected every piece of the date and tried to figure out where I went wrong. Being born without a penis. That's where I went wrong. If only I'd had a fairy godmother patting my shoulder consolingly while giggling into her fabulously embroidered handkerchief.

Now, eight years later, those first-date jitters are back. But they are of a completely different variety. I stare across the table at Jeremy, and wonder if I will make it through the date without trying to kill him.

The good news is, he is most definitely straight. Straight in an all-American beautiful way that makes Josie look like last week's lunch meat. I focus on his features, a strong face housing thick lashes that frame deep brown eyes. Eyes that are watching me closely, a smile playing across the sexy mouth that hides a perfect set of pearly whites. A smile. He should not be smiling. I frown at him, which prompts a laugh from his side of the table.

"Stop scowling." He reaches across and grabs my hand, capturing it before I can slide it under the table. "It only makes you sexier and..." He pauses, carefully examining the surface of my hand, his large palms dwarfing my smaller one. "I can't have pissed you off already. We haven't even ordered."

Ordered. My villainous thoughts get distracted by the concept of restaurant food. I, since my one successful venture into the light, have started to tinker with the idea of grocery shopping. Stopping my food-by-mail program and entering the world of raw meat, fresh fruit, and local produce. Surely my nutrition is a worthy excuse to leave the apartment. I close my mind to that justification and look at the menu, gingerly touch the edge, flip it open, and stare at the possibilities.

All thoughts of death and mayhem disappear when I see the steaks, scattered among the images casually, as if it is no big deal to have a hunk of red, fresh meat—one that will be touched by the sizzle of the grill and nothing else. I swallow, worried that I will physically drool all over the laminated pages.

We are interrupted by a waitress, an exhausted stick of deep wrinkles and frizzy hair, who barely glances our direction as she pulls out her order pad. "What'll you have?"

Jeremy looks at me. "Please, go ahead."

My eyes dart across the page, indecision gnawing at my gut as I scan from one delicious entrée to the next. "I'll have the filet, please."

"Side?" she drawls.

"Baked potato, please. Loaded." The thought of·fresh sour cream and, *ohmygod*, real butter sends a shot of euphoria through me. Jeremy sends me an odd glance and I realize, my cheeks stretched tight, that I am beaming.

"Salad?"

"Yes, please. With Ranch. And could I also get a side of broccoli?" My eyes trip and stall over the vegetable list. "And mushrooms," I quickly add, her pen stalling as she glances my way. Her pen. It is cheap, a Bic whose end has been chewed down to a twisted, gnarled end of missing plastic. I wonder, my eyes catching on it, if—jabbed quickly enough—it would stab through the tanned skin of her neck. "And green beans." Her mouth twists in a grimace of sorts. "Please," I add. *Please.* Please let me stand over your body and watch you die. I'll add a *pretty please* if you promise to bleed heavily.

Jeremy orders quickly, and FrizzyOMonday flees, as if she knows she is escaping death. I watch her retreat, pulled back to the present by Jeremy's voice.

"Hungry?" His wry tone gives me pause, and my gaze flicks back to him.

"I'm sorry. I didn't think about the cost." My eyes drop to the menu. "I planned on paying for my portion."

"It's a date, you're not paying for your half. And I don't care about the cost. It's just…" He shrugs, smiling at me as if I am an interesting display. "You're so tiny. I guess I expected, with all the diet boxes that are delivered, that you'd be a dry salad girl."

I grin. "The diet plans are easy. And don't require much thought. I haven't…it's been a while since I've had real food." I don't expand on the thought. He knows. Knows that I've locked myself in my apartment for three years. Knows that, other than my road trip of mayhem two weeks ago, this is the first time I've left the sanctuary of apartment 6E.

"Maybe I could cook for you sometime."

I smile weakly. "Let's see how tonight goes."

"You've been good so far."

"She hasn't brought the steak knives out yet."

He laughs, as if it is funny, as if there is no real threat of danger. I frown.

"Stop doing that," he warns. "And please, relax a bit. I'm not gonna let you hurt me." *I'm not gonna let you hurt me.* An odd statement for a first date, but one that fits us well.

"Don't be so sure you can stop me."

"Can you be naked again the next time you try? I enjoyed that." His serious tone catches me off guard, and laughter suddenly bubbles out of me, uncontrolled in its erratic path.

It is, quite possibly, the strangest first date in history. But I behaved. I gripped my steak knife tightly and avoided putting it through his skin. I focused my attention on the food, diving full force into the deliciousness that was unpreserved, unboxed cuisine. He was amused, chewing his food slowly as he watched me, staring with an awe that was unnerving. Undeserved. Then he ordered every dessert they had, and watched with unreserved glee as I dug in. We left the restaurant by six and, fifteen minutes later, we're back at my doorstep, the sight of this side of the door unfamiliar, foreign.

I place my hands on the steel, noticing that the 6E metallic sticker is slightly crooked and barely hanging on, and that my doorknob is brass, while all of the other hardware silver. Of course it's different. Mine is the only one designed to lock someone in as opposed to keeping strangers out. I turn to Jeremy nervously, fingering my key as I try to figure out what to do.

I am out of practice, and unsure of my level of control. I feel panic grip my chest, the hallway entirely too small, the warmth and scent of his body, *right there*, and all I have to do is reach out and we will touch.

He leans against the opposite wall, his posture loose and relaxed, as far away from me as he can reasonably be, my tension easing slightly at the move. "Thank you," he says softly. "For the date."

I blush, the words ones I should have thought to say. I am out of practice, but am fairly sure that the girl typically thanks the man, especially when he foots the bill for half the menu. "Thank you."

"I'd like to kiss you, if you're comfortable with that."

I hesitate. This is stupid. We spent three days together, two weeks ago, our bodies wrapped around each other during the night, his mouth on mine countless times during that period. I know his kiss, know that I want it—want more than just it. But two weeks ago—I was broken during that time, and he was healing me. Now, I am back to normal, and my urges are as strong as they've ever been. I worry over what will happen when he is that close, worry how my psychotic mind will handle the experience. Whether it will slink to the background and lie low, allowing me to enjoy the experience. Or, if it will bare its teeth and come out to play. I drop my keys on the floor and hold out my hands. "Could you hold me still? Just in case." I avoid his eyes when I say the words, my gaze fixated on my wrists, outstretched and waiting for his touch. Then I feel him step closer, see his strong hands wrap, one wrist in each hand, and pull.

He drags me forward, his hands spreading mine and swinging them around my body, till they are joined at the small of my back, the new position bringing his body flush to mine, his arms wrapped around me, my face in the crook of his neck, his breath quickening as he walks us backward till our hands hit my door and his body pins me to it.

It is too much, the rush of sensations. Sensations that I have forgotten, either intentionally or through neglect. The hard press of hips against mine, the hard brush of him against the thin material of my dress, one leg sliding in between and spreading my legs, my pelvis grinding, without thought, on his thigh, the movement causing a quick intake of breath to hiss through his lips.

"Deanna..." He whispers my name as he lowers his mouth, and there is a brief moment of quiet as our lips pause, inches from each other.

"Like this?" he whispers, and all I can do is nod a response.

The need. It is stronger than my blood lust; it is overriding any thought in my head. I want this man so bad. I want him alive, and I want him to fill me with that life, that sweetness.

Our mouths meet and I taste the sweet flavor of a mint, feel the rough brush of a tongue against mine, and lose any thought in the sweet clash of restrained lust.

CHAPTER 2

House Arrest Countdown: 3 Months

TWENTY-TWO MONTHS. MARCUS has spent twenty-two months locked away like an animal. Surrounded by the dregs of society, half of them too stupid to understand the confines of the situation they were in. Almost two years in a place where he'd had to shit five feet from a felon. Far too long. For a man of his standing, with no priors, weak evidence... the five-year sentence had been ludicrous. The fact that it had taken his attorneys twenty-two months to get him out of there—unacceptable.

But now he is free and the bitching can wait until Monday. Now, at 6:14 p.m. on a Friday night, he stands on the pavement outside of the prison and breathes free air. Air that, on this side of the chain link, tastes different. It is filled with hope. Rebirth. Never again will he step inside that fence. Never again will he feel the grip of confinement around his wrists.

He had been stupid.

Sloppy.

Made mistakes he will not repeat. He will think more, act less. Be smarter.

Marcus steps toward the waiting car, the sleek Bentley radiating the reflecting sun rays like a beacon to his soul. The bracelet, heavy on his right ankle, reminding him of the three months of supervision ahead of him.

The door opens and he leans over. Grins into the waiting face of his attorney. "I'll bitch at you next week about how long that took. For now, let's go celebrate."

Doors click, hugs are exchanged in the awkward space of the car, and then the attorney leans forward, overriding his suggestion with a few tossed words to the driver.

"Come on," Marcus growls. "I've been locked up and fed dog food. Jacked off to visions of a porterhouse so bloody it'll stain my teeth."

"Easy Marcus." The thin man shoots him a look. "Watch what you say."

"Shit. Everyone lost their sense of humor while I was gone?"

There is silence in the car for a moment and he realizes how crude his words sounded. He went into prison a gentleman, had come out an animal. He pulls at the collar of his prison-issued shirt, a cheap material that now feels normal. First thing, when he gets inside, he'll change. Take a shower in his stone grotto and scrub the scent of criminals away. Pull on a thousand-dollar suit and remember what it feels like to be a man. Remember what clean fingernails feel like. What fresh fruit, quality meats taste like. Remember what being a human entails. What being Marcus Renza, one of Florida's biggest landholders, entitles him to.

An hour later, the car turns, the secured gates of his neighborhood passing by, and his mouth turns downward slightly. Trading razor wire for iron gates. Prison guards for an anklet. One prison for another. But three months of house arrest will be easy compared to what he has just undergone. Three months of having his house, his bed, his staff. Meals prepared twenty-four hours a day. A pool, gym, and tennis courts on his property. His office. Real estate holdings to review, employees to kick back into line, respect to regain after two years away. Work would distract. Work had always distracted.

Yes, three months will be easy. He watches a woman jog past, her sweat making the yellow sports bra she wears hug wet and tight to her curves. His hand stops its drum on the armrest, his neck tensing as he fights the urge to turn and see the curves of her ass, to watch her retreat.

Fuck. Maybe it won't be that easy. It's been so long.

CHAPTER 3

JEREMY'S KISS PUSHES for more, his hips pressing me against the door, his hands pulling my wrists down slightly, causing my chest to arch into his, my head to come back, my mouth to break from his for a moment. When his lips return, they are soft, barely brushing across my mouth, a tease that I need more of, and he pushes forward and deepens the kiss, my mouth greedy in its response. I am restrained, his hard leg between mine, my dress pushed up, the rough feel of his jeans rubbing a delicious friction against my thin panties. A small sound escapes my lips and it breaks him, his left hand taking over my wrists, wrapping them both in his strong grip, his right running smoothly up my leg, slipping under my dress and moving upward till it hits my hip.

I struggle against his restraint, wanting to run my hands through his hair, lift up his shirt, travel over the lines of his abs, dip my hands under the waist of his jeans, and feel the heat of his bare skin under my palms. His thumb rubs a delicious pattern on my inner thigh, and I lift my leg higher, wrapping it around his body and gripping him to me. His mouth is perfect, not too pushy, taking his time and enjoying my mouth while turning every knob on my body to full-fledged arousal. Then he withdraws, gives me one soft brush of his lips before releasing my hands and stepping back, my leg arguing, pulling at him before giving up and joining my other, my body slumped against the door, my eyes on Jeremy, questions pushing at my mouth but none yet spilling out.

"Good night."

"Good night?" I sputter. This is unexpected. My ego may be overinflated from webcam chats with fifty-year-old men and confused transvestites, but I'm used to being sought after, ten hours of my day spent virtually between the sheets with strangers. Now, with a flesh-and-blood man in front of me...I get a kiss and a "good night."

He glances at his watch. "You told me to have you inside by seven."

The elevator picks that time to groan, a loud rumble that will turn into a screech, the laborious journey just noisy enough to make its occupants wonder if this will be the trip that doesn't take, if this will be the moment that it settles into place and says "Fuck you, I'm not moving another foot." It does make the climb, and I tense as I watch the doors open. Another view I have never seen. This long hall, and the motion of the doors. I've heard them a thousand times, always envisioned the bodies that step off, the looks on their faces, the scent of their skin. A figure shuffles off, and I feel a moment of recognition at the scrawny build, previous sightings distorted by my peephole. A pale hand swipes at short dark hair, the man shifting the backpack higher as he glances at us from down the hall.

"You're barking up the wrong tree," he calls out, his voice bouncing off filthy walls as he moves closer. "She won't open that door."

I smile at the voice, non-muffled without the door between us, and glance at Jeremy to see if he understands the man's comment. His face surprises me. Tense, his back leaving the wall, his posture stiff as he straightens. I have forgotten that he knows Simon, that they have bitched countless times over the package of pills that he delivers monthly.

Simon pauses, a hitch in his step, when he is ten feet away, his eyes warily recognizing Jeremy. "Oh. Hey, man."

Jeremy says nothing, nodding at him in acknowledgment of the greeting.

The druggie's gaze jumps left, and stares me up and down, his eyes taking their time. "What—delivery boy bring you to see the freak show?" he cackles. "I've got stuff a lot more exciting in my place. If you want..." He steps closer, smiling, and I see Jeremy's fists clench.

I smile brightly, using the young innocent smile, the one that my clients love, the one that dissolves all tension and puts them all at ease. He moves closer and I jump into action, bringing my knee up quickly, into the soft flesh between his sweatpanted legs, the hard impact causing his eyes to tightly close, his torso doubling over as all air leaves his chest in one brittle exhale. He wheezes and I bring my forearm up, under his chin, and press hard, pushing him back against the wall, my four-inch heels putting us at eye level with each other. "Hi Simon," I drawl, watching his eyes jump to mine, a hesitant recognition at my voice in their red-rimmed depths. "Welcome to the freak show."

CHAPTER 4

JEREMY PULLS ME off. Not that it is really necessary. I have no weapon on me. My knee-to-the-crotch move is pretty much the only move I have—and it's been in my repertoire since middle school, back when a properly timed middle finger was just as argumentatively effective. Had Simon not been surprised, not still been overcome from the assault on his nuts, I wouldn't have been able to push him back, to get my forearm under his chin and hard against his throat. He was already recovering when Jeremy pulled me off, already gaining his wits and understanding the situation before him. A few seconds later, he would have pushed me off. So I'm glad Jeremy stepped in. Saved my credibility while still letting me feel like a badass.

Jeremy moves before me, glancing at my face. "Are you okay?"

Are you okay? An outside observer would think he was being protective, was asking if I was hurt, or offended, or any other manner of state that would send a knight in shining armor rushing to my aid. But I know what he is asking. He is asking if I am under control. If that show of violence was a spark that will lead to a full-blown forest fire. I feel a buzz of warmth that he understands. That he appreciates what is possible.

I look at Simon, whose expression sits somewhere between incredulity and admiration, most likely in relation to my looks over my barely there ass-kicking abilities. "Nine o'clock?"

He nods, looking down. "Yeah. Sorry about the...Yeah. Nine. I'll be here." He stumbles sideways, avoiding the glowering stare of Jeremy, and hurries down the hall, the jingle of keys announcing his arrival at his apartment door.

Jeremy swears under his breath and reaches for my hand, grabs the key ring I loosely hold, and jams the aluminum piece into the lock, twisting and pushing until the knob gives way. Then he pushes open the door and steps inside.

"What happened to good night?" I ask, my feet still in the hall, my arms crossed as I watch him wait, his hand impatiently holding the door open for me.

"Get in, please. Before that piece of shit comes back."

I grin at his tone, which is more of a growl than enunciated speech, enjoying the pained look on his face and move past him, tossing my bag to the side, enjoying the look of it falling to the floor. *I am normal. I go out and come home and toss my purse casually on the floor.*

"And stop looking so happy," he continues. "That punk is dangerous."

"Happy is not a bad thing. And Simon is harmless. He's not going to bite the hand that feeds him."

"He didn't know what you looked like before."

I shrug, sitting on my bed, and unstrap my heels, my feet aching. I watch him, facing the door as if he expects it to open, a frown on his face. "Your protectiveness is cute, but I'll be fine." More than fine. In fact, I am fingers-crossed hoping Simon will walk back down the hall and knock on my door before he locks me in, will try to talk his way inside. I am suddenly anxious for Jeremy to leave, hoping he will scamper on so that I can unlock my safe, pull out my knives, and have time to sharpen them just in case. I close my eyes, tighten my fists, and try to block out the thoughts. Try to think of something other than how easy it would be to kill my keeper. How easy it would be to throw out the possibilities and take action into my own hands. Walk to Simon's door instead of hoping he'll open mine. Put my heels back on and saunter down that hall, my stiletto knife hidden in my purse. He'd open the door. Open the door, welcome me in, and then see what the true meaning of "freak show" was. The freak show would be my redecoration of his apartment with his blood. His skin growing cold under my hands as blood drained from his body. My eyes flip open when I feel a hand on my shoulder, the touch startling me.

"Are you okay?" Jeremy's eyes flit from my face to my hands, my fists clenched so tightly that the skin is white.

I nod, releasing my fists, flexing my hands, and shaking them loose. I try to focus on his face, to listen to the words that he is saying, but I can't hear anything, the roar in my head increasing as I think of Simon, of the interest in his eyes—my opening—the possibilities that Jeremy's presence is inhibiting. The roar subsides a bit when I meet his eyes, distracted by the flicker of desire in their depths. Desire. Very different from my own, but present just the same. I clench my fist, draw in a shuddering breath, and spit out the words before my want to kill buries the possibility. "Kiss me. Now."

CHAPTER 5

THERE IS NOT a moment of hesitation in his response. I think he moves before I even finish the order, his hand sweeping up to move my hair aside, to cup my face, his lips on mine, my body falling back against the bed. He is above me, the weight of his body warm on mine, and it is different. Completely different from our previous nights of cuddles and comfort. This is raw, needy heat, thoughts of Simon obliterated by the assault of sensations that are suddenly barraging my brain. I close my eyes and let him in. Let his mouth kiss my lips and his body settle atop mine, my legs instinctively spreading, wrapping around his waist, pulling him tighter into my body.

My virginity suddenly sits up and takes notice.

It is funny how a mind works. Three minutes takes me from killing to lusting to debating. Why *am* I still a virgin? There is no morality front that is keeping my legs bound. It has really been more of a question of opportunity. I made it to age nineteen by blind luck, then imprisoned myself for three years. Jeremy is the first person I've kissed since then.

Is tonight the night? The night that I say good-bye to my v-card? Some would say I lost it a long time ago. Lost it the first time I pushed a plastic dick through the thin hymen, the small bit of blood causing the irritated client to accuse me of being on my period. Little did he know that he was my first. That he witnessed a pivotal moment in that six-minute Internet chat. A chat I'm pretty sure he requested a refund for.

I push against Jeremy's chest, breaking our kiss, his ragged breath matching my own, a question in his eyes when he looked down at me.

"No sex."

"Okay." He shrugs. "I didn't bring protection." He lowers his mouth to me as if my statement is no big deal, as if he isn't straining against his zipper, the ridge of him obvious as he grinds against my body, my thin panties letting me feel every inch of his want. I run my hands down his body, tugging up on his polo, dragging the material up and over his head, his mouth reluctantly letting go of me long enough to dip out of the shirt.

I love the feeling of his skin underneath my hands. The hot surface flexing and breathing beneath my palms, my fingers skipping over and pressing into abs, clear and defined, then sliding up and over the muscles of his chest. I slide my hands lower, till I hit and slip under the leather of his belt, the rough material of his jeans, a slight intake of breath pausing our kiss, his mouth lifting off of me long enough for the word *stop* to slip out.

"I don't speak crazy," I whisper, my hands quick on the leather, the brass of his button, the clasp suddenly free, my hands encountering soft cotton behind his zipper. I pull the top hem down slightly and am rewarded by a brief glimpse of a skin-stretched-tight, glistening head.

Cock.

A real live cock. Twitching, responding, panting for me. The last one I saw was during the first few weeks of community college, when a Friday night kegger led to a heavy make-out session on an upstairs black leather couch, my new acquaintance's short stub pumping a load into my hand just moments after I pulled it from his pants. He laughed with embarrassment, belched, and stood up to refill our beers. I never saw him again. Jeremy's cock is entirely different. It is different than KegBoy's, it is different than the fifteen dildos just twenty feet away. It is *there*, I can see it, and I want nothing more than to tug down his pants until it pops free.

"You touch that, I won't be able to stop," he mutters.

He wants me. I hear the yearn in his voice, can feel the fever in his touch, the jump of his skin when my hand moves lower. The knowledge empowers me, feeds my confidence, and I am shocked when he pulls away, moves down the bed, sliding my dress up and his hand down, its touch hesitant on the lace of my panties. He looks up at me and I nod, unsure of what I am even agreeing to, just knowing that I need more. Anything that he wishes to give me.

His hands dip under the edges of my boyshorts, tug at the material, and I lift my hips to help him, the silk sliding down my legs quickly, his fingers trailing along my skin as he takes them down and off my body. "No sex." He says the words as if reminding himself of the fact.

I prop my body up at his words, resting on my elbows, my eyes watching greedily as he kneels beside my bed, spreads my legs, and runs his hands down the inside of my thighs. "Is this allowed?"

I don't know what he has planned, what he is asking permission for. I only know that the throb between my legs is screaming for attention, and the look in his eyes is hot as hell. It is a raging fire, as needy as my own, both of us desperate for something more than we currently have, his right hand sliding further on my thigh until he is close enough to move his thumb slightly and it brushes across my sex.

I inhale, someone else's touch so different from my own. My fingers spend hours on that area, other objects bumping across that skin hundreds of times a day. I should be immune to touch, should barely feel the calloused ridge of his finger, should play the "cool" card and shoot him a "what else do you have?" look.

But I don't. Just the slight brush of his thumb brings me to life, pouring sensation through every nerve in my body. He moves the digit again, returning it to my thigh, and I involuntarily buck from the touch, my body instinctively moving closer to his hand, wanting more of what I just so briefly experienced.

"Is this allowed?" he repeats, his eyes on mine, my mouth practically panting as I stare at him, bare-chested between my legs.

"Yes," I gasp, clenching my inner muscles in an attempt to satisfy the need that is growing there.

He grins, hunger in his eyes, and lowers his mouth to my needy skin. The first touch of his tongue causes my mouth to drop open. My eyes involuntarily close and my head falls back, temporarily blotting out the delicious image of his mouth on me.

I've never had a tongue on my clit. Never had the hot, wet sensation, vibrating suction, the delicate play of a talented tongue against pleasure-packed bundles of nerves. It is shocking, how incredible it feels. My nervousness fades, my body relaxing as my legs drop open, giving him full access to whatever he wants. My elbows relax and my upper body collapses upon the bed. Somehow, my hands find their way to his head and I twist my fingers through his short hair. My orgasm is building, growing at a rate faster than I have ever been able to bring it. I worry, for a brief moment, that it will come too quickly, that I won't have time to enjoy this incredible sensation he is creating.

Then, I stop worrying. I stop thinking. I lose myself in the beautiful experience he is bringing to my body. I don't think about how close my fingers are to his neck, or the vulnerable proximity of his eyes to my fingernails. I am too engrossed in the arrival of ecstasy. And when it comes, it is the most perfect form of insanity I have ever experienced.

CHAPTER 6

I COME BACK down to earth, my legs shuddering around Jeremy's head, the orgasm better than anything I have ever brought myself. I have the sudden realization that I have pushed through a door—the door of awareness. I will never enjoy my orgasms the same, will always compare them to this moment. I close my eyes and wonder what sex will feel like. How his cock will differ from my toys. How the unknown, undirected motion will stack up against my stimulated thrusts. I relax my legs, letting them drop from his shoulders, and feel his hands on my skin as he stands, open my eyes to find him smiling, a crooked, sexy gesture that I can't help but return. "You look pleased with yourself," I mumble.

I don't know dating protocol. Is now when I suck his cock? My limbs are too relaxed, my brain too lazy to do anything other than lie here. He falls onto the bed next to me, the mattress jumping at the additional weight, and both of us stare up at the ceiling. He reaches his arm around me, and I lift my head and allow his arm to steal underneath, relaxing back against the strength of his shoulder.

"Is this okay?" he asks.

I smile. "Yeah. This is cool." I enjoy the moment, the warmth of him next to me, and curl slightly to the side until I am nestled in the crook of his body. "Are you okay?" I blush, trying to find the right word, my personal dictionary too stocked with crude terms to be ladylike. "Do you want to get off or are you—"

"I'm fine." He presses a soft kiss onto my head. "I didn't intend to barrel in here and take advantage of you. In fact…I had big plans to be a gentleman."

"Is that what that peck in the hallway was all about?"

"Peck?" His scoff makes me smile. "From your reaction, I think it worked pretty well."

"Easy, Casanova." I poke his side, admiring when my finger hits hard muscle. "Just making sure you don't get a big head."

"I understand. Your biting comments are your way of secretly stroking a man's ego."

"Stroking is one of my talents," I tease, the comment earning me a groan, his body rolling into mine, his hand gripping my back and sliding me closer, until I am flush against him. Then, he reclaims my mouth with one, long, heart-stopping kiss.

Ten minutes later, the witching hour near, we say our goodbyes. An hour later, there is the slide of dead bolt through metal, and Simon locks me in for the next eight hours.

CHAPTER 7

House Arrest Countdown: 2 Months, 3 Weeks

A WEEK AGO, Marcus had walked through palatial doors to an empty house, the stale smell not overcome by the traffic of maids and repairmen. It felt like someone else's home, the sweeping banisters, the chandelier that towered thirty feet above him, all staring at him as if unsure of who this man—his clothes cheap, face unshaven—was. He had moved through the entire house, visiting rooms he hadn't seen in years, nodding to unfamiliar staff as he tried to reacquaint himself with his former lifestyle.

Now, he still feels awkward, as if he is living another man's life, an imposter in a world he once dominated. It's the minor things that point it out. The smell of refinement—something his nose is relearning, each scent bringing back memories and a piece of the man he used to be. A cigar, freshly cut, its smoky scent and the change in it once lit. The citrus scent of polish. The whiff of it from his housekeeper's rag as she wipes a banister. The scent that hangs off Persian rugs, custom drapes, and fine leather. Merlot, the draw of it against his nostril sweeter given the fact that the bottle bears his winery's name.

The smells comfort him. Move him closer to the acceptance that he is home. And the other, more vulnerable smells of emotion, are slowly but surely giving him back the confidence, the swagger, that prison has robbed him of.

Fear. It floats off the elderly woman who cleans his house, as she avoids eye contact and scurries out of the room when he enters. *Subservience.* The smell of weakness, shown in limp handshakes, quickly nodding heads, flurries of activity in response to his words. *Respect.* The best smell of them all, the one that will be confirmation that the axis has righted, that life is back in order, that he is once again king and un-fucking-stoppable.

He frowns at his ankle, at his constant reminder that he is, in fact, stoppable. It blinks. All the fucking time. He'd had to stuff his feet under the covers last night just so that damn light wouldn't keep him awake. Had to feel the restrictive weight of sheets and blankets pressing on his toes. Kicking did nothing, the weight settling back down as soon as his movement stopped. Fucking bracelet. Pinching the hair on his ankle. Makes him want to shave his leg like a fag.

At 6:04 a.m. he sat at his desk. Pen in hand. Papers spread before him like a mountain of cash. Coffee almost gone, the white mug almost lost in the sea of paper. Each sip reminding him of the dwindling supply. Where was the girl? The one who should have refilled it by now. The black one they hired, probably because he isn't attracted to dark women, likes his sluts pale and quaking. Black women have too much attitude. Talk back. Roll their eyes. All behavior which deserves a strong slap across the face. He takes a final sip, draining the cup, his anger mounting when his office door opens and she steps inside, a coffee pitcher carried on a tray in her hands. *Finally.*

He ignores her. Focuses on the property rent roll before him, reading the same numbers over and over, the words blurring as she moves close, refills his cup silently. She smells like cake. She moves away. The door clicks shut as his eyes move to the next line.

He finishes the column, makes a note in the margin, and reaches for the phone.

"Good morning Marcus." His attorney's voice speaks of an awakened man.

"I want this anklet off sooner. This is bullshit. I'm a respected man for Christ's sake. I have a business to run; can't do that from the house."

"It's been six days. I can't petition the judge till you've been out for at least a month. Just try to behave."

"How can I not? Jesus, couldn't you have at least stocked the house with some ass?"

Silence. "It's three months, Marcus. Three months during which the judge will be examining every move you make. As will the McLaughlin family, the press, and every one of your enemies. You need to stay away from women. Preferably forever. But at least during this time. Otherwise, you'll be back in prison, simple as that."

"I've been locked up for a year and a half. It's been so long my housekeeper is looking attractive."

"Masturbate," the man says flatly. "Then focus on something other than sex."

Marcus hangs up the phone. Takes a long pull of coffee. Decides, when the girl returns, that he'll ask her for breakfast.

The black bitch never comes back.

❖

"Where's the girl?"

A man he doesn't recognize rises from a seat at the kitchen table, silverware mid-polish before him. Black uniform, the slacks and monogrammed button-up indicating he is a member of the staff. No name tag needed because he doesn't give a damn about their names. This one has red hair. Ugh. He'd never met a redhead he cared for. Case in point Katie McLaughlin. That bitch would stalk him to the grave.

"I'm sorry, Mr. Renza, which girl?"

"The one who filled my coffee. It's been an hour. I'd like some fucking breakfast without having to walk halfway across this house to get some. I have things to do."

The man blinks. "I'm so sorry. Diana was fired, Mr. Renza. She left."

"Fired?" He puts his hands on his hips. Glares with all the strength possible considering he is still in his bathrobe. "By who?"

"Mr. Theland did. I was brought in by the—"

He turns, unconcerned with whatever bullshit is about to come out of the man's weak mouth. Another example of his punishment. How he is free, but isn't free. His decisions are not his own.

Marcus moves down the hall, his bare feet smacking on the unpolished granite, entering the bedroom with one stiff push on the door, yanking at his sash and dropping the robe to the floor. Falling back on the carefully made bed, he yanks at his pajama bottoms with a frantic hand, his fingers digging at and withdrawing his cock, its length already hard and ready. He squeezes his eyes shut, clenches his toes, and wills his mind to focus on images that will take him to release.

Jerk.

Tug.

The over-conditioned prick does little to respond. He spits on his palm and tries harder.

Recloses his eyes and tries to focus. Tries to push past twenty-two months of abstinence and remember the curve of a woman's ass. The squeeze and grip of her body as he thrusts inside. The way her breasts bounce when she fucks. The moan when she is broken.

Somehow, despite the faint memories, he manages.

CHAPTER 8

I SIT AGAINST the door and eat apple pie. It doesn't really taste like an apple pie. It tastes like an apple Pop-Tart warmed in the microwave, with sprinkles of bland crunch on top. But I'm bored and not ready for bed, so what the hell. I chew, the consistency soggy as it is pushed around by my tongue and ground into nothing by my teeth. I chew and stare, my eyes glued to the window as they've been for the last seven minutes. I don't know why I find it so appealing. *Appealing*: wrong word. *Tempting*: better. I have survived, for three years, by not focusing on this window. I avoid it most days. Alternate between covering it with paper and ripping it bare and staring outside. Back when I moved in, when I was idealistic and scared, and doing everything in my power to restrain my urges, I painted it shut. Added a fresh coat when I went rose-petal-pink crazy on my cam bedroom a year later. Tug on that window, and it doesn't matter how many push-ups I do, it isn't budging. But suddenly, swallowing a thick glob of apple, I want it open. I want the scent of night, to stick my head through and see stars.

That night, when I drove to Annie, I saw stars. A blanket of them stretched carelessly across the sky, as if their existence was no fucking big deal. For nine hours I got to see them. And now, as I crunch my way through stale apple substitute, I suddenly want, even have, to see them again.

I toss the paper plate to the side and stand. Walk to the kitchen counter and open the drawer. Grab the only knife I keep readily available, a butter knife. Wild woman I am. I grip the knife in my fist and walk to the window. Slide the edge down the jamb and start to scrape the paint.

Scrape. I don't focus on the task, or the growing pain in my hand from the effort. I sit on a stool by the window and scrape at the dried pink paint. Wonder, with each dig of metal into pink, if I will regret this. Is seeing stars worth the temptation of fresh air? Worth the removal of a barrier? I break through the final piece of paint and set the knife down. Move the stool aside and flip the window's latch, placing my hands on the wooden frame. Pause for a beat as I analyze this poor decision.

Yes, this is wrong.

But my sanity is worth a little risk.

I need this step. I need to prove I can handle this step.

I yank, the window sticking an inch up, the crisp night air sneaking through the crack. I tug harder, the whistle of air blowing stronger as the wood behaves underneath my palms and slides all the way up. I smile despite my better judgment, and lean through the dark hole.

Stars. A galaxy of them, stretching above me. I stare, my breath gone for one moment, stolen by the awesomeness of our galaxy. Wonder at the view from the heavens. Wonder whether my family is up there, watching me, watching this step. Wonder if they are proud, or if they are screaming at me to get the hell back inside. That is the issue with being my own police, the responsibility to decide if the decisions I make are right. Annie was right. I know that, I have to believe that. I return inside for a brief, depressing moment and grab a blanket, gingerly sliding a foot through the open window and sitting on the ledge, the blanket around me, my forefinger running over a small blister on my thumb. *I opened the window and it is okay.* It is night; I am, in a small way, free. My reward: the stars, stars I have missed, stars I've spent three years imagining on the ceiling above me. I lean my head back against wood and look up.

And here, under this sky of impossibility, I feel the first slice of understanding at the enormity of things out of my control. I am one of thousands underneath this sky, not someone particularly special or unique.

Yes, I've killed. Yes, I still want to kill. But, looking up at thousands of lights that could harbor unknown galaxies and universes, could hold my missing family, I feel a bit, there, somewhere... yes... a flicker of hope.

There has to be a plan. I have to have a purpose. I am, despite all that rots in my core, a good person.

I sit, my head resting on the frame, a pile of pink paint shavings beneath my dangling foot, and stare until my eyes become heavy and I finally move to bed, leaving the window open, the fresh air my excuse.

Star light. Star bright.

First star I see tonight.

I wish I may, wish I might.

Not kill those whom my heart holds tight.

CHAPTER 9

"I WANT TO see you naked."

I fight a yawn. Shocker. This guy is original. With a name like PluckTheBirds I would have expected more. But that's what I get for a guy whose webcam is turned on, yet facing a blank wall, his need to speak versus type indicating a desire for full hands-on masturbation. I smile, shimmy out of my teddy and step closer to the cam, slowly pulling off my shelf bra as my eyes watch the cam clock. It's a delicate balance, stretching out the minutes without pissing off the clients. But it's something that I, in my online persona as JessReilly19, have mastered. I turn, my back to the cam, and crawl onto the bed, bending over before the cam and sliding my panties over my ass when he speaks, the words giving me pause.

"You like pain?"

I pause. PluckTheBirds better not be wanting to pluck my hairs, or watch me scrape on nipple clamps and tug my girly points to bloody bits. There are other girls on this site for that. Girls that get wetter the more pain that rips through their body. Girls that rival me in craziness. "In what way?" I almost stop my panty removal process, ready to sit up, lean back and press the "End Chat" button.

"I like pain. I'd like you to tie me up. Hurt me, cause me pain."

I relax, kicking my leg to the side, watching my panties fly across the room.

Yeah. Yeah, I like pain.

❖

Twelve minutes later, I am about to come. My excitement builds at the realization. It rarely happens in a chat, my body too bored with the constraints of digital interaction. But this man, this sub, wants pain. It's something I rarely do; the clients wanting that normally go for the dominatrix types. But today has been slow and my fingers are numb from the vibration of my toys, so what-the-hell, I'm here, my legs spread, my fingers strumming across my clit in a frantic movement that would make Keith Richards proud. And I am pouring my soul out to him. Our role-play has me straddling his body, his hard cock inside of me. My hands wrapped tight around his neck. His hands tied, spread-eagle to the bed, helpless to stop me. The frantic pumps of his hips as he tries to squirm free pushing his cock deeper and deeper, the thrash of his body creating additional friction against my clit. He is hard despite himself. Unable to resist my body. The soft touch of my fingers, even as they dig into the muscles of his throat. I make him stare into my eyes as he gulps for air.

I can physically hear his gasps, his begs as he, as excited as I am, pleads for his life. And when he comes, when his breaths become short and fast and finally stop—I imagine that I am done. That the life has left his body, that he is dead and I have killed him. And that final image pacifies my sick mind for the rest of the night.

That night, I sleep like a baby.

CHAPTER 10

TWO NIGHTS LATER. I pull a load of laundry out of the dryer, the job made easy by the fact that 90 percent of the items are in delicate-garment bags, mesh pouches that protect my lingerie and subdivide the majority of my laundry, a few pairs of sweats added in. I hold the phone in the crook of my shoulder, glancing at the wall clock as I move.

"I've got to go. I have a call scheduled in a few minutes."

"I should be headed to my sister's house anyway. Is it Paul?"

I grin at Jeremy's response. "Yes, it's Paul. I've got to stop talking to you about clients. I'll lose my rep for secrecy."

I *shouldn't* talk to him about my clients. I've always freely discussed them with Dr. Bryan, my sex therapist, our conversations protected by the beautiful cloud of doctor/client confidentiality. But my conversations with Jeremy don't have that protection. If he wanted, he could put a billboard on the side of I-10, broadcasting my clients' secrets across four lanes of freeway traffic. I'm not sure who would pay attention. No one knows who IWearMommasPanties42 is. I could find out, if I cared enough to sic Mike on them. But I don't dig, and Jeremy doesn't know usernames or specific intimate details. I've only discussed a few clients with him—my regulars. Paul, the sweetheart who calls me daily, madly in love with a figment of my imagination. Frankie, my latest FinDom client, a relationship which will last until he depletes his bank account. DoctorPat, my resident physician, who prescribes me the pills I pay Simon with in exchange for watching him corrupt his ass with whatever phallic-shaped item he has handy.

"Paul gets more conversation time in than I do."

I hesitate in my steps to the bed, unsure at the tone in his voice. Is it jealousy? I am so out of practice that I don't know. But it seems, from the subtle hints he occasionally drops, that the emotional clients bother him more than the physical. Which, in some ways I get. In other ways, this entire relationship is screwed six ways to Sunday, an hour-long chat with a lonely man being the least of our hurdles.

"We still on for the movies tomorrow night?" he asks.

I upend the laundry basket onto my cam bed, tossing the plastic bin to the side and beginning the super-exciting process of unzipping and dumping out the mesh bags of lingerie. "I don't know if you can call four o'clock night... but yeah. I haven't made other plans." My other cell, the one I use while camming, vibrates against the wood of my desk. I speak quickly. "I got to go."

"Bye, babe." There is a smile in his voice and my own face responds, curving upward.

"Bye."

I end the call and answer the second, moving to my computer as I speak.

"Hey, Paul."

"Hey. I'm in the chatroom."

I scroll through my site, find the private chatroom with Paul's username in it, and click. Start the clock, then put my laptop down, moving back to the laundry. "Got it. I'm in. How's your day going?"

We settle into conversation, the words flowing easily. I know him, in all honesty, better than Jeremy. I can predict his responses, can tell you the name of every member of his family, his best friend growing up, the last five repairs he did to the barely-a-classic Bronco he's driven since high school. And he thinks that he knows everything about me. I stopped making up things on our third chat, when I realized his memory could be listed as a registered weapon it is so sharp. I use as many real names and details as I can, dutifully recording everything that I tell him on a notepad I keep for our chats. During our calls I live in a world I once knew—that of a college freshman, sharing details of my old roommate, Jenny, a girl who is probably now pregnant and married, but—in my warped sense of time—lives in the connected apartment and never buys laundry detergent, hangs wet towels all over the porch, and goes through relationship drama with every male she can find. He knows about Summer and Trent, though—in my fairy-tale world— they are still alive, anxiously waiting for me to get home for break. Trent recently developed an obsession with video games, Summer is trying out for Pee Wee cheerleading. I love our chats. I love the admiration and warmth that fills his voice, the way he pictures me. In Paul's mind, I am perfect. And, in the world I create on our calls, my life is perfect. No thoughts of murder, no blood in my past. My family is alive and normal; they love me. My world is open and free; I am a normal college student with normal problems. Finals. Best friend drama. The difficult decision of whether I should spend spring break in Cabo or Panama City Beach.

I fold and sort thongs, panties, boyshorts. Line push-ups, underwires, and camisoles in my drawer. Hang up teddies, silk robes, and schoolgirl button-ups. Organize my leather crops, dildos, and ball gags. Strip off sheets that smell of lube and replace them with a fresh pink set. Lie back on said sheets and stare at the ceiling. Wish I saw stars instead of beams. Listen to Paul's smooth voice and glance at the time. One hour twenty-one minutes so far. I close my eyes and laugh when he jokes.

There is a knock on the door, and I sit up with a frown.

Jeremy? I don't know who else it could be. But this is odd, especially since he should be chewing on a ribeye at his sister's house right now. I move to the door and look through the peephole, right at the time that another knock sounds.

Simon, his black hair sticking out in all directions. My frown deepens, and I hold the phone away from my mouth, covering the receiver with my hand. "What?" I call out to him.

The druggie's head snaps up, his eyes at the peephole. It's a weird experience when someone looks directly at you through the warped viewing glass. When you look back, knowing that they can't see you, despite the proximity and directness of their stare. "Hey. I just wanted to see if you were home."

"I'm always home."

He laughs awkwardly, looking up and down the hall before looking at the peephole again. "Right. Can I come in? I thought maybe we could hang out. Get to know each other. I wanted to apologize for the other night...I brought beer." He holds up what looks to be a six-pack.

He brought beer. Like six bucks' worth of alcohol will change our entire relationship, cause me to open my door and welcome a stranger inside, to "get to know each other." I'll get to know him all right. Every inch of what lies underneath his skin. I bet his muscles are dry, the drugs in his system eating at any extra blood or fat. It'd probably be a breeze to skin him. I almost salivate at the thought and am brought back to earth by Paul's voice in my ear. "You okay?"

Paul. Oh, right. The guy paying me seven bucks a minute to break his heart. I step away from the door, move the phone in front of my mouth. "Just a sec. My neighbor's asking for something." Asking for me to cut him open. Feast on his skin with every utensil in my safe.

I almost move to it. Roll my fingers over the safe's dial to unlock the heavy door. Just in case. Just so I won't have to struggle with it while Simon is here. Just so I can move the weapons to strategically convenient places around the room. Almost. Instead I take a deep breath, move away from the safe, back to the door. "Go away, Simon."

"But—I..." He continues holding up the beer, a pathetic waste of a gesture. Ice-cold soda and he may have been granted entry. A root beer float, the ice cream still bobbing on top of dark carbonation? I'd have broken down the door in my haste to let him in.

Instead, I rest my forehead on the door, my eyes stuck to his image. "Leave me alone," I bite out, my hand gripping the phone so hard I worry about breaking its cheap frame in half.

"What's wrong?" Paul's voice sounds worried. I ignore it, staring through the peephole.

"Fine, sorry." Simon backs away, holding up his other hand in a calm-the-fuck-down manner. "I just wanted to apologize. Maybe it's a bad time."

"It's always a bad time!" I yell the words, hoping my hand will muffle the words from Paul, and that the scream will get things through Simon's skull before I lick the warm beer off his dead body.

I take a deep breath, holding the air and then blowing it out. Count to five because I'm not patient enough for ten. Turn and step away from the door. Wish it were nine at night, and I was locked in. Curse Simon for ruining a moment that felt normal. I take a few more breaths and return the phone to my ear.

"Sorry about that. My neighbor's a pain in the ass." My voice is so light I impress myself. So calm that it takes Paul a moment to respond.

"Uh...okay. Are you sure you're okay?"

"I'm fine," I say smoothly. I lie back on my sheets and will my hands to stop shaking.

Six minutes later, Paul hangs up and I end the chat session. One hour thirty-one minutes. $636.09 earned and Simon is still alive. Life is, as much as it can be, good.

CHAPTER 11

BACK WHEN LIFE was good, Marcus had a system. It had been designed by his head of security, Thorat, after one of Marcus's "dates" had called the cops and complained of rape. A prostitute, complaining of rape. It was laughable. Thorat had padded the pockets of the cops who arrived to take a report, and the police report and girl were never heard of again, a problem taken care of by his ex–Special Forces employee. After that mishap, Thorat took control. Used his considerable knowledge and corrupted intelligence to devise their system, one where Thorat provided the girls and disposed of them afterward. Marcus simply had to show up and enjoy himself. It kept his hands clean and his world simple.

Marcus would wait at the marsh cottage, the thousand-foot structure that was his personal fuck den. Have his time with the girls, take as long as he needed, get his fill, enough to last a few months, possibly even a year. They'd struggle. The more hours that passed, the more the drugs wore off, the more they fought. Some more than others. The worst were the ones who failed to break. He'd only had one, a girl seven years ago. That girl hadn't made it through alive, was the one black mark on his record. He didn't like that ending—all the work of a fight without the reward of them yielding and pliable. The rest of the girls had all ended up there; he'd broken them, he'd won. It was what he was: a winner.

Always had been, always would be. And the girls had each learned that. From his fists. From his belt. From his cock. They'd all eventually quieted down. Begged. Offered him anything and everything, then given him even more.

He'd take his fill and leave. The longest session had been seven hours, shortest was two. He'd leave and Thorat would return. Give the girl a dose of forget-me and then dump them on the street. The ending the whores deserved. The lucky ones woke up and found their own way home with no clear memory of what had happened. The unlucky ones got found by someone else. Someone different than Marcus but after the same thing. The countless other breeds of animals that roamed these streets.

Thorat's system worked. It had been well planned, weaknesses examined, kinks worked out. Gave Thorat job security and the chance to exercise his old skills. Gave Marcus the fix he needed without the risk. And he hadn't been greedy, had regulated himself. Made each experience last, holding him over for months, even years, at a time. He and Thorat had had fourteen perfect exchanges over the course of ten years. Katie McLaughlin had been the bitch who brought the system down.

CHAPTER 12

I SIT ON the window ledge, the glass open, the cold air refreshing on my face. One leg dangles out. Dangerous. I love the danger. Love the risk. What if I fall? This height would probably kill me, but maybe I'd get lucky. Broken bones, damaged organs. An ambulance ride, strangers' hands along my body. Touches. Interactions. Conversations. An adventure. I watch the convenience store at the corner. Thirteen people have entered and left in the last forty-five minutes. Some drove up, some walked, one individual, skinny and white, has paced before the front for the last twenty minutes, looking more jittery than I do at one a.m. on a killing night. The sun is settling over rooftops, moving lower, night falling. I should be camming. I've taken too long for dinner. But as night falls, the interior lights illuminate the store and it glows. Like a beacon. I can now see inside. See the rows of food. If I squint hard and imagine a lot, I can see the slow spin of the hot dog turner. I roll away from the window, swing my leg inside, and stand, sliding the window down, the tracks sticking as if reluctant to obey.

I locked myself up for three years before I stepped out of my apartment for one long-ass day. That day, when I felt the foreign weight of shoes moving me up and along the grit of concrete? When I took a breath and registered scents, breeze, sunshine? It terrified me. I worried that I was facing an adversary I might not be able to resist. Normality. It is a tempting and crafty bastard. I worried that I would take that short trip, then not be able to return. Not be able to shut myself back inside, relatch the lock on my world of isolation. I worried that I would paint over my situation and convince myself that I can handle the outside world. Lie to myself because I would want normality so badly that I would risk others' safety to get it.

Is that what I'm doing now? Lying to myself? Telling myself that I am strong enough because I am *not* strong enough to resist it? Is my will to be normal greater than my thirst to kill?

I let my brain ponder the question for one short moment, the length of time to properly dress, then I pull open the door. Stuff my hands into the pockets of my jacket, and step, one tennis-shoed foot before the other, along the orange carpet.

CHAPTER 13

I CAN DO this. I can handle this. A snack, that's all I want. There is a taped poster on the glass window. One that advertises Good Humor ice cream bars. I've been thinking of ice cream all night. An ice cream Snickers Bar. That's what I really want. One just soft enough that the caramel runs into the ice cream, and one bite creates a delicious combination of chocolate, caramel, nuts, and cold cream on my tongue. Wash it down with an ice-cold can of Dr P, and I just might orgasm all over myself. I push on the stairwell handle and pound down the stairs.

Baby steps. Ice cream Snickers Bar. Dr Pepper. Return home. I can handle this. I can prove that I can handle this. Fuck you, Dr. Derek. Fuck you, killer instincts. Ice cream. Dr Pepper. Home.

I round the final flight of stairs, pushing through my concerns with one firm hand against the exit bar, the outside sky darker than I expected, night rapidly falling. I might miss the sunset. I might return to my apartment and it will be gone.

Night: a stupid mistake. I should have done this during the day. On my lunch break. Night is reckless. Night is dangerous. Not just for others—for myself. This is the neighborhood where criminals hog the air, where the howl of a siren is as common as the chirp of a bird. I should have a weapon, something to defend myself with.

Defense. Sure. Another lie to myself? I'm too deep in my own shit to know.

I trip over a broken curb and right myself. At least my urges are being quiet. I should have four to five hours of sanity left. At least forty-five minutes before Simon swings by to lock me in. I will be fine. I can handle this. I move down the sidewalk, gripping the inside fabric of my jacket pockets. Keep my hands in.

In my back pocket is a twenty. I felt so mature slipping it back there—like I was a kid with Mommy's credit card.

Look, I am an adult.

I must be an adult because I have money.

I am an adult because I left the house on my own.

I am an adult because I can handle myself. Buy a snack and not try to kill anybody.

I step into the street, a blared horn scaring the shit out of me, and I jump, jogging forward, out of the way of an oncoming car. I manage to survive the street crossing and face the store, my eyes following the skittish steps of JitterBoy, who approaches me as I move.

"Got any cash?"

I shoot him a look that I hope accurately communicates my level of incredulity at his question. "Not that I'm giving you."

"Please." He holds out his hand as if I'm going to give him something. *Give* it to him! I stare at his palm for a beat, shake my head, and shoulder past him, my arm brushing against him, and I suddenly want to chop off that limb and throw it away forever.

Is this what life is outside my door? Druggies like Simon, Jit-terBoy? People who think they can approach strangers and ask for money? Like a simple "please" will grant them free access to whatever is in my pocket? I yank my jacket sleeve down, far enough to protect my hand from germs, and grab the door handle, the word *Pull* helpfully provided next to a faded image of Joe Camel and a sign announcing that they have only fifty dollars in cash.

I step inside.

CHAPTER 14

I AM SUCH a good girl. I prove, with the direct route I take, that I can do this. I spy the yellow cooler against the back and walk directly to it, not passing GO, not taking two hundred dollars or the life of the little old lady who checks out the gum aisle. I slide open the cooler and examine the chocolate. Oohh…Godiva chocolate–covered vanilla. Gas station fare has gotten fancy in my time away. I stay loyal, breathing a sigh of relief when I see the Snickers, king-sized, at the back. I grab one, think about two, *I can come back for more*, and shut the lid. Eleven steps to the right. Sodas. Rows and rows, stacks and stacks. I hesitate briefly at Cherry Coke but keep moving, grab a can of Dr Pepper, and shut the case.

I am doing so well! Thoughts behaving, mind clear. A simple errand that is, obviously, no trouble to my psyche. My eyes notice more. Tampons in the row before me. Cleaning supplies. Red Bull. A sewing kit. Phone cards. I could shop online less. Come here more. Just across the street, no reason not to. I don't have to order bottled water online; they sell it here.

I step to the register, one man ahead of me. My eyes skip over him. Bald. Old. Small. Still too big for me to tackle. He steps up to the counter, slides over a lotto card, lead dots peppering its surface.

I stand in place, shifting my weight from one foot to the other.

My feet are hot. Itchy. They aren't used to the constriction of socks and shoes and the blow of an overenthusiastic gas station heater.

Something's wrong with the man's lottery card. Bits of discussion float over the man's shoulder with the scent of…I sniff, trying to hide the action. Sawdust? I glance over his backside. Worn jeans, dark wash. Boots. A red T-shirt, pulled up on one side enough to show the hint of…I squint, move closer. Bend to the side slightly for a better look. *I think it's a Leatherman.* My heart picks up pace, drumming a happy rhythm in my chest.

My father had a Leatherman. It was a Christmas present, selected by my mother, and wrapped in ribbon and stuck under the tree. I watched him open it, earbuds already put in, my iPod rudely blaring any thought of family time from my head, the entire present-opening experience set to the tune of Mötley Crüe. I didn't notice anything particularly special about the present, smiled politely when he oohed and aahed over the nine tiny knives, the fourteen other accompaniments that would open wine corks, unscrew eyeglass threads, tweeze, puncture, hole punch, saw. I smiled, I listened to my music, and I wondered if any of the other yet-to-be-unwrapped presents under the tree were mine. During the next two years, I occasionally had need of his gift, would wrap my small hands around the metal tool, cutting wire or unscrewing the back of the remote. I never thought about the many ways it could be used to torture. Kill.

But now, with NeverGonnaWinMillions taking his sweet jolly time before me, his pencil now working on a new card, slowly filling in circles, the scratch of lead driving me I'll-kill-you-now crazy, I can think of all sorts of ways to use that tool. How the fourteen accompaniments could complement the nine knives in a variety of he'll-scream-so-loud ways. My hands tighten on reflex, and I feel the ice cream bar squish slightly, melting in my hot hands and this furnace of a store. *Motherfucker.* If this jackpot-chaser costs me any bit of chocolate nut bliss, I'll start the mayhem right now.

I clear my throat, a suggestive action that prompts no response whatsoever. Scratch. Scribble. He pauses, looks up to the ceiling as if he is trying to remember a nostalgic date. Scribble. Fill. I sigh as loudly as humanly possible, and wonder how long it would take to sever his pencil-gripping hand with the baby saw enclosed in that Leatherman. I move closer and crouch to tie my shoes, the act an excuse to examine the tool closer, my eyes noting that it, just sitting in the harness, could be pulled out with one quick snatch. Flipped open so the sharp needles of the pliers are exposed. My fingers twitch around the candy. If I yank it out it'll take a moment for him to respond, a moment to turn around. Am I fast enough?

I step back as the man straightens and pushes his scratch card forward. *Thank God.* I release a shaky breath and move an extra step away, closing my eyes tightly as I spend a moment cursing myself. My weakness. Weakness that almost ruined this moment. The man before me moves, stuffing his ticket in his back pocket and nodding to the cashier, his steps relaxed as he steps toward the door. My eyes try for one more glimpse at the Leatherman before I step to the counter, my eyes catching on the lit screen beside the register, advertising in proud letters a Hundred-Million-Dollar Jackpot! I set my items on the counter.

"Sorry 'bout that." The man wheezes, his words whistling out through a month's worth of beard growth. "The big drawing's tonight. Everyone's coming in." He glances up, the corner of his mouth lifting. "Feeling lucky?"

Am I feeling lucky? I ponder the question, then shrug, anxious to move on before my mind takes a psychological journey that wanders into crazy town. "Sure. Give me ten quick picks. It draws tonight?"

"Yep. At ten. The display in the window'll show the numbers, if you're in the area that late." He sniffs loudly, a day's worth of snot sucking through his nose, then rips off a ticket and drops it on the counter, counting out my change on top of it. "Good luck."

"Thanks." I gingerly scoop up my haul and step out, the burn of the door's cold metal delighting my fingers. I nod cheerily to JitterBoy and step off the curb, quickening my steps as I cross the street. Almost home. I inhale deeply, wanting to remember this. The roll and pitch of concrete underneath my shoes. The whip of hair across my face as I cross the street. The numb sensation under my palm, the soda too cold to hold, yet nowhere else to put it. Ten steps. Five steps. Three. One. I juggle items and pull on the door, the air inside only slightly warmer, my jog up the stairs increasing into a run as I worry about my ice cream.

I don't need to worry. It is perfect when I finally open the wrapper. When I sit on the windowsill and bite into ice cream bliss, the crisp crack of an opened can of soda the perfect accompaniment. I sit there until my Snickers is gone and night has fully fallen, the lotto window display blinking happily at me. Saturday night. Maybe this could be a ritual. Saturday ice cream and soda snack. Buy a lotto ticket and spend the evening off camera. My end-of-week celebration of non-violence.

I stand, chug the rest of the soda, and toss the can. Then I head back to the lights. Time to work.

At ten forty-five, in between chats, I wander back to that window. Pick up my jeans and fish my ticket out of their pocket. Watch the scrolling marquee and verify that, out of ten quick picks, I have not one winner. Not two dollars, not two hundred million. Better luck next time. Maybe next week. I did it, despite my hiccup. I proved that I can handle it.

CHAPTER 15

AT 2:18 A.M. Bush plays through the sound system, the glass bottle of Budweiser vibrating against the metal desk in time to the bass. The world outside is quiet, but the lines of the Internet are alive, a buzz of late-night activity. Mike switches screens, fingers furious on the keys, a message tapped out as insults and trash-talking occur across a thousand miles of cyberspace.

Behind him, there is movement, a body rolling over in a bed. Jamie, her red curls sticking to her curves as she breathes his name. The woman he pays to keep his life in order, coming twice a week, Sundays and Thursdays, armfuls of groceries in chubby hands. She stocks the fridge, cooks up a storm, and then settles in on the couch. There they typically smoke weed, watch TV, and shoot the shit. Eat. Inhale. Hold. Exhale. Laugh. Repeat. At some point he'll move closer to her, throw his arm around, and pull her in. She has meat on her bones, enough that her sink into his chest feels like a comfortable pillow. One that breathes, provides comfort, smells of vanilla and woman. Sometimes she'll unzip his pants, take out his cock, and carry him to a high-infused nut. Sometimes she won't. They've never fucked, never kissed, but he likes to have her. She breathes life into the space, into him. He glances back at her, hits a few keys and turns down the music a little. Sometimes, in his life of solitude, he forgets common courtesies. How others live. Jamie is drunk, the line of bottles along the windowsill evidence of their night. Soon, he'll join her. Finish this up and crawl into bed. Pull her against him. She'll let him. She always does. He likes it when she stays. Likes the scent of a woman on his sheets, the huff of breath on his chest as she sleeps. He wonders, for a moment, if she'd come without the money. He doesn't pay her to drink with him, suck his cock, sleep in his bed. But if he didn't employ her for the other things, would they still be friends? Would she stop by? Hang out?

He focuses on the screen, taking his time, moving the mouse carefully, superimposing Deanna's face on the drunken coed's sexy frame, the background clearly showing the bar's name in neon lights. The light is all wrong, pointing a giant, clear arrow to the falsehood of the pic. So he continues. Highlights her face, then adds bar shadows, the slight glow of neon light. A bit of grain, evidence of poor lighting captured by a cheap camera phone. He doesn't rush, he checks the work carefully, and when done, clears the photo's cache history and e-mails the image to Deanna, along with four other similar creations. Tomorrow she'll post them to her Facebook wall, and another layer of the lie will be in place.

Her, aka JessReilly19, popular coed. Drinks Miller Lite with her fake ID. Likes live music and kegs.

Him, aka HackOffMyBigCock, fellow college student. Loves working out, football, and lap dances. Dabbles in hacking when he isn't being the big man on campus.

We all live different lies.

CHAPTER 16

JEREMY KNOCKS ON my door at six, my smile not flinching, my game amping a bit, the back arch and finger play moving to level OhMyGodI'mGonnaCum. The client responds, and my coulda-been-fifteen-minute chat ends a hundred seconds later at seven minutes. I smile, wave, and hop off the bed when the END CHAT message fills the screen.

I yank open the door, casting a sympathetic glance at Jeremy. "Sorry, babe."

"It's fine. I know the drill." He pushes off the opposite wall, tucking his phone in his pocket and bends down, lifting a box and ducking through the door behind me, his foot kicking it shut, his eyes sweeping over me appreciatively as he leans in for a kiss.

"Let me put something on." I'm getting used to wearing clothes again. Feeling the warmth and friction of cotton, the cushion of one more layer when sitting on the hard concrete of my floor. The first time Jeremy came by after work, he couldn't focus, his eyes tripping over my naked form, heels still on. He, in as few words as possible, politely told me to put some clothes on before he ate me alive. At the time it was really cute. Now, in the retelling of the story, it sounds creepy I slip on sweatpants, shrug into a sweatshirt and peel off my heels, tossing them toward the bed. "I got another one? Who's it from?"

He sets it on the table, one he built last weekend, if "to build" means assembling five pieces of wood, then using a hundred screws to hold it together. He insisted I needed one, and I'm embarrassed how often I've sat at it since. I still like leaning against the front door. Listening to the world outside, my secret perch, the peek into the other Sixers' lives. But it is nice, especially when he's here, to have a table. Room to spread out food. Something to lean on, put a laptop on. A sign that I am normal. That not everything has to have a base purpose for existence in this apartment. "Couldn't tell. A random name, somewhere in New York. There's more in the hall."

The right side of my apartment holds a sea of boxes, 100 percent of them delivered by Jeremy. I'm not a FedEx girl; that relationship ended on its first delivery when the guy refused to leave a package without seeing my face. Jeremy's with UPS, has been since our first interaction three years ago, when he left my thousand-dollar computer in the seedy hallway after only a brief argument. He's since delivered countless more brown squares, the story of our courtship told in the mountain of boxes that fill my loft.

He heads back to the door, holding it open long enough to snag two more packages and haul them inside. The top box is small and square, the second one larger. The sight of it makes my feet pause, my mouth freezing in a half grin of tentative glee.

"Is that...for me?"

He says nothing, just gives me a wry grin, dropping the large package next to the fridge.

I can't stop my smile. It turns into some kind of split-your-face-open expression, one that hurts my cheeks in its intensity. Not the brown box of a delivery, but a gift: plastic stretched tight over four cases of Dr Pepper. Four times eighteen equaled one shitload of fresh, never-been-opened carbonation. All for me, to fill my fridge and instantly satisfy every craving my body decides to conjure up. I knock him down with the force of my hug.

PART 2

"Please," he whispers, his voice tight. "Deeper."

CHAPTER 17

House Arrest Countdown: 2 Months, 2 Weeks

A QUIET HOUSE. Quiet, a luxury Marcus never recognized until he lived in a concrete block with seventy other men. A quick glance at the clock confirms the time. 11:14. No surprise his cock is awake. It's used to a nighttime ritual of being jacked, the pitch black of his cell hiding the tight grip of his features, the twist and flex of his feet.

Now, he stands from his desk, free to move about, free to turn on every damn light in the house and fuck his way through every room should he choose to. Except there is no one here to fuck. A problem, especially given his pent-up need. His fingers twitch, reach for the cell that lies on his desk, a faithful companion that still worked upon his discharge. Funny—it's been two weeks, and he's still surprised by his ability to pick up a phone without waiting in line. His fingers scroll down and find the number for Patricia, a woman he has known for ten years. He hesitates over the number. Patricia is all that he knows, his only connection to expensive pussy. He can't call an employee, a friend, everyone's panties in a wad over the McLaughlin bullshit. He presses on her number and lifts the cell to his ear.

"You've got to be kidding me." The steely voice immediately brings Patricia's thin frame and sharp eyes to mind. The tone of her greeting leaves little doubt as to her current opinion of him.

"Pat…" he says warmly. "It's been a long time."

"Too short, Marcus. Don't *tell* me you want a girl." The arch of her voice makes it clear what the correct response to that accusation should be.

He sinks into his desk chair, forces his voice to remain light while his fingers reach for something to break, the snagged pencil snapping cleanly in half. "No, no. I'm just calling to touch base. Clear up any misunderstanding."

"Misunderstanding?" The cold lilt of her calm voice chills him. A tone with more bite than he can provide with the buckle of his belt. Women shouldn't speak to men in this manner, and he suddenly doesn't want to hear the next words out of her mouth. "You dropped a girl in an alley in town I wouldn't toss a used cigarette in. The fact that she was found is a miracle. Not to mention what you did to her. You listen to me, *shithead*." Her sentence ends in a hiss and he can imagine her, leaning over her desk, her conservatively perfect nails biting into the phone as she snarls. "You think I'm gonna let you step within ten miles of my girls, you are crazy. As far as your sex life is concerned, you are dead to this town. *Dead*." She punctuates the end of her sentence with a firm click of the phone.

"Jesus *Christ*," Marcus swears, looking at the cell phone screen, confirming the snub before tossing it down, the plastic piece sliding across papers before coming to a slow stop. He stares at the phone, recounting the conversation. He had underestimated the reach of the trial coverage. The effects of his tarnished reputation. The fact that Katie McLaughlin is preventing him from getting a prostitute is fucking ridiculous. And he isn't *about* to stoop to getting a street whore. Not, he reminds himself, jiggling his foot, that he has the ability to drive to one.

No matter. There have to be a hundred Patricias in this city of wealth and sex.

He powers on his computer, waiting for the machine to warm up. He clicks on the Internet icon, staring blankly at the search box before typing "escorts in Miami" into the field.

He selects the first link he sees, the screen quickly filling with a grid of videos, videos that appear to be live, all women, in various stages of undress, on beds, stages, one posing in the shower. Confused, he scrolls down then up, his eyes following the tabs on top, the word *ESCORTS* nowhere in sight. Is this an interview process for clients to meet the hookers? Or an online version of prostitution? For the hell of it, he follows the simplistic sign-up, deposits a few hundred bucks and, intrigued, settles back in his chair, clicking on one prominent face, a smiling brunette, the words *JessReilly19* underneath her image.

CHAPTER 18

I RECLINE, RUN a hand lazily over the comforter while I read the chat streams in free chat. This is the waiting room, the place where I look tempting and smile and laugh and convince one of the waiting men to press the "Take to Private Chat" button, starting the clock ticking, starting the quick, steady drain on their credit card. $6.99 a minute. It has built my empire and put hundreds of men into debt.

BBQKing: damn ur hot

LSUfreshman: pls show your tits

JoeyBaby111: are your breasts real?

I laugh, running a hand slowly down the dip of my bra, pulling slightly at the lace to show the boys a little more skin. "Joey, my breasts would be a lot bigger if they were fake. These girls are all mine. LSU, I can't show my tits in free chat but would be happy to show them in private."

LSUfreshman: im broke

---HungBlackCock enters room

MommasBoy: do u do family chat bb?

Divorced4646: take off your panties and turn around

---freebird71 enters room

"I'll do family chat, MommasBoy." I smile, let my hand wander lower, tug on the top hem of my panties. Family chat is easy, the boys typically spilling their load as soon as the word *Mother*, *Sister*, or *Brother* is uttered. The Internet brings out all types, including those men who want nothing more than to sniff their sister's panties. Joy.

420allday: let me peek at ur pussy please

BBQKing: do u do anal in pvt?

MommasBoy: I want to do a roleplay with u as my Mom

HungBlackCock: that's disgusting

MommasBoy: black cock is disgusting

Divorced4646: put on some stockings. Sheer ones.

HungBlackCock: u wouldn't find your daddys black cock disgusting

---shavedandhard4u enters room

---jeff001972 enters room

MommasBoy: that doesn't even make sense

I ignore the arguments, rolling my finger over the remote and zooming the cam into my cleavage, letting the high definition do the work for me. I'm surprised I'm still here. Normally I'd have been taken to private by now.

- FREE CHAT ENDED - freebird71 HAS STARTED A PRIVATE CHAT

I zoom out enough that he can see me smile. "Hey, free."

freebird71: hey

"What are you looking for tonight?"

freebird71: cunt

I try not to frown, hide the struggle by rolling my body over, letting him see the curve of my ass, my face shielded. "I don't like that word."

freebird71: I've never done this before.

I hear the ding of the message and roll back forward. Read his message and note the complete lack of apology in the words. Try again for a smile. It is late. I am starting to get jittery. Needy. I hope he's not a chatter. It's easier to pretend to be normal when my fingers are shoved inside of me, the gasps and gritted teeth attributed to arousal, and not the thin containment of madness. "What's your name?"

freebird71: marcus

"And Marcus, would you like me to keep my clothes on? Or get undressed?"

The good news with this guy is, time doesn't seem to be a concern. The worst clients are the ones who want you to strip and dip in the first fifteen seconds. They pant through the words they type, rushrushrushing you like it is the final curve of the Kentucky Derby. At the rate this chat is going, I can stretch it out. Get a half hour and a couple hundred bucks out of him.

freebird71: keep them on for now. but pull up your shirt so I can see your tits

I'm wearing a tight tank, cut low in front, with no bra underneath. I drag it over my nipples, high enough that both of my breasts are revealed. I settle onto my side, zooming out the camera until I am fully in the frame, my panties bright pink against my skin, my hair down, framing my face. I look, in this position, in these clothes, like a naughty teenager, getting frisky on her webcam, willing to do anything for approval. It is a look the men go crazy for.

freebird71: small tits. They're pretty.

"Thanks." I let my hands trail, one pulling gently on my nipples, teasing the skin until they pout, like tight red berries against my skin, the other hand pulling on the edge of my panties, letting them tighten against the lines of my sex.

freebird71: what can I make u do?

Make me do? I consider the question. Newbies can be controlled in ways that seasoned cammers can't. They believe what you tell them, not knowing any differently. But he'd eventually find out the rules, would know any lies I chose to spin. And...

since I enjoy what I do, there is little reason, if any, to lie, at least about the actions allowed on the site. I wet my lips. "You can *ask* me to do almost anything. I can't break the law, so anything illegal is off-limits."

freebird71: whats illegal?

I grit my teeth. This guy is a real winner. "Defecation or urinary acts. Pretending to be younger than eighteen. Bestiality."

freebird71: everything else goes.

There should have been a question mark at the end of his text. He's either an unintelligent newbie, or…or I'm almost at the stage of ending this chat. Several things about him I'm not crazy about. "You can *ask* me to do anything," I repeat. "Doesn't mean I will do it."

I end up doing everything he asks for. It isn't hard. He isn't creative, kinky, or illegal. He wants me, once he gets warmed up, naked. Then fucks me from behind, my ass in the air before the camera, bent over, gasping his name when I pretend to come. He wants to slap my ass and tell me what a nasty girl I was. Wants me to tell him it hurts, that it is too big, wants me to tell him how hot and wet I feel inside, then how big he feels in my mouth. When he is close, he asks for a facial and I kneel before the camera and look up into it. Beg for him to come on my face, then take his imaginary cum like a good slut.

It feels oddly restrained, he types slow as molasses, and I never warm to his brand of romance, but it is long. And long means money and distraction.

At the end, once the typing stops and there is a long moment of silence, I switch the cam to an overhead feed and lie back on the bed, my breath slowing, the exertion of faking it more intensive than you might expect. I breathe and stare at the blank screen. Wait for him to say something. It's compliment time, the bits of space when words gush onto the screen, should the client wait around that long. Most have their finger poised over the "End Chat" button, wanting to jab it as soon as their orgasm starts, anxious not to spend a penny over what is physically required by their bodies. But freebird71 hasn't been cheap so far, so I wait and look pretty. Let him think he has sated my voracious sexual appetite.

freebird71: I'd like to do that in person. Where do you live?

Ha. Right. I reach out quickly, hitting the "End Chat" button for him, setting the stage early for this newbie. If he really wants to know, he can piece together the false clues that Mike has sprinkled so creatively around. The University of Iowa sweatshirt that hangs over my desk chair. The Facebook account that is third on Google results when you search for Jess Reilly. The area code of my cell phone, my address which is forwarded here. We have worked hard at the illusion. Backed it up with social media accounts, fake friends, user profiles, and campus registrations. When clients dig, there is a slew of information for them to find. Easily. So easily that there is no need to dig any further. They find what they want and no more questions are needed. The system is set up specifically for this type of client, the kind that makes my skin crawl and who doesn't seem quite right.

------RETURN TO FREE CHAT?

I pull on my tank top and underwear and reenter free chat.

CHAPTER 19

------END CHAT: JessReilly19 HAS LEFT THE ROOM.

------RETURN TO FREE CHAT?

MARCUS STARES AT the screen. That was *it*? The chat's over? He moves the mouse, presses "YES"; the screen returning to the home page, a grid of moving bodies framed in usernames and prices. His cock softens against his hand, and he pulls back his sweatpants' waist and stuffs it inside. He glances at the upper-left-hand corner of the screen, where his balance, which had previously lit bright green with the figure of three hundred dollars—now had yellow font. $76.32. Hmm. Not bad. Cheapest orgasm he'd had in two years. Cheapest female orgasm. The prison ones had all come from his hand or from men, the explosion slightly sour in its delivery. It was hard to come while staring at a male mouth wrapped around his cock. Even if they did suck better, did understand where to focus their attention and where to ignore. Josh had been his favorite. A young kid, twenty years old with a flop of hair that almost covered his green eyes. He had been taken early, Marcus shoving down on the boy's shoulders while explaining clearly the way that the power structure in this prison worked. Better treatment. Full canteen balance. Protection from the thugs that roamed those halls. All in exchange for fifteen minutes of his mouth. The boy had complied, his eyes tightly squeezed shut, a skinny stream of liquid weakness running down his cheek as he had gagged on Marcus's cock. But that was the first time. Eight months later, Josh had a taste for it. Was sucking off half of C block, and living the life of a king.

In there, with nothing but masculinity surrounding him for almost two years, the female guards worse than the men, Marcus had almost felt himself slip into fag territory. Had jacked off to the thought of a cock once or twice instead of a pussy. So it was good to know, well worth two hundred bucks, that pussy still turned him on. That girl, Jess Reilly, had more than done the trick. The high-def camera had told him exactly what he was missing, had made him feel like a man again, and he wanted more of it. To know how she breathed, to feel the pant of her around his cock, how tight her ass was and if it got hot when it was fucked.

But she had ended it, her expression changing slightly, becoming more guarded when he had asked the simple question of her location. She was a whore; surely it'd be good for business to leave the camera behind and really have the client. Money would convince her. It always did. He'd throw a few thousand on the table the next time, and she'd sing a different tune. They all fell for the allure of cash, whether it be physical bills or diamond earrings. Sluts are sluts, and when they've been fucked enough, giving it up one more time means nothing.

He spins in his chair, turning away from the computer, and stares out the large window that comprises the back wall of his office, at the far-off twinkle of city lights. The dark break between them hiding the fruit trees. Half a grove of Florida's finest, fifty of the most valuable acres in the state displayed before him in a dark sea of green. The hours of the night stretch before him, empty hours with nothing but time to think. It is always the empty hours in which the devil lies. He had raped his first girl during empty hours—an eighteen-hour bus trip, the maddening minutes stacking upon each other, each stop bringing aboard fresh trash and making him only more aware of the teenager beside him. He'd spent the first six hours fighting it. The seventh hour devising a plan. The eighth, ninth, and tenth hours gaining her trust. The twelfth hour muffling her screams as he took her virginity in the fifteen minutes of a stop. He'd left her, bloody and crying, on the ground behind the convenience store and had boarded the bus with barely a minute to spare. Had relaxed with the success of his endeavor as the bus jerked its way back to the interstate.

That was twenty years ago. Back when he was a poor kid from Philly heading south, hoping for pussy and fortune. Willing to do whatever it took to get either. He'd gotten off the bus six hours after taking the girl, the scent of her still on his hands, his feet hitting the dirt of Miami at an hour of night when only trouble walked. He'd had eighty bucks in his pocket and he'd felt unstoppable.

Marcus lets out a breath and closes his eyes, remembering the feeling. Wishing it to return. Now, back in his life, he feels incomplete—he needs that amp. Needs the affirmation that he is in control. That he can bend wills and take what isn't meant to be given. He needs that high from twenty years ago and can't get it inside this house. Can't get it with the police watching his every move. Two more months and some change. Then he'll be free. Then he'll find a girl and take the final piece of his life back.

CHAPTER 20

WHILE JEREMY KNOWS the feel of my lips, the curves of my naked body, Dr. Derek knows my soul. He's seen the black pit of it, knows the things I think, things I can't imagine confessing to Jeremy. Things that would make teenage boys plug in a night-light. Things that scare me more than anyone, since I hold the keys to their containment.

Derek has never made me feel ashamed of my sickness. He has, out of everyone, judged me the least. He has always been supremely unaffected by the dark confessions that come from my lips, has not flinched. And while, in some ways, he knows me better than anyone... in other ways he is ignorant. He doesn't know what I spend my days doing. Doesn't know about the bed, the cameras, the toys. He doesn't know about the men who whisper through my speakers, about the graphic way I can describe a sexual act. He thinks I design websites, spend all day with plug-ins, shopping carts, and graphic design. I initially lied to control the conversation, to steer our talks away from my daily activities and to focus them on what mattered. Stopping my fantasies, fixing my brain. Making it possible for me to reenter the world.

Now? Now that we have talked my sickness to pieces, looked at it from every possible angle, made little progress in two years of appointments—I could bring my job up. But why? For what purpose? I think, when I turn the psychoanalysis on myself, it is because I am embarrassed. Embarrassed to be both sexual *and* insane. He knows so much about my brain, yet still—in some crazy way—treats me like I'm innocent. I don't want to ruin that side of our relationship. And I'm pretty sure stuffy straitlaced Derek will not approve. Of the words I say, the actions I perform. He'll turn it into something dirty, stack a psychological sentence on top of it, give all sorts of clinical reasons for my motivation. Make me feel guilty for it.

So I haven't told him. And I most likely won't.

CHAPTER 21

"HOW'S WORK?"

The question makes me pause, a spoon heaped with mint-chocolate-chip ice cream halfway to my mouth. It's Edy's, Jeremy's beautiful ass bringing me an entire half gallon of it. My fridge, which has never held more than bottled water, is suddenly being used in ways it probably forgot it could. I finish—no use wasting a spoonful of deliciousness—and wonder about the calories as the cool ice slips down my throat. I need to be careful. I've lived off diet meals for the past three years. Probably couldn't have gained weight if I'd tried. Now, with Jeremy showing up with bags full of carbs, calories, and desserts, I might pack on a few. Join the group of girls who mark the "generous proportions" checkbox on their cam profile.

He waits, unhurried, his steady look indicating I'm not going to mint-chocolate-chip-swallow this away. I shrug, the sharp pain in my head announcing with gusto the arrival of a brain freeze. I wince and wait for it to pass. Wow. Have forgotten what *that* feels like. "Fine. Busy day."

"Any new clients?"

I glance over, the deliberately casual forming of his words raising a red flag in some part of my brain not concerned with ice cream. "Yep. I have new clients every day."

"Anything interesting?"

I raise a brow. "I feel like you're hinting at something."

He sits back, glances at the framework that covers my bed. "Not really. Just curious what goes on. I know you told me you do cybersex, and I've seen your setup, but I guess I don't really know what that is."

"Cybersex?" I scrape the spoon along the bottom of the bowl, getting a generous amount of green, and raise a hypothetical middle finger to the risk of brain freeze with one big-ass spoonful. *Ouch.* Splinters through my skull, ones that dig deep and twist on their painful way down. I recover, making a face that no one would consider sexy, and vow allegiance to some bit of restraint. "It's not that complicated. Want to watch a couple of chats? Before you leave?" It's his third visit of this sort. A drop-in. I have a boyfriend, and he has "stopped by" after work. I feel so normal. And the thought of killing him hasn't even crossed my mind. The previous two visits, we were lazy. Stretched out on my bed, his hand running through my hair. A few times his fingers took the slow and delicate path up my shirt, or under the hem of my shorts. The last visit, I didn't even get back online. We just kept talking, his hand rolling me over and tugging my body into his, his hand tracing patterns on my skin as he spoke against my neck. About his family. About his childhood. Neither topics that included death or blood.

He shakes his head. "No. I don't want to make you feel uncomfortable."

I set down the pint. "I don't think it's possible for me to feel uncomfortable at this point. Just watch one or two."

His jaw sets, a new look—one I haven't seen before. It is cute, in a stubborn sort of way. "No, I'm fine. I don't want to see it. Just explain what happens. I'd feel awkward watching. Like I'm invading your space. That's a personal thing you do. Just tell me how it works."

I tilt my head, trying to think about the best way to describe my chats. How each one is different. Orchestrated by the client and traveling whatever direction that mind might wander in. "I've....got a better idea."

CHAPTER 22

I SMILE INTO the camera and wait for a command. I am in lingerie, a red lace set sheer enough to tease but modest enough that he'll want it off. I wet my lips and listen to the shake of his breath.

"I don't know what to say. I've never done this before."

I smile. "Tell me what you would do if you were here. Would you want me to come closer? Or would you want to come to me?" I zoom the camera in, using the remote in my hand, letting it pan over my breasts, down my lace-covered stomach, and to the bit of silk between my closed thighs.

He groans softly, and I feel my own breath quicken. "God, the picture is so clear. Can I—Can I tell you what to do?"

I smile. "Yes. This is about you. Tell me what you want me to do."

"Open your legs a bit. I want to see...yeah. Zoom in on that spot. Please." The *please* is an afterthought, stuck awkwardly to the end of the sentence, as if he is unsure if what he has asked for is appropriate. I smile, my face out of frame, amused at his hesitancy. This will be fun. He has no idea what I am capable of. For once, I feel confident in our physical exchange, as if I have the upper hand.

I recline on my side, zooming the camera in until it is centered on the spot between my thighs, a side angle, one that shows the detailed cut of my panties. I draw one leg up, bending it at the knee, and run my hand softly down my leg, until he can see the edge of my fingers. "What would you do, if you were here? Would you move this aside?" I dip my fingers underneath the lace and tug slightly, just a hint of movement, enough to show him that I am shaved, enough to tease him, to cause his words to come quicker, and to flow without thought.

"Yes." A rough whisper.

"Yes, what?"

"I would move that aside. Slide them over—all the way. Slide them over and let me see your pussy."

The word is so strange, coming from his voice—so unexpected that I break character for a moment, look up in surprise, and have to find my bearings, my composure. I tug on the silk, harder than is needed, and grind my hips slightly, wanting to regain the lead, wanting the shake and uncertainty back in his voice. I pull the panties fully to the side, exposing my most private area to the high-def camera's eye. Slick. Shaved. Wet. I run a finger down, traveling to the lips of my sex, the slit that is already ready and wanting, begging for attention, this experience catching it off guard, and it is raring to play.

"I want you to pull out your cock, Jeremy. Pull out your cock and stroke it for me."

My arm, the one that was supporting me, collapses, and I relax on the bed, turning my face and angling my body so that my upper body is in the background of the shot, him able to see when I lick my lips and stare into his camera. I picture his face before me, the intense look in his eyes when he is aroused. I have seen that look before, seen the thin control when Jeremy's kissed my lips while his erection raged against his pants. And right now, imagining that look in his eyes, I want him here, before me. I want him to yank down his pants and fully thrust, let me feel every thick inch until—

"God, I want to fuck you so badly." He pauses. "I'm sorry, I shouldn't have said that—"

"Tell me." I pant, sliding two fingers inside of me, my legs spread wide for his eyes, my cunt needing more than the weak assault of my fingers. I need him, rigid and hard, without a condom, nothing but the heat of his skin inside of me, thrusting, filling, taking me and breathing life, lust, experience inside of me. "Tell me what you want."

"I want to make love to you. I want—"

"More!" I gasp, pushing myself up and spreading my fingers, letting the camera see the throb of muscles inside of me, staring into the camera with need, letting him see every bit of truth in the words I am about to say. "I *need* you. I *want* you. Don't tell me what you think I want to hear. This is about honest need, want. Tell. Me. What. You. Want."

CHAPTER 23

JEREMY THOUGHT HE knew the sides to her. The complex, twisted sides of this woman. The woman who tentatively responds to his kiss, as if she is afraid of breaking if pushed too far. The woman whose eyes light with fire, and who carries a dark thread of insanity, one that should make him run but only draws him closer. One who should cling to him, given the amount of her solitude, but instead is strong, independent, even dismissive at times when he expects her to be needy. Jeremy thought he knew the sides to her, but he was wrong.

This girl on the screen is all woman. Her legs spread, beautiful body unashamedly before him, she has not one trace of insecurity, does not need to be coddled or respected. She wants one thing, one thing that is thick and hard beneath his palm, straining for attention so hard it hurts, begging for release. Deanna stares through the screen with eyes that burn, complex and confident, and challenges him for more. He stands, facing the computer, and wishes like hell that he had his own cam, not just this headpiece, a way for her to not just hear but *see* the level of his need. He takes off the kid gloves.

"I want to take you on your back, with your legs wrapped around my waist, your heels digging into me as I hold down your wrists and thrust inside of that body. I want to fuck you deep. Slow, hard thrusts that have your muscles squeezing my cock. I want you to feel every bit of me as I move. I want to watch your tits bounce as

I speed up, as I lose control and fuck you without thought. I want to release your hands and have you dig into my back. Pull you to me and feel your soft breasts against my chest as I pound into you." His breath runs out, his cock releasing a clear stream of pre-arousal, his hand fisting up and down the shaft, watching as this beautiful woman plunges her fingers inside, her body contracting and moving, rolling in time with her fucks. He growls, feeling a surge of ownership overtake him, an animalistic urge millions of years old pushing him. He wants every bit of this woman. He wants to protect her, reassure her, hold her in his hands and make her his with his cock. "Fuck, Dee. You are too perfect, too right for me. I want you in ways that are bad for me. I want to pick you up and fuck you against every surface in your apartment. I want you to fall apart in my hands and come with my cock inside you, fucking you through it. I want to be yours. I want to be the best and the only man you ever take. I want you wrapped around my cock as I come inside of you. And I want to kiss your mouth and take your breath and fill you with every bit of myself."

She stiffens, her back arches, her fingers a blur of pink moisture on his screen, and she moans, a bit of her hand shown gripping the sheets, her body lifting a bit off the bed, the beautiful sounds of her orgasm breaking any last hold Jeremy has left.

He can't stop, his hand gripping the shaft tightly, and he whispers her name, his body freezing as his head drops back and his orgasm arrives.

CHAPTER 24

A MAN NEEDS a release from time to time. Needs to feel the full brute force of his power. Needs to untap all his potential and see the result. In Marcus's younger days, it was done in a fight, leaning over a younger opponent. Punching then kicking, till the boy was a broken mess of a coward. Life changes as you grow up. As everyone else keeps growing and you stay the same, a five-foot-seven midget. Forced to look up. A man's head shouldn't turn up. Not a real man. And his fists could no longer win respect—not against a larger man. So Marcus found new weapons. Clawed his way to new heights. Gained power. Money. Money can create all manner of intimidation. And in that intimidation, he regained his footing. His confidence. But he still needed confirmation. That was where the girls had come in. The girls had given him the feeling of power and masculinity he missed from his youth.

On November 11, three years prior, he had finished in four hours. Turned away from the girl, zipping his pants as he walked to the cottage's round table, gathering his keys and wallet and returning them to his pocket. He examined the front of his pants for blood. Nothing. Lifting the white dress shirt from the far chair, he shrugged into it.

Silence in the space. He glanced back. The whimpering had been good while it lasted, her gasps and screams silenced, first by his belt, then by his cock. But total silence was a problem. He walked to the bed, pulling up her head, her eyes closed, the muscles of her face slack. He swung the back of his hand and slapped her, the snap of her face satisfying, the brief start of her eyes reassuring. Still breathing. Good. He wasn't an animal for Christ's sake. Killing was for animals. He was a man of control.

He left her tied, his eyes sweeping appreciably over her outstretched arms, the marks of his fingers visible in the bruising. Her legs, still spread open, the twitch of his cock affirming his virility.

Shutting and locking the door behind him, he dialed his phone as he walked to the car, his lungs expanding and contracting, the axis of the world righted, his confidence regained, masculinity intact.

"Thorat. I'm done. Get her back."

It had been November 11. Less than twenty-four hours before Katie McLaughlin had ruined his life.

CHAPTER 25

THE "END CHAT" message dings, and I press the button on my remote, my lights shutting down with one quiet sigh. I relax against the mattress, not surprised in the least when my phone vibrates, muffled by sheets, my hands fumbling across the fabric before finding and unveiling the phone. I answer it with a smile.

"Hey, baby."

Jeremy's voice is throaty, as if he has just woken up and is flexing his throat muscles back into action. "Hey." I grin at the thickness in his voice, and imagine him stretched out on his bed, chest heaving, cock heavy in his hand. Sated.

"Well?" I wait.

"I think I just fell in love with you."

I think? It is close, close enough that my heart races and chest tightens. *Do I want that? Am I ready?* I laugh the statement off, rolling onto my back. "That's what they all say."

"I want to see you. Now."

My smile widens, and I prop myself up, glance at the top. "It's too late. It's almost ten."

"Tomorrow?"

I blush. "Tomorrow."

"Is that how they all are? Your chats?"

My smile drops at the vulnerability in his tone. Suddenly, every bit of my cybersex prowess is a potential negative, his thoughts quite possibly running through a wood chipper of what-ifs. "No," I say softly. "None of them have been like that."

It is, in some ways, true. It is, in other ways, one of the most harmful lies I have ever told him. I've been that aroused before. Have come to the sound of a man's voice plenty of times. I enjoy my job. I enjoy the escape it gives me. I understand that a boyfriend might have an issue with what goes on under the lights of my set. It's more than understandable. It is expected. And I wonder, my high fading, how much of an issue this will turn into. I wonder if my budding love is worth the extinguishing of my online life. I can't stay in 6E without the cyber interaction. I will go crazy. Crazier.

"Night, baby." His voice holds trepidation in its sweetness.

"Night."

I hang up the phone, wishing it were earlier. Wishing I could overcome his worry with physical contact. Wishing he could come over and pin me against the wall, put his mouth on my skin. But it's late. This time of night? I'm as likely to kill him as kiss him. And that would be a tragedy. Because despite our issues and the cavernous void of my secrets, I think I'm falling in love with him too.

CHAPTER 26

FREEDOM CAN BE a drug. The more you get, the more you want. It was easier when I completely restricted myself. When I locked myself into my apartment for three years and forgot what freedom tasted like. Now, just a few days inside and I am starting to feel claustrophobic. I'm itching for the stolen moments of fresh air and stars, yearning for the smells of life being lived, the sounds of people laughing, couples fighting, the brush of someone's hand against your own. Jeremy helps. His visits are the best part of my day, each package delivery a mini-visit. I'll turn off the spotlights, put my computer to sleep, and we'll eat lunch, cross-legged on the floor, our backs against the wall, or at the table, noisily slurping soda and eating. Eating typically leads to kissing, and we've had a few make-out sessions, there on the floor, food cartons pushed out of the way as he reminds me of the one thing better than takeout. But he doesn't stay long. Not during the week, when we're both on the clock and my horny clients are anxiously waiting. He'll kiss me softly and leave, taking my mail and garbage down, his uniformed backside tugging temptingly at my psyche as I close the door.

Those visits hold me over. Get me through the rest of the day until Simon locks me in. I'm returning to the window more and more, my self-control grateful that I am on the sixth floor. Too high to contemplate jumping or climbing down the brick face. The click of my door's lock is my nightly alarm clock—the reminder to my struggling subconscious that the witching hour is near, my own dark fantasies itching to take flight. On the bad nights, that's when I turn off the cameras, bidding good-bye to the flushed faces and hungry demands of my clients. On the bad nights, I explore my own sick fantasies. I am like my clients—on the edge of danger, playing with the fire of fantasy and hoping I don't slip. Hoping I don't fall over that dangerous edge and act out on my desires.

I was there to stop Ralph, to save Annie before his fantasies become reality. But who is there to stop me? Who will keep me in check? Who will stop me before I kill another?

For now, it is Simon. Simon, who religiously turns the lock that keeps me in this apartment. The lock on the door that three inches of steel guarantees will keep me inside, will keep others safe.

Yes, even though I've allowed myself some freedoms, a few steps into the world of normalcy, I haven't lost my awareness of the need for control. I still need assistance at certain times. Like night. Night is still the hardest. Night is still when the urge to kill is greatest.

Tonight is a bad night. I hear the lock turn and relax, the tension in my arms loosening as I shake out the limbs. *Locked in.* Others are safe. From me, at least.

CHAPTER 27

I AM BARELY in free chat when my speakers chime, indicating the start of a private chat. I straighten up out of my lazy, sloppy pose and into one that puts all of my assets on full display.

   ---freebird71 just entered into a private chat with you

   freebird71: hey

I smile. "Hey. How's it going?"

   freebird71: good. I video chatted with you the other night. Remember?

His username doesn't ring a bell. It takes something extreme to get me to remember someone. One guy chatted with me twenty-three times last month. I remember *him*. Though with the username ElephantCock4You—he was hard to forget. So was his eleven-inch dick. NuttyBuddy73, who painted his penis with peanut butter and then licked it off? I remember him too. But freebird71 doesn't ring a bell, not that I'd ever admit that to him. "Of course I do!" I say brightly, flipping screens and opening the word document I keep in the background, type in his username with a few quick strokes. Two notes beside the resulting cell. *Marcus. Asked where I lived.* I lean back on the bed. Smile as I part my legs in a way that draws attention to my underwear's hot-pink crotch. "It was..." I tilt my head to the side as if deep in thought. "Marcus, right?"

freebird71: right.

freebird71: good.

freebird71: get naked. I want to see you.

I get naked.

I arch.

I touch.

I pull open the toy drawer and get creative.

The eight-inch white dildo is declared to be his favorite. I pretend it's my favorite too.

He finishes by putting me on my knees, having me look up into the camera. I lick my lips and open my mouth and beg. Lick imaginary cum off of my lips and tell him it tastes delicious.

Chat timer: 37:02. He wants more. A second round.

I hop off the bed. "I'm gonna grab some water."

freebird71: ok

I glance at the wall clock. 3:15 p.m. Briefly wonder at this guy's time zone, if he is in his office or his pajamas. It's so hard to tell when they just type. When I can't hear the tone or volume of their voice. I prefer the cammers who turn on their audio, whose voices travel through the lines and paint the pictures of the confessions of their souls. My favorite are the whisperers. Makes the entire thing feel clandestine, the idea that they are risking their jobs or their lives in order to virtually fuck me. I pull on a thong, open up the fridge, and grab a Voss. The fridge clicks shut as I uncap the bottle, swig the cool water, and walk back under the heat of the lamps.

He's still there, the screen unchanged, the clock in the upper-right-hand corner letting me know that my stroll to the fridge just earned me somewhere around the neighborhood of two dollars. I take another sip, watching my video feed, seeing the flush of my cheeks, the tint of naked skin. I move the bottle down. Rub the cold plastic over the tops of my breasts, my nipples instantly responding, pebbling hard, the high-def camera catching every reaction, the wet path of the bottle leaving a smear of glisten across my skin.

freebird71: do that again

I ignore him for a moment, leaning my head back and taking another long pull of water, moving my free hand to the camera's control and zooming in further.

The art of seduction is now second nature. The tease. Giving them what they don't know they want, and then withholding long enough to make them pant.

freebird71: do it again

I move onto the bed, sit Indian-style, and frame the camera on my body, mattress to shoulder, putting the bottle in the hole between my ankles and my crotch, the cold plastic wet against the silk of my thong. It'll leave a damp spot. He'll like that. I set down the cam remote, run my hands across my breasts, dragging the moisture across, gently pulling the tips of nipples, squeezing the flesh of breasts, lowering my mouth and lifting a pink tip into my mouth.

freebird71: jesus I want to fuck you so badly.

freebird71: how much?

A danger zone but I don't stop. For one, I'm enjoying this. For two, this is a potential whale, a man unconcerned with minute counts, who has apparently come back for a second chat in one week. At any given moment, I've got fifteen to twenty whales, and am always looking for more, always needing a fresh supply.

I choose to ignore the question, lifting the bottle and returning it to my breasts, my damp thong clinging to me where the bottle had been.

freebird71: how much would you charge if I flew you here for sex?

I let the camera see a smile and empty the bottle down my throat, tossing it to the side without looking. "I don't do that, Marcus."

freebird71: $1000

I fight back a laugh. A thousand bucks is an average offer, but that's coming from six-minute chatters, ones who save up to drop fifty bucks on an orgasm. This current chat is running on fifty minutes, three hundred and fifty of his dollars spent without hesitation. A thousand-dollar offer from him is almost insulting.

"I'm a camgirl, Marcus, not a prostitute. Just drop it." My smile paints the words with a brush of friendliness but my hand moves closer to the mouse. I tried, gave him a chance. The "End Chat" screen will do more to put across my stance than words. It always does, the clients coming back contrite and behaving.

His response flicks up in the moment of pause before my finger presses on the mouse.

freebird71: fucking tease.

------JessReilly19 HAS ENDED THE CHAT. RETURN TO FREE CHAT?

I reopen my client spreadsheet, add in his IP address and a note. Flag it for Mike to gather intel. He's a potential whale, but he's also a potential problem. It won't hurt to know a little more about freebird71.

CHAPTER 28

House Arrest Countdown: 2 Months, 1 Week

MARCUS'S HAND STOPS its forward progress, his cock instantly weakening, the surge of anger doing nothing to revive its flaccid length. Two chats with this bitch, and she had hung up on him in both of them. The first one, whatever. He had already come, had just been making polite conversation. But this time? This one? His half-there cock amped up in his hand? Her bitchy little "just drop it" comment? That was something you said to a subservient. Not your employer. Not when he is Marcus Fucking Renza. A sound collects in his throat, one low and empty, the growl of a caged animal, his hand shaking slightly as he reaches forward, moves the mouse, and clicks on the button to return to the home page.

The fury builds. The disrespect. The dismissive look on her face. He closes his eyes, pictures her sweet naked body, and how much he can remember about life *before*. Thinks about the feel of her skin and the gasp of her breath. What he would do if he were with her. She would submit. She would beg. She would surrender. She would respect. He lets out a controlled breath, attempts to regain his focus, his hand jerking the soft skin of his cock as his eyes skim the available chat rooms.

Another girl. There would be another option. One better than her.

He clicks on a brunette with a similar body. The room behind her gray as opposed to pink. He watches the girl smile, flip her hair. Lean forward and type into her keyboard with long, electric-blue fake nails. Ugh. At least Jess Reilly had been clean. Whole-some. As clean and wholesome as a girl who swallows a fake cock could be. He watches her type and wonders what she is doing. Then a line of text appears in the window, a line that quickly moves as a hundred responses follow it. Why isn't she talking? He can hear music softly playing in her room, so her microphone is working. He clicks on the "Take to Private" button, and the other participants disappear.

No change. The girl looks into the camera for a minute, a bored expression on her face. Then she reaches forward. Clicks a couple of keys.

HotSexxxyGirl4You: hi

He drops his cock. Reaches forward in response.

freebird71: why aren't you talking?

The girl stares at the screen. Blinks. Blinks again. Then her lips move, and broken English comes out. "I can talk. Not much."

Her accent is thick, an ugly foreign paint over the English words, her voice rough, as if it hasn't had much practice with the syllables. *This* is what he is paying seven bucks a minute for? With Jess Reilly, he'd felt the rate was a deal. Now, he feels like a poor man visiting a street hooker, an interaction guaranteed to end with an STD and a stolen wallet.

He types.

freebird71: don't talk. What do you do?

Another long blink. Like she doesn't understand the question.

HotSexxxyGirl4You: I do everything for you. You turn me on.

He sighs. Contemplates returning to free chat and finding another girl. Instead he returns his hand to his cock and decides to test out what "everything" means.

Fifty minutes later, the chat interrupted at one point with an automated request for more funds, he ends the chat, pulling a tissue from the box on his desk and wiping the length of his cock. "Everything" had been plenty. The girl had put in a ball gag. Spread her legs and fisted her pussy. Slapped herself across the face with the metal end of her handcuffs till her lip was busted and tears came. She got on all fours and barked like a dog when he told her to. Gagged on anal beads after having had them inside of her. Had brought herself to the point of tears by the time he had come. Seven dollars a minute had bought her self-respect and let him rip it to shreds.

He kept waiting for her hand to move, to push the button that Jess Reilly had wielded so easily. But she didn't. She listened, she performed, she didn't give him any lip. She was motherfucking boring, even when her lips were bleeding and her ass was being violated. He felt like he was at a donkey show, not the high-class pussy he was accustomed to. Jess Reilly, despite the stick up her ass, is quality. Is American, for God's sake. Is what his cock, even now, post-orgasm, wants.

Shutting down his computer, he stands and heads to the shower to wash off the virtual feel of slut.

CHAPTER 29

CaliCouple111: hey

I LEAN FORWARD, wave to the camera, and call out an enthusiastic hello.

CaliCouple111: can we turn on our cam?

I don't know why clients ask. It's not an act that requires permission, and considering that my rate goes up when they share their cam... I can't imagine why any cammer would respond with anything other than an enthusiastic YES! But their question reveals two things. One, there is more than one of them. Two, they are polite, unsure. *New.* I grin. "Of course! Send it! I can't wait to see you guys."

A window appears on my screen, showing me a bedroom, two figures perched on the edge of a bed, hands clasped. Fully dressed. Fully. Like, shoes and socks, the man wearing a tie, the woman wearing three layers of clothing and jewels. I smile broadly but examine every piece of the image, my mind working overtime.

Expensive backdrop.

Heavy wood, professionally decorated room, floor-to-ceiling drapes, paneled walls, the edge of a fireplace along the left side of the frame.

A high-quality camera, one that doesn't lose focus, crisp, clean, and high-def.

Attractive couple. Late forties.

The woman's cardigan hides an impossibly busty chest.

The man's suit hangs well over a body that seems in shape. They look plucked from a Tommy Hilfiger ad, and seem a little too proper to be on a cam. I feel underdressed in my thin T-shirt and hot-pink thong.

The man speaks, a dark tone with words that roll out, laced with bits of prep school diplomas and breeding. I imagine he went to Dartmouth, works in a firm, drives a Mercedes. "Good evening, Jessica. My name is Ted, and this is Susannah."

The woman smiles, and I return the gesture, sliding onto my side into a comfortable position. "It's a pleasure to meet you both. What are you guys interested in tonight?"

"Susannah would like to see me with another woman. We thought you might be a baby step to that goal." I like his voice. It drags fingertips of sexuality up my skin and causes my thighs to tighten.

"Sounds fun," I say softly. "Did you have a specific scenario in mind or would you like me to start?"

"I'll start." He stands, pulls off his jacket, and tosses it onto the bed. Starts the casual and sexy process of loosening his tie. I sit up, onto my knees, and take advantage of their distraction to move a toy into the eye-level attachment that affixes to my stand. "Susannah, kneel down before me."

I fight a smile, his words matching my thoughts. I wait, his tone telling me enough. He is in control.

She kneels, her dress pants tight, and looks up into his face as he unbuttons his shirt and shrugs out of it. Nice. Muscular, trim. He works out but doesn't obsess over it.

"Can you move the camera in a bit?" I move closer to the end of the bed and switch camera inputs, to a higher one that sits above the toy, one that looks down on me, much as he would.

She hops to her feet, moves offscreen, and then I see the camera pan in, see him turn to face me, the camera framing him in perfect clarity. He flips the leather of his belt out and yanks the clasp of his pants. A burst of arousal comes at the anticipation, as his wife kneels before him, a smile curving over his mouth as he palms the back of her head softly. Reaching forward, she places a tentative hand on his zipper and turns to me, looks into the camera and I stare a little bit into her soul.

We may be a hundred or two thousand miles apart, but it is amazing the connections that can occur on camera. I understand why the clients think they know me, have a right, a claim to me. I feel it too. But they are one of thousands to me, and I am—for many of them—the only one. It is a dangerous seesaw of inequality, one I balance on with no clear understanding of its butterfly effects.

CHAPTER 30

House Arrest Countdown: 1 Month, 3 Weeks

MARCUS ISN'T THE only one who prefers Jess Reilly. He realizes that quickly, his first two chats lucky in his easy snag of her attention. She is one of the most popular women on the site, her window constantly grayed out in a private session. He spent a few nights refreshing his screen, hoping to grab her the minute she returned to free chat—only to be bested by another user doing the same thing. It was infuriating, to wait like a lackey, begging for a chance to pay a whore.

Then, after trying for two weeks, he got her.

"I know you." She smiles into the camera, and he feels the juvenile warmth of importance. He reaches forward to type but is stopped by her voice. "We've chatted before, right?"

❖

I was aided. Returning clients' names are shown in blue versus red. One time out of a hundred the system glitches, and I give a warm welcome to a person who has never seen me before, but this time I am rewarded by a quick line of text.

> freebird71: Yes. I've been trying to chat with you but you are always in private.

I frown in a manner that conveys regret and wish I were some-where else. Somewhere with people, living, breathing organisms that have blood in their veins and who scream when injured. Tonight is a bad night. One where my mind won't stay on cam-ming, and my hands want to squeeze a throat until it cracks. "I'm sorry. The site's been busy lately. If you sign up for my fan club it can send you a text or pop-up when I enter free chat."

freebird71: brilliant

I smile. "Yes. It's nice." Nice that it charges the customer forty dollars a month just for the ability to encourage their spending. Nice that it reduces the amount of time I fend off the free-chat clingers.

freebird71: the other girls don't talk.

"Most of them are foreign. Or in a place where they can't be heard."

freebird71: why not

"Why can't they be heard? Maybe they live with family, or a roommate."

freebird71: do you?

An odd question but one I've gotten a hundred times before. "No. I'm in an apartment on campus. I got lucky and got a one-bedroom." I smile, as if *WAHOO! This is a feat worth celebrating.*

freebird71: boyfriend?

Another common question, ranked right up there in popularity with *How many toys do you have? Do you do anal? Are your boobs real?* I shake my head again. "Nope."

freebird71: why not

I give the answer that always works. One that clients believe. "My job doesn't really work with a boyfriend. Most guys don't want to date a girl who gets naked on the Internet." Yes. Lucky me. With a boyfriend who turns a blind eye to my homicidal ten-dencies *and* allows me to cyberfuck strangers all day long. I smile brightly and ward off a yawn. My mood tonight is strange. I am bitter and angry, and don't know why. After this chat, I am getting offline. I'm too close to blurting out the wrong thing and damaging my online image.

freebird71: I want to fuck you

And...looks like the chitchat is over. I am almost relieved, despite the fact that my throat is tired of moaning and my body has been worked over enough times today to classify as spent. "How do you want me?"

freebird71: on your knees in front of the camera. Get a flogger.

I shake my head. "I don't do that sort of stuff." I flip screens and look at my client spreadsheet, read the note I have next to his username: *Wants a personal meet.* I can't imagine the girls who meet these guys in person. The risks they take when we already make enough. More than enough.

I get on my knees, switching the camera input to the cam above me, the one that looks down on me from the height of a typical man. "Do you want me to suck your cock?"

freebird71: yes

"Black or white cock?"

A long pause.

freebird71: white. Stop talking and suck me.

I clip a nude RealSkin seven-incher on the stand before me and grip it in eyesight of the camera, looking up into it. Tilting my head, I stare into the camera. "Please." I don't move. I don't suck. I wait.

Thirty seconds pass.

freebird71: please what

"*Please* suck me."

freebird71: are you serious?

I let go of the cock, let it hang before me, and stare into the cam and wait. Another minute passes. Another seven bucks earned.

freebird71: fine. PLEASE suck my cock. This is ridiculous.

I oblige, grabbing the toy and looking up into the camera, letting my tongue play over the head of it before I give it a slow and sexual journey down the back of my throat. I close my eyes as I pull off, taking my time, letting my hand work. I tease him for a good three minutes, then start the business of a full-fledged plastic cock suck.

I have almost forgotten about him, my mind elsewhere, my mouth going through automatic motions—suck, gag, bury, tease—when I hear the chime of a message.

freebird71: turn around. doggie style. muffle your mouth.

It's a request I wouldn't normally think twice about. Muffling my voice into a pillow—it's about as tame as domination gets. But tonight...this client...I pull my mouth off of the cock, sliding the attachment and camera both lower, till they are at a more appropriate level. Standing, I strip free of my panties, taking my time before dropping back to my knees, my ass to the camera. I slide into the doggie-style position, giving him a view he will appreciate, pushing back until the toy is at my entrance. Then I wait, turning my head and looking into the camera. Bob my ass a bit, so that the toy teases me without going in.

freebird71: fuck me

"Please," I say with an edge to my tone.

His response comes quickly.

freebird71: fuck you

I laugh. Sit up. "One more chance, freebird. Say please or go find another girl."

freebird71: fuck you

I reach over and end the chat. Lock down my computer and turn off the lights. My hands shaking slightly, I step to the window. Run my hands over the latch. I need just a glimpse of the stars. Just a breath of the air. One minute's worth, then I'll sleep. I touch the metal of the latch. Press my hands against the glass to stop them from shaking.

My level of need for the action is suddenly scary. An indication of my loss of control. I watch my hands tremble against glass and wonder at the danger behind it. I have to control myself. Cannot *need* any of the freedoms I allow myself. Cannot grow addicted to the outside world as I have grown addicted to the thought of death. I pull my hands from the window. I may not be able to handle the scent of freedom. I am getting weaker. I suddenly don't trust myself or any of my justifications. I turn my back to the window and move to the shower.

✦

His mouth set, Marcus reaches for the mouse, clicking the button that takes him back to free chat. *The little bitch.* Thinking she holds the power. Thinking she can make him beg like a dog. There are a thousand other girls on this site. Who cares if they don't speak English? Who cares if they have tattoos and piercings? Who cares if they let him use them without argument? That snobby bitch. Making him say "please" like he is a child. He is *paying* her. She should take her money like a good whore and say, *Thank you. Yes, sir. Whatever the fuck you want.* Not sit there with her stony stare and demand that he kiss her ass. God, if only she were in front of him. He would break her. She would beg him. Cry for him. Scream to God then scream to him. By the time he was done with her the only name she would know would be his.

Refresh. He jabs at the button over and over. Searches for her among the sea of slutty faces. But she doesn't return, the late hour probably sending her to bed. *Bitch.*

He jacks off to the thought of smacking the smirk off her face, his hand moving in tune to the sound of her screams.

He will get her respect, put her in her place. Preferably in person. He is a powerful man. It will happen.

CHAPTER 31

"GOOD AFTERNOON, DEANNA."

"Hey, Doc." I bite into an apple, moving the phone away from my mouth as I chew.

"How are you doing today?"

"Haven't killed anybody yet." I smile, expecting—hoping for a chuckle. I should know better. Disapproving silence meets my ears, and I make a face into the receiver. "It's a joke, Derek. I'm good."

"Are you taking your meds?"

"Yep," I lie smoothly, the word coming out casual, so perfect I decide to elaborate a bit, just because I'm bored and we have a half hour to fill. "I'm thinking about getting on birth control. Will the medicine affect that?"

Total silence. I grin, wishing I could see his face. "Why?" he finally manages, his voice tight and uncomfortable.

"Why what?" I crunch happily away.

"Why would you get on birth control?"

"For the same reason that normal people do. To avoid pregnancy."

"You're having sex?"

"I'm thinking about it."

"Deanna, I don't think that's a good idea."

I frown. "I'm not asking your permission. It's my body. My life."

It's not that I'm surprised by Derek's response; he hasn't exactly been on board with my relationship. But my flippant tease of Derek does bring to mind the risks associated if Jeremy and I *do* take that next step. The risks that are more emotionally damaging than physical. I don't worry about physically hurting him during the act of sex. He has held me at bay enough to dissuade that fear. Plus, any homicidal thoughts seem to flee the moment my arousal begins. But emotionally…I think we are both in danger. I'm in danger of falling for a man who will one day discover the black actions of my soul and leave me. He's in danger of falling for a girl who may one day kill him.

"It's too dangerous, Dee. What if you lose control? When an individual is swept away by passion, they often lose common sense, the ability to make good decisions…" His voice trails off.

"I'm not gonna stop midfuck and strangle him with my libido," I say dryly, chucking my apple core in the direction of the trash and groaning when it misses.

"When are you planning on being intimate? And will it be during the day or at night? Have you thought these details through?" His voice has increased in agitation, and I would bet a million dollars he is standing right now, pacing behind his desk, his face twisted in frustration.

I roll my eyes, standing and walking over to the apple, picking it up and throwing it away. "Killing doesn't seem to be on my mind when we are…please don't say 'intimate.' It makes you sound ancient. And you're…what—under fifty, right?" It is a weak attempt at sleuthing. I know so little about this man, other than that he has a smooth voice that could make a killing in phone sex, should he ever be so inclined. I've considered siccing Mike on him, but that seems invasive, like something that shouldn't be done to a friend. Plus, the fantasies of Derek make it all the more fun. Chances are he's George Costanza with a mullet, and there's no way I can fantasize to that image. Better that I envision him leaning back in his chair, a Josh Duhamel type, with glasses, his suit unbuttoned, twirling a pen lazily as he reaches down and adjusts his hardening cock.

"How long have you been considering this?"

I pretend that there's a bit of a hitch to his tone, a thickening that indicates arousal. "A while." *Definitely under fifty.* "And please, just call it what it is. No more 'intimate' terminology."

"Which is?"

Okay, I'm not crazy. There is definitely a bit of a sexual drawl in that question. I grin, letting my voice drop and my tone change. "Fucking, Derek. Crazy, screammynamelouder fucking."

Silence. Maybe I took that answer a little too far.

"Time's up, Deanna." he says shortly, and I glance at the wall clock, silently arguing with him that we have eight minutes left. "Your medication will not affect, or be affected by, birth control. Please note that I strongly suggest you refrain from any sexual activity as it could trigger an episode. Especially at night."

A click, absolute and decisive, sounds through the cell phone's receiver, and he is gone. I look to the other side of my apartment, to my bed of sex, cameras, toys, and lingerie spread all over its surface. Refrain from any sexual activity? Bitch, please.

CHAPTER 32

HackOffMyBigCock: u there?

JessReilly19: yep

HackOffMyBigCock: you flagged a client about a month ago. A freebird71.

JessReilly19: Go on

HackOffMyBigCock: his name is Marcus Renza. He was just released from jail.

JessReilly19: Awesome. For what?

HackOffMyBigCock: rape and aggravated battery

JessReilly19: Swell. Thanks for the speedy warning.

HackOffMyBigCock: you flagged 32 people last month. my caseload got backed up. Plus I'm assuming, from your smartass tone, that you are still alive.

JessReilly19: For now.

HackOffMyBigCock: want me to block him from your sites and social networks?

JessReilly19: No. he's a potential whale. I'll tread lightly. If he misbehaves, I'll let you know to cut him off.

HackOffMyBigCock: I could do more.

JessReilly19: Stop stretching your morals on my dime. I can take care of myself.

HackOffMyBigCock: never doubted that babe.

JessReilly19: Thanks for the heads up

HackOffMyBigCock: anytime. The rest of the list was clean.

JessReilly19: Got to run. Horny men waiting.

HackOffMyBigCock: bye sexy

CHAPTER 33

VILLAINS COME IN all shapes and forms. I'm sure no one would have suspected my mother, her gingerbread apron tied perfectly over pressed pants and paired with a spotless smile. Or me, the barely-looks-eighteen beauty in a pink cami and white panties, kneeling on my bed and smiling into my webcam.

I know better. Regardless of the exterior smile, regardless of how sweet, or handsome, or friendly someone may look, I should never trust them. I should never let them get close enough to hurt me. Even Jeremy. In some ways, especially Jeremy.

I've been turning it over ever since my conversation with Derek. Debated the point of undertaking an unwinnable journey. My side of our relationship has become, in these deliberations, a struggle to keep him emotionally at bay. I have physically let him in, let him run those strong fingers over every inch of my body, my skin thirsty for the touch, my mouth eager for the contact. But I won't let him touch my heart. It isn't fair to let him love me, not when he doesn't really know what it is he is loving. He doesn't know what he holds in his hand, who he kisses over takeout. He thinks he knows, he thinks he is aware of my dark desires to hurt and thinks that that makes him educated, protected. But when he doesn't know what I've done with that need, what lives I have taken...can his love be true without that information?

Our relationship started out so guarded, my fear of my actions setting so many parameters and restrictions on our time that we barely discussed anything other than the basics. And as time has gone on I have carefully trained him to avoid certain subjects. My work is discussed freely. But any discussion of death is avoided. He has tried to ask about the past, about where I went that night when I borrowed his truck a couple of months ago. But I have stayed silent and he, respectful Jeremy, hasn't pushed the issue.

A part of me thinks that I should tell him. Should give him some idea of what lies beneath my skin. He might take my fears more seriously if he knew. Might do more to ensure that I am returned to my apartment at night. Might understand why I insist we avoid steak knives, glass bottles, or anything with a point sharp enough to kill. So I consider, at weak moments, telling him things. Sharing my past—at least some of it—my moral compass wavering over exclusion points and disclosure limits. Trust, a loosening of the purse strings that contain my secrets, might be necessary for a viable relationship. And maybe, after he knows what I am capable of, he won't run. He'll stay.

Maybe. Or maybe, for the first time in this crazy courtship that we call a relationship, he'll show some common sense and run the hell away.

I consider the possibilities, turn over the words I'd use to confess, but my mouth has stayed quiet. I can always tell him. But I can't take back the truth once it is spoken. And honestly? I don't know how my heart would react if he left.

Yes, my silence is selfish. Admitting the fact does little to convince my mouth to speak. Selfishness is the least of my problems.

CHAPTER 34

I WATCH THE clock in Jeremy's truck hit 7:40 p.m. I am pushing it, breaking my own rules, outside later than I should be. Dr. Derek would not approve, but Dr. Derek can go screw himself. *I want to do this. Try this.* And if I fail, then Jeremy is here to stop me. I have no weapons on me; he'll return me home soon, in time for lockup, so everything should be fine. I just want one night. One night of normalcy. I deserve this after behaving for so long, trying so hard. I've left the apartment at this time for the last two Saturdays. Bought lotto tickets and ice cream and not killed anyone. So tonight should be easy.

Now, I accelerate. We just left dinner, a barbecue restaurant where I ordered ribs and Jeremy let me pay, reluctantly accepting once I pointed out that he has fronted my dinners for months now. He still has some barbecue sauce on his mouth; I can see it out of the corner of my eye, a dried bit of yummy, begging to be licked off. He turns, catches my eye, and reaches over, loops his hand through mine. I smile, my eyes returning to the road, the rough hum of the engine reassuring me.

Jeremy wanted to drive, thinks it establishes some form of caveman masculinity, but I haven't driven in so long and am not passing up the opportunity. To have the windows down, wind ripping through my hair, the fresh blast of air, however cold it may be, reminding me that I am alive. Alive and living. The seat is warm on my legs and back, my body glued to them, the heater placing a gentle touch on my arms and face before the night air steals it away. I take the exit that Jeremy indicates, the ramp curving steeply, my foot on the brake long enough to pause, then there is a small squeal of truck tires and we are heading up. I didn't even know there were hills in this area, flatness seeming to be the only game in town. But here, fifteen minutes outside of town, we are curving down and then up the swells of a hill, Jeremy tapping on my arm and pointing, my foot easing off the gas, and we pull off and park.

At eight, a winter fireworks display is scheduled. I haven't seen fireworks since my family was alive. That night five years ago, we had packed up snacks and blankets and headed into town, spread out on an open bit of park lawn and watched the sky light up above us. Trent had cried from the noise, Mom had deserted us to get the car, and Dad had pulled the twins into his lap, shooting me a reassuring smile. Trent had quieted, Dad's arms strong around him, hands covering his little ears. And we had watched the remainder of the show, the display of colors, taking our time, waiting until the end before collecting our things and meeting Mom at the car.

7:58 p.m. I can do this. I step out of the truck, no one in sight, just him and me, alone on the side of the road, high enough that we can look down on the city. He unrolls a blanket, puts it on the hood of the truck, close to the windshield, and holds out a hand. Helps me up onto the hood, then joins me, his arm wrapping around me and pulling me back, reclining us both against the windshield, the sky above us dark.

Stars. My fascination continues, not hampered by time. Ever since I scraped off the old paint and freed my window, I have snuck an almost daily look at them, the rare nights off a continued attempt to prove to myself my level of control. Sometimes just a glance, sometimes a stare, sometimes I sit on the open sill and take my dear sweet time, watching them until my vision blurs, and I stumble over to bed. It is as if seeing them reassures me that I have a choice. I have freedom, I just choose to celebrate it inside my apartment. I interrupt my star worship and lean against Jeremy's shoulder, loving the fit of my body under his arm, his other hand coming around to fully wrap me. I close my eyes, smiling when I feel his lips, warm on my forehead, his hand brushing back the hair to bare the skin for his kiss.

"Thank you," I murmur against his shirt, "for bringing me here." I look up, into his eyes, the close proximity letting me see the thick eyelashes that frame his green eyes.

He shifts, his hands moving lower until they are around my waist and he lifts, surprising me, my hands gripping his shoulders, my legs moving as he drags me atop his lap. I shift, repositioning my legs until I am straddling him, my knees against the blanket, his hands soft on my waist, his face looking up into mine. "I love you," he whispers. He pulls at my coat, lifts his mouth to mine, but I stop him, place a hand on his chest and look into his eyes.

Vulnerable. They look vulnerable. He *loves* me. I forget, for a moment, to breathe. It is here, the moment I have fought, hoped against while secretly desired. *I am loved.* Me: dirty, rotten me. The man hasn't even *had* me, our touches restricted to heavy petting and third base, our dates mostly centered on food or bringing me items I have been deprived of. "You don't know me enough to love me." I grip his jacket, pin him into place with my eyes, make sure that he hears the words I hate to say. "The things that I think of, the things that I have done...I am not worthy of being loved by you."

"We don't choose who we love, Deanna. You are beautiful to me. Perfect to me. Despite what you struggle with. Your struggle..." His eyes leave me for a moment, searching for words; then they come back to me, wisps of smoke leaving his mouth in the chilled night air. "Your struggle is part of what makes you beautiful. You don't see what I see. You don't see the good person that I know that you are." He runs a hand up my back, tugs firmly on my hair. "Don't argue with me. I know how I feel. I just wanted you to know. I've been holding it in too long. I love you."

He tries to pull me to him, to kiss me, but I stop him again, my hand firmer this time as words spill out that I have no business saying. "I love you too." I make sure that he sees me, understands me, the second time the words coming out softer. "I love you."

It is a horrible thing to say, this is a terrible moment for the future of our relationship, for the future of my rules and control and safeguards. But his mouth tugs into a grin, the widest I've ever seen it, and I don't fight it when his hands cradle my head and pull me to his mouth. Behind me, the fireworks begin their display, the shake of the ground fitting the moment when our lips meet.

I kiss him and push aside the howl of my conscience. In this moment, I don't want to think about the future and what disasters it may hold. I kiss him and celebrate the rush of love and passion and elation. I am a girl in love with a boy and—at eight on a Wednesday night—am getting kissed underneath fireworks. Hello normal, I am Deanna. Nice to make your acquaintance.

In that moment, in that kiss, I choose to believe anything is possible. I choose to forget all of the horrible things that "anything" can include.

CHAPTER 35

House Arrest Countdown: 1 Month

TONIGHT IS THE night, the time to reintroduce the idea of a face-to-face meeting. Marcus can't wait any longer, his impatience won't allow for that. He smooths his hair down, forgetting for a brief moment that she can't see him. He'll use the fucking *please* word that she has such attachment to. Will mask his anger during the chat. Charm her. He has the ability, just hasn't used it the last two years of imprisonment. Then at the end, when she is smiling and hearts and flowers are filling the space between them, he'll bring up meeting in person. Will offer more money. Ten grand if need be. But she *needs* to say yes. He's already decided that she will be his reward. For two years without pussy. For two years of imprisonment he didn't deserve. Breaking her will be empowering, will give him his cojones back. He'll probably have to kill her. Dirty his hands in a way he has never done. In this return to glory, it's important to him that she knows it is him—he needs to have her break with his name on her lips. That will be the best part of it all, her fall from superiority. Her transition into her rightful place of subservience.

It takes three hours of attempts to get her into a private chat, but finally she is on his screen, lit up in crisp high-definition, gorgeous on the new, bigger laptop he had ordered in.

"Hey."

He can tell by the slight hesitation that she recognizes his name, despite the weeks that have passed since he last had her. Weeks that he spent with other camgirls, discovering the same thing, time after time, blonde after brunette after redhead: they weren't her, they didn't have it. There is something about her that calls to him, a mystery behind the smile that he wants to reach out and bring to the surface. He isn't the only one. The men all fight for her like pigs at feeding time, anxious to throw their money at the tiny girl with the big smile.

He types. Behaves.

She smiles. Performs. Undresses. Dances on camera for him when he asks nicely. Spreads her legs and lets her hand dance across the lips of her cunt. Moans and closes her eyes when she touches the place he's been waiting for. She skillfully takes him up the hill of arousal, his cock stretching and hardening. Unbending in his hand, it sticks straight up, the speed of his hand slowed only by his desire to prolong the experience.

When he is close, he has her kneel. Imagines his belt tight around her neck, his yank on it bringing her on and off of his shaft. At a moment when he is close, too close, needing a moment to cool off, he drops his hands to the keyboard and makes his move.

freebird71: I'd like to meet you in person. Please.

Her smile doesn't stop, just shakes from side to side in a "no" motion.

He tries her favorite word a second time, his teeth already gritting as he types the painful six-letter word.

freebird71: Please.

Another shake of the brunette head.

He hesitates before continuing, his hand above the numbers, unsure of a starting bid, her unwillingness to cooperate annoying. Finally, his fingers move.

freebird71: $5000. I'll pay for travel or come to you.

"I already told you no." She leans back, resting the weight on her hands and feet, coming off her knees, her legs opening slowly, teasingly, the light catching and illuminating the pink place between her legs fully. His cock stands at attention between his arms as he types.

freebird71: $7500. No kink. Just a few hours.

She says nothing but sighs. *Sighs.* As if she is exasperated. His hands tighten, cramping, as he waits above the keys, then types a final bid.

freebird71: $10k. That's it.

She leans forward, and his interest piques. A blur of skin as she moves, then is gone, the screen black.

------JessReilly19 HAS ENDED THE CHAT. RETURN TO FREE CHAT?

He roars, a push of emotions coming from a very dark place and moving out, his inability to do anything but sit in his house infuriating. He jabs at the mouse, preparing to rip apart the screen, then he sees her window reopen in the free chat.

She is back. His hand stops its movement as he leans forward, stares in incredulity at her thumbnail, the arch of her naked body across the screen. Her nerve was incredible, the blatant disregard of respect. And the effect on his body was immediate, his cock coming back to life, the return empowering.

He quickly clicks the mouse and reopens a private chat with JessReilly19.

CHAPTER 36

GOD, THIS GUY doesn't quit. Maybe the END CHAT message wasn't clear enough. I paste a smile on my face and hiss through my teeth.

freebird71: did you end our chat?

"I'm not a prostitute. If you can't respect that, then I'm not interested in chatting."

freebird71: you just virtually fucked me and then screwed me over by leaving me hanging. now get on your knees and suck my dick.

My smile is genuine now, it lives in incredulity and power. Forget my desire to take human life; even pushing that character trait aside, this guy obviously has no idea who he is fucking with. This site, with the exception of its horrible commission rates, is all about us: the talent. They don't listen to the customers, don't care if this guy drops a thousand dollars a day on the site. We, the camgirls, have the power. We can block a bad client with one click of the mouse, can ban him from the site with one phone call. No questions asked, no explanations needed. Cams.com last year made over a million dollars from me, money that buys me all the power over clients I could ever want. This man thinks he can order me around? Cop an attitude? I've been too nice already. Time to let my inner bitch reign.

I chuckle, rising to my bare feet on the mattress, zooming and changing the camera angle via remote so that it is looking up at me, the image on the screen one of control and power. "Don't fuck with me, freebird. You have grossly misjudged your position of power in this dynamic. I don't work for you. You pay me, *you beg me*, for my time. And that, my friend, is now over. Fuck you and your limp dick. You get on your knees and suck it yourself." I hop off the bed, off camera, and reach for the mouse. Leisurely slide it over to the "BLOCK" button and pause for a moment. Watch the screen to see if this guy has a response. Then I click the mouse, and separate our lives forever.

------freebird71 HAS BEEN BLOCKED FROM YOUR ACCOUNT.
    RETURN TO FREE CHAT?
------YES/NO

I ignore the question, stepping around the bed, and head to the kitchen. Pick up my phone and call my model rep, his voice connecting quickly.

"Hey, Deanna."

"Hey, Jeff. I got a guy I need you to ban."

"Let me log in." Clicks on keys. "Okay, what's his username?"

"Freebird71."

More clicks. "Sitewide ban? Want it on our affiliate sites too?"

"Everywhere. Burn his ass."

A low whistle. "Remind me to not piss you off."

I grin. "Don't I always?"

He laughs. "All right, hon. Done. I blocked his e-mail, phone number, credit card, as well as his IP address. He's covered."

"Thanks."

"Don't mention it. I'm sure I'll bring it up the next time you chew my ass out."

I hang up with a smile, tossing the phone down and move back to the bed where the message remains on the screen.

------freebird71 HAS BEEN BLOCKED FROM YOUR ACCOUNT.
   RETURN TO FREE CHAT?
------YES/NO

I update my spreadsheet, add today's date and the word "BLOCKED" next to his username. Then I e-mail Mike one short sentence.

I've blocked Marcus Renza AKA freebird71.
Please put him on one-strike access on my
website.

I learned the first year, early on, about the crazies. It's best to cut all access from them. The camsite's blocking handles 90 percent of them, but sometimes they continue to seek me out. Go to my private site. Try to schedule appointments there. Mike polices that arena. I'll let blacklisted members watch my feed, subscribe. Pay up and jack off to the hours of content I upload daily. But they take it any further than that? Click on the "Email Me" link? Or the "Schedule Time with Jess"? Gone. See ya. Straight to the Blacklist of the Blacklist. And I never hear from them again.

I click on the "YES" button and smile, returning to free chat, the room filling up with names, messages of greeting populating in the white box. And my night continues.

CHAPTER 37

THAT BITCH DID something. She made her big dramatic speech, the one that took Marcus's cock to a whole new level of flaccidity, then clicked something. Something that ended their chat. He waited for her to return, waited for her face to pop back up among the other girls, but she didn't appear. Ten minutes later, his computer wouldn't even bring up the site. A message, one that said FUCK YOU in three short sentences, is the only thing that came up when he refreshed the screen:

> YOUR PROFILE HAS BEEN REMOVED FROM THIS SITE. ANY OUTSTANDING CHARGES WILL BE MADE TO THE CREDIT CARD ON FILE. THANK YOU FOR YOUR PATRONAGE.

He gets on the phone and calls the customer service line, a phone call that takes thirty minutes to initiate, seeing that he can't pull up the company's website. The rep he gets is American, the first surprise he encounters. The second is in how he is treated. As if *he* is in the wrong. As if there is nothing they will do, as if he is a criminal and kicked out of their stupid, exclusive club. He asks for a supervisor and is refused. According to the Midwestern idiot, he is no longer a customer of Cams.com and therefore isn't afforded the basic decencies a normal client receives.

He hangs up.

Tries again to visit the website. Blocked.

Tries to remember the girl's name. Jess something. Riley.

An Internet search of "Jess Riley camgirl" brings up a hundred thousand results. The first ten sites he clicks on won't open, a similar message stating his inability to access the site. Bullshit.

He slams the laptop shut, swinging an arm out and taking his lamp off of the edge. A satisfying crash of breakage, the room instantly dark. He breathes hard in the empty office, his pants still unzipped, his fury mounting in the quiet hush of scorn.

This is not over.

Around his naked ankle, the red blink of his monitor flashes an incessant pattern—one that screams through the dark room—its beacon never as infuriating as in that moment of lost control.

This is not over. He'll have her if it is the last thing he ever does.

CHAPTER 38

2:24:03 p.m. TUESDAY
HackOffMyBigCock: hey babe
HackOffMyBigCock: you around?
2:59:11 p.m. TUESDAY
JessReilly19: I am now. What's up?
HackOffMyBigCock: just wanted to give you a heads up about
   Jeremy
3:01:59 p.m. TUESDAY
JessReilly19: who?
HackOffMyBigCock: you know who
JessReilly19: what's the heads up?
HackOffMyBigCock: todays his birthday
JessReilly19: wow. Talk about some advance notice. Thanks for
   nothing.
HackOffMyBigCock: I'm sure you'll figure something out.
JessReilly19: I still have no idea who you're talking about.
HackOffMyBigCock: whatever. I've got to go. Hot date.
JessReilly19: at 3 in the afternoon? Don't forget to pay him.
HackOffMyBigCock: you need to work on your insults
JessReilly19: I'm rusty. Too busy being sweet and adorable.
HackOffMyBigCock: you're not that sweet
JessReilly19: Mike
HackOffMyBigCock: what

JessReilly19: stay the fuck out of my business. Seriously. It's creepy and way out of line.

HackOffMyBigCock: would you have rather nct known about his birthday?

3:04:03 p.m. TUESDAY

JessReilly19: I don't even know a Jeremy.

HackOffMyBigCock: you're welcome

JessReilly19: bye

HackOffMyBigCock: we're still good right?

JessReilly19: I don't have much of a choice. My friend list is pretty short.

HackOffMyBigCock: I'll take that as a yes

---JessReilly19 HAS LEFT THE CHAT---

CHAPTER 39

House Arrest Countdown: 3 Weeks

MARCUS'S FIRST ATTEMPT at a non-cyber prostitute was a disaster. The woman had smelled of cop the minute she walked in the door, the attitude wrong, the questions staged. He'd feigned confusion and sent her on her way, his anger mounting. That's what he got for calling a fucking yellow pages ad, like he was the dregs of society. He should be feasting on high-class pussy, drowning every night in champagne and breasts, their hands crawling over his body, their subservience only increased by his fists.

So... the first attempt a cop, the second woman this piece of trash. He eyes her on the bed, her legs spread, scars running up the left side of her thigh, her right eye faint yellow from a healing bruise, the afternoon sun streaming through the window, amplifying her imperfections.

He strokes his cock, nudges her legs wider, and stares at her. Wills his cock to respond. No response from it. He isn't surprised. His cock isn't stupid. How can he expect a response brought from this woman? He's never stooped to this level before, with the exception of his prison time. And now... for her to be his return to sex? No. He'd made a mistake in even trying. Especially when the only thing on his cock's mind is the brunette with the cocky eyes that flash with darkness.

He stops, tucks his cock back into his pants. Counts out three bills and tosses them on the bed.

"Get out."

Reilly. Not Riley. That had been the Internet girl's last name. He walks into his office, shuts the door, and starts up his computer. He feels a calm wash over him as he finds her personal website and his screen fills with her image.

CHAPTER 40

FOR JEREMY, TODAY has sucked. Thunderstorms all day, the kind where the sky throws up and dumps every bitchy emotion it has all over your body. The kind where puddles form everywhere, deeper than they appear to be, every fifth one he steps in causing his foot to sink ankle-deep in dirty water. His socks have molded to his feet, the wet squish in every step reminding him of how cold it is, this storm bringing with it a blast of frigid air. He didn't grab his jacket this morning; he's stuck using the light windbreaker that stays in his work truck. So he is cold, miserable, and wet when he drops off his final delivery, smiles at the housewife, takes back his pen, and jumps back into the truck.

It's been three and a half years since the first time Jeremy heard her voice. Four months since he first kissed her lips. Six days since he confessed his love. One day since he last saw her smile. He's lost track of the month when she took his heart in her rebellious hands.

All he wants to do is be at her place. Walk in that door and feel her arms around him. He puts the truck into drive and heads for the distribution center. He'll swing by the house first, change out of this uniform and shower. See what she wants to eat, then make it to her place by seven.

Seven gives them two hours. Two hours till that druggie locks her in. He hates the situation, but has learned to keep his mouth shut. A person doesn't really argue with her. Not when her eyes blaze quickly, and she has all the cards and he is left guessing at her hand. A situation he'd never accept from any woman other than her. There is so much he doesn't know, so much that she holds close to the vest. She says she needs to be locked in at night, so he doesn't argue. She says she wants Simon to do it, doesn't want to put their relationship in that situation, so he doesn't argue. He takes what she gives, and keeps his mouth shut about how he feels about it. But he doesn't like it. Doesn't like so much unknown. Doesn't like the feeling of a girlfriend who keeps secrets. Doesn't like the fact that he's scared of the secrets. Doesn't like that twitchy-eyed prick Simon has anything to do with her. Especially after his eyes all but raped her in the hallway.

He doesn't like any of it, but he takes it. Takes it and asks for more. Puts his heart closer to her with every interaction. Why? Why when so much of him is scared of her secrets? Scared that they will be too big to overcome. Scared that they will force him to step away, sanity not allowing any other option. No, he doesn't want to know anything that will end this moment in time when their lives are connected. He'll take it as long as he can. Take as much of this beautiful stranger as he can get. The secrets he'll overlook. Her job... that will one day be a bigger problem. His patience with it is waning, especially after he saw her on camera. Felt the reaction he had to her digital image. Realized how much of a connection can be made through a digital porthole. Understood what other men are experiencing with her. He hadn't realized how much could be communicated through a phone call and corresponding video. Hadn't realized the risk that his fragile relationship undergoes every time a new client pops up on her screen. What if she makes a connection? What if she falls for one of the strangers that seek her out?

He will go along with it all until the moment he can't take it.

She says she loves him. If he can continue on, cement her love until it reaches a place of unshakable bond, then he will bring up his issues. Will work with her toward a solution. But not now, not when her love for him is so young and vulnerable.

An hour and a half later, with a bag of subs in hand, he knocks on her door. It's unlocked. It's always unlocked during the day. Another thing he hates. Another thing he doesn't understand. It'd be a bad enough practice in a good area, much less this dump where police cars are often curbside, hookers lounge against telephone poles, and the homeless sleep on the benches out front.

She opens the door, the door he could have just pushed in, and turns, sauntering away while pointing toward the kitchen. "Put the food down."

He groans, shutting the door and locking it, his eyes on her ass, the curve of it accentuated by the sheer lingerie that hugs it. "Babe. You're driving me crazy."

She turns, rolls her desk chair till it is against the back wall, and points to it. "Put the food down and sit."

He cocks his head, confused. Takes two steps over and sets the subs down. "Am I in trouble?"

Her mouth curves into a smile. "Yes. Sit."

She is saying yes, but she looks anything but mad. Mischievous would be a better descriptor. He walks slowly to the chair. Sits down. Watches her face as she steps closer, her stripper shoes putting her at an insane height, his mouth in line with her belly button. He reaches out, wanting to touch her, but she shakes her head, clucks her tongue disapprovingly and steps back, out of his reach.

"Hands on the arms. Don't touch me."

"I'd love to know what I've done wrong."

His dry tone makes her smile, the twinkle in her eyes tugging on every string in his heart.

"You," she whispers, standing before him, raising her arms and reaching back, behind her head, undoing some tie that causes the lace to slink off her front, her bare breasts suddenly on display for him. He feels his cock respond, thickening and hardening, pushing against his jeans, insistent in its rush. She reaches back again, pulls at the fabric and the entire ensemble suddenly drops, leaving only her skin, still in heels, her confidence so fucking sexy his cock hurts. "You," she repeats, stepping forward and leaning over him, her breasts brushing against his shirt, her teeth taking a soft nip of his jaw before her mouth moves to his ear. "Didn't tell me it was your birthday."

She kneels, a pillow under her knees, running her hands confidently down his shirt and thumbing the buckle of his belt. He inhales when her hands dip under his jeans, her fingers wrapping over the denim while working the button, and she smiles.

You didn't tell me it was your birthday.

"I would have, had I known it would lead to this." He doesn't have a condom. The oversight is glaring, in big huge letters that a blind man would have trouble missing. He hasn't needed one, the unspoken boundaries in their relationship clear. They touch, they kiss...but they haven't gone there, haven't gone there enough times that he's stopped carrying one. Yet another question he doesn't ask and another answer she doesn't volunteer. Maybe he won't need one. Maybe, with his back to the wall and her settled in on her knees, this will be a blow job, no condom necessary. He almost hopes she doesn't ask. He won't be able to say no if she pulls him to his feet and leads him to the bed. A man's willpower is only so strong, and turning her down is Numero Uno on the list of things he is unable to do.

Then her fingers pull his cock out, an organ that has only strengthened in the few minutes that have passed since she disrobed, a cock that swells even more in her hands, her eager look surprising as she examines it. Squeezes it gently, runs her fist up and down its length, her other hand lightly traveling over it, trailing the veins just under the skin, cupping his balls lightly. He stares at her face, wondering at the delight there. As if this is something she has waited for. Imagined. Almost like she is pinching herself to see if this is real. This girl, this girl who has so much fear of herself in her heart... he will never understand her many sides. And here is a new one, the explorative innocent, eager and ready to please.

Then she lowers her mouth, taking her enthusiasm to a different level, and he gasps, his pelvis spasming, his hand falling and entangling in her hair. Maybe not innocent. This mouth, working his cock in ways he has never felt, is anything but innocent.

In this moment, his most vulnerable organ in her mouth, the impossible happens, and he falls even deeper in love.

CHAPTER 41

House Arrest Countdown: 2 Weeks

MARCUS SHUTS DOWN the computer, his sex drive sated, the latest Jess Reilly videos spurring his arousal in a way that the white-trash hooker had failed to do. He gave up on ordering in pussy after that night. Decided to wait until his house arrest ended, then celebrate his freedom in the proper fashion, his sights once again set on Jess Reilly.

He has jacked off to the camgirl every night this week, the "Submissive" section of her website being of particular interest to him, her normally feisty eyes staring into the camera, focused right on him, their stare softer, more willing, the shudder of her obedience making his cock stand at attention every fucking time. She *is* perfect. She is exactly what he needs. The obedience in these videos shows that she is already capable of it. He may not have to work too hard to pull it out of her. She will be so sweet when she cries beneath him.

With a second thought, he turns the computer back on, relogs into her site and stares at the "Contact Me" button. It has been five weeks since the bitch banned him from the camsite. Her loss, as the number of hours he'd spent on her videos could have meant serious income. Now, it feels like the right time to reapproach her. He'll start with an appointment on her site, have a chat session where she'll breathe his name into the camera and tell him the sexual words he needs to hear. Make him come. He has two weeks till his house arrest ends. Enough time to work his way back into her good graces, offer her even more money this time. The dollar figure is really irrelevant considering that she'll never see the money anyway. He should go big. Throw out a large enough figure she won't be able to say no. Fifty thousand—that'll catch her attention. Cause her to make plans, meet him, and give him the Welcome Back gift he deserves.

He reaches forward, nudges the mouse toward the "Contact Me" button and clicks once, his mind going over the words he will open with. A negotiation. Like hundreds he has successfully pulled off. He just needs to swallow his pride and take her shit.

BLOCKED ACCESS.

His stomach drops at the screen, its colors screaming red, boiling the blood in his system, his hand moving with urgency back to the address bar and retyping her website in.

BLOCKED ACCESS.

Cocksucking motherfucker. He leans back his head and screams his anger, his fists clenching, and any post-orgasm glow vanishes.

He will kill her. He is Marcus Fucking Renza. Who the fuck does she think she is?

CHAPTER 42

November 11—Two Years Earlier

WHEN DADDY'S MONEY *rained, it poured. And when you've been cut off, it sucks. Katie McLaughlin glances toward the bartender, green eyes meeting brown, and shakes her head, red curls bouncing. She pushes off the counter, her hand reaching out and snagging the leather elbow of her roommate. "Hey." She leans in, close enough to smell Dior and smoke. "Spot me twenty."*

"I'm out." The blonde shrugs. "Unbutton your blouse. Let 'em work." She moves away, bouncing through bodies, her hand tugged forward by a Mohawk with sunglasses. Neon lights dance off bodies, and she is lost in the crowd as soon as the bass beats out the next song.

"You look like you need a drink," the voice yells, and she can still barely hear it over the music. She turns, the swell of bodies behind her jostling her forward into the proximity of the voice, one who holds out a bottle of Michelob ULTRA. "This is what you were drinking, right?" He smiles. Nice smile. Shaved head, short enough to bring the word military to mind. A tall body that stretches his polo tight, biceps big enough to impress. Midthirties. A little old but he works it. She reaches out, accepts the cool bottle with a smile, and notes the Breitling on his wrist.

"Yeah. Thanks."

"*I saw you nursing one earlier.*" He nods toward the bar. "*Pretty girls shouldn't drink alone.*"

She lifts up the bottle. "*I'll drink to that.*"

"*To company,*" he says solemnly.

"*And strangers,*" she adds, clinking bottles with him and turning up the beer, letting it rush down her throat, the energy and fight of the club pushing them closer, a hard jostle from behind causing a spurt of alcohol to run out of her mouth. She laughs awkwardly, wiping her mouth with the back of her hand, the stranger shooting a hard look at her bumping offender, his arm moving protectively around her, the touch of his fingers sending a jolt of arousal through her buzzed mind.

"*I'm Katie.*" She switches beer hands and holds out a palm, shaking his as she blushes, the smear of beer still wet across her lips.

"*Benjamin.*" He has to say the name twice, the crowd noise scrambling the syllables in her brain.

"*Benjamin,*" she repeats with a shake of her head. "*I'll never remember that in the morning.*"

He laughs. "*No.*" He shakes his head with a wide smile. God, he has pretty teeth. "*You probably won't.*"

It was 12:02 a.m. Nine hours later she would wake up in a hospital.

CHAPTER 43

"THE GUY DOWN the hall has become a problem." I floss my teeth, talking through a long string of peppermint dental hygiene. I shut the medicine cabinet door, hiding eleven more containers of the floss. The downfall of shopping exclusively online. Bulk inventory of everything.

"In what way?" Dr. Derek's voice is calm. It's always calm. For once, I'd like to see him freak the fuck out.

"The I'm-gonna-fucking-kill-him way."

"Which guy are you talking about?"

I roll my neck, the muscles sore from a ridiculously long blow-job session with a client who I will never service again. Forty-five minutes of plastic dick in my mouth cost him three hundred bucks and a front row seat on my block list. The taste of cyberskin is still on my tongue. I lean over and spit, rinsing out my mouth before refocusing on Dr. Derek. "Simon. The one who locks me in at night."

"What's the problem?"

"He saw me. In the hall one day. So now he's trying to flirt with me." It had happened again. A knock on my door, at an evening hour. I didn't respond to it this time. Instead I unplugged my microwave, hefted it above my head, and stood to the side of the door with it raised high. Waited and prayed that he would try the knob. Find it unlocked. Walk in. Let me slam the thirty-some pound appliance on his head. He hadn't tried the knob. He'd knocked again. Waited. Knocked. Waited. Waited so long that my arms ached and I developed a cramp somewhere in my upper back. When he finally gave up, wandered back down the hall to his apartment, my arms were so weak they could barely carry the damn thing back to its normal place on the counter. I had collapsed on the floor, shaking out my arms and cursing my lack of muscle tone.

"This is why you shouldn't leave the apartment. If he hadn't seen you, this wouldn't be an issue."

"You try staying in your bedroom for years at a time."

He is silent for a moment. "Your concern is that you will be able to talk him into unlocking the door?"

"Yes. Or just invite him in during the day. And it's not a concern. It's a fact."

"And you want to kill him?"

I scrunch my face in incredulity. "Do you think I *like* paying you money? Why the fuck would I hire you if I don't want to kill people?"

He sighed in a manner that reminds me of my father, and I suddenly have the urge to cry. Can feel the swell of emotion that used to push its way out in tears. I was grateful when he spoke, grateful to have something to focus on other than the memory of my father. "I don't understand why you suddenly think you can rejoin society. Hang out in the hall. Go on dates and have sex and cross the damn street for snacks. You're living as if you *don't* have these urges. As if you *don't* need me. Why? Why the sudden changes? Have you improved? Because from my end of the line, you seem the same."

I blink in surprise. A good part of my sessions with Derek is spent trying to goad him into emotion. Because I'm bored, or because it's fun, there is no rhyme or reason why. Hell, five minutes ago I was lamenting his lack of reaction. For him to snap at me, his tone laced with irritation and frustration, and a dash of…was that damaged ego? The tones are completely foreign, and I grin.

"I apologize, O great psychologist. Yes, I want to kill Simon. I want to cut his stomach open and reclaim every white pill I've ever paid him with."

"You realize those pills don't stay there. They are digested by stomach acids, pass through the body in a matter of hours. You'd be lucky to find a small part of a pill, even if you sifted through his entire long intestine all afternoon." His voice is so matter-of-fact, so instructionally Derek, that I almost miss the humor. I gawk at the phone, the man on the other side a stranger.

The man doesn't rant. Doesn't get emotional, or frustrated, or jealous. And he doesn't joke. Not even a little bit. And certainly not about anything as macabre as killing.

Who was this stranger? And could I, despite the lectures, be actually enjoying our session?

I hang up on him just for the hell of it. It helps me convince myself, in some small way, that I have the upper hand. At times it seems my whole life is a fight for the upper hand.

CHAPTER 44

FIVE DAYS AFTER the birthday blow job, I hear the elevator and shoot to my feet, swinging open the door before Jeremy gets to it, my purse in hand. *My purse.* It feels so strange in my hand, the extra unnecessary weight one carries around for the purposes of... what? What is so imperative that we, as women, must carry an extra appendage? Men manage to survive just fine without carrying around a personal supply of Band-Aids, tissues, medicine and Q-tips. My purse is shiny and new, a whoopee-I'm-rich purchase back when I didn't have the sense to realize a shut-in doesn't need a purse. So dammit—I'm using it. A giant, empty purse with only two things inside: a driver's license and a checkbook.

"Hey." Jeremy stops short in the hall, his eyes sweeping appreciatively over me. "You look... ready."

"Ready?" I roll my eyes and pull my door shut. "Wow, you're as out of practice as I am. How about hot? Sexy? Beautiful?"

I breeze past him and am caught off guard when his hand catches me, rolling me to one side and pinning me against the wall, his body suddenly *there*, hard and strong against me, his breath hot against my neck. "Hot. Sexy. Beautiful," he whispers, my body weakening underneath his as my chin lifts up and he captures my mouth in his.

Thud. My purse hits the floor as he dips into my mouth, his

tongue dancing over mine in a slow, confident sweep, my hands stealing under his shirt and gripping his back, wanting him closer, harder, everywhere against me.

His mouth pulls off and I catch my breath, looking up into his eyes. "You in a rush?"

I grin, reaching for the front of his shirt and pulling myself upright, appreciating the smooth way it slides over his chest muscles. "Yes, as a matter of fact, I am. Let's go, Romeo."

He scowls, taking one last kiss before bending down, picking up my purse and handing it over. "You ready to tell me where we're going?"

"In the truck," I promise, accepting my bag and moving toward the stairs.

❖

"You want to buy a car?" the skeptical look on Jeremy's face is identical to the one I often imagine Dr. Derek wearing, and I shoot him a warning look.

"Yep. Head north. All of the dealerships—"

"Are off Route 1," Jeremy supplies dryly.

"Right. Deliveryman. I forgot."

His lips twitch at my tone but he doesn't respond, changing lanes and heading north. "What kind of car do you want?"

I look out the window, absorbing the city during the day. People everywhere, in cars, on foot, all living their lives with blatant disregard for their daily freedoms. They talk without thinking of death. They live without holding themselves back from violence. I stare at a stroller-pushing mother and imagine our truck plowing her down, the scream and crack of her bones underneath the tires. If I roll down the window, I'll get a front row seat to their pain. "A convertible," I mumble.

We enter the four-lane road that is our destination, and Jeremy moves to the slow lane, peering out the window. "Where do you want to start?"

I scan the signs and point forward. "There."

He gives me a confused look. "Jaguar?"

"Yeah."

He puts on his blinker, taking his time pulling into the dealership and parking, his truck out of place among the sleek vehicles. I open the door and step out, my sneaker hitting the hard concrete, a small thrill shooting through me at the contact with the outside world. It is still new. I am still grateful. And that emotion is a reminder that I need to be careful. I need to behave. This purchase will open my world up. I need to make sure I don't open it too far and suck hell in along with it.

I step forward a few steps and stop, my eyes feasting on a midnight blue beast in the front row. It glistens under the sun, a hint of glitter in the paint. I don't move, don't take my eyes from its lines. It would look down its perfectly created nose at my high school Honda Accord and snort, smoke puffing from the vents on its sides. It is sex, speed, and attitude all rolled into one. It looks like a car that would make side bets with its owner, and rub its hands in glee at the prospect of mayhem.

I can buy this. I have money to burn, and this can be mine. It has been years since I have bought anything frivolous. But for my ticket to freedom, it feels like the time is right to splurge. To open the door, sit in its leather, and celebrate the unorthodox definition of success I have attained.

I hear the scuff of feet against pavement and break my eyes from the car, colliding with the image of a thin man, his suit pressed, his eyes passing from Jeremy's truck to my jeans and finding us both lacking. He tilts his head with a perfunctory smile. "Anything I can help you two with?"

"We're just looking," Jeremy offers, and I send him a look that stops him cold, his eyes questioning as his mouth stops moving.

"That one," I say, reaching out and pointing to my car. "I want that one."

The man continues to smile, an impressive feat that manages to convey annoyance without breaking the mold of professionalism. "The F-TYPE S. That is our V8 model, a fine car. Perhaps you'd like to step inside and discuss pricing?"

"No." I step forward, running my hands along the glossy paint, the car seeming to swell underneath my touch. I can imagine her purr, can hear her throaty growl when she loses all control. "I want to drive it."

CHAPTER 45

House Arrest Countdown: 10 Days

"MR. RENZA?"

Marcus looks up from his desk to see a man, tall and lanky, a thin tie knotted around his neck, rolled-up sleeves revealing tattoo-covered forearms. He frowns. "What?"

"I'm Nick. John said you wanted to see me? I'm the tech guy."

He eyes him for a long minute, the man's image not consistent with the pocket-protector nerd he'd been expecting. Another minute passes before he pushes on his desk and rolls away, gesturing forward with a hand. "Come here."

The large room grows smaller with the new presence, the man's stench invading Marcus's personal space, his seat before the desk barely containing the constant movement of his body, finger taps, hums, bouncing legs. The man has not one bit of control, an infuriating condition. Marcus glares at him, pulling a notepad from his center drawer and ripping off the top sheet, his pen pushing it across the table at the man, the camgirl's website scribbled across its surface.

"This website? This is what you want info on?"

"Yes."

"Okay…" the man drawls out. He drops his messenger bag on the closest chair and digs into its depths, pulling out a tablet.

"Let me pull it up. You said on the phone you were blocked from it?"

"Yes."

"Your IP address is probably toast. But my iPad won't use your Wi-Fi, so it should let me in…yes." He sets down the tablet on the desk, at a place where they can both see the screen. "Damn, she's hot."

Marcus's hands grip at the arm of his chair. His control is slipping, another indication of prison rotting his composure. Two years ago he wouldn't have blinked at that statement. Two years ago he wouldn't have felt ownership of a girl he met on the Internet. Fuck, two years ago he wouldn't have been wasting precious time *on* the damn Internet. The man runs his fingers over the surface of the device, pressing on links at a speed that sickens Marcus, the linger of his eyes over Jessica's body angering him even more. "So…I'm sorry—what info did you need?"

"Can you unblock me?" Marcus asks, his fists clenching against the top of his dress pants.

The man laughs, sitting back in Marcus's chair, his eyes staying on the intro video, one that shows a naked Jessica giggling into the camera, her small bare breasts heaving in erotic slow motion. "Nope. Ain't happening, man. Power to the geeks, that's the beauty of the Internet!" He makes some ridiculous hand pump gesture that pokes at a part of Marcus he had intended to leave in prison. The man continues, oblivious to his foul. "Your IP address is your social security number, man. And every time you visit a website, you're shoving that shit into their face. A website can block your IP, or…say…every IP within a certain zip code or state, or country. And then you're done. Nothing. Nada. No access for you. And I can't do anything about it." He laughs as if the idea pleases him, stopping when a low growl is emitted from Marcus's throat.

The man has the sense to quiet down. "What were you doing when you were blocked?"

"I clicked on the 'Contact Me' link." Marcus says tightly.

The idiot reaches forward and taps the link, the familiar "BLOCKED" status twisting Marcus's stomach. "Well that's new," the man says, surprised, a hint of admiration in his tone. "Looks like it's got you on limited access that triggers a block if you do certain actions on the site. Chances are whoever set this up tied in the area's IP addresses. So you've got two options." He looks up, the words giving Marcus a glimmer of hope.

"Go ahead," Marcus spits out, ready to strangle the information out of the man.

"You can get a tablet and use the cellular provider's IP address. Or I can mask the IP address or set it up to use your cell phone's hot spot. But it'll only give you limited access. You click on that link, or any other triggering link, and you'll be blacklisted again. And eventually you're gonna run out of connection spots unless you get in your car and drive. Which…" The smirk on his face tells Marcus that he is aware of his house arrest. Forget reestablishing his manhood via Jess Reilly; maybe he'll just work this guy over. Teach him some damn respect.

The asshole keys a few more entries and then looks up. "Anything else, man?"

Man? I am not your man. I am your fucking employer. Treat me with some goddamn respect before I shove six inches of it up your ass. "I want to know who owns this website and how to find her."

"Find her?" The man looks intimidated for the first time, his tattooed Adam's apple moving up and down with his swallow, and he glances back at the "BLOCKED ACCESS" title on the screen. "I thought you were stuck here, couldn't…"

"Get me the fucking information," Marcus growls. "And get the fuck outta my chair."

The tattooed man takes his time, the slow shuffle as he stores his tablet and moves away from the desk, lighting a new flare of anger in Marcus as he returns to his seat, glares at the man, and thinks of prison. This kid would have been his bitch within the hour, respectful eight ways to Sunday.

He watches the man's slow exit and calls out to him as he pulls at the heavy doorknob. "Tonight. I want the information tonight."

No response, not a "yes, sir" or a "right away." The lack of response burns, and the numbers in front of him blur, his focus pulling, his desire to explore her site competing with the disrespect of the kid. Who hired that piece of shit?

He controls himself, taking a moment before reaching over and yanking up the phone. He calls the redheaded servant, who jumps on the line before the second ring. *Finally*. Someone with some respect. The kid was growing on him, despite the red hair. "I'm expecting some information from that asswipe who just left here. As soon as he delivers it, fire his ass."

CHAPTER 46

THE LOOK BETWEEN Jeremy and the salesperson puts a dent in my "I'm not going to kill anyone today" outlook. I growl under my breath and open the door, sliding into the driver's seat and opening my purse. I pull out my driver's license and hold it out, waiting.

Five seconds pass.

Ten.

Twenty.

I turn, looking up at JagPusher. "That's what you need, right? For a test drive?"

"Ma'am, this car has only eight miles on it." The man's smile is gone, a terse exasperation in its place.

"And?"

"And it costs a hundred and four thousand dollars," Jeremy whispers loudly from behind the man.

"It seems like, at that price point, you'd be a little more helpful," I snap, facing forward again, the license still dangling from my hand.

I wait for a long, silent moment, then feel the jerk of plastic as he takes it. There is a pause, and I look over to see him examining the front. "My apologies, ma'am. I didn't realize you were a distinguished resident of Mulholland Oaks Apartments. Please give the cockroaches my regards upon your return home." He smiles acidly and spins, a flutter of suit and presumption, and strides toward the dealership, my license firmly in hand, as if he has evidence and is headed for the principal's office.

I wrap my hands around the steering wheel, gripping the leather tightly, and imagine his neck between my palms, the whites of his eyes as I strangle the life from his chest. The heavy weight of his body as it slumps, dead, against me. I exhale a slow breath and enjoy the vision for one, final, moment before I push it aside.

I feel the car shift as the passenger door opens and Jeremy settles in. I open my eyes and glance his way.

"Nice car," he remarks casually.

"Yep."

"Am I a little off base or does—"

"You're off base," I interrupt him.

"Really? 'Cause the sticker says a hundred thousand dollars, which is a—"

"A hundred and four thousand," I correct him. "Don't presume to know my financial situation."

That shuts him up and he sits, silent, for a moment, before fully turning to me. "You have a hundred thousand dollars?"

"Yep."

The return footfalls are double in number and I groan, opening the door and preparing for battle, stepping out and turning to face the oncoming pair, my unhelpful salesman and his older suited counterpart, a man whose irritated expression screams of a supervisory title.

"Ms. Madden," JagPusher begins. "You have no car currently, or previously, registered in your name."

I fold my arms, catching a glimpse of Jeremy in my peripheral vision. He sits, facing forward, a confused expression on his face, which is adorable enough for me to want to cover him in kisses. "Your point?"

"I don't think we're the dealership for you," the manager says with dismissive authority.

I lean against the car, feeling her straighten underneath me, and grin, my arms still folded over my T-shirt. "You've got five minutes to sort out your dick-measuring contest, then I need a key to test drive this car. *This* one. Not another F-TYPE, or your shitty-ass XFs, or some used Lexus that you have on the back lot. If you don't get me a key, I'll call Jaguar corporate, preorder an identical V8 from the next closest dealership, and bitch enough about discrimination that I'll have it delivered directly to my fabulous apartment at Mulholland Oaks and let your dealership cover the shipping along with any servicing for the next ten years, just to help cover my pain and suffering." I raise an eyebrow at the men and wait long enough to see indecision in their eyes before sliding back into the driver's seat and reacquainting myself with my new baby.

Jeremy and I are left alone for less than five minutes before JagPusher returns, passing me a single black key, and stepping back with a pained look. Two minutes later, Jeremy and I are screaming down Highway 244.

Screaming might be a strong term. *Softly whistling* might be more appropriate. Whatever you'd call hands at ten and two, my foot whisper-soft against the pedal, the car traveling twenty miles under the speed limit and still in second gear. I can practically hear the car scoff at me. But other than my road trip down Murder Lane and the Fireworks Date, I haven't driven in three, almost four years. So forgive me for not giving this car the proper strap-on fucking it deserves.

"We're getting passed by minivans." Jeremy's voice is quiet, a touch of humor in it that indicates he is smiling.

I don't look over. Can't. I'm too scared to take my eyes off the road. I push slightly harder on the accelerator and watch the speedometer creep up to thirty-seven miles per hour, then relax my foot and put on my blinker.

"Where're we going?"

"Back to the dealership. I'm happy with it."

"We've gone a mile, tops. You haven't even left second gear."

Truth is, she scares me a little. I can feel the coil of energy in her body, know, with her quick jump from my pedal, what she is capable of and I respect that—the bundle of madness barely suppressed. I will learn to unleash her. But the fact that I fear her is reason enough for me to buy her. We are connected. We are more similar than Jeremy or JagPusher will ever understand. We both carry a demon inside.

CHAPTER 47

I CONSIDER REFUSING to go into the dealership upon
our return. My reluctance half due to the fact that the employees
seem to be presented, like fresh delicacies, in glass cubicles ready
for my choosing, all waiting expectantly for death. The other half
of my resistance to entering is pure stubbornness on my part, my
adolescent desire to stamp my feet and crow my wealth and purchase ability exuberantly as I dramatically create a scene in the
middle of the parking lot.

But I behave. I park carefully, palm the shiny new key and
walk in, Jeremy's hand finding mine and squeezing it. I look at
our union, at his fingers looped through mine, the unexpected
contact confusing in its normalcy. How long has it been since I
held someone's hand? Annie was the last, her seven-year-old palm
slightly sticky in its grip. But...before that? Years. Years climbing on years of neglect. I detangle my hand from Jeremy's and
step through the glass door he holds open. I made the stupid decision to profess a love that I'm still unsure I should allow myself. I
probably should, in an attempt at crisis management, insert a little
space in this new relationship.

Once I pull out my checkbook and explain that I'll be wiring
cash for the car, all attitudes dissipate. There are smiles, waves,
offers of champagne, and a disgusting display of ass kissing. After
a halfhearted attempt at negotiation, they knock a few grand off

the purchase price and begin the paperwork process. Jeremy and I step from the office and settle into the lobby's couch.

"You can go," I offer. "I'll drive home."

"I don't mind. It shouldn't take long. Did you want to get lunch?"

Lunch. I glance at my watch. One fifteen p.m. Normal people would be hungry. But all I want to do is get in my new car and drive. Celebrate my new independence. Even if my way of celebrating is driving in the slow lane with hazards on. "No. I need to get home."

I push through my door an hour later, wincing when the knob slams into the white plaster with a thunk that sounds of damage. I move past this week's collection of packages and pull out my cell, dialing a number I know by heart. It is not Wednesday. It is not two o'clock. But I need to speak to him. Need to hear his calming voice and rational thought process. I have done too much. I have gone too far. I am *not* ready for this. The decision I just made pushes on me with stern, unyielding fingers, shoving my self-worth down into the ground.

He answers and I breathe a sigh of relief.

"Deanna? What's wrong?"

"Nothing. I just . . . I just need to talk for a moment."

"It's daytime. Are you okay?" *You shouldn't be uncontrollable during the day.* His unspoken thought only increases my stress level.

"It's nothing to freak out about. I—just—"

"You what?" Dr. Derek's voice drops an octave, fully into calm psychiatrist mode, and I relax slightly, examining the key in my hand briefly—a forbidden burst of pleasure shooting through me. I set it on the counter and move to my bed, sinking onto the surface and peeling my shoes off.

"I bought a car."

"You bought a car."

"Yes. Jeremy drove me."

"So...you bought a car. In person."

"Yes. Was that a mistake?" I let out a long breath, trying to understand why I am shaky. What it is about the last hour that has me so worked up. But I know what it is. It's the same reason I am calling him now. Because I feel like I've gone too far. I've accelerated my assimilation to an unhealthy level.

"Why didn't you ask me this *before* you bought a car?"

"It was kind of an impulse decision." And it had been. Purely impulse. A fleeting thought in the shower that I had grabbed with both hands, squeezed with unrestrained glee until its head had popped off, spewing out a new Jaguar that I now have no earthly idea what to do with.

What was my plan? To rejoin the human race? Run errands? Go for Sunday drives? *This* is my home. *This* is my safe place. These walls are what have protected me. Protected others from me.

"I don't like the new path you are taking. I understand that you are tired of isolation—"

"No, you don't understand. *Stir-crazy* is a term for a *reason*. You try to spend three years breathing the same air. Forget killing other people; I'll start chopping at my own neck pretty soon."

"Deanna. You were content, you were happy. Four months ago, you were perfectly adjusted and comfortable with the idea of living in that apartment till you were old and gray. What happened? What changed? Why *now* are you champing at the bit for change?"

Because four months ago I stepped outside. I stepped outside and felt the sun. I kissed a boy. I drove across the country and killed someone. All things I can't confess to. Can't discuss with the one man who could help me move past them. "Nothing happened." I lick my lips and search for an excuse. "I'm just...I don't know. I changed. Maybe it's my period."

The unmentionable period. The one word that causes every man to shut his trap, change the subject, move on and away, ready for anything but to discuss *that*. Every man except, apparently, Derek.

"Don't be ridiculous, your period has never had that effect before. Is it Jeremy?"

My stomach clenches. "No. Don't try to take that away from me."

"I can't take anything away from you, a fact evidenced by your continued denial to listen to any of my advice." His words are terse, and I smile. This is comfortable, this is what I know. Derek preaching, me arguing. I feel a bit of my tension ease.

"Can you take the car back?"

I laugh. "I didn't ask if it was refundable, but I'm pretty sure the answer to that question is no."

"You're enabling yourself. That car is a key to some very dangerous doors. You need to get rid of it. Immediately."

And just like that, the purchase turns sour. I knew. I knew before I dialed his number. I knew when my heart was racing in the stairway that I'd made a mistake. That I am biting off more than I can chew and that this piece of candy will pull me around by the mouth until it drags me off the cliff and into hell. But hearing the words from his mouth, knowing the wisdom behind them...it cements my fuckup. Quite possibly my most expensive fuckup ever. I slump, sliding off the end of the bed and leaning back against the mattress. I listen to Derek's steady breath, and wish he were here to hold me. Hug me. I bet he's a good hugger. A good, responsible hugger who makes you feel like he is taking some of your worry with the embrace. I close my eyes.

"I've got to go."

"Deanna—don't—" He pauses. "Just don't drive anywhere. Give yourself a few days to think. Promise me you won't drive till we talk tomorrow."

"Okay."

I hang up the phone and look at the car key. Lying lonely on a worn linoleum counter. Waiting for something more. A life to explore. I close my eyes, drop my head back against the bed, and feel its pain. Another thing we have in common.

I need to get online. I roll over and push myself onto my feet. Distraction will help.

CHAPTER 48

NICK HOPPER SITS in a parking lot, the adjacent restaurant's free Wi-Fi sending a weak but usable signal to his laptop even after the hours pass and the interior lights go out. He starts with a few simple searches, tracking down the Internet DNA of one Jess Reilly, Internet superstar. There is the face that someone shows, the makeup that smears a pretty façade over their online presence—then there is the truth behind the makeup. The un-Photoshopped images, the fat body behind the close-cropped Facebook profile pic, the lease that sits in the glove box of the Porsche. He finds the makeup easy enough, the camgirl's location too clearly displayed, a P.O. box as easily found as clicking on the "Contact Me" tab of her website. She can't be that stupid, can't be that stupid and still be alive and online. Some psycho, some version of the man he has just left, would have tracked her down by now. Corrupted that sweet smile in ways that keep single women up at night.

Nick's heard the stories about the man who signs his paychecks. He's been at Renza Development for two years, his start date a couple of months before the man was sent away. The rumors had swirled during his initial weeks of employment, rumors backed up by the courtroom drama that was broadcasted on truTV for the whole world to see. The man is seriously fucked up. Two years later and Nick can still picture the chick, Katie something-or-other.

The girl's face had looked like that of a stroke victim, the right side unresponsive when she spoke, the testifying doctor stating that it was a result of tissue damage. She sat on the stand and revealed that the damage was done with his fists, his belt, and—at one point—the toes of his dress shoes.

He closes his eyes to the memory and types on. Peels back the façade of Jess Reilly and digs deeper. Her cover is impressive, going five or six levels deeper than is necessary. He slurps a Big Gulp and breaks a few more federal rules involving privacy. Focusing on her website, skirting past the private registration and moving closer, the scent of her fills his car as he hacks his way closer to the brunette's truth.

It isn't a quick process. Someone with skill had set her up. But he finds a few holes. Pushes them wide open and crawls in. And finally, hours later, he has an address. A long way from her fake Iowa address. An even longer way from Marcus Renza's Miami mansion. Maybe Mr. Renza won't go there. He can't, right? He is under house arrest. For now at least. Nick writes down the address with a reluctant hand. Then he starts the car and heads back to the mansion.

CHAPTER 49

HackOffMyBigCock: hey killer

"EASY THERE." I stick out my tongue and lean over, open up the drawer that contains my outfits of the schoolgirl variety. "You in the mood for green or red plaid?"

HackOffMyBigCock: just get naked. skip the outfit.

I pause, stockings already in hand, surprised. We've chatted for three years, and he's about worn through every schoolgirl outfit I have. Straight nudity is a new thing. "What—your prep school girlfriend dump you?"

HackOffMyBigCock: keep laughing. Ill find a new fetish. Maybe turn into a furry freak. Make you spend some of that cash on some big ass costumes.

I wrinkle my nose. "I don't have enough closet space for furry fans. And I'm sweating my ass off as it is. I can't imagine being under these lights in a twenty-pound kangaroo outfit."

HackOffMyBigCock: fuck kangaroo. I wanna fuck polar bear ass. youd be a sexy polar bear.

I laugh, spinning on my knees till my back is to him, and unclip my bra, glancing over my shoulder at the cam, and give him a teasing smile.

HackOffMyBigCock: turn around. Let me see em.

Mike is the only person on this earth who knows about my

wealth. I'm pretty sure there is very little about me he doesn't know. I didn't think he knew about Jeremy. Didn't think he had made that level of invasion into my habits. Guess I was wrong on that front. But, my love life notwithstanding, the bigger deal is that he knows who I really am. Knows my family history, my address, my banking info. Even knows about that night in Georgia. Knows that I left with blood on my hands. He's the one who orchestrated the money transfer to Annie's family. I trust him explicitly. I don't have much of a choice. He, for a long time, was my lifeline to the world. He provided me my false identity, my Internet access, my firewall that (he guarantees) is impenetrable. And, that night in Georgia? I'm pretty sure he committed enough felonies to earn a jail cell right next to mine. He knows and protects me in a way that Jeremy will never be able to, is my friend in a way that no one else covers. Yet I've never seen him. Only memorized the sound of his voice. The grate of his chuckle when he laughs. The hiss of his breath when I bring him to orgasm. It is a strange relationship. He gives me so much and I pay him with the unemotional gift of cash. It doesn't really seem fair, but he hasn't complained yet so I keep my mouth shut and appreciate it.

I obey his directive and turn, covering my breasts initially before sliding my hands lower, uncovering inch by inch of skin, my breath quickening a bit.

HackOffMyBigCock: fuck bb. my cock is so hard.

"Show me it." A futile request, yet one I always throw out. He never shows me his cam. I lean back on the bed and pull my panties off, now fully naked before him.

HackOffMyBigCock: give me camera control

"Please," I growl.

HackOffMyBigCock: pretty please u gorgeous fucking woman

"That'll work." I grin. I lean forward, waiting, then clicking when a box pops up, asking for remote access. I'm pretty certain he has a way to get around my permission's control, but I appreciate his not going there. The extra step of granting him access makes me feel like I have some semblance of control. I click on the permissions box and then lean back, watching the screen as it pans out, my cameras working without touch, zooming and focusing as he takes control of our session.

HackOffMyBigCock: lie on ur side. then open those legs for me.

"Do you want me to touch myself?" I watch the screen and wait for his response.

HackOffMyBigCock: no use a toy. 1 of your small vibrators. Hold it gently on your clit. Turn slightly so I can see your pussy.

I angle my body toward one of the cams, keeping my knees bent and my sex open. I grab a toy and turn it to low, lying down on the bed and running it gently over my clit, whisper soft. My body instantly responses, lubricating my inner walls, my clit standing at attention and straining for more contact. I close my eyes. "Turn on your mic."

There is an electronic beep, and I hear his breath, the sounds of a life somewhere else, far from me and my apartment of solitude.

"Hey there."

"God, you are beautiful." His voice is gruff, heavy with need. I love his voice. It brings to mind a face I will never see, a touch I will never feel.

I smile, my eyes closed, and imagine his mouth on me, replacing the toy, making an unhurried path across my sex. "I want you to fuck me so bad," I whisper, the statement eliciting a thick groan from him.

"Tell me. Tell me what you'd do to me."

"I'd get myself ready on your bed. Touch myself while I listen to you work. Imagine your hands on my skin, your mouth in between my legs." I arch my back, needing more stimulation, and turn the vibrator up, moaning softly when it bumps hard against my clit.

"Come here. I want you to crawl to me on your knees."

I don't move. "Not just yet, I want you hard and ready before I take you into my mouth."

He swears. "God, you are a tease. There isn't a thing on this planet harder than my cock right now."

"I'm picturing it right now." I move the toy lower, and slip the tip of it into my sex, the intrusion perfect. I open my eyes, hearing the movement of the cam, and watch on-screen as he zooms in, focusing on my lips around the toy. "I want to feel every ridge on your cock as you tease me with it. I want you to slide the tip of it in and out of my cunt and feel how hot and tight I am for you."

A low, guttural sound comes from him, and I arch my back, pushing further, my body greedy for more, the view of my sex pulsing around the hot-pink plastic erotic, even to me. Even to my eyes that have seen this view thousands of times.

"Please," he whispers, his voice tight. "Deeper."

I push it fully in, and the sounds of his orgasm rip through the speakers.

Some men are quiet when they come. There is a sudden pause, no sound at all. No soft breaths, no gentle moan. Their entire body clenches in a death grip of silence. Other men are vocal, moaning, speaking, gasping loudly as they expel their pleasure all over the keyboard. I had a shrieker once. A high-pitched shriek that blew out one of my speakers and made me fight back a smile. Mike is a groaner. He groans my name in a deep, guttural voice that runs a possessive touch down my back. His orgasms are long, enjoyable, and I feel a shot of arousal zip through me as he finishes. I squeeze my core around the toy, waiting, hoping that I might follow suit, my orgasm triggered by his. But the arousal fades, my attempts at catching it futile. I slide the toy slowly out, the camera zooming in on the action, his interest still piqued, and I hear him sigh as the length of it is exposed. "Fuck," he sighs. "If I didn't know better, I'd think you just avoided sucking my dick."

"You complaining?" I move the mouse, turn off his access to my computer, and switch the video feeds, choosing the cam that shows my face. I grin, and hear him chuckle in response.

"Not at all. You always take care of me."

"As do you," I shoot back, my eyes studying the timer for our chat. Seventeen minutes thirty-eight seconds. "Talk to you soon?"

"You know it, babe."

He clicks off and the "ENDED CHAT" message fills the screen. Eighteen minutes. A hundred and twenty-five bucks. Though for Mike, I'd have done it for free.

CHAPTER 50

THE MAN BEFORE Nick stands like a roadblock, framed by the arched doorway. A bright red roadblock, the man's flushed skin almost matching his hair in intensity. "It's late, Nick."

He glances at his watch. "Mr. Renza said he wanted it."

"I'll give it to him in the morning."

"It needs explanation. Can you just check—"

"Why don't you just tell me the explanation, and I can pass it on?"

Nick looks past him, his gaze sweeping over a perfectly kept space as he tries to think. Fuck it. He has a girlfriend at home waiting. "It wasn't easy to get. The girl has a really complex misdirection set up. The whole appearance is that she's in Iowa. At a college there. It's really tight. All the roads led the place they should. I almost stopped looking and brought you the Iowa apartment info I found."

The houseman sighs as if bored. "Just give me the info." He holds out a hand, the sleeve of his button-up riding up to reveal a watch that looks too dainty to be on a man's wrist.

Nick hands over a single piece of paper, the address on it. "I woulda had it sooner, but it wasn't easy to get. I had to track it down through the hosting account on a sub website, an old URL that isn't being used anymore—"

"I'll let him know." The man snatches the piece of paper, turning, his hand on the knob as he swings the door shut.

Nick sticks out a hand, stopping the door. "He told me I'd get a bonus."

The man's eyes glare at his hand, as if it is offensive. "It'll be in your paycheck." His gaze drags to Nick's face, the edge of his mouth curving slightly. "Your *final* paycheck. Your services are no longer needed, Mr. Hopper." He shoves at the door, Nick's hand moving just in time as the wood clicks shut with a loud finality.

He stares at the walnut surface, confusion giving way to irritation. Well...shit. Staring at the knob, he contemplates breaking down the door and getting her address back. Instead, swearing under his breath, he kicks at the nearest planter, the ceramic pot falling over with a satisfying crack, dirt spraying over the marble surface. His boots stomp down the gritty steps as he leaves.

CHAPTER 51

November 12—Two Years Earlier

"WHAT THE FUCK *happened?"*

The voice of Katie's father. Loud. Louder than when she crashed his Range Rover into the country club's entrance. Louder than when she had announced her teenage pregnancy, only to lose the baby three weeks later. Katie McLaughlin blinks her eyes and tries to focus, but can only see white. White fuzz. She closes her eyes tightly. Tries again.

"We aren't sure." A strange voice. One she doesn't recognize. Soothing. That's a mistake. Her father doesn't like to be soothed or coddled. Hugged or loved. He likes to be respected. A soothing individual doesn't, in his mind, respect him. The soothing stranger continues. "She was brought in by a couple of girls; they found her on Sixty-sixth Street just after four this morning. Curled against the back door of Maloney's."

"What the fuck's Maloney's?"

"Mr. McLaughlin, she's lucky to be alive. We pumped her stomach as soon as she arrived, which removed much of the drugs before they could take full effect. She'd been heavily drugged. Had we not gotten to her when we did, who knows the effect of that cocktail on her system, on her brain and memory receptors for that matter."

"She takes drugs."

No! Her brain screams the word. She doesn't do drugs. Hasn't for four years. He should know this, she has told him. He doesn't believe her. She blinks, fire-hot liquid pooling, vision unchanging, her brain infuriated by the white cloud that won't lift from her eyes. Tries to turn her head but can't. There's a brace of some sort keeping it in place. Swallows. Tries to speak. Her tongue is not cooperating, nothing is coming out.

"These weren't recreational drugs. They were Rohypnol, GHB. We cleared them from her system, and—other than short-term memory loss—there shouldn't be any lasting effect."

"You don't know my daughter. She's a drug addict."

The soothing voice starts sounding like someone with a backbone. Katie perks up, listening, while another part of her brain wonders where her mother is. "Mr. McLaughlin, focus. Your daughter has abrasions on her wrists and ankles indicative of being tied up. She has anal and vaginal tearing consistent with rape. Her right cheek-bone and eye socket are fractured as if she was punched repeatedly by a strong fist. She has broken ribs and lash marks as if from a whip or belt. This is not from a party or her own doing. She is a victim."

Katie stops breathing, her chest constricting as it struggles for air, her body suddenly chiming in with all of the places that ache, bleed, are broken. She stops trying to see past the white, stops trying to listen to her father, and only tries to think. To open up last night's window and remember. Then memories pour in, and she reopens her mouth. Gasps in a breath while she wheezes out a scream. Her lips, her tongue, finally working, opening and shutting as sound actually comes out.

She can speak. This is good. She doesn't hear her father's response to the stranger's voice. His thoughts, his words, no longer matter. She is too busy screaming for her broken soul.

She remembers, her memories going back to a dim bedroom, no

clear understanding of how she got there. She remembers waking up in the room. The man before her. The smile on his face . . . the . . . oh my God . . .

She remembers.

She remembers.

She remembers.

And suddenly, she wants nothing but to forget.

PART 3

"Can you rip his head off for me? Start pushing at his forehead until it snaps the fuck off? Yank in and rip out tendril after tendril of veins and organs until he is a hot dripping mess of blood?"

CHAPTER 52

MARCUS SIGHS. THIS should be a joyous occasion. The literal unshackling of oppression. Trumpets should sound, friends should surround him, bitches should cheer. Instead, the removal of Marcus's anklet is done without ceremony, his attorney looking on dourly at the rate of four hundred an hour. When the metal piece finally falls, the demon inside of him flexes itchy wings, and Marcus tries to keep a grin off his face. Finally, he'll have a normal range of activity. To dine in his old restaurants. To visit his properties. To return to the life of the elite. His old self would be making plans, calling business associates, celebrating with champagne and filet tonight.

Instead, he has only one thought. Only one goal. The reward that has, over the last three months, grown into an obsession. And now, with the bitch's address burning a hole in his pocket, it is the only thing he can think of. He shakes his attorney's hand, gives him a grim smile, then turns to the redheaded houseboy. "Gas up my car and pack me a bag. I have work to take care of."

CHAPTER 53

18 hours later

EMPTY TIME. IN moments of weakness it has led to violence. But empty time has also been the creation point for much of Marcus's wealth and most of his plans. Empty time can be precious if used properly. Can give him valuable moments to strategize. To think. To figure out the things most people rush right over. To judge past decisions and learn from his mistakes. Now, he drives. The open road before him, hours both behind and ahead. Empty time. Planning time.

It feels strange to drive, his initial hundred miles hesitant before he regained his confidence. Before prison, he rarely drove. Had people for that, every moment useful, a million-dollar property often brokered in the backseat. Real estate development and management is a nonstop process, one where a missed opportunity can mean lost market share. Now, he sees all of the benefits of being behind the wheel. Freedom. Obscurity. At this moment in time, this moment in space, no one on earth knows where he is. What he is doing. Before, with Thorat, a driver, and security staff, there were too many pieces. Pieces that all became liabilities when it came time for his trial. People had to be paid, controlled, intimidated. Thorat handled it all, keeping the silence while enjoying a healthy bonus and protection from Marcus in return. All of

Thorat's efforts useless, the jail cell still clanging behind him with finality. Yes, Thorat's procurement of the women, the delivery and cleanup crews, had all been convenient, his fuck house had been ideal, complete control of the environment liberating, but it had tied a hundred strings of evidence to him in the process. He had been stupid and egotistic to think he'd never be caught.

Here, on the open road, he has so many more options. And nothing but time to plan the perfect ending for Jess Reilly.

It has been weeks since their last chat, but she's been present every day in his mind. Like a flea you can't find on your skin. Taunting, teasing him. He'd had to satisfy himself with hand-fucks to her website's videos, her recorded voice coming through the speakers. Soon, he'll have her. In the flesh—not through the computer. His hands will be able to touch, his mouth to taste. She will be his coming-back act. And he won't necessarily have to kill her. Not if she behaves. Fucking might be enough, his cock in her, his hand on her face, forcing her eyes to his. She might behave, speak and tell him what he needs to hear. How good his cock feels. How much she wants him. How she was a little bitch for blocking him. How sorry she is. How he can fuck her any way that he wants. He will tie her down, spread-eagle. Fuck her face, her ass, the slutty place between her thighs. Maybe leave her there for an hour while he explores the town, has a celebratory steak and a nice merlot. Return when she's reached the point of panic. Fuck her through that stage. Let her scream into the gag until she's hoarse, beg until she cries. Take her again. Break her until the only thing she knows is his touch, and the only voice she recognizes is his. Then, depending on her spirit, he will decide what to do. Holding her life in his hands, he'll be in the ultimate position of power.

He'll just need to be smart. After Katie…after being locked up, listening to the wisdom of those beside him in jail—it is better to be safe. It is probably, from this point on, too risky to leave a girl alive. But the look in her eyes will help him make that decision. The lost, blank look is best. Those you can leave without worry; they aren't coming back. They'll bump around in their life until they kill themselves or get adopted. The ones who spit fire till the end...those are the ones you have to kill. They don't appreciate the attention and never learn respect, even when beaten and broken. They're the ones who come back and bite you in the ass. Katie had been that girl. Katie he should have ended. He frowns, all experiences with Jess Reilly exhibiting her fire, showing nothing of the submissive innocent on her website's videos. If only he had an additional tool. A child or a parent to threaten, break her with. He needs more information than the simple address the tech asshole provided.

He checks the GPS. Seven hours more. Then he'll be at her address. An estimated 10:30 p.m. arrival. A late hour, but not unthinkable. She'll be up whoring. He'll try knocking first, the dignified approach. If that fails, he'll resort to his tools.

If two decades in real estate and two years in jail had taught him anything, it was how to pick a lock.

CHAPTER 54

10:22 p.m.

SIMON HAS NOT *locked the door.* I sit on the floor and stare at the metal door before me. Count the scratches on its surface for the third time. Again I reach the number forty-seven. They are scratches of my own making, from nights when I went mad and tried to rip my way to freedom. Three years of insanity shown on that surface, should someone pay enough attention to look.

Simon has not locked the door. I noticed the oversight at 9:50, leaving a chat midsession, my feet bringing me to standing, my naked body heaving as I stared at the door, my eyes trailing down the thin crack between door and jamb and failing to see the thin view of dead-bolt lock. I ended the chat, leaving a fifty-year-old husband in Nevada hanging with his junk in his hand. I'd gingerly walked to the door, not touching its surface, not doing anything but looking. Verifying, my eyes close to the crack, that I was, in fact, unsecured.

10:23 p.m. It does not escape my attention that this is the precise time of night, roughly five years ago, that my mother was halfway through killing my family. That's not why I am shaking; this is not necessarily my genetic hour of killing. For me, the killing is not restricted to night—my last kill occurred at the time of day when most individuals were diving into a bowl of Cheerios.

But night is my weakest; night is my most vulnerable time. Hence my mandate that Simon lock me in.

Simon has not locked the door. He might be on the way now. Realizing, in whatever drug stupor that's claimed his body, that he is late. Flooring his Kia's gas pedal, not wanting to anger his source of pharmaceutical assistance. I move closer to the door, my bare feet sliding out, gripping concrete floor, my ass dragging across the cool surface as it plays catch-up with my heels. Closer now. Close enough that I see a dried line of blood, no doubt shed in a past attempt to break down my door and kill someone.

It hasn't been long since I've had blood on my hands. Too short, really. Too short for me to want it like this. I had hoped, some twisted form of hope, that by killing, I would pacify the blood-thirstiness of my soul. That's how it works in books. The serial killer kills every once in a while, and that death tides him over until the next psychological breakdown. But I only got a few days of solace, a few days where my mental state was so ruined that I could only sleep. Sleep and lie with Jeremy and let him take care of me. He had been so caring, so worried. I wonder if he'd have been so nurturing had he known what I had done.

I let the sharp blade sink into Ralph's skin and yank left, cutting the throat as I have, through books and videos, been taught, the blade jerking in a wet sweep across his neck until it breaks loose of the skin.

I close my eyes and savor the memory. Wrap my arms tightly around my knees and rock back and forth, focusing on the images in my head, the way his blood pooled in the dirt, the look in his eyes, the steal of death across his features. The power. The rush. This is what Dr. Derek has taught me, this is what I know. When the urges get too strong, I am to contain myself and let the fantasies run wild. But I am not contained, my door is unlocked, and I can't focus on anything but the opportunity before me. Time is wasting. Any minute I could hear the scrape of metal on metal and my opportunity will be gone. I bounce to my feet and stand, my breath quickening as I fight what I want with what I know. I know I shouldn't. But I am weak. My hands shake. My heart pounds. I step forward and wrap my hand around the knob. Mentally prepare myself as—very faintly—my brain screams at me to stop.

I'm not leaving to kill.

I'm not leaving to kill.

I'm not leaving to kill.

I repeat the words and pretend to believe them. I can do this. I can leave the house at night. Just cross the street. Ice cream. I've gotten ice cream before. Ice cream and lotto. Maybe scratch-off or maybe I'll buy my Powerball early.

I'm not leaving to kill.

I twist the knob and pull open the last barrier before me.

CHAPTER 55

FINALLY AT HIS destination, Marcus slips gloves on, working finger by finger through the leather, flexing his hands when complete, his heart thudding quicker than it ever has, excitement flooding him.

Finally.

Now.

He has waited so long.

He turns off the car and surveys the shitty street before him.

CHAPTER 56

I AM NAKED. A piece of my sanity speaks up, the warm air of the hall hitting my skin, a sharp contrast to the icy chill of my apartment. I pause, the heel of my foot stopping the closing of the door. I look down at small breasts and bare legs. No weapon. Not that I need one. Not that I am leaving to kill. No one ever strangled someone to death with sexuality. I step back, like a jerky video set in rewind, left-right-left until my door swings shut and I am back in 6E. I move to my bed, bend before the stack of clothes, and grab sweatpants and a T-shirt, pulling them on without undergarments, my movement quick. I snatch a hair elastic off the bathroom sink and pull my long hair back into a messy bun. Grab a baseball cap of Jeremy's and tug it on, a quick glance into the mirror letting me know that I am good.

Ice cream.

A paper ticket that might hold a fortune.

Proof that I can handle freedom.

Without allowing myself to think, I push aside cardboard towers, squeezing back into the far corner of my apartment, my hands shaking in excitement by the time I reach my safe.

I spin the dial, 22-31-14, the gritty scrape of metal on metal giving way, and the door swings open. My eyes dance over the selection as the reality of what I am doing pushes its way into my mind. Is this who I am? A girl who can't take a single night without supervision? Ice cream. Lotto. I step back. Stare at the 9mm that leans against the right side of the space. It's loaded; I keep it loaded, with one in the chamber. I step another few steps back and fumble on the bed for my cell. Have trouble finding it among the tangle of my sheets. I dial the number I know by heart and hold it to my ear.

It rings and rings. With every ring the sound fades, and all I hear is the pounding in my head. The bellowing knock of insanity, it bangs at the inside of my skull and pushes me forward. I step forward as the phone rings, closer to the safe. *Ring.* My hand reaches out, tugs out the gun. *Ring.* It is cold in my hand but warm with possibilities. *Ring.* I heft it, feel the weight of it, then put it in the pocket of my sweatshirt, my finger light on the trigger. *I will not kill anyone.* It will be my protection. Ice cream. Lotto. I prefer my killing to be done with knives; I like blood, appreciate the close contact of manually cutting through a soul and watching it run, like uncontrolled tears, out of a body.

I know. Probably shouldn't stick that into the "Favorite Activities" section of a Match.com profile. I hang up the phone when his voice mail begins. Stick the cell in my pocket and head for the door, my conscience unable to be heard above the ringing in my ears.

I realize, at the moment that I step on the elevator, that I forgot shoes. My bare feet squish against the carpet, my mouth curling into a grimace as the stick of carpet lingers when I step forward. I freeze, midstep, in the middle of a pad that no doubt contains vomit and urine in its fibers. Bumping the "1" button with my elbow, I breathe through my mouth, trying to think of anything but the wet consistency of rotted carpet against my soles. I grab a moment of indecision and close my eyes. Pray. Pray that I won't kill Marilyn from 6B or a family of four unpacking food-stamp groceries in our parking lot. I don't need a gun to buy ice cream. I jab at the "6" button with the intention of returning the gun. *I will not kill anyone. Please help me God.* I don't know if it's a worthy prayer. If God even listens to psychopaths.

The car settles on the ground floor, and I hear the shudder of door open behind me I should stay on. Ride this beast back up to the sixth floor and return the gun. Without turning I pull my bare foot from the wet suck of carpet and step back, grateful for the hard concrete it hits, my second foot following quickly, any extra precautions disappearing with the close of the doors before me. It's okay. I can handle this. I won't use the gun. I will not kill anyone. I have a burst of confidence in my mantra, in myself, a moment of euphoria at the possibility of a successful field trip. It is nighttime. I am outside my apartment and *armed*, yet I will not hurt anyone. I put my hands in my pocket to stop their shake, the call of dark beckoning, my awareness narrowing as I focus on the task before me. I step to the left and push on the handle, the exterior door popping open, the world of cars and road open before me, the convenience store across the street glowing bright. In a normal neighborhood, the one I grew up in, the street would be quiet, the respectable families asleep or tucked away behind brick walls. But here, in a zip code that boasts the highest crime and lowest reportable income in the city, the streets buzz. I am surrounded, bodies sprinkled around the street, leaning against buildings, cars. I watch a prostitute skitter across the street toward the convenience store, wearing a pair of heels that cheaply mimics some of my own. Her end will come soon enough. It might be a blessing to have it through my hands, quick and final as opposed to a rough ending or slow death through disease. Plus, she is female, an easy target.

I pause in my step onto the street, realize the path of my mind, the grip of my hand around the gun and spin to the left, walking in a direction that has no destination, the only thought in my head one of flight. Flight from my own thoughts, from the horrific individual that lies inside my bones. *I wasn't supposed to kill anyone tonight. I didn't want to kill anyone tonight.*

My run from myself is redirected by the hand that closes around my elbow, a firm grip, the body tied to the hand too close for me to see, the hold pinning my elbow to his side as I am shoved forward.

I don't scream, I don't fight. It takes me a delayed moment to bring my mind out of my own self-loathing and realize what the hell is going on. I realize what is occurring around the time that the faceless stranger forces me left, into the dark space between two buildings, his grip tightening on my arm to a point of pain.

CHAPTER 57

EVERY JOB HAS its risks. A hacker's life just contains more. It is part of the allure. High risks, high reward. Risks make Mike's heart beat, his blood pump. It is what makes a mediocre life worth living. Plus, it gives him access to pussy. Women love the hacker angle. It makes a normal guy seem dangerous, connected. Makes them think he can, with a few strokes of deft fingers, accomplish anything he wants to. Unspeakable power harnessed by the sheer strength of self-control alone.

Mike closes the screen, watching Deanna's recorded show disappear with one reluctant mouse click. Ripping off a chunk of paper towels, he cleans off his cock, and rolls the chair back, tossing the damp towels into the trash can below the desk. He frowns, the towels missing their mark, batted away from entrance by the overfull can, bottles, takeout containers, and a healthy collection of used paper towels towering precariously over the rim of the basket. A quick debate over emptying the can is ended by a knock on his home's front door, the song echoing through the empty house. Loud and decisive, the knock authoritative enough to make his hand freeze and brain regroup. Rolling the chair forward, he clicks on the security system, and opens the cam that displays the front porch, the dim porch light displaying a man, his features unclear, his stance straight enough to scream *COP* via the high-def feed. Cops, in his world, equal Feds—the fear of hackers everywhere.

Mike's hands go into a frenzy as the man's fists pound again at the door. Firewalls get closed, feeds get killed, and he disconnects from the online file server. This pig can take every piece of his computer and it'll be months before they realize half the stuff they don't have. He locks down the computer and moves to the door, getting to the handle just as a third set of knocks begins.

◈

The door swings casually beneath his hand, his features relaxed, a friendly grin hiding the acceleration of his heart. His mouth curves more naturally into amusement as the man's eyes drop, surprised, to his face. There is a moment of hesitation in the stranger's face and then he smiles. Smiles. An unexpected response, one that puts a seed of fear in his stomach that feels unnatural. Despite his life, his situation, fear is an unfamiliar emotion. Mike reaches for the door, filled with the sudden and unexplainable urge to slam it in the man's face and flip the dead bolt.

"Can I help you?" His eyes pick up on the stranger's details. His shoes, black and shiny, with little tassels on the front. Dark gray slacks. A black sweater that looks too expensive for a Fed. A briefcase in hand, which fits every stereotype he would have envisioned. Keeping his face bland, Mike's examination continues. A wiry build and hard face, one that a smile does nothing to soften. Smaller and shorter than the security cam indicated, the man's strong posture making him appear bigger. Midforties. With eyes that are pure bad news. A cop he wouldn't trust to watch a dog.

"May I come in?"

"You got a warrant?" It is the wrong thing to say, a comment that screams *I've got something to hide.* But the man only smiles wider, and Mike feels the prickle of unease return.

"I'm not a cop. Why don't you let me in? I think you'd rather we have this conversation in private."

Not a cop. Right. Just a random stranger who feels the need to stop by at ten o'clock at night. Everyone knows you shouldn't let a stranger in. Knows you should refuse entry, close the door with a polite but firm rebuke. But most people haven't broken enough laws to earn them a lifetime behind bars. Mike has waited for this knock since he was thirteen, and hacked into the Ask Jeeves search database, causing every search query to return images of giant penises. He moves aside and lets the man enter, shoving at the door with his hand until it clicks fully closed.

CHAPTER 58

"WHAT'CHA DOING OUT here, white girl?"

The man is young, the sideways cap proclaiming his love for the Lakers while housing a forest of kinked hair. LoveLakers2Death looks toward the street for a quick moment before his gaze returns to me, his free hand stopping midhitch of his pants as he catches sight of the gun.

"Now? Hunting," I reply. I press the 9mm into his stomach, staring into his face as my mouth curls into a smile. This idiot. So helpful, bringing us both to a private location. Had I known it would be this easy, I'da left my apartment earlier. *I will not kill anyone.* I hear my conscience and grip the gun tighter, fighting a losing battle against ignoring it.

The man releases my left arm, and I shake it out, the imprint of his fingers no doubt having left a bruise. Raising both hands, he glances back to the street, this time for a different reason.

I watch him with interest, wondering at the man I have the ability to kill. His mouth chews at something, his eyes dart with manic regularity from me to the street, yet he is silent. I expected protesting. Begs. I dream of begs in the dark of night. Begs and screams. Yet here, it appears this man will die silently. It's quite disappointing, if I'm to be entirely honest.

"On your knees," I order. "Open your mouth."

I watched a show four years ago, back when I lived in the

decadent world of cable television, a *Forensic Files* episode, where they showed a collection of crime scene photos. One was from a suicide where the man shot himself through the mouth. The blood spatter was spectacular, painting the wall behind him with splatter and gore. If LoveLakers2Death is going to go silently, it may as well be pretty. I wonder at the hat, if it will fly off or if brain matter will hit and be contained in its yellow and purple cavity.

The man doesn't move. His eyes flick to the gun, then to my face.

God, I wish I had my knife. A stupid oversight on my part, one that made no sense. With a gun, there is only threat, then action. And action is loud and attention getting, especially from an unsilenced 9mm. I study the man and try to think, my brain sluggish when competing with the hum of need in my head. I push the gun deeper into the man's ribs. "On your knees or I'll shoot you in the side and *then* in the mouth. Look in my eyes and decide if I'm fucking with you."

Maybe it is the tone in my voice. Or the smile on my face. Whatever it is, the man obediently drops to his knees before me. And I've never felt stronger. I am fine without my knife. My kill can still be beautiful. I don't know this man, he may not deserve to die, but I *need* this, my four-month hiatus from murder a lifetime long. I lift the gun to his mouth and push it against his stubborn lips.

"Open."

At the moment he complies, his eyes pleading as his lips shake, my cell rings.

CHAPTER 59

WHEN I ANSWER the phone I hear people in the background and I feel a pang of jealousy that cuts through my bloodlust. Maybe that's all I need to solve my condition. The jealous distraction of another life. A life where I am out of this skin, surrounded by laughing people. Living my life.

"Just a minute." His voice is low and seductive, as if I am important and worth answering the phone for, worth stepping away for. As if he and I share a secret, and he is pausing his life to focus on me.

The voices muffle and fade, and I look at the 9mm against white teeth, then the man's eyes, which dart from me to the phone then the gun, the eye contact turning cross-eyed at the end. His tongue moves, and the gun shifts slightly in my hand. I smile at him and wonder how far the sound of the gunshot will travel. Try to remember how much this gun kicks and if I should use both hands.

"Deanna." I love when Derek says my name. I feel high on it, or maybe it is just the fact that I am seconds away from killing. Whatever the reason, right now I am un-fucking-stoppable.

"Derek." I hope he likes when I say his name.

"Is everything okay?"

His question breaks me in a way that shouldn't happen. Maybe it was fingers of concern that lace his words. *Someone cares.*

Someone, in some form, loves me. The real me. A girl who is very broken inside. A different someone, in another form, loves this man before me. A mother. A prostitute. A child.

"I'm in a bad place." I speak quickly, watching the man's eyes before me catch. LoveLakers2Death is listening Interested. I push the gun harder into his mouth and glare. Try to focus on him, but Derek is speaking and this situation is, with his one short question, falling apart.

"Tell me."

"Simon...he didn't lock the door." My voice is not my voice. It hitches when it speaks. It is weak, it trembles. It is the side of me that is scared of the side of me that is about to break open my world and destroy it. It is a voice that breathes hard and not calm.

"Where are you?"

I don't answer. If I speak, my voice may wobble. If my voice wobbles, the man before me may move. I suddenly don't know why I am here or what I am doing. I wanted ice cream and lotto. Wanted to prove that I could handle the night. That I didn't need a druggie to lock me in at night like a caged animal. Wanted to exist as someone other than myself. How did those wants become this situation? My fingers moments away from taking a stranger's life? I hang up the phone and shove it, with trembling fingers, into my pocket.

"Lie faceup on the fucking ground," I bark, my voice behaving. "If you do anything other than what I say, I will kill you." I step backward once, just out of reach of the stranger who likes the Lakers, whose life I almost took.

Muffled by fabric, my cell rings. I watch the man sit back, his hands up as he lies back on the dirty ground his eyes on the gun, which I now handle with both hands.

"Bye, motherfucker." I step back, the gun on him for seven full steps, until the ground beneath my bare feet changes and I am back on the street, my gun slipping back into the pocket of my sweatshirt. Then, with my cell buzzing against my stomach, I run home like the scared white girl that I am.

When I get home, I can't open the door. Simon has mother-fucking locked it.

CHAPTER 60

MIKE USHERS THE guest into the living room, his worn furnishings consisting of a couch, recliner, and coffee table. The furniture had been left by the previous tenant, someone with cats, and white hairs still litter the surface, any rough movement creating a snow effect in which the hairs float up, irritate any available allergies, and then rehide, waiting patiently for their next opportunity to invade.

The stranger sits back on the couch. Looks around, his eyes picking up on everything, something akin to confusion in his gaze. What was he expecting? Mike mimics the action, trying to see the room through foreign eyes, not picking up on anything suspicious, no computer equipment in this room, at least none visible at this moment in time.

He waits for him to speak, wondering f he will search the apartment, and if he will find the laptop that sits underneath him, beneath the couch, its battery no doubt dead, its code still fully functioning and incriminating.

The man clears his mouth and asks his first question, one that both calms Mike and introduces an entirely new possibility for his visit.

"You the boyfriend?"

He fights the urge to look around, to see if the uninvited guest is speaking to another individual. "What?"

"Where's the bitch?"

The bitch. A worrisome title for some poor girl in some place other than here. Mike blinks slowly, hiding the moment of elation at the realization that this man is in the wrong place. "Who?"

"Jess Reilly." The short man drags out the name, injecting lust and want and disdain, all into the three syllables.

Fuck. He is in the right place. Mike swallows, shrugs his shoulders to the best of his limited ability. "I don't know who you are talking about." This is unexpected. He can feel his body tensing, his protective instincts coming forward in one surge. This man, with his shifty eyes and expensive clothes, the darkness that seeps from his skin—he has no good reason to want her, no good reason to be here.

The man scoffs, rolling his thin neck, loose fat still bulging on the sides when his head tilts. "My web guy said this is her address. So where is she?"

"How'd he get this address?" In the horrible moment, the hacker in him is curious about which of the intentionally left rabbit holes was picked up and followed.

The man growls. Physically growls, like a chained dog, a response that doesn't match his meticulous appearance. "I don't fucking know. He looked into her website."

"I work on websites," Mike responds slowly. "Build them, manage them. Perhaps you're looking for someone who owns or puts content on one of those websites. But I have thousands of clients, I don't personally know a Jessica." *Thousands* was a gross exaggeration. Hundreds, maybe. If you added up every client he'd ever had. But there was only one Jess. Had been from the first time he had dealt with her.

The man's face hardens. He holds up a finger, pulls out an old cell phone. Dials a number and waits.

"Tell that tattooed computer prick to call me."

Then he hangs up, Mike's eyes picking up on the delicate flaring of the man's nostrils. The burn of his face. Embarrassment? At being mistaken? The man sets down the phone on the side table. Stares into Mike's eyes while his left hand fumbles in his pocket, pulling out something. Mike's palms sweat as the man flips his wrist, and reveals a blade.

"Whoa." Mike raises his hands. "I just build websites."

"That's it? Nothing else? Nothing the FBI would be interested in?"

Mike narrows his eyes and tries to figure out the man's point. And where he was going with the veiled threat. "I build websites. And write code. I'm a developer."

"Again, anything the FBI would care about?"

"What's your point?"

"That answers my question."

"Good, then you can leave." Brave words that don't match the quick thud of his heart as he watches the blade flip through the man's hands. Open. Closed. Open. Closed. "I build websites," he repeats, his record set on repeat. "Sorry that I can't help you more."

"And I just need to know about hers. Give me her name and address, and I'll walk out of here and leave you to your next game of Halo."

He chuckles in response, cursing Deanna's beautiful face as dread crawls up his uncooperative spine, his mind moving rapidly as he studies the stranger before him and tries to place his connection to her. A client? Has to be. The list of possibilities a hundred names long.

"Sexy jess dot com. That's the site."

Mike works his mouth, cultivating a blank look as his mind searches desperately for a plan. "Doesn't ring a bell. I coulda built it years ago. Chances are, any information I do have is old. I can tell you this. I haven't heard of the URL or a Jess Reilly. And I don't have a girlfriend. I don't even leave this house."

Out of the entire statement, only two of the four sentences are true. He doesn't have a girlfriend, and he hasn't, with a few rare exceptions, left this house in the last eight years.

CHAPTER 61

AT TEN YEARS of age, any thought of being a physical badass was abandoned. That was the age when Mike Rollins put down a baseball and picked up a keyboard. When his world became smaller and centered on things that required little physical effort. Books on code were read, online chat forums and computer clubs joined. Visions of designing video games or social networking sites became the new fantasy. Hopes focused on becoming the next Internet billionaire, surrounded by women and friends and admiration.

Quick money called, and greedy adolescence listened. Mike pushed aside developmental projects and focused instead on breaking the genetic code that is the Internet. Once you understand it, it's easy to curtail it. Once you can curtail it, you can start to control it. Build fake trails that will lead your opponents turning in circles until they fall on their ass. Create insurmountable roadblocks that are truly only paper thin. Hide someone so deep that you are the only person who can pull them out.

The truth:

Deanna Madden, aka JessReilly19, is twenty-two years old. She lives on 163 Oakmont Place, Apartment 6E. She has, unfortunately for Mike, a boyfriend, one Jeremy Pacer. She has a net worth of $2.3 million, half of which is hidden away in the Cayman Islands in a place known only to her and Mike. She is an orphan, her parents and younger siblings killed four years ago in a manner one can only describe as brutal.

The appearance:

Jessica Reilly is nineteen years old, a sophomore at the University of Iowa. She lives in an on-campus dorm on a student budget. She is single, widely popular, and, as evidenced by her Facebook wall, hasn't met a frat party or house party she'll turn down.

This man will never track her down. It is impossible. The cover was tested recently, just a year ago. After all the groundwork was in place, Mike posted a challenge to Hnet. Offered a thousand of Deanna's bucks to anyone who could find one hole in her story. A hole that led to something other than a dead end or him. Forty-nine hackers accepted the challenge. Forty-nine who, within three weeks, admitted defeat. This man, with his rudimentary knowledge of the Internet and his Motorola Krzr, doesn't stand a chance. And his guy in IT either sucks or is on the same side Mike is, which involves keeping this psycho as far from her as possible.

CHAPTER 62

I BANG ON Simon's door like a madwoman. What if he is not home? What if he locked my door and left? *I can't stay in this hall.* I have nowhere else to go.

He opens the door within minutes and I am treated to the sight of Strung Out Simon. It is ugly. In the background is a girl, her body draped across a black leather couch that looks to be a Big Lots special. His jaw works, back and forth, his bloodshot gaze shooting from me to my door, me-to-door, me-to-door, no doubt wondering how in the hell I escaped.

"You were late," I gasp, my vision blurring, my hands coming up and gripping the door frame. I think I'm crying. How do four sentences with Derek turn me into such a girl?

"I...I'm sorry." He looks at my door again. And me.

I want to, despite the breaking of my composure, pull out my gun right now. This asshole is a worthy subject. But even I, in my manic state, realize the stupidity of that. Morality and eyewitness aside, Simon is too close, I need him. And what I really don't need is him, and the crack whore behind him, to know that I am psychotic. "Unlock the fucking door," I grit.

The idiot looks down, at his own doorknob, which rests, unlocked, in his hand. His cheeks flex as he tries to understand. Behind him, the girl starts to laugh, a pig squeal of a sound. I close my eyes and try not to think of death.

I shouldn't have left.

I shouldn't have left.

I should have cammed like a good girl, then went to bed. Simon should have locked me in. I want to kill him so badly, it physically pains me.

"Unlock MY apartment," I growl, pointing with a hand to my door. "NOW."

"Oh." He digs in his pocket, moving through the doorway, too close to me. I don't like the smell of him, don't like how his stare brushes up my outfit like he can see through it. I step back and wrap my hands around the two items in my pocket.

"You know you're ringing," Simon says, smiling as if he is funny, his hand taking too long to pick out the key. I stare at his key ring and wonder if, shoved far enough down his throat, it would choke or kill. "Your cell?" he adds helpfully, as if I don't know that my cell phone is ringing.

"Unlock my door before I kill you." The words break out of me in a barely controlled stream of rage.

He squints at me as if deciphering the words, while his right hand turns the lock and the door cracks open. I shove past him, slamming the door the moment my feet enter the sanctuary of my apartment. "Lock it!" I scream, my eye at the peephole.

He looks up and down the hall as my hand closes around the gun. Shakes his head before twisting the key in the opposite direction. I sink to my knees as I hear the tumbler move, my hands pulling out the cell and engaging the call.

"I'm fine," I say. "I'm home. I'm locked in."

"Jesus Christ!" Derek thunders into the phone, the emotion greater than I have ever heard. "Do you have any idea what… what I've been picturing?"

"Yeah," I whisper, my voice unable to reach much further than that. "I'm tired, Derek. I need to sleep."

"We need to discuss this, Deanna. Where were you when I called?"

"I'm in the apartment, Derek. I'm safe. So is everyone else. I didn't do anything."

"That's not good enough—"

"I'm going to bed," I interrupt. "I'll call you in the morning."

"Promise me." His tone makes me pause, makes my thumb stop in its journey to the "End Call" button. It is pleading, concerned. I love it.

"I promise," I mumble. "Tomorrow morning."

Then I end the call, pull the gun out of my sweatshirt, and crawl, with filthy feet, into bed.

CHAPTER 63

MIKE TENSES WHEN the man stands. He fights the reaction, trying to keep his body relaxed, his hands from shaking, when the man moves toward him, the knife held loosely in his right hand, a flip of his wrist spinning it, letting Mike know in one easy movement that he has held it countless times. Used it. This short, thin man with his dark eyes and soulless smile... he cannot get to Deanna. Yet Mike, made even shorter by his chair, seems to be the only thing standing in this man's way. The asshole rolls his wrist, then gestures with the knife.

"Let's move to your computer."

Stepping back, out of the way enough to allow Mike to wheel, through the living room, into the bedroom, his eyes skipping everywhere as his brain tries to think, tries to work through the best way to pull up the information that shouldn't be given.

Logging in, he bypasses the mainframe, doing a simple search in the database for Jess Reilly. Jess Reilly's name in the computer will only bring up the numerous creations that confirm her false identity, all true knowledge housed under her real name. He opens a client file, stealing a piece of paper from the printer and writing the address in clear, neat print. *Jess Reilly. P.O. Box 2499. Des Moines, Iowa.*

"A P.O. box isn't worth shit," the man interjects. "I need a street address."

"She probably lives in a dorm," Mike murmurs, turning back to the computer and pulling up Facebook, to the page where he spends a good part of every day.

"No. Stop bullshitting me. My tech guy said she's not at the college."

"Was that the same guy who told you she lives here?" He regrets the sarcasm as soon as it comes out, covering it with a shrug, turning to glance over his shoulder. "That's all I got, man. It looks like I sent the bills to her P.O. box, she paid them. Last job I did was build her website, and that was..." Reaching up, he scratches the back of his head in a gesture he hopes is convincing. "Uh...a few years ago. Long enough that I don't remember it."

Dropping his hands to the arm of the chair, he forces himself to keep his head forward as the man walks behind him, and there is suddenly the edge of the sharp blade against the delicate cords of his neck. The next exhale, cautious in execution, causes a prick of pain, and Mike's hands shake slightly when he lifts them from the keyboard.

"Are you sure?" the asshole says slowly, dragging out each word.

The shake of his head is a mistake, the blade showing exactly how sharp it is, the gentle movement across the edge burning hot against Mike's skin, and he inhales slowly, as carefully as possible. "I'm sure," he says softly. Slowly. "I told you. I don't know anything."

The knife is removed so quickly that it skitters across his neck in its exit, a searing heat of pain quick and light, the fear shaking him more than the hurt, the shock of it all freezing the hacker in place for a moment before he pants in relief.

Stab. The movement is unexpected, the man moves quickly, jerking his hand in a downward motion to the shoulder, the smooth cut of blade passing through clothing, skin, and tissue. Every thought process is instantly immobilized, sudden, intense pain screaming through Mike's body, the agonizing pain bringing to mind the time, back when he had full use of his body, that the snot-nosed neighbor from three houses over slammed his fingers into the car door, the five intense seconds of pain before the door was yanked open by a frantic parent's hand. Only this pain doesn't stop. It continues, screaming bloodred across every pore in his body, dots appearing in his vision as he struggles for breath, for speech, for thought. Gripping his shoulder tightly, shaky fingers discovering what his awkward glance is too short for. *The butt of a knife.* Blood, lots of sticky liquid underneath his fingers, soaking his shirt, his world gasping as the fuckhead before him says something that his mind can't hear because it is too obsessed with the struggle to stay conscious. He won't betray her. This psychopath, who will stab an innocent man without a second's pause, cannot get near her. Who knows what she has done to him, if there are other Ralphs out there, what grudge this man holds against her beautiful self, and what he might do to avenge that grudge.

More dots. His torso sways and he tries to stay upright, wheezing aloud, the sound of the asshole's curse ringing out, the man suddenly standing before him, his eyes in his vision, arresting. They are so close they could kiss, the stranger's breath too clean for the dirty ass that he is. *Anger.* Mike's brain focuses on the avenue, anger over pain, and the dots cease enough for him to understand the words.

"Look at me, you prick. Convince me that you're telling the truth. Don't be a hero for her."

A hero? He's never claimed to be one. He's a worthless excuse of a man, but one who has done right by one person: her. Fuck this man and his knife. Fuck the shell of a life that exists in this chair. This man has no plans of leaving him alive.

"I can give you money," he gasps out, a plan formulating, the details sorting as he breathes through his teeth and tries to handle the pain.

The man laughs, close and hard in his face, and he was wrong, this breath is not clean. Not a speck of this man is. His eyes are hard and dead, his manner almost gleeful, his compassion nonexistent. "I have money." The man sneers.

A believable statement. Mike owns a duplicate version of the watch on his wrist. Bought it when he did his first big deal, back when he was an impressionable hacker who sold his morals for cash. Got his first half-million-dollar payday and wanted some flash. Something that a girl, looking at his webcam, would notice. Be impressed by. So he plunked down thirty grand for the Breguet, his own wrist for a short time matching this bloodthirsty maniac's. Now, it sits somewhere in a sock drawer. Mike would have sold it by now, should have sold it by now, but time passed and distractions occurred. And now it is too late. Thirty-thousand-dollar watch sales are the kind of thing that FBI searches pull up. Find suspicious. Can be the final straw that pushes a judge to stamp "Approved" on a warrant. He's smarter now. All his cash goes to the Caymans. Like Deanna, he stows it away for a rainy day that will probably never occur.

"I'll give you everything I have. Over a million dollars. Every dollar I've saved for five years." He allows the panic that he's held at bay to sink in, tears spilling and his voice breaking in the way that a pussy's would. "Fuck, I wouldn't give that up for some skank. Please. I'll give you it all." The words come out right. Like he is terrified, ready to sacrifice anything and everything in exchange for his life.

The blurred image before him straightens, and he gasps through his sobs, his shoulder seizing, and all he can wonder is if the knife in his shoulder is doing permanent damage. His shoulder, the joint that gives his hands life. Why couldn't the man have stabbed his leg?

"Set up a transfer. Every dollar you have. You're right, I don't believe you'd do that to protect this slut."

CHAPTER 64

THE MONEY HAD been a stroke of personal brilliance, one that came to Mike amid the searing pain and threat of death. Hopefully Deanna wouldn't mind losing a million bucks in exchange for a cryptic warning. He frowns, his mind reanalyzing the plan from her perspective. It *is* a rather expensive warning. But it is too late to change course now. At least if this asshole kills him, the warning—expensive or not—will get to Deanna. A way to catch her attention and put her on the defense. Mike carefully straightens before the keyboard and begins the process, leaving his personal funds intact. He also ignores around two hundred million of his clients' funds, thirty different Deannas, spread throughout the United States, a quarter of the money clean, most of it dirty, all in easy access of his handicapped fingers. Instead, Mike beelines for one place, Fifth Third Bank, worming into and going straight to one account: Deanna's US holdings. Combined balance: $1,342,109.12

"You know the account number you want the funds put into?"

The man thinks for a moment. Pulls out his cell and calls a number while Mike makes every attempt to stay conscious despite the hole in his shoulder.

"It's Marcus."

Marcus. The asshole has a name. Marcus . . . Marcus . . . a light-bulb clicks. He's most likely Marcus Renza, the client Deanna blocked just a month or so ago. The rapist who had just gotten out of prison. Mike's breaths shorten, a new wave of panic overtaking him, the weight of his responsibility increased. He is the weak link between this monster and her. A sudden image of her smile pops into his head and he closes his eyes. Tries to find strength that he hasn't needed since he was a child. The man speaks from behind him.

"A few months ago. Got an account number? I got that million for you, what's remaining on our hotel debt. Consider anything extra as additional interest."

The fucker laughs, a short sound that actually contains humor. "Sounds good. It'll be there soon." He leans back over Mike, the hard edge of his elbow digging into his arm, but Mike says nothing, watching as the man scribbles a long number down.

"I'll need the routing number," he mumbles.

"Routing number?" Marcus speaks into the phone, then waits, scribbling a second figure on the pad before pushing it across the desk and stepping away. Continues his conversation like no one is bleeding to death before him.

Mike makes an initial transfer, from her account to his, with one word in the memo line: *RUN*. Then, three minutes later, moves the funds again, making enough stops on the way to prevent this asshole from ever backtracking his way to the original account number.

"Done?" The man's mouth, close to his ear.

"Yes," he hisses, reaching across his chest in an attempt to examine the wound. "Are we good?"

"We're good. You fuck with that transfer, I'll come back and peel the skin off your crippled body. Understand?"

The concern is more, at this moment, with the present situation. In the corner of his mind, a glimmer of hope surfaces that he might survive this ordeal. He nods. "Yes, sir."

The man likes that, a beam coming over his face as he pats his good shoulder. "Sorry about the shoulder. I've been lied to a lot."

There has never been a moment when a handicap is more hated than this. If there were only a knife or a gun in this weak excuse for a home. If only the legs attached to this body worked and he could spring from this chair and kill this man. Mike looks away and prays for the man to leave.

The hand at his shoulder lifts, the man examining the fingers of his glove closely, a look of undisguised disgust crossing his features. Probably blood. Cripple blood often offends. Mike's eyes close, afraid to watch, hearing the man step back, the bathroom door squeaking open, additional light filling the dim bedroom when he flips on the light. The scrub of terrycloth heard. The run of water.

Fuck. Something's wrong. An alert of some sort, blaring through Mike's brain, not loud enough to cut through the pain. Not loud enough to stop his head, which is now nodding, the dots of nausea returning. He needs an ambulance. He needs help. He—

"You piece of shit motherfucker."

That his brain hears, his head snapping back as he cranes his neck over, sees the photo the asshole grips in gloved fingers, her sunny smile shining at him across the room. His eyes close.

Yeah. That was it. The picture. Two years old, printed out because he couldn't help himself. She's in underwear, covering her breasts with both hands and laughing. He'd taken a screen-shot, captured the moment, one of her real ones. The ones that made him think he was different than the others. That they had some sort of real connection that the others only dreamed of. It was his screensaver for a bit, then he printed it out. Taped it to the corner of his mirror so he can see it every morning. Reminds him that there's a life outside this house. A girl, like her, out there, that he will one day be with. Be good enough for.

"Just kill me." His eyes are closed when he says the words, when they stumble off of his lips, but he means every word of them. He will protect her to his death, a final destination that seems to be quickly approaching. There can't be a pain worse than this one. If there is, his fragile state can't handle it.

Steps sound against the floor, his presence felt as he nears, and Mike repeats the words, just in case this son of a bitch missed them.

"Just kill me. I won't tell you anything."

✦

He'd like to say that he made it. Retained his silence. Was the hero. That when his eyes opened and the rapist is there, kneeling down before him, at a height that puts their eyes level, the stranger's face close enough to bite, that Mike doesn't shake. He wants to say that he stares him down and isn't nervous. But then the man reaches over his body to the side table, and what he lifts up causes Mike, the parts of him that still have movement, to shake. Shake like the ten-year-old boy that he still very much is.

Wire cutters. Heavy duty, with green plastic grips, the kind that allow a handicapped man to cut through computer mainframes, hard drive harnesses, and impenetrable plastic casing. With dead eyes he watches the man's hands, long fingers that don't match his short stature, that damn Breguet watch glinting in the dark, the cutters loose in hand, carried with the same easy nonchalance that the knife had afforded, the knife that still sits, butt-deep, in Mike's shoulder. Mike moves his hands to his lap and clenches them tightly, looking to the side, away from the hand, away from the eyes, and swallows nervously.

He had wanted to do it. Had wanted so badly to be strong for her. To be her hero.

CHAPTER 65

MIKE'S EYES WATCH the sharp blade of the cutters, a stare of desperation as the man pulls his hand closer, placing his right index finger in between the metal blades. Mike tugs against his hand, straining to free the finger, all movement halting when the asshole squeezes the handles. Just an inch, just enough to bring the blades closer and to create a sharp pinch of pain. He freezes, looking up into the man's face.

I am weak. She deserves a better protector than me.

"Please. Just kill me," he whispers through weak tears of anticipation.

"Who is she?"

"Jessica Reilly."

The man squeezes the blades enough that he screams, a gargled, girly sound that he should be ashamed of, but isn't. Ashamed got left behind when he realized that he was going to die. "Stop wasting time. We've done enough of that already." This man is used to being in control. To giving orders that get followed, are respected. And the more subservient, the more he seems to swell, grow confident in his footing. There is no way to gain an advantage. No way to win.

"Know what's worse than death? Your life, how I could make it." He depresses fully on the clippers, and Mike bucks against the chair, the pain so intense it brings fresh tears, the spots in his vision giving him a brief hope that he will pass out from the pain. Oblivion would be heaven right now. He blinks rapidly, afraid to look down, the drag against the hand telling that the digit has not yet been severed. But the moment had been felt when those blades touched bone and literally tested the strength of his marrow.

He closes his eyes tightly and the final piece of his strength breaks.

"Deanna Madden. She lives in Tulsa, Oklahoma. Please, stop. Please. Just kill me."

His head is spinning, his fingers throbbing, the blood flow unnecessarily rushing to a place it doesn't need to exist. *This man will kill me.* He will torture until he learns everything, then he will kill. There is nothing else that can be done to protect her. Her fate is already sealed.

Through despair, Mike hears the clink of metal and moves his eyes slightly to the desk, to the tool that was just set down. The metal blades are wet. Red. He closes his eyes as a wave of nausea sweeps through him.

There is warm breath on his face and he opens dead eyes to find the monster staring at him. "Show me everything. Prove who she is. Then, I'll decide whether to kill you."

Not the most encouraging statement. This prick should work on his pep talks. The man rolls the wheelchair around, repositioning Mike's broken body in front of the keyboard; struggling to think, he lifts broken hands to the keyboard. His world glosses over red, and he struggles to stay upright, absent of even the consciousness to curse his own soul to hell.

I have failed her.

CHAPTER 66

HUNDREDS OF HOURS of work get deciphered in four easy minutes. Mike tries to drag out the process, but his finger is the only impediment. And while it still functions, the cutters stopping short of the bone, each brush against something brings a new wave of agony. The dickhead produces a bottle of pills, says it is codeine. Promises relief once he gets what he wants.

So Deanna Madden's world is opened up to him. Mike shows him the truth, a copy of her actual driver's license, borrowed from the Tulsa County DMV. Shows him her original lease, the term, the address. The man wants to see pictures, and so Mike opens up his Deanna spank bank, his skin crawling at the way the man's breath quickens and pants like an adolescent teenager over her images. The images are the best of the best, three years' worth of hard-selected shots from over twelve thousand images. They have the ability to get Mike off in five minutes. This asshole would probably last two.

He tries, in one remaining act of nobility, to hide Jeremy. Flips quickly past the folder with his images, just a couple, taken from social networks in a moment of jealous stalking. But the man's eyes are quick, his hand jerking out and stopping the mouse's scroll. "Who's that?" He points.

Mike shrugs. "Not sure. A brother?"

The man doesn't need to ask his name, Mike's OCD organization provides that in the helpful image titling, the photos titled

JeremyPacer01, JeremyPacer02, and JeremyPacer03. The man's hand settles on Mike's bad shoulder and squeezes it tightly, the movement bringing a rush of pain so strong he cries out. "Or boyfriend?" the asshole digs.

"Or a boyfriend," Mike responds dutifully, any self-respect he once had circling the drain of this man's hell. "But he doesn't live with her," he adds quickly. "So he shouldn't be an issue."

"How do you know that?" The man's hand threatens a second squeeze.

"Please don't," Mike begs. "Please. The boyfriend has his own house. Lives about fifteen minutes away. I swear. They both live alone."

"Give me his address too. In case she's there."

Guilt is almost as heavy as pain. It weighs him down, pulling his heart apart with sharp, dark fingers. He has failed her in the most invasive ways possible. And now Jeremy, though he could give two shits about him. Sure, there was more that he could have shared. He didn't volunteer the fact of her wealth, the question not thought of or inquired about by this man. And why would it? No one thinks the tiny girl with the innocent smile and shitty-ass apartment is a millionaire. And no one, including himself, has any idea what she is fully capable of.

For the first time all night, Mike fights the ridiculous urge to smile, the gesture hidden in a grimace of pain at the act of picking up a pen. Writing awkwardly, he keeps his index finger up, the handwriting scraggly and rough as he records both of their addresses for this man's sadistic needs. *Yes, I have failed her. Yes, I am leading this maniac directly to her door.*

A flutter of hope rolls persistent in his stomach, and the pain, for a brief moment, subsides.

I hope she cuts him to shreds.

CHAPTER 67

MARCUS WALKS FROM the house, pulling on the fingers of his gloves, noting the stubborn scar of discoloration, barely discernable on the black leather. He inhales, thickness in his chest, what feels like the beginnings of congestion clogging his airflow. Fuck. A cold is, right now, the last thing he needs.

He probably should have killed the cripple. The guy had seen his face, not that his face was anything distinct or recognizable. Any other situation, he would have killed him. But if something was wrong, if the girl wasn't there...the cripple is the only tie he has to her. So he'd left him alive. Trussed up like countless sluts he had had before, the ritual of tying the knots peaceful in its familiarity.

The kid back there will eventually be found. Eventually be freed. Whether or not he'll be alive at that point is up to him and his own inner strength. Marcus just needs two days. By then he'll be at the girl's house. By then the boy can warn her all he wants... there'll be no one there to answer his calls.

Two days. It shouldn't be an issue. The cripple is self-sufficient, seems to care for himself despite his handicap. Has a van parked in the back, so doesn't need a caretaker and doesn't have a day job to be missing from. He is a ghost, a hacker, the nerd's profession as clear as day with his evasions to Marcus's FBI mentions. The perfect tool to not be missed, the perfect tool to keep his mouth shut about what had happened today.

Threats and promises. They have been Marcus's bread and butter in his life of excess. The boy won't speak. Not when his bank account is drained and he'll need more cash. Not when he doesn't want police attention any more than Marcus does. Before leaving, Marcus had threatened the boy with calling the Feds, taking his amateur hacking empire down, should the boy ever call the cops. Then, an end-of-tunnel light: the return of some of his money, a hundred-grand hush gift, should the boy deliver on his begged promises and keep his mouth shut.

Marcus is jittery, this wait for her lasting too long. The months of house arrest, tacked on to the twenty-two months in the pen, and he is dealing with sex withdrawals from hell. He needs to touch a woman, needs to feel the rise and fall of her skin, her breath, the soft wet wrap of her mouth around his shaft. His cock had been about to burst, knocking on that door. And now he has to wait even longer. A couple more days that stretch before him like years. He doesn't pity the experience that the camgirl will undergo as a result of his level of need.

Getting in the car, he gives one last look at the house and starts the engine.

CHAPTER 68

JEREMY STARES DOWN, watching her sleep. She is so beautiful, so peaceful when she sleeps, all of her fight gone. He's almost forgotten how serene it makes her look—his last opportunity to see her sleep four months ago—a three-day period when exhaustion had dragged her into sleep for ten hours at a time. She'd been a stranger to him then, their lives unexpectedly colliding—the beautiful girl with the cold shoulder returning from a trip and launching herself into his arms, fully surrendering into his care. She'd let him feed her, hold and kiss her, her sleeping body trusting in its innocent press against his own.

Four months ago, he might have just been in the right place at the right time: the only source of a vehicle on that fated Thursday night of her departure, the only available warm body on the Friday night of her return. Whatever the reason, that situation had gotten them here, to a relationship. *Love.* He still doesn't believe it, that he's become this lucky. That this delicate beauty with the balls of a giant and the soul of an angel has chosen him. Accepted his love and created her own.

He watches her sleep and wonders at the nap. It's eleven a.m.—the time in which she normally cams, her schedule very regimented and rarely deviated from. He pulls the blanket higher on her, noticing her clothes, another oddity on a woman that spends the majority of her time naked.

He straightens, his time tight. He needs to go. Doesn't have time to linger, his minutes owned by UPS, packages impatiently waiting in the truck. Leaning over, he presses a kiss to her head before stepping to the kitchen, and setting a bag on the counter, soup inside. He gives her one final glance, her breaths even, her face tranquil as it peeks from a mess of dark brown hair. Saving the image in his mind, that of his wildcat asleep, he heads for the door, his feet pausing on the threshold, a foreign item snagging his attention. Spinning slowly, his mind questioning the sighting, his eyes lock on the gun, a 9mm lying casually atop a giant Charmin Ultra box.

A gun. He didn't know she had a gun. Then again, he didn't know she had a hundred grand to drop on a car that she hasn't driven since. More questions that he is afraid to ask, terrified of the answers. He steps toward the gun, eyeing it warily, her cell phone lying next to it as if to provide indisputable evidence to its ownership. He stares at the gun as if his examination will morph it into something else. Anything else but a weapon that can kill with careless abandon.

If he knows only one thing about her with certainty, it is that she avoids weapons. Tries to cut steak with a butter knife for God's sake. Doesn't keep plastic grocery bags in the house because they can be used to suffocate.

Yet here, lying out as if it was used yesterday, a gun.

He stares at it, then her. It, then her. And, in the pit of his stomach, a seed of doubt grows a little larger.

CHAPTER 69

"TELL ME YOU haven't driven."

That's how he starts our session. I cross off any chance of an enjoyable chat and pop my gum loudly into the phone, a habit I know he abhors. "I haven't driven. But I can drive. I'm fine. We'll never know if I can handle things like this if I don't try."

Dr. Derek sighs, the sound heavy. "You've lost control, Dee. The car, the trips outside...your boyfriend. We haven't changed your medication and you've had no reduction in your...desires. I'm starting to think that you are a danger to others."

A *danger to others*. The four words that can get me put in a padded cell, my arms through a straitjacket. Medication dispensed via syringe if necessary. My jaw tightens, and I regret every time I have opened my mouth and told him the truth. He has never taken this path. Never threatened me before. "I'm not a danger." I say the lie quietly, in the sanest voice I can manage. I cannot be locked up and medicated. I will behave. I will restrict myself more. I can do it. I can do anything to avoid that.

"What happened the other night? The night you called me. You still haven't told me about it."

"Nothing. I had a panic attack. I stayed in the apartment. Simon showed up."

"To lock you in."

"Yes."

"Listen to yourself, Dee. You need help." He pauses, and I tighten my fists as I wait for what is next, as I wait for what I already know is coming. "Maybe now is the time. When you get help. When you move somewhere where you can interact with others in a controlled environment."

"I'm not being locked up."

"You're already locked up. Might as well be getting help through the process."

"You don't understand. All these calls, all these years, and you don't understand."

"Neither do you."

I hang up the phone, stare at it. Stare at the blinking duration of our call, twenty-one minutes too short, and wonder what he will do.

He could commit me. If he thinks I'm a harm to myself or others, he could have me committed. I have impressed him, so far, with my dedication to seclusion. But he doesn't know what happened in Georgia. If he finds out, I'm certain that he will fill out that form. First, turn me in for murder. Then, send me to the loony bin. Either way, seems like it'd be bad for our friendship.

But any action Derek eventually takes will be difficult. He doesn't have my address. I filled out a client information sheet when I first hired him. Put on it a bogus address. Requested that billing be done via e-mail. He knows my real name: Deanna Madden. Nothing else. All he has is my phone number, a number that Mike has protected in some superhacker fashion that guarantees me anonymity. So if he does call the goons, they'll knock on a few empty doors, waste a few hours wandering through Harrisville, Utah—then scratch my name off their list and move on. Committing potential criminals is pretty low on their priority list.

I could end it right now. Pay his bill and move on. Find a new psychiatrist, be less truthful about the depravity of my mind. But what little success I've had these last three years, I owe in part to him. He knows me. Will call me on my shit. Has the greatest chance of keeping me in line. I, in some way, shape, or form, need him.

CHAPTER 70

SOME TWENTY-ODD HOURS after the psychopath left, Mike's chair pushed far enough out of reach to tease, his wrists handcuffed to the bed frame, a strip of duct tape firm and sticky against his mouth, someone rings the doorbell.

Three years ago, before Jamie, there was Tiffany. She was perky, one of those girls who had too many aspirations: fitness trainer, nutritionist, talk show host, celebrity—the least and most attainable of which was life coach. She was hired as an assistant, but viewed Mike as a life coach project, someone to practice her insanity on before she reached the point of charging for her inspirational pushiness. They didn't last long together. Six months. Long enough for him to find Jamie. Six months of healthy food, no soda, no weed, cheery Post-its next to his sink reminding him to Brush Your Teeth! and Don't Forget to Smile! Six months of misery. The sole reminder of the Tiffany servitude now exists in a white box that sits atop his fridge. It connects wirelessly to a cheap doorbell mount on the front door, and plays a cheery tune when the doorbell button is suppressed. There were twenty-two tunes to choose from, but it was December when Tiffany installed it, so "Jingle Bells" was chosen. The button, a cheap white piece, permanently affixed to the brick with liquid nails, sticks if pressed too aggressively, causing "Jingle Bells" to play on repeat until the button is gently worked free.

The visitor this morning was an aggressive type. Probably a delivery. Jamie knows his hatred of the bell. It's been discussed, amid clouds of reefer smoke, sticking the entire box into the fireplace and lighting the shit on fire. But it has become a source of humor, a way to bring back up the ridiculousness that was Tiffany. So they had left it. And now, that decision is causing this aggressive visitor's push of the bell to stick, starting an incessant repeat of "Jingle Bells" to blare loudly through the space. Propped up against the bed, Mike sends a curse out to whomever is listening.

One round of cheery chorus.

Two rounds.

Three.

Four.

Thirty.

Seventy-two.

He vows to stop counting at one hundred, but gets up to two hundred and thirty-nine choruses before he manages to, while in the confines of holiday hell, his right shoulder now just a roar of dull pain, fall asleep.

CHAPTER 71

I HOLD UP a pair of lace pink thongs. "These?"

Missy0002: next

I bend over my dresser, arching my back, rummaging through the layers of lingerie. I pull out a pair of black underwear, with more bows and ties than would ever reasonably fit underneath clothing. I keep my back and ass to the cam and turn slightly, dangling the panties off a finger. "How about these?" I glance at the screen.

Missy0002: yes bb. put those on slowly.

There's an art to putting on panties in a way that is sexy and not awkward. I lie back on the bed, raise my feet in the air, and slide the black cloth slowly down the length of my legs, trying to stretch out the action as long as possible. When I get fully down, I roll onto my side, smiling into the camera and shimmy the silk over my hips, my fingers sliding over the panties and making sure that everything is in place.

We are thirty-six minutes and five panties into the chat. I have gotten little-to-no feedback from Missy, who seems content to pick out underwear, watch me put them on, and sit there silently for a few minutes as I model them. I'm bored, have been since the third pair, but at seven bucks a minute, this is easy. No anal, no ice cubes, no nipple clamps. A little boredom is fine at two in the afternoon.

The site freezes, my image halting in a facial expression that can only be described as a yawn. I wince, and lean forward, refresh the feed. My webchat window disappears and an error message displays. I frown, check another website. It's not my Internet. Other sites load without fail. I return to my website and check a sub-URL, but everything is down. I growl, hoping that the site properly closed the cam session, charging panty boy properly before spazzing out on me. Then I stand, turn off the lights, and grab my phone. I call Mike first, leave him a message, then call the hosting server.

It takes four menus of prompts and fifteen minutes of elevator music, but I am finally connected to Nancy, a woman who sounds nothing like a Nancy, her Indian accent so strong I can barely understand her. We have ten minutes of awkward communication before I come to the questionable understanding that my payment method was declined. I argue the issue in a manner that, despite my best attempts, comes off snobby in all three of the ways I try to word it. "It's a bank draft. There's tons of money in that account."

"I understand, but the payment has been declined. We cannot activate your hosting until you give us a new payment method."

I curse under my breath and give her my debit card number, listening to her repeat the information in painstakingly poor English. "Yes," I mutter.

There is silence for a long moment, then she announces: "Declined also."

"I'll call back," I promise, hanging up the phone, urgency in my movements, and pull up my bank's website, ready to call customer service and hop on a new ass. My anger turns to panic upon log-in, when my eyes rest on my balance and see a bright red $0.00.

Technically, if you look under that number, I have $-1,137.88. I stare at the figure, in shock, then click on "Recent Transactions."

My eyes skip over my traditional purchases, zeroing in on the $37,219.22 withdrawal dated yesterday. An ACH wire, one that emptied out my personal checking account to the penny. I click with dead fingers, back to my accounts tab, and click and drag through menus until my money market accounts are displayed. All three accounts show a zero balance. I stop breathing for a moment, my chest seizing.

I don't check the accounts often. I prefer to let the stacks of money pile up, unobserved, an effect that heightens the drama when I do take the time to log in. It's probably been months since I logged in, so I don't know the extent of what is missing. I could go through the torture of clicking on each account and calculating the sums, but it's a waste of time. Over a million dollars is missing.

I reach for the phone and call the only person who could be responsible. His phone goes straight to voice mail. I hang up without leaving a message, then call my bank.

Ten minutes later, my worst fears are confirmed. I am, in the eyes of my financial institution, broke. Every one of my accounts has been cleaned out, the funds wired from my accounts, using my passcodes. No, they cannot get the funds back. No, they don't know or won't disclose where the funds went. They did provide me with a day, yesterday, when I lost my savings. They did have a copy of the wire transfer, which they promised to e-mail over. They also mentioned, several times, that I have negative balances in two of my accounts, and asked how I would be taking care of those.

They are rude and unhelpful, the sugary-sweet tones of prior calls gone, replaced by a bitchiness of the you-owe-us-money variety. I hang up the phone and punch a hole through the thin Sheetrock of the nearest wall.

Money. It was so precious to me when I first moved here. When the deposit on this apartment was a struggle, and I had no clear idea of what to do for income. But I had stopped thinking about money over three years ago. I have forgotten what the panic feels like. It feels like shit.

I sit on the edge of the bed, my chest tight, forcing myself to breathe, to think. Foregoing the possibility that some random identity-theft individual out there hacked into my world and stole every dollar I had, Mike is the only one who could have done this. He has full, unfettered access to my life. My computer, my money, my identity. Part given by me, part taken or provided by him. There have been times when I have questioned the wisdom of such access. But I need him, need his connections and access, have needed the digital walls he can build to keep my identity safe. And I have always paid him well. For him to steal *everything* from me…it is unthinkable. I pause, halfway through the process of picking Sheetrock bits from my knuckles. It. Is. Unthinkable. Mike, damn my naïveté, wouldn't have left me completely penniless. We are, in some twisted sense of the word, friends. He *had* to have left me something. I move quickly, at the keyboard in an instance, bringing up the website for my offshore bank, my fingers hesitating, unsure of the login credentials, and open my e-mail and look for the one Mike sent a few years ago with login instructions.

I can't find it. I can't, two hours later, after painstakingly reading every e-mail he has ever sent me, find any information on logging in. I know he sent it, I know I read it, have—once or twice—logged into the site. I know the accounts are there. I filled out and scanned in registration and account forms, wire authorizations. I've spoken to the bank four or five times in the last year. There should be a million and a half, maybe two, in that bank. I glance at my watch, the hour too late to get anyone on the phone. I breathe deeply, send false reassurances to the part of my brain dumb enough to believe me. The offshore money will be there.

A million and a half is more than enough. I will be fine. The money will be there. I'll call them in the morning and, within minutes, they will confirm that fact. I will change my PINs and protect the money. The money will be there.

My computer dings, the alert of an incoming e-mail. I open it quickly, my bank the sender, the one-page attachment containing lines of numbers that tell me nothing, only one thing capturing my eyes. The memo line. Repeated four times, one for each of my money market accounts, one for my checking account. The same word, all caps in each instance. *RUN.*

I stare at the words, my brain dull, no clear explanation coming to mind, my forehead scrunching when I frown. Read the words again. They now stand out from the page, are in look-at-only-me font, nothing else legible but those words.

RUN.

RUN.

RUN.

RUN.

What the fuck is going on?

Where the fuck would I run to?

And who the fuck am I running from?

I close the attachment and move a shaky hand to my cell, wanting to take care of my most urgent need before my brain runs itself straight to crazy town. I enter the number for Cams.com and press "Send."

Cams.com never closes. Their 24-7 line is answered promptly and they are, apparently, used to demands for money. I currently have $24,194 in my payout account, a pay period not yet complete, and am not scheduled for an ACH deposit until next Thursday. But, according to the cheery-voiced customer service rep, they can deposit it in my bank account early tomorrow morning, for a minimal service fee of 50 percent. Fifty fucking percent. In very colorful language I tell him to process the payment. I hang up and hope to God Mike is done emptying these accounts. Done sending me cryptic messages without explanation.

RUN.

He's not a dramatic guy. Not someone I've pissed off recently or who is in the habit of playing elaborate jokes. I have to assume that he has either skipped town with my money or that something is very wrong. And if something is very wrong, what do my funds have to do with him? With his memo alert? Are the funds a tool of communication or a piece of the puzzle?

I have too many questions and no answers. Let me revise that. At the moment, I have too many questions, no answers, *and* am broke, an uneasy predicament to be in.

CHAPTER 72

MARCUS RETURNS TO the interstate, a fresh tank of gas giving him renewed vigor. Pumping gas. Such a simple act, yet one that—prior to this trip—he has no recollection of. Not since he was a teenager, before the money and the respect and the hired help. In some ways he misses the simple pleasures of handling his own affairs. In other ways, he hates the stench of gasoline on his hands.

Soon. Soon he'll have her. It had been frustrating to discover that he had the wrong address. Had driven a thousand miles out of the way for nothing. But he'd gotten a million dollars out of it. Not a bad travel stipend. And...even more valuable, he'd discovered the boyfriend. A key that could turn the lock of Jess Reilly's submission. A threat against her boyfriend—that would bring the pleas, the subservience. The willing participation in whatever he chooses to act out. The respect. Nothing gained respect quicker than the threat of loss. And to achieve maximum impact, you had to threaten what was dearest.

The man in the wheelchair was easy. It didn't take hours of thought to figure out that attack angle. His hands. They were his lifeline. Without them, his mobility, job, and independence were limited. It took just the threat of removing digits for him to speak, fast lines of speech tumbling out, anything that might be useful thrust eagerly forward, as long as the wire cutters didn't make the final squeeze that would claim a capable digit.

He shifts, settles deeper into the seat, his thought returning to the girl. As a female, her trigger points will most likely lie in relationships. The hacker had said her family was all dead, a statement he believed. So she is alone. The boyfriend most likely the most important person in her life. Jeremy Pacer. The ticket to her submission. Marcus will go to him first, then her. A little work to ensure that his reward is perfect. Her willing submission. Respect. Anything and everything he wants from the little brunette with the deflated attitude. He reaches down, pressing on the base of his cock, the hard-on coming fast. Tries to distract his mind from arousal and focus on an intelligent plan.

Jeremy Pacer. Age thirty-one. 23 Prestwick Place, Tulsa, Oklahoma.

That is all he has, all the cripple could provide. He needs more. He hates dealing with fucking men. This one had been easy. He'd known from the moment the door opened that he could handle him. This next boy, a muscular man. Probably stronger. His eyes flick to a passing billboard. Prepares for the next exit. He'll call Thorat. Get some help. The ex-head of his security would assist. Owes him that. Marcus had stayed strong during the trial, kept his silence, had protected the man's involvement with Katie McLaughlin. Now was as good a time as any to call up his old employee and ask a favor.

Fifteen minutes later. Pay phones, scarce before, have disappeared completely. The Waffle House sign above him casts a yellow glow on the interior of his Mercedes, turning the cellphone screen before him sickly. He stares at Thorat's number, contemplates taking a risk and calling from it. Closes the cell before he makes a mistake. Puts the car in park and gets out.

"It's Marcus." He fights the battle between holding the phone to his ear to muffle the conversation and not wanting the germ-covered appliance that close to his skin.

Thorat's voice warms instantly. "It's been a long time."

"Yes." Marcus's time in jail had lost the employee, the man moving on to more exciting opportunities than guarding an empty compound. Thorat had parted happily, with a hefty severance package, one that acted as insurance against the secrets he kept. Marcus clears his throat, moves away from the counter, shooting a look at the man behind the counter. You'd think a hundred-dollar bill would buy some fucking privacy. "Look, you got me something a few years ago. The injections. Remember?"

"Yeah. You need more?"

"Two. FedEx them to the Ritz in Cleveland. Just mark the package 'employment contracts.' Put the company name on it. Can you get it there tomorrow?"

The chew of silence for a minute. It was one of the things he always appreciated about the man. When he gave you an answer, it meant something. Not like half of the flappers in his employ, men who spit out "yes, sir" with no idea what it means. "Yeah. It'll be there by noon. Just two?"

"Make it three. Also. You know how you took care of the Sandbar?" The Sandbar. Also known as Billy Littleton, a county commissioner who had made it his mission to stop every wave of forward progress on an airport they had constructed in Kansas City. Thorat had worked some magic with zip ties, a handful of contracts, and some piece of baking TNT. A half hour with Thorat, and the Sandbar had become an inward tide of forward progress.

"Yeah."

"Include some instructions, telling me how to do that. Make 'em clear. I don't wanna blow myself up in the process."

"It's impossible. You'll be fine. Will be simple for someone as smart as you."

"Watch that flattery, Thor. You've been around those yuppies too long. I've got to go. Get it there tomorrow."

"Will do. I've missed you, man. Welcome back."

Handing back the receiver, he watches the attendant hang it up, then looks for the bathroom. His hands are in desperate need of a washing.

He returns to the interstate, his foot heavy on the gas. 23 Prestwick Place. He's never killed a man. Is a little concerned with the size of Jeremy Pacer. But Thorat's injections should take care of that. Marcus had seen them take down a grown elephant, the demonstration very convincing in its proof. Plus, he has the element of surprise. But not a lot in the way of time. Eventually, someone will discover the crippled hacker. And, depending on the shape the man is in, if he is alive or dead, coherent or insane, there is a chance he'll talk. Might call her. And she'll run. So time management is important.

He drives into the dark night, the roads empty, him and tow trucks sharing the lonely lanes. He drives and thinks. Empty time. His reward so close. He smiles in anticipation.

CHAPTER 73

I WAKE WITH thoughts of Mike. I have so few friends, Mike
being at the top of the list. It's sad that someone I have never even
seen, know so little about, holds the top spot on my list. But he
is my enabler, my protector, my partner in crime, the one who
helped in the events that led to Ralph's death. I feel, or felt, in
some way, like that kill solidified our relationship. Took us to a
level beyond cybersex and Internet crime. It is sobering to realize
that I may have thought wrong. May have been just a mark, a
pretty girl to steal a million bucks from. I roll out of bed and reach
for my phone, placing an international call to my Cayman Islands
bank.

It takes me five minutes to verify that my funds are secured,
untouched. For some reason or another, Mike hasn't touched a
penny in their vaults. I ask to change the security passwords, and
get passed to three or four different representatives before I get the
right department. Twenty minutes later, I breathe a sigh of relief
and hang up the phone. My money is safe. He left that alone.

Something is not right, the idea of Mike taking my money off
in so many ways. I work through other possibilities. Who else
would have had access? *No one.* Who'd know about all of my
US accounts? *Him.* Who hasn't, for the first time in three years,
answered his phone? *Him.* Who'd put a cryptic message in the
memo line, one that was either a helpful message or ominous

threat? *Him?* But again, there is no other option. It had to be him. Thinking otherwise is naïve.

I dial his number, lifting the phone to my ear and sorting out my words. Again, I get his voice mail, and again, I hang up without leaving a message. I think last night was the first time I've ever even heard his voice mail. He always answers. Doesn't have any reason not to be available. His nondescript voice mail speaks louder than words ever could. He is, for a reason unbeknownst to me, gone. With my money. And any friendship we may or may not have shared.

I lean back and scream in frustration, a long howl of crazy that somehow, in its aggression, makes me feel a little better. My anger at the situation mounts, mixing with the clusterfuck cocktail of unknowns. I cannot *remember* the last time something important has been out of my control. Cannot remember the last time I had so many questions with no clear way to get answers.

Half of me hates him, wants to tear out his heart and stuff it down his mouth. Wants to torture him for making me value and care and then disappearing without explanation. That half of me envisions him spending my money with a bleach-blond bimbo, laughing at me and my naïveté as he fucks his way to happiness and guzzles champagne.

The other half of me knows that that cannot be true, trusts the man that I've known for three years. That half of me stares at the word *RUN* and understands that this has a purpose. Half of me worries that Mike is in danger and I cannot save him because I know absolutely-fucking-nothing about the man. Half of me wants to crawl into a ball and cry over what could have happened to my friend.

Neither of those halves are interested in running. For one, I don't have anywhere to run to. For two, I'm a fight over flight girl. I see *RUN* and I think *WAR.*

Maybe I should be preparing.

But how do you prepare for the unknown?

CHAPTER 74

IF YOU WERE to walk into Dunbar Diagnostics, crawl up a hot flight of stairs into their attic, and troll around long enough, you'd eventually stumble on a file. It states that Mike's trip to the fair netted thirteen broken bones. Only one mattered. A vertebra in his lower spine, one whose crack caused a rupture of the spinal cord. A very important vertebra, one that secures the framework of guardrails and caution tape that protect the life-giving bundle of nerves we all take for granted. Vertebrae are weak, not strong enough to stop the steel of a ride from snapping your lower body movement into oblivion. Hello paraplegia.

It could be worse. Paraplegia is different from paralysis. Different in the fact that he has feeling in most of his legs. But they are weak, too weak to function. His brain tells them things; they just don't listen. At least his dick works. It works too well at times, pushing and protesting about the unhelpful limbs attached to it. Paralysis would be worse. Lack of sexual function, lack of urinary and bowel movements—that would really suck. So he is lucky. That's what he tells himself in the dead of night. Lucky. When he stares up at the ceiling and thinks about ending it all. Poof. Done. Just like that.

There are some upsides to continuing life. His existence is comfortable, thanks to the profitable side of hacking. Women are plentiful, if you don't mind paying per orgasm. He doesn't need the outside world. Between hookers and Jamie, his needs are met.

Jamie grew up with a brother worse off than Mike—a car accident completely paralyzing his lower half. His body is at the stage where normal bowel and urinary functions are problematic, and daily functions take four times longer than a healthy human's. He lives on his own, has a regular job, manages through his condition. Jamie grew up with that, accepts it as normal. Doesn't blink twice if Mike falls from his chair or if he gets pissed at his useless legs. He never worries about pity with her—if anything she keeps him in line. Keeps him from feeling sorry for himself. He is so much luckier than her brother. Lucky that his dick works and that he can feel when she reaches over and grips his thigh. Lucky that he can piss in a toilet and not through a catheter.

Jamie. She comes on Sundays and Thursdays, and is his only hope at rescue. He closes his eyes and wonders what time it is. Wonders how fucking long "Jingle Bells" will play before the cheap plastic innards say "screw this" and give up. Why the hell did he never put a clock on the wall in this room? It wouldn't have taken any time. Five minutes to stick a nail in the wall and hang twenty bucks' worth of sanity up. His mind is already playing games with his psyche. Right now, he's fairly certain it is late in the afternoon on Wednesday. Pretty sure. It can't be before noon. There's no fucking way that only five hours have passed since the sun came up. He tries to see his shoulder, gauge the amount of pain. The codeine has worn off. He moves the shoulder as little as possible, hoping that the knife is stemming the flow of blood, hoping the arm is salvageable. He wiggles his fingers, rolls his wrists, moves his other arm as much as he can, and wishes the fucker had used longer handcuffs.

Not that he can really complain. He has his fingers. He has his life. And all it took was putting her head on a platter.

He is horrible. He is weak.

He hates fucking "Jingle Bells."

CHAPTER 75

MARCUS HAD LEARNED a lot in prison. A lot about human nature, how caged humans, despite our upbringing, drug habits, or skin color, are all the same. We want to fuck, to eat, to live. We want freedom, we enjoy control, we want to kill. It is an animal instinct, one society tries to squash, to raise out of us, but it is the natural urge that lies in all of us. Some of us have learned how to feed that need. Enjoy it in the underworld of human life. Pick our victims carefully. Learn how to properly control them.

The men Marcus shared cells with were animals. He hated them, despised their dirty skin, the way they spit when they spoke, the naked look of their bodies in the showers. But he learned from them. Listened to their conquests, their failures, their mistakes.

Lenny Blackwell. In cell H8. Term: thirty-two years. He raped and killed four women that the law was aware of, nineteen that they weren't. He taught Marcus that bodies were the weak link; if you can destroy the body, you can destroy the evidence. He also expanded Marcus's lock-picking skills and explained how long it took to strangle a woman properly.

Bruce Hornt. In a shower stall. Term: forty-two months. He tortured a next-door neighbor for six hours till the man admitted to fucking his wife. He taught Marcus what worked with torture, what didn't. What had finally caused the man to break.

Mikel Stevens. In the yard. Term: seven years. Six counts of kidnapping. He taught him that you don't have to kill the victims if you have one of their loved ones handy. Taught him that a fighting victim will become putty if they believe someone else is in danger.

Marcus was locked up because the judge thought he was dangerous. He left that prison a smarter, better predator. *God bless our justice system.*

He changes lanes and risks a ticket, increasing his speed. Excited to get to his prize.

CHAPTER 76

MY FRUSTRATION REDUCES a little bit at lunch, when I check my bank balance and see the Cams.com deposit. Twelve grand. I got twelve grand and they got twelve grand just for a fucking wire. Bullshit. I feel my heart rate increase again, just from the ridiculous fee. I take a deep breath and call my hosting company. Tell them to rerun my debit card, wait on hold for a ridiculous twelve minutes, then crack a smile when they inform me that my site is back up. *Finally.* One short-term problem solved. I have cash.

And I still have the Cayman money. My nest egg. I can build back my US funds. It'll take a year, maybe two, but I'll build it back. I push the missing millions out of my mind and focus on Mike. I need a new hacker. Someone to dig for information on Mike. Find out his address and full name. Then pack up Ftype-Baby and RUN right to his door. Then, depending on what I find, I can either hug the man to death or chop him into pieces. I feel something on my cheek, and brush at it, surprised when my finger comes back wet. Wet. *My eye teared up.* I stare at it in surprise. Blink rapidly and dare my body to produce more weakness.

I eat a roasted turkey breast and mashed potatoes boxed dinner. Drink water and check e-mail, hoping against reason for something from Mike. I don't know what I'm expecting. A heartfelt apology with a treasure map to my fortune? Another clue, this one leading me to discover the big bad monster that I am to run from? I'd take either but get nothing. Nothing except twenty-two client e-mails, covering everything from fawnfests to marriage proposals. I distract myself from growing anxiety and return them all, most with template letters I keep saved on my desktop. Thirty minutes. Twenty-two letters. I'm still jittery when I finish.

I use the restroom, brush my teeth, and floss. Redesign my toilet paper pyramid.

I am useless, an emotional ball of confused. Camming has always worked to distract me, but I can't imagine getting online right now. Smiling for strangers when I only want to know what has happened to Mike.

I hate him.

I'm scared for him.

The seesaw between the two will drive me mad.

CHAPTER 77

UNLESS MIKE IS completely insane, it's now been two days, making today Thursday. Two days that Mike's sat here, his head against the iron frame of his bed, his wrists handcuffed out like he's Jesus. Two days without food or water. If only that fucker had come on a Wednesday, successfully avoiding Jamie while giving him only a day to hang. Thank God he hadn't come on Monday. He might not have made it—two days are about all his weak mind and body can take. He's already going crazy. Last night, he couldn't sleep. Could have sworn whispers from the corner of the room were singing along with holiday hell. The chorus is chanting through, his damn fingers tapping along, every spare thought in his head drowning in its words. Jamie's bang brings him back, wakes his conscious up from the slippery slope of death. His mind swims upward and he blinks, eyelashes stuck together, crude grit in the edges of his eyes. Trying to swallow, to call out, there is no spare saliva, and she wouldn't hear him through the duct tape anyway. He feels drained, like he has sat under a heat lamp until every pore in his body is dried into a dead leaf that will crumble under a firm touch.

She bangs again, a firm pound on the front door, and he can picture her, a hip cocked, hands weighed down with groceries, a frustrated breath blowing a curl of red hair out of her eyes.

She doesn't have a key, a past decision he now curses. But his sexual needs are frequent. Should she decide to pop by unannounced, he didn't want her walking into a fuckfest. Plus, he's not an invalid. And she's not a nurse. She's a friend—one that is paid. One who saves him from having to battle the inconveniences of the outside world. Those inconveniences, the hassle of getting a chair in a vehicle, over a curb, through a crowded restaurant— those are why he just stays here. And…fuck. The stares. The looks of pity. He left all that behind. Online, no one knows that shit. Online, he is a god. Online, he is the man he was always meant to be. The man that adorable, cocky little kid should have grown into.

He can hear her. She calls his name, frustration turning into something else. Worry. Worry is good. He strains to hear more, but there is nothing. Then he hears the incredible sound of the bedroom window lifting, and the curtains parting to reveal one frizzy head. She looks the wrong way first, toward his computer, then turns her head back, toward the bed, and freezes. Their eyes lock, and if there was a way to smile without ripping half the skin off his lips, he would.

"Shit." The word a hiss. She shoves herself forward, through the low window, and lands in an uncoordinated heap of legs, arms, and red hair, a foot swinging out, and he hears the crack of glass as there is an awkward collision. It is one of the most beautiful things ever seen.

She flings herself to her feet, rushes to him, and pulls, with trembling fingers, at the edge of the tape. There is no notice of pain, only the feel of her soft touch, the concern in her eyes, the warmth of possibility that he will live. As soon as his mouth is free, there is the dart of a dry tongue as he licks his lips and speaks. "Water." She reaches for the water bottle on the bedside table. The one that he's stared at for days, just far enough from reach to literally drive him insane.

She twists off the cap and holds it to his mouth, watching, her eyes wide, as Mike greedily chugs the water. The enormous relief of having liquid, of rescue, the release of every horrific nightmare held at bay, rushes him. A breakdown is coming, he can feel a snap somewhere inside as the magnitude of what has been survived hits him. He struggles to meet her eyes, struggles to find words as the black cloud of oblivion moves closer, threatening him with its sweet insanity. "Call Deanna," he manages, the words more watery than he would have expected.

She meets his eyes, confusion in her own. He fights, his lips moving, a moment passing before sound comes out. "Don't tell her...about me. About..." there is a struggle to explain, nodding to his legs, and her eyes soften, a gentle hand placed on his chest.

"I won't. But Mike, where are the keys? The keys to the handcuffs?"

"No cops," he whispers. Then blackness washes over, and he speaks the words that have chanted through his mind for days.

"Jingle all the way. Oh what..."

CHAPTER 78

CALL DEANNA. JAMIE stands in Mike's bedroom and tries to make sense of his words. Who is Deanna? And why—with his body chained to a bed, a *knife* jutting out of him, blood over half of his torso, is he asking for her? She should call the police. An ambulance at least. Mike's jaw is chattering, words humming through his mouth in an insane chorus, out of rhythm with the chimes that are echoing through the house. She snags a chair, drags it to the kitchen, and stands on it, running her hands along the top of the fridge till she reaches the box, the ridiculous Tiffany box that is blaring holiday cheer in the middle of freaking February. She gropes for its power cord, yanking the hell out of it until the music ceases and her mind can think.

Call Deanna. She walks over to Mike's desk, looks for a phone. Nothing. Walks over to his chair, pushed into the corner of the room, far from the bed. A pain grips her heart as she imagines him chained to the bed, away from anything that could help him. How long was he tied up? Who did this? The TVs, computer, everything is still here. She leans down, digs through the pocket sewn into the side of his chair, and her hands close around the hard metal of a phone. She pulls it out, presses a button, and the screen floods with light. Fourteen missed calls. She dismisses the alert, a red battery indicating that there is 2 percent left of life. Swearing, she hurries to the bed, grabs the charger, and plugs it in, breathing a sigh of relief when the charge indicator displays. Then she scrolls through the contents till she sees the name. Deanna. Six letters, no description, no picture attached to the contact. Nothing to tell her anything. She presses the "Call" button and waits, the phone to her ear, unsure of what she will say.

"Hi, fuckface."

The voice sounds pissed. Beyond pissed. The tone of the girl drags a long, sharp razor across Jamie's skin. This voice doesn't belong to the image she had in mind, that of a frilly bimbo, one of Mike's hundred-dollar whores. This voice lives far outside Jamie's life of pasta ziti and *Real Housewives of Miami*. She swallows. "Hi."

CHAPTER 79

"HI." THE MYSTERIOUS bitch, calling from Mike's phone, says *hi*. Like we are sleepover buddies painting our fucking nails.

I had been on camera when the phone rang, a range of emotions flooding through me at Mike's name on the display. Relief, then a sudden flare of anger. He *is* alive. He *is* fine. Has been fucking me around for two days just for the apparent hell of it. At the female's greeting I set the phone down, pasting a smile on my face, and blow a kiss into the cam, exiting out of nude chat, a chorus of good-bye messages suddenly flooding the chat room screen. I end the chat and yank the black cock from between my legs. "Who the fuck is this?" I stand, naked, the cool air from my AC refreshing against my hot skin. I close my eyes, let out one long breath, and relish the cold breeze. Try to figure out the emotions that are full-out battling in the tight confines of my chest. I let out a long breath, struggling to release the anger that is growing with every stuttered word from MysteryBarbie's mouth. It isn't working. I want to rip someone apart, make a throat scream so loud that I come from just the sound of it, my orgasm spreading as the agony lengthens.

"My name is Jamie. I'm..." She pauses for a moment, like she doesn't know what the fuck she is. I am furious, every emotion I've felt for the last forty-eight hours, every shred of hate and love I have for Mike flooding through my veins. I hold back words and wait for her to finish her pathetic sentence. "...I'm a friend of Mike's."

"Can you rip his head off for me? Start pushing at his forehead until it snaps the fuck off? Yank in and rip out tendril after tendril of veins and organs until he is a hot dripping mess of blood?" I breathe hard, unsure of where this raw aggression is coming from, but it mixes with the hot tears burning from my eyes and feels good. He *was* partying with my money and a slut. I *lost sleep* over him. I *worried* over him. I *mourned* for him. I clench my hands into fists, my cunt growing wetter with each violent word from my mouth. *Yes.* I need him dead before me, his eyes unmoving, his blood covering my skin, warming my surfaces, pleasing my heart.

There is a sound, something like a stutter, a skittering of words across an unclean surface. Great, MysteryBarbie probably doesn't want to bloody her manicured hands. "He just told me to call you. Something's happened. I just—" A gasp sounds through the phone, then something wet, like a sob.

I roll my eyes. Is she crying? "Stop blubbering and put Mike on. I'll hash this bullshit out with him."

"I can't!" Somewhere, MysteryBarbie finds her backbone and the balls to actually scream at me. "You won't let me explain! I just got here, and he is tied up and *stabbed* and almost dead!"

My feet stop. They have been moving, a pacing motion that keeps me in place but works off some of my nervous energy. They stop and I pause the action of breathing for a quick moment. She has my attention.

"How long has he been tied up?"

"I don't know," she sobs. "I was here on Sunday. I come on Sundays and Thursdays. His cell phone is at two percent, so...a day? Two—three? I don't know how long a battery lasts. And he was thirsty, he looks—horrible."

I can't find my heartbeat. I think my guilt may have eaten it. I grip the phone tighter and wish I could take back every curse I just uttered. "He isn't speaking?"

"Yeah, but it's gibberish. He's just singing 'Jingle Bells.' Over and over. He asked me to call you, then started in. I think he's in shock."

"What did he say exactly?"

She pauses. "'Call Deanna.' Well—first he asked for water."

"'Call Deanna.' That was it?" *I hated him for nothing. Almost dead. Stabbed. Shock.*

"Yeah. That was it." There is something in her tone, something that makes me think she is lying, but she's not in front of me, and interrogation isn't nearly as effective if torture devices aren't involved.

"Did you call the cops?"

"No. He told me not to."

"So he did say something else!" I snap the words, my frustration at a breaking point.

"Sorry—I forgot that part."

"Don't forget anything else."

She puffs into the phone. "Why'd he want me to call you? Are you a nurse? Can you come over?"

"Shut up, let me think for a minute." I sit on the bed, my skin already cold, time too precious to waste with the thermostat.

RUN.

Call Deanna.

Why call me? Why the wire memo? Why reach out unless this is about me? I can't rescue him. I can't nurse him back to health. *This might be my fault.* So help me God, if I caused this...I grip the phone so hard I hear the case crack. *RUN.* "Look around. Tell me what you see."

"I came in the window because he didn't answer the door. He

was in the bedroom, tied to the bed. Handcuffed to the bed. His mouth was taped shut."

"Any damage to him?"

"Other than the knife in his shoulder?" There is a beat of silence. Some rustling, and I can suddenly hear the rhythmic sound of a man singing softly, almost whispering the sound.

I picture her leaning over him, his arms spread-eagle against the bed. The face I have never seen, duct tape hanging from one cheek. "Is he still handcuffed?"

"Yeah. I don't have a key. I haven't seen one anywhere."

This bitch is useless.

"I don't see anything—God, there's so much blood everywhere." A sob breaks from her.

Blood. Pools of blood. A heaving chest. "The knife is still in him?" I flex my hands. A knife. Jabbed into his shoulder. I wonder if that's how the man got him onto the bed. Just the threat of it probably would have worked. People freeze when a knife is held against their skin. I fight my excitement reflex. I miss that freeze. I miss that power.

"Yeah. I'm not gonna touch it. The blood is caked around—" She breaks off, the sudden silence ominous.

"What?" I demand.

"Oh my God," she chokes out. "His finger...it's almost cut off. I can see bone—" she gags, and I have the sudden image of MysteryBarbie vomiting all over the crime scene.

"Get away from him. Have you checked the rest of the house?"

"For what?"

I growl into the phone. "Blood, dead bodies, a masked man waiting to slash your throat?"

"Do you think I'm in danger?" Her voice squeaks slightly, and I fight the urge to roll my eyes again. Fuck it. I roll them.

"Just check the house." Shit. I need him. I need him to tell me what the fuck is going on. I need him to tell me if he is the one who took my money, or if he stole it for someone else. I need to find out what he said to them, what he told them about me. I need to know if this was about me, or if my missing money was just a side effect of some other deal he had cooking. I need to know if this is my fault. I need to know if I should prepare for war.

Damn. Damn. Damn. Damn. Damn.

RUN.

Four minutes later, I hang up the phone, knowing little more after MysteryBarbie's pussy-ass tour of the house. I swear to you that my grandmother had bigger balls than this chick. Plus, she was hiding something. Her answers to my questions all seemed carefully designed to hide one gigantic secret. I wanted to know one thing: whether that secret had anything to do with me. Anything else, I didn't care. Let him smuggle coke, or grow weed in his backyard. Or have a wife and five kids. I wanted my money and my hacker back. And my friend, if I want to get all gushy about it.

She was an emotional mess, wanting to know how to unhand-cuff him, how to pull him out of shock, whether she was in danger of the handcuffing-finger-cutter coming back. I told her to cut off his wrists and let him sing "Jingle Bells" till he starved to death. Her stony silence let me know her level of humor. A part of me wasn't joking. The knowledge that Mike had suffered through one hell of a forty-eight hours melted my anger, but I wasn't ready to put the BFF necklace back on until I knew which one of us had fucked up. Chances are, it was me. I swallowed a mountain of guilt and told her in the nicest words I could, to start Googling answers to her questions. I'm not a freaking nurse.

I let out a sigh, and make a slow, measured spin, looking at my apartment with new eyes. Mike knows a very long list of information, including, in big bright fucking letters, my address. *RUN.*

The message makes a little more sense now, the pieces falling into logical place. Mike is the only person, other than Jeremy, who knows who JessicaReilly19 really is, and where she lives. Mike. Jeremy. And now, a new man: FingerCutter. A man. Probably just one. I can handle a man. *RUN*. Mike must have given him my information. The man must be on his way here.

I fight against it, but a small smile breaks through anyway. Yes, I could follow Mike's directive. Add my twelve grand to the Cayman fortune and leave this life. Run. Hide. Buy a new identity and cut all ties. Leave behind the man I love. The only friend I have. Live safely in a new bubble of fakeness. That option sounds horrific.

Or, I can wait. Wait for the man who comes. And take my time on him when he arrives. Punish him for torturing my friend.

My smile widens. Stretches so tightly it hurts.

PART 4

"Skip to the fucking point."

CHAPTER 80

WHEN YOU KNOW someone is coming, the biggest enemy is time. I knew where, I knew how. The only thing I didn't know was when. I call back MysteryBarbie and ask the question I should never have overlooked.

"Where are you? What city?"

"Worcester."

"Where the fuck is that?"

"Google it." She hangs up the phone and I smile despite myself. MysteryBarbie might have teeth after all.

❖

Worcester turns out to be in Massachusetts, some fifteen hundred miles away. I have to assume he came straight here. If he had flown, he'd be here already. Driving would take him…I do a quick calculation. Twenty, twenty-two hours. Not counting bathroom breaks and an overnight stop. Which means I have little time.

One feature I offer on my website is a live voyeur feed that displays my cam chats. I scroll through three years of saved cam history and pick a day fifteen months ago. I embed four hours' worth of video files into my site and start streaming the video through my "live" feed. Anyone checking my site will see me, naked and happy, pleasuring myself for strangers. I leave it playing and unclip my corset, loop by loop, walking to the dresser and yanking open a drawer.

The transformation from vixen to ordinary is less than a minute. I lace up tennis shoes, pull my hair into a ponytail, and stand, shrugging into a jacket, too hot for summer, but one that will hide an instrument of death.

I take a deep breath and wonder if I should call Dr. Derek. Wonder if I am mentally equipped for this errand. It is funny how quickly things can change. A few days ago I was reeling myself in. Chastising my poor decisions and promising myself in big capital letters that I Will Stay Inside. Not repeat my recent mistakes. Cut back my freedom and regain control. Do a better job of keeping others safe, of policing my own actions.

Yet here I am, about to leave the house. Drive my car. Run an errand with no purpose other than to properly outfit myself for war. And to make matters worse, I'm walking out in the world armed with a weapon. It's a necessary item, FingerCutter's location unknown, the knife tucked in my jacket, one that is needed for my own protection.

I stand at the door, my car keys in hand, and take short, measured breaths. Will my resolve to stay in control. I will be fine. It is during the day. The knife is contained—I will not pull it out unless assaulted. I take a moment. Breathe. Focus. Prepare.

I have a sudden thought and turn, hurrying to my pink desk, yanking open drawers, and sighing in relief when I see the roll of clear scotch tape. I cut off a piece, hold it carefully, and walk to the door. Yank it open before common sense stops me, and come face-to-face with Jeremy.

"What are you doing here?" My eyes skip over his empty hands, no package present for delivery.

"We're going to an early dinner. Remember?" He glances at his watch. "Thursday at five, right?"

I swear under my breath, pulling the door shut and locking it. Not the dead bolt—Simon is the only one with that key. But the lower lock, part of the knob, a weak barrier that has never been tested. I hesitate, looking at it, then rise on my toes, sticking the tape firmly along the crack at the top of the door. I jump slightly, trying to get the tape to be flat and invisible. Jeremy moves closer, his fingers replacing mine, his height making the task easy. He looks down at me, his fingers sliding over the tape. "You expecting a visitor?"

"Not sure," I mumble, trying not to inhale his scent. He is so close to my chest, the warmth of him intoxicating in its life. I step back. "I can't do dinner today. I'm sorry—something's come up."

"Something's come up?" His brow furrows, a look that is adorable. I wonder, briefly, if eyebrows were cut out of a face, how much they would resemble caterpillars.

"Yeah. I'll talk to you next week." I need him away from me. This is bad, his presence at a time when someone is on their way here. Jeremy will only complicate this situation. Worst-case scenario, he gets hurt. Best-case scenario, he sees me rip a man to shreds with glee. Both disastrous, one a scenario I may not ever recover from. There is already the ongoing possibility that I put Mike in danger. I cannot, will not, endanger this man also. I turn, my walk picking up speed until it is a jog, and I bang through the stairwell door. This is so familiar. We have been in this situation before. Last time I needed his help, his truck. Now, I'm in a different place. One that doesn't want to get another innocent individual hurt.

I exit the stairwell out the back, hoping he isn't following, my steps quickening in the parking lot, the blacktop littered with tricked-out Cadillacs and tired Corollas. And there, in the midst of dented fenders and duct-taped windows, she sits. Like a coiled snake, ready to strike. Gorgeous, feline, and dangerous. I feel wetness between my legs, the rub of my jeans heightening my excitement and anticipation. I am not the same tentative woman who drove this monster home. I am being hunted. And, in the face of that danger, am releasing all constraints. War has no room for indecision. It's time for me and her to kick some ass.

I press the button, listen to her chirp, and slide around the front of her, rolling my hand gently over her polished surface and pull on the handle. Thank God I paid for her before the theft of my money. It's almost, in retrospect, like getting her for free.

"Where are you going?"

Shit. He followed. I pause, one foot in the *ohmygodImabouttodrive* car. I glare at him. Use my bitchiest voice. "I'm in a hurry. I'll call you later." I sit in the car, glancing up when his hand stops the closing of my door.

"That's it? You're standing me up for dinner and you won't tell me where you're going?"

He sounds pissed, a tone I've never heard from him. I stand up enough to pull his hand off the door, then scoot back inside, slamming the door before he has a chance to think about it. As an afterthought, I roll down the window, worried, in my hurry to kill someone, that he might try to follow me. "I'm sorry, I promise I'll call you later. Something's come up; it's kind of an emergency."

"An emergency…" His stare doesn't leave my eyes, the hard look in his one that worries me. He is mad. Doesn't believe me. Doesn't, from the suspicion on his face, even trust me. It figures that my relationship would have an emotional breaking point *today*, at a moment when—at any second—my adversary could come striding across the parking lot.

I look into his face and say the only thing I can, a sentence that we may never recover from, but that I hope will get through.

"If you *do* love me, you need to let me go right now. Trust in me, in us, and go home."

I push the giant "START" button and let the roar of the engine drown out his response. I can't listen. Can't know. Can't allow him to be in danger and me to be emotional. Love is weakness. And right now, I need every bit of strength I have.

I carefully pull forward, out of the space and out of the lot, leaving Jeremy standing alone, in a sea of cheap cars.

Damn. I suck as a girlfriend.

CHAPTER 81

WITH MYSTERYBARBIE'S CALL, everything changed.
Those fantasies that I hide from, that I push out the door with
every ounce of my underdeveloped muscles? I suddenly need
them. I need to embrace that evil, need to go back down that
path. I am not afraid, I am not worried about that part of myself
stepping up. I know, without hesitation, what will be in my heart
when I fully unlock that door. The darkness has not disappeared.
It, like that tree in Florida, has flourished despite my best attempts
at starvation. My struggle over the last two months has only fed
this monster's need. Fed its appetite with juicy giblets of freedom.
It has, despite my best attempts, strengthened.

FtypeBaby and I break each other in well. We hit Bass Pro,
Lowe's, and Home Depot, before a curious store associate is kind
enough to point me in the direction of an army-surplus pawnshop. I put the top down and head north, reaching the destination
far too quickly for my newly freed tastes. I leave her in a front spot
and push open the pawnshop's door, the weight of it enough to
work my arm muscles. For a girl with a steel-reinforced apartment
door, that says a lot.

I know, the minute my tennis shoe hits the concrete floor, that I
have come to the wrong place. The right place for a gas mask, the
wrong for every single aspect of my twisted personality.

Knives.

Guns.

Machine guns.

Handcuffs.

Nunchakus.

Fighting stars.

Things I don't even know what they're called but they look badass awesome.

My hands shake slightly and I shove them in my pockets, which puts them in close proximity to my knife. Like, bumping up against close proximity. I take a deep breath and try to focus on the man behind the counter. Sixties, bald, with enough wrinkles and character for me to know that he has killed before. Probably served enough tours to make my future death count look like a paint-our-toenails Tupperware party.

His eyes glance at my car, the gleam of the hood loud, even in this dark pit of death. "You need directions?"

I meet his eyes. "I need a gas mask. I was told you carry them." I don't look around. I can't. I will go apeshit crazy if given the chance. Fill up a shopping cart like those contestants from *Supermarket Sweep*. Shriek with glee while I stuff samurai swords and grenades in FtypeBaby's trunk.

He sticks a toothpick in his mouth, leans one liver-spotted arm on the glass case before him. "A gas mask? You a survivalist?"

"And fentanyl. If you have it." I shrug as if certain he doesn't, a challenge in the gesture. He probably doesn't have it, fentanyl in chemical form more common in a terrorist cell than a pawn shop. My eyes catch on the low display rack beside the counter, and I bend, snag a Taser, one that advertises enough volts to put down a thousand-pound cow, and set it on the counter.

"And fentanyl. A gas mask and fentanyl and..." His eyes drop. "A Taser." He walks around the counter until he is crossing before me, and my muscles tighten. He is close enough to touch, my hand knocking against the switchblade in my pocket. I shouldn't have brought it. But, knowing that FingerCutter was coming— it would have been stupid to leave the house without some sort of protection. He walks on, toward the door, his eyes on my car. "That your car?"

"I drove it here, didn't I?"

He turns, faces me, a frown stretching and pulling the wrinkles on his face. "I didn't ask you that."

"It's none of your damn business. Do you have what I need?" He'd better. He has to. The town isn't big enough for a fourth possibility. Unless I knock off a family of survivalists, this is my only and last hope. Me and ToothpickDick need to sort this hierarchy shit out so I can get on my way.

He sighs, tongues the wood in his mouth, and saunters to the right, down an aisle, till he is almost out of sight. Then reaches up and picks up a plastic piece with tubes and glass. A mask. I hope my sigh of relief isn't audible. "This is the smallest one I have. You just need one?"

I nod.

He shakes his head, moves back to the counter. "Young pretty girl like you. Walks in and wants one gas mask. Seems suspicious."

"Do you have the chemical?" I interrupt this bullshit waste of speculation.

"Well now that makes me even more suspicious." He sits on a stool, one with dog-bitten legs and nowhere convenient to rest a foot. His legs stick out, like a kid's.

"It's a yes-or-no question."

He chuckles. Slowly. As if he knows the time-eater will drive me crazy. I can feel the madness creeping. Can feel my slippery grip on morality sliding. Dark thoughts sneaking in, every line of the smirk of his face expediting the process.

"Fuck you," I spit out, grabbing the mask from the counter and digging into my pocket. I fish out two hundred-dollar bills and slap them on the counter.

"Now wait just a minute." He pushes to his feet, shuffles down the counter, then bends over, hidden from view. "I don't have any incapacitating agents per se, at least that's my line for any suits that walk in the door, but I think this is what you're looking for." He straightens, lifts a box out, and sets it on the counter. I move closer, glance at the contents while trying not to drool all over the counter. "What is it?"

White aerosol cans. Fifteen or twenty. Lined up in a neat row like jewels in a box. Shimmering under the dim light of the overhead fluorescent. I place my hand gently on the edge of the box, my irritation forgotten. "What is it?"

"Capsicum. It's not gonna knock anyone out, but will wreak havoc on their senses. Can cause blindness, will definitely disorient someone, give them one hell of a headache, blurs vision, dizziness, pretty much a one-two punch of fucking you up. It's the same stuff that is in pepper spray, but this is an aerosol form. Set four or five of these in a room, pop the tops, let the mist fill the room. You'll have about fifteen minutes of knock-you-down air before it'll start dissipating. Just keep your mask on. It'll linger in the air for a few hours; even the afterburn will cause your eyes to tear up and your throat to close."

"I'll take 'em."

"How many?"

"All of them."

He tilts his head at me, brown eyes scrunching underneath brows that have never seen the beautiful sharp end of tweezers. "All of them? Who're you going to war with?"

I don't respond, reaching into my pocket for more cash. "How much?"

He works his mouth and I can practically hear the inflation rising. "Sixty each."

"Twenty." I have no earthly idea what capawhateverhesaid goes for. Have never heard of it. ToothpickDick could be selling me mini-cans of hairspray, my attempt at mayhem giving me one hell of a stiff hairdo. But the price had been tossed out with suggestion, like there is some room to haggle.

"Naw, I can't do that. Not for all of them." He works the piece of wood, flipping it straight out, and I wonder suddenly, if I stiff-hand his face, if it will puncture anything important, or just slide down his throat and cause him to hack like a furball-afflicted cat. "Thirty."

I make one last volley. "Twenty-five."

He answers by withdrawing a small stack of cans, shutting the box lid, and sliding it across the glass toward me. "Cash. I'll sell you fifteen."

"Cash." I grin, count out four hundred more bucks, and lay it on the counter, backpedaling with the box in hand, not waiting for change.

Then FtypeBaby and I get the hell outta there, gas mask and arsenal in hand.

CHAPTER 82

AFTER TWENTY-SOME HOURS of driving, and one overnight spent in five-star luxury, Marcus reaches 23 Prestwick Place. A small house underneath big trees, the thin lot cozies right up to the neighbors, a fact that sits ill in Marcus's stomach. Neighbors are a bitch. There is a reason his house sits on fifty acres. Neighbors hear screams. Neighbors report if a naked bitch stumbles out on the lawn with bloody wrists.

This yard is clear. No vehicle present. Now is the time to go in, while the house is empty. Damn the neighbors, damn the daylight flickering through the trees. He parks on the street, a few houses down, and pockets goodies from Thorat's package: zip ties and a syringe preloaded with ketamine, the veterinary anesthetic that will knock a grown man on his ass within twenty seconds. A grown man fighting, less time. A quick pop of the trunk and his casserole dish from hell joins the party.

He locks the car, his eyes sweeping over the Mercedes' lines. A little conspicuous. He should have borrowed a car. Rented one. This neighborhood, same as the cripple's, isn't the type to host hundred-thousand-dollar cars. Picking his way through fallen leaves, carrying five pounds of mayhem, he watches the house. Dark windows. Empty drive. No one home. More trudging. Over the curb and through the yard, his head forward, like it is normal, like moving around to the back of the house, over a forgotten hose and past the water meter, is routine. He's pleased to see a fence around the back of the house, the privacy it affords. Lifts his head and focuses. Tries the back door, skips the windows and tries the doggie door. A big one, built for a large dog. Lifts the flap, but a plastic piece covers the hole. A plastic piece that three hard kicks knocks loose. He sets down the dish and examines the opening. Dirty. Made for an animal that licks its own ass. He pushes aside the irritation and shimmies through on his belly. Disgusting yet easy. The best side effect his small stature has ever afforded him.

Dark inside. Silent, his breathing the only sound. No dog. No roommate. Good. He takes a quick tour, retrieves the casserole dish, then gets in position. Settles in and waits.

It doesn't take long. Less than an hour later, the sound of an engine. He listens, counts the sound of a single vehicle door open and close. The weight of feet on the steps outside. Unhurried, relaxed strides. The knob twitches, keys jingle, and the door swings open. Marcus waits, watches. The man, big with strong shoulders, steps inside, swinging his foot behind him and kicking the door closed without looking, the man's head dipped in distraction as he sifts through a handful of mail.

Exposed. Unguarded. Perfect. Marcus steps forward, the syringe ready, jabs and depresses it, in one combined movement, into the man's neck.

CHAPTER 83

NINETY MINUTES INTO the real world, and I am already chewing my nails to the quick. I sit at a red light, the sixteen-year-old kid beside me breaking every bone in his neck to stare at my car. I turn up the radio and breathe. Try to focus on the purr of the car and the pound of a hard rock beat. I need Mike. Mike would tap into whatever world he belonged to, the one that provides fake IDs and paper trails and illegal firearms without hesitation. As it is, I am relying on Google's version of a phone book, driving around a town I don't know like an asshole tourist. I have some items. Are they enough? Or am I creating excuses to avoid heading back home? I should go home. Time is short.

"Hey."

The word is shouted. Loud. Loud enough to be heard over Nine Inch Nails, which is a feat in itself. I turn my head, pin 16WishesIt-WasInches with an unfriendly stare. "What?" I don't speak up, let his baby eyes read my expression and my lips.

"Nice car."

I nod, smile grimly, and face forward. Will the light to change while considering running the damn thing. He'd get in the car. No problem. It'd be simple. He'd let pussy and horsepower take him anywhere I'd want to go. I could try out my new toys on his hormone-laced body. Afterward, stuff his body in FtypeBaby's tiny-ass trunk.

The light changes and I floor the gas, leaving twenty feet of rubber on Thompson Ave.

I pull in, the same spot open. I yank the car into park and step out, unlucky enough to encounter Simon, his ripped-jeans self standing one vehicle over. He whistles at the car. "I wondered who that belonged to."

I say nothing, opening the trunk and shouldering out the cardboard box, stacking the mask on top and looping my fingers through the plastic handles of my Home Depot haul.

"You need help with that?" Simon the Helpful.

"Nope." I push down on the lid with my chin. Listen to it settle gently into itself, the simple act of the trunk closing beautiful in its own understated way.

He holds the building's door open, his eyes skipping over my items as he hurries to the elevator and presses the button.

Silence. His eyes dancing. Examining. Probing. I can hear the unasked questions. They are pushing on my skin, crowding around my ears and mouth, wanting to crawl in and rip from my brain answers to satisfy every curiosity of his drug-fueled head, my inclination to drop the box and bags and cover my ears huge. But that would be crazy, because he hasn't uttered a word.

The doors open and we step, as a unit, onto the elevator car.

"You don't have to lock me in tonight."

"Really? But the..."

"The pills will still come on the first. I just don't want you to lock the door tonight. Pick the normal routine back up tomorrow." I work through the details for a moment, trying to see if I'll have need of Simon at any stage in the plan. "Will you be home today—tonight?"

"Yeah. I'll be around."

"Around." Just wishy-washy enough to guarantee that—if I

need him—he won't be there. I could ask for his phone number, but don't trust myself to have it. Especially now that he seems too interested in friendship. That's the problem with having a pussy. Every man around wants to dive into it.

I step off the elevator and onto the sixth floor.

CHAPTER 84

MARCUS LEAVES THROUGH the front door, pulling off his ski mask before exiting. Locks it behind him with gloved hands and goes down the worn front steps, his movements confident. Slow. No rush, no need for anyone to give a second look. Passes the boy's truck.

This golden boy is his insurance policy. If she tries to scream, struggles when he touches her, kicks and punches, and clamps her jaw before his cock, he'll pull out the magic card. Wave Jeremy Pacer temptingly in front of her and explain the plight he faces. Explain the ticking clock, and what will happen when it counts down to zero. Even a strong individual breaks under the threat of danger to another. Breaks under the thought that their stubbornness will cause another's death. He'll attain her breakage. He'll get her compliance. Will enjoy the evening in the proper fashion. Civilized. With her eyes full of fear and respect.

Several firsts for him, taken care of. First time subduing a man. It was almost disappointing, how easy it was. The injection had done all of the work, the man wheeling around at the contact, his hand going for his neck, by the time he realized what was stuck there, by the time his eyes focused on Marcus and his fists swung into action...

Collapse. The kid had landed one punch, a good one. Marcus rubs his jaw, remembering the jar of the impact, the boy's fists never making the journey to round two. It is fine. Pain is a reminder of life, of the ability to feel.

Another first. The bomb. Thorat was right. The instructions were incredibly simple. Unwrap package, put into oven. Program oven. Done. A fucking caveman could do it. A caveman with a set of balls. The kid's oven timer was now programmed for fifteen hours, after which it will heat to six hundred degrees. Thorat's instructions didn't indicate how long it would take the ammonium perc to explode, just said to leave at least fifteen minutes' time to get the hell away. It might happen before the oven finishes heating. It might take an hour. But once it ignites... it's a beautiful thing. He'd seen it once before, four years ago, still remembers the damage. In this case, a two-pound pack of AP exploding will set fire to all that it touches. The kitchen will go quickly, then the house.

So he's leaving the house with a fifteen-hour window. It should be plenty of time. To find the girl, incapacitate her, and find out what kind of bitch he was working with. Spend a good six to eight hours celebrating his return to freedom, reaffirming the type of man that he is. To drink in the cocktail of sex and power and to know that he is, once again, all man. Afterward, if she behaves, he'll swing back by. Turn off the oven altogether. Let the guy sit there in safety until he is found. And if he dies? Starves to death there on the floor? So be it. Life is never as precious as when it is threatened. We all need a little death in our lives to remind us to keep living.

The beauty is, neither of them will ever know who he is. The hacker is clueless; the boy never saw him, and the girl, if left alive, will only remember his mask. It will be the perfect execution, performed with intelligence and planning. Another first for him. He should have taken control of these activities a long time ago. More work but more empowering. This girl will be sweeter than every one before her. This will also be the first time he will use leverage over torture. It will be interesting to see the difference a reluctantly willing participant makes.

Of course, if the plan fails, if she doesn't submit, then he won't return to Jeremy at all. Should she fight, be stubborn, fail to treat him with respect? He'll let the man die on the principle of it. Stay with her, let her watch the news and crumble before he fucks her to death. Her cooperation. Her attitude. That will determine whether Jeremy Pacer burns to death or not. Whether he feels gracious or not. Fifteen hours will give him enough time. Plenty.

Soon. Everything he has waited for, soon. He gets in, starts up the engine, the heat blowing out lukewarm at first blast. He digs in his pocket, pulls out her address, and reprograms his GPS. Six miles; fifteen minutes away. So close. Hopefully, it will be in a nicer area than this middle-suburbia dump. Adrenaline flowing, he turns around, heads left, then right, then left. Gets on the freeway and drives through downtown, the tall buildings soon dropping off, the cityscape turning cheaper and cheaper until he is in what can only be described as the slums of Tulsa. Slums. Not what he was expecting from the bubbly brunette with the nice bedroom. No campus in sight. Frowning, he comes to a stop at her address, pulling off into a metered spot and checking the address. Looks left, at the structure, a worn façade with no balconies, one long box with at least six levels of small windows sporadically scattered on its surface. The entire building seems to sag, as if holding up the weight of its floors is a losing battle. A worn awning on its front displays its name, in plastic letters that have seen better days. MULHOLLAND OAKS APARTMENTS. A phone number is below it, along with a giant star advertising weekly rentals starting at $199.

This can't be right. If he didn't know better, he'd say the hacker lied. But he's seen the legwork. Seen the proof. This is, to the best of the hacker's extensive knowledge, her address. But why would a woman with her level of income live in a tenement building? He rolls down the window, puts the car in park, and looks out again, without the obstruction of tinted window glass. Notes what appears to be a drug deal going on one car over. Glances at the building again. Dingy and dark, it squats on the piece of land like a fat hamster someone forgot to put back in the cage. Some windows are covered in newspaper, one in cardboard, and there isn't a car on the street that has matching hubcaps. Tries to imagine her parking on this street and walking in. She has to make enough to live somewhere else. Hell, he alone had dropped an easy grand on her. Maybe it's drugs, she snorts her income away. Or has some version of a virtual pimp who takes all of her profits. He stares at the building, doesn't like it one bit. His visions of tying her down, spending his time fucking her every way but normal . . . those fantasies had been orchestrated on clean sheets, a place with running water. Not this Dumpster of existence. He sighs, rolling up the window. Adjusts the settings of his seat until he is fully reclined, grateful for the tinted windows, his eyes on the front of the building, flicking once to the locks, to ensure their safety position. If the boy's neighborhood was rough, this one was Compton. He leaves the engine running, ready to make a quick departure should a street punk decide to try for his car. He'll wait. Wait till the sun finishes setting. Wait a few more hours, till she is sure to be tucked away inside, getting ready for bed. Then. Then he'll strike. He rubs his jaw and allows himself to smile.

It is almost here.

CHAPTER 85

THEY SAY IDLE hands are the devil's workshop. For me, it is not my hands, it is my mind. Without distraction, it dives into dark places it shouldn't go. Places that make little boys scream and psychopaths celebrate. I've spent years avoiding those places. But now, as I sit in the dark and wait for this man? I open the cage and let my idle mind wander free.

Butt on the ground, my back against a box of Jenny Craig cardboard entrees, I run my mind over the plan and hope that I am not wrong. Hope that he is on his way, and that I can act out this stockpile of fantasies. The law says that if my home is entered, that I have the right to defend myself. Self-defense. A beautiful word that opens a world of possibilities. Yeah, let's call this self-defense. Not that a defense will be needed. I don't plan on getting cops involved.

I sit and wait. Work through the worst-case scenarios in my mind. He may be a hulk of a man. Might walk in covered in tactical gear. Might open an automatic weapon in the middle of my loft and destroy my well-crafted plan in the course of seconds. I frown, my palms sweating despite the cold room. Whoa. I came up with three disastrous scenarios without even thinking hard. Give me another hour and I'll have a hundred more possibilities. My confidence plummets, my brilliant plan suddenly full of holes. I bite at my nails and wonder how long before he arrives. Try, for the third or fourth time, Mike's number. I haven't talked to MysteryBarbie again, my calls ringing through to voice mail. According to her story, he didn't answer my calls before because he was tied up. That should no longer be an issue. I don't like that he is not answering. Maybe she took my advice and chopped his fucking hands off in an attempt to remove the handcuffs. Homegirl didn't seem real bright.

Now that my anger has subsided, I really need to talk to him. He could tell me if this brilliant plan of mine is for naught—my killer instincts celebrating an event that will never occur. I did kinda jump the gun a bit. Embraced MysteryBarbie's words and created the perfect scenario in my head. Someone coming for me. Someone I can kill without guilt. I let out a sigh and continue the waiting game. Hope that my badass self doesn't fall asleep against two weeks' worth of herb-roasted turkey breasts.

Maybe I should walk away. Now that I've gone through the motions, made the plan, outfitted my apartment to the hilt. I could still walk away. Call the police and have them come here, sit in the dark with me. Let them arrest the man should he break through the door. It is the right thing to do.

I should be stronger, I should be able to fight off the blood rush that holds my veins hostage and takes over my body. Maybe I should try to handle this the normal way. Curl into a ball, hold my body tight, shut my eyes and let my mind play out a sick, twisted fantasy. As sick as I want it, as blood-filled as I want to take it. I can be and do anything I want to do in the confines of my mind, with my eyes closed and body controlled. Because I am being good. I am doing the right thing.

Okay, so a new plan. I'll mentally act out my fantasy and then, in the brief moment of sanity after a fantasy exploration, call the cops. Quickly, before I lose my fortitude. It is a good plan. The right thing to do. Safe for all involved parties. I take a deep breath and mentally prepare myself to give up this opportunity. Mourn, for a brief moment, the death of what was going to be a kick-ass takedown. Then I curl into a tight ball, my arms gripping my legs tightly, my head dropping, eyes scrunched close and imagine the elevator, its announcement of this asshole's arrival.

For the thirty-first time since I stepped back into this apartment, my arsenal in hand, the elevator suddenly moves, wheezing and screeching its way up the tower of our building. I stop breathing, my tight ball loosening as I raise my head and tense. Wait to see if I am imagining this or if it is real. It is. It's real and my good intentions are too fucking late.

I tried. I really did try. I had a plan and a goal to be good. I said good-bye to my opportunity and wrapped myself into a ball. I was walking away, was going to let the police handle this. I tried. I failed. Fate intervened and kicked my good intentions' ass.

I wait, my head up, ears straining. The lights are off. When I first turned them off, it was a shock, my eyes blind in the dark. But now, three hours later, they have adjusted. Even if they hadn't adjusted, even if I were blind—I know every inch of this apartment, my familiarity a by-product of three and a half years spent in nine hundred square feet. I can jump, crawl, or handstand my way through this space blindfolded. He does not know this space. He will not have any idea of what he is walking into. I hear the elevator shudder to a stop. The sixth floor. Jackpot. This might be *it*, the chances one in fourteen that he is headed to me. I stand, my back leaving the boxes, and listen. Strain for footsteps, wish that we had a hardwood hall as opposed to silent carpet. Move to the peephole, see a stranger move closer, closer. See his pause at my door.

Then, I see the soft motion of the knob. It's a new one, swapped out two hours ago for the crappiest one Home Depot carries. It moves gently. Quietly. And I know that he is here.

I ignore the knock when it arrives. I am too busy.

He thinks I am unaware. He thinks I am helpless. He has no idea who he is dealing with.

CHAPTER 86

APARTMENT #6E. MARCUS stares at the sticker on the door. The edges are curled, as if one strong breeze might pull the brittle sticker off. He leans close, lifting his hand and covering the peephole. A presumptuous action, one that assumes she's sitting on the other side, her eye pressed to the glass, for no reason whatsoever. Reaching down, he gently works the knob, verifies that it is locked. *Smart girl.* Too bad this knob is shit, one that a credit card could work open with three plastic attempts. It looks new. She was probably trying to be safe. Should have spent more. Should have gone with a brand that isn't carried in Dollar General. Safety shouldn't be skimped on. He reaches up and knocks. His mouth curves at the recollection of a prison session, Mikel squatting in the dirt, hands rubbing vigorously on his knees as he spouted the proper rules of home invasion. Marcus had listened with half an ear, relaxing in the sun, occasionally glancing over at Mikel's intent face. But some of it had stuck. Rule Number One: Don't break in if they'll open the door. Breaking in puts a mark on edge, gives them a moment to reach for their phone, call the cops, a neighbor, or grab a gun. No one thinks a killer will knock. A smiling face disarms. Marcus obeys, paints a casual, offhand look on his face, lounges against the door frame, and runs the lines through his head. *Just moved in. Got locked out. Do you have the super's number? I'm John.* Hand out, that bland smile that people look through and forget. She'll help. No one wants to appear an unhelpful bitch, even if they are one. Inside, he'll subdue her, use a syringe if need be. Don a mask and leave it on until the work is done.

There is no answer. He glances at his watch, surprised at the lack of response, notices the scratch on its face. Wonders if that happened during the struggle with the boy. Fuck. He'll need a new face. The watch hands point to ten p.m. Maybe she is out. The skank letting some guy grope all over those great tits, someone other than him. He frowns. Her bringing someone home will be problematic. Rolling his bottom lip between his teeth, he thinks. Knocks again, harder this time.

He's been in this hallway too long. It's just a matter of time until someone walks by, sees him. She's not home. Three knocks is enough. Two minutes is enough time for someone to get off the toilet. To call out a "just a sec." He reaches for his wallet. Pulls out a credit card and slips it into the jamb.

It takes less than three tries and the lock pops, the door swinging inward from his weight. Darkness inside. Silence. Marcus grins, sliding in and shutting the door, letting the blackness envelop him, his feet making the only sound, a slick step as they step on what sounds to be plastic flooring. He pulls out his wallet and, by feel, returns the card to its spot. He is fumbling through the process, his back to the door, when everything changes.

Simultaneous explosions.

Lights blare on, more than humanly possible, the glare and intensity of them staggering.

A sea of exposure blinding him, causing his hands to raise, his eyes to squint, and that is when his mind has the delayed sense to register a hiss.

Pop.

Hiss.

Pop.

Hiss.

Pop.

Hiss.

The pops increase in speed, the hisses multiply, and his legs flinch as hard items roll and hit the door behind him, the leather of his shoes. One jumps and catches the delicate bone of his shin.

The gas hits his senses. Covering his eyes, pressing hard into eye sockets, trying to prevent penetration, not realizing that his hands, his fingers, are already covered, his inhalations and gasping breaths taking in the fog, a fog which instantly disorients, his brain taking a dip into acid town, nausea and pain gripping his mind and shoving it into a blender of fuck you. He drops to his knees, the light covered for one grateful moment, and he cracks an eye to see the reason for the reprieve. Blinks, despite the pain it creates, opening his eye wider for a painful moment as he endures the agony for one last grip at his sanity.

But it is too late. He has lost it. Must be crazy. An angel of death. Dressed in tight black, her head that of an elephant, disproportionately large, the long trunk winding down and around. She moves closer and points. His body collapses when the first jolt of electricity hits.

CHAPTER 87

TOOTHPICKDICK WASN'T JOKING. Three cans would have been more than enough for my apartment. As it was, I used ten. Puncturing the tenth can, the front door already a bright white cloud, I pulled at the gas mask, paranoid that some of the vapors would get through, my bare spots of skin tingling from it, the urge to take a shower strong. What if my mask is faulty? What if it's too big? From the sounds of the man before me, his moans, ones that scrape a happy trail through my consciousness, the cans of whatever the hell I bought are doing their job. Doing it well.

I arm the Taser, step forward, clouds of chemicals parting slightly, and aim, at a distance that cannot be missed. Then, I pull. Fire. Smile with satisfaction when he crumples at my feet. I feel capable. Organized. Superior. My hands shake with excitement.

This will be fun.

CHAPTER 88

I USE ZIP ties, not trusting my ability to tie knots, and having seen too many prisoners cut through duct tape with a conveniently found piece of glass. Thank you, Spike TV. Plus, he had them on him, in his pants pocket, my body pat discovering them early on, along with a syringe that I keep for the pure hell of it. Also found: ski mask, knife, keys, and enough condoms to piss me the hell off. Looks like the man had planned for years of fucking. I keep the Taser ready, the tins still attached, a new blast of current shooting through him every time he even thinks about moving.

The gas is still here, showing no sign of dissipation, and I start wondering why I took ToothpickDick's knowledge vomit without even a cursory verification through Google. What if this shit takes days? How do I eat, shower, talk on the phone, with a gas mask on? Should I open the window? Let the toxic air float through the city, causing sore throats and blurred vision at every turn? At least it is working. More than working. I zip-tie his hands together, at his back, the act a struggle, his hands fighting me for a spell before I get the loop in place and yank. His eyes are shut tightly and he's blubbering. This man, twenty years my senior, armed with elements of destruction, an infidel knife—impressive—and expensive trappings, is blubbering. Rivers of tears down his face, nonsense hiccupping in big gushy teenagechickattheendof*Titanic* sobs.

I am crouched at his feet, my hands too small to fully wrap

around his ankles, when he shoots a foot up and catches the underside of my chin. Hard. Hard enough to knock me back, the back of my head slamming against the floor. The impact causes tears to spring, a gasp coming from my mouth. Panic sets in when sudden heat sears my eyes, acid from the room creeping underneath my dislodged mask. I reach up, yanking the mask back into place at the same time that the sharp tip of his shoe finds me a second time, this kick connecting at my thigh.

Motherfucker. I wheeze, my eyes blinking rapidly as I roll out of reach, my throat burning as I grab at my thigh, rubbing the spot where I can already feel a knot forming. Anger erupts, my hand grabbing along the floor until I locate the Taser and sit upright, sending a long volley of jolts into this bitch of a man that I may just lose control over and kill.

I wait for a minute before moving, let my rage simmer and eyes recover, hating the rapid pant of my breath. I must remember my size, my limitations. Need to squash my confidence a bit.

I give him another jolt of juice and crawl forward, straddle his shins for more leverage, and zip-tie his ankles, moving as quickly as I can, breathing easier once his feet are under wraps. Then I duct tape his mouth shut and turn off the lights. Sit in the misty dark for a moment and let my heartbeat slow. My eyes readjust, following the line of his prone body, stretched out on the floor, his chest heaving, cries muffled by duct tape, his instruments of attack moved to the kitchen counter. My breath is hot in the mask and I exhale slowly, evenly, trying to get my body under control, trying to tame the madness to a point that it will be productive. I have done it. I have subdued him. He is tied up. My objective attained. Now, I just have to control myself. Gain information. Find out why he is here. Find out why he hurt Mike. For the hell of it, ask where my motherfucking money is. Have fun. Yes, in the midst of fact discovery, I will have one hell of a good time. My own personal present to myself.

CHAPTER 89

JAMIE PUSHES MIKE'S chair through the glass doors, the frigid air hitting them both at the same time. Good lord. He needs to move to Florida. Somewhere where the girls have real tans, somewhere you can open your windows and enjoy fresh air without a parka. Somewhere the sun lights up more than dingy slush and worn faces. She slips slightly on ice and the chair jerks a bit as she catches herself with the handles. "I don't need you to push me," he mutters, rubbing his arms and wishing that one of them had had the foresight to bring jackets.

"Shut up. You don't need to be using your hand or your shoulder."

"They're fine." *Not really.* With stitches, wound dressing, and gauze, he feels like a fiddler crab, one arm dressed to twice its normal size. But at least he isn't in pain. The cocktail of meds has helped, along with the injections that make half of his body numb. He feels high, a woozy, sleepy state that barely allows brain function. "What time is it?"

"Eleven."

Eleven. So this is what the city looks like at eleven at night. Pretty fucking boring. Dark streets, every fifth streetlight out, the city's budget too tight to allow something as economically wasteful as new bulbs. "Where's my phone?"

"I told you, it's at the house. And you've already bitched me out about that twice, so shut it. We'll be back there in ten minutes. I'm sorry that, in the midst of freeing you from your bed and carrying your jingle-bell-ringing ass to the car so you didn't bleed to death, I didn't think about your precious cell phone."

"You found me tied up—that doesn't seem like an odd situation—one that I might need my cell phone to get out of?"

"*I* got you out of it…the in-shock, wasn't-in-shape-to-talk-on-the-phone-anyways person that you were. And no, you should have mentioned that. After telling me not to call the cops. Or after telling me to call that bitch. At *that* point in time, you should have said 'And, should we leave this house, bring my phone.'"

"She's not a bitch."

She yanks the chair to a stop next to her car, a motion that is twice as abrupt as it needs to be. "Oh, she's a bitch."

"She's probably just pissed about her money." He watches her open the back doors to her Mazda. A car not equipped to carry a wheelchair, but they didn't have many options. Mike's big van, the one parked at his house, hasn't been driven in years, the battery dead, the tires rotten. His parents thought it would make him more independent. Nothing is as independent as staying home, in a place where everything is easy, where no one stares, and where mountains can be moved and new people created in a few hours with his computer.

"Yeah." She shoots him a sideways glance. "She mentioned something about wanting her money back. You need help getting in?"

"No." He pushes himself to the edge of the wheelchair. Uses his arms to support his weight, swinging himself into the low enclosure, bringing his legs along once his butt is in. "You got the chair?"

She nods, flipping clasps and dismantling it. "Yeah."

"Then let's get back home. I need to call her."

He shuts the door with his good hand and leans back, his head against the headrest. By the time she finishes with the chair and climbs into the driver's seat, he is asleep.

✦

Deanna's not answering. She's not answering and he doesn't know if it's because she is pissed or dead. He has four missed calls, calls that accrued during their stint at the hospital. Calls that occurred while Jamie was launching into a detailed explanation to a nurse who didn't care, an unnecessarily elaborate story about a masked intruder who stabbed him and then took off. The nurse nodded, looked busy, scribbled, then whisked him away to surgery while lecturing him on his poor state of nutrition. Calls that rang to voice mail while he was pumped full of antibiotics, fluids, and painkillers. While they repeated the whole song and dance to a pair of uniforms, who nodded respectfully and avoided eye contact. His condition makes people nervous. And they can't imagine a cripple would lie. No messages were left by Deanna, his voice mail still full from his two days of imprisonment. Jamie also left that important task undone while scrambling around with her head cut off.

His head droops, eyes closing involuntarily, and he catches the action, jerking his forehead back and meeting Jamie's irritated eyes. She snaps her fingers. Points. Like he's a well-behaved dog. "Get in bed. I'll try her again soon."

He reaches out, snagging her hand and pulls it to his lips, pressing a soft kiss on it. "Thank you," he says. "For saving me. For everything. For putting up with me."

She blinks rapidly, her eyes swelling with moisture. "I'm just glad you're okay."

He squeezes her hand and drops it, trying to think through the cloud of medication. Should he call the cops? Deanna might be like he was. Trussed up, bleeding to death on the edge of insanity. Waiting in hopes that her lover boy may show. Lover boy might be out of town. Or fucking around. Or dead. Something tugs at him, like an important to-do item that he has forgotten to cross off. The other possibility is that Deanna is dead. He tries to think, tries to backtrack and remember what just occurred to him. Tries to have a rational thought, one that she will approve of, but his eyes close and he nods off. He barely notices when Jamie drags him into bed. Doesn't notice the fresh sheets she has put down. Doesn't feel the blanket she pulls over his body. Doesn't see her sit in the chair, his cell on her lap, and watch, with worried eyes, as he sleeps.

CHAPTER 90

I DID A poor job of shopping. I missed the good stuff: A drill, wire cutters, a hammer. Everyday items that could cause excruciating amounts of pain. I had shopped like a fucking Girl Scout, buying items of restraint as opposed to pain. Thinking that I had weapons at the house, that no more were needed. But my weapons were boring when compared to all of the torture possibilities that could have existed before me. I guess I didn't expect to torture someone, never thought that would be a viable possibility in my future, never shopped with that scenario in mind. My fantasies have never been about inflicting pain without extinguishing a life. I look at the contents of my safe and listen to the whimper of my visitor, my extended zap of Taser combining with the gas to take the fight completely out of this monster. FingerCutter has become a pussy before my eyes, having a bout of hysteria after the Taser, his panic reducing to whimpers in the last twenty minutes of silence. He needs to calm the fuck down. He needs to man up a little, find the backboned individual that kicked the shit out of my chin. I can't question him like this.

I stand, walk over to the window and open it. Send a silent apology to everyone in the surrounding blocks as I let the poisonous fog out. I can't take any more of this mask.

The room clears quickly, the cool blast of air sweeping in and sucking it out. Hopefully that will cause him to stop. Between the wheezing and sniffling and sobs, I'm on the razor edge of killing him just so my apartment will be quiet again.

My cell rings.

CHAPTER 91

JAMIE ISN'T EVEN sure she should call the girl, but Mike had been so insistent over it, had been so irritated over the lack of his cell when he had finally stopped his jingle belling and came back to sanity. Jamie dials the number and waits, breathing a sigh of relief when the girl doesn't answer, a cheery voice mail coming on that sounds nothing like the bitch from earlier. She hangs up.

Less than a minute later, the cell rings, "Deanna" showing up on the screen.

Jamie fights the urge to do a Hail Mary. "Hello?"

"You called?"

"We just got back from the hospital. Do you want to talk to Mike?"

"Yes."

She crosses to him, shaking his shoulder gently, watching his eyes and speaking as soon as they open. "Mike. It's Deanna. Did you want to talk to her?"

He blinks, his eyes looking around, then finding hers, and she waits for him to come to, starts to repeat the question but he nods. Pushes himself to a more upright position and holds out his hand.

"Hey."

Jamie can't understand the response, but can hear the snap-fire volley of words through the earpiece. "I don't know who he is." Jamie watches closely, her mind trying to put the pieces together

but coming up short. "He didn't mention anything about that..."
His eyes close and she steps forward, thinking he is asleep, reaching for the phone, but is surprised when his voice comes, shaky in its message. "I told him who you are. *Where* you are. You need to get out of there. *Now.* He's got to be on his way, but he doesn't know." His eyes open and he glances over, his eyes opening a bit as if surprised to see her there. He covers the mouthpiece. "Can you give me a minute?"

Jamie can feel the set of her jaw and knows how it must look. Like she is stubborn. She tries to relax it, attempts a gracious smile, and nods, backing up and reaching for the knob, stepping into the hall and shutting the door. Then she leans forward, presses her ear against the wood, but can't hear anything.

CHAPTER 92

"HE DOESN'T KNOW what?" I pace the hallway, a jacket thrown on over my tight black sweats, the gas mask hanging from my hand. I couldn't answer the cell with the mask on, so I stepped out of 6E and called his cell back.

"He doesn't know that you . . . are . . . whatever you are. Capable of things."

"What *does* he know?" I crack the door slightly, peek through to make sure FingerCutter is still prone and behaving. The bit of acidic air makes my eyes water, and I close the door, light-headed for a moment.

"Your address. Everything's kind of hazy, I was in a lot of pain, but I know I gave him that. And your name."

"And at what point did you decide to spend a million of my dollars to send over an unhelpful warning?" I don't fight the hard edge that comes into my voice.

"I'm sorry, Dee. He stabbed me in the fucking shoulder. I had to give him something . . . thought that that would distract him, convince him that I was telling the truth. It worked, till he saw a photo of you. Then he—" his voice cracks a little. "He started to cut my fingers off. I broke—I couldn't . . ."

A piece of me inside, a piece that I thought died in my family's kitchen, rolls over in my heart. I clear my throat and go for a hard tone. One that doesn't give away the sentimental tug inside of me.

"Next time give him your own money. And from what your guard dog told me, it was more like *part* of a finger. Unnecessary skin. You need to man up. He was probably just fucking with you. It's a finger, Mike. You have nine more." My words come out level and in control. They hide the heartache that I'm experiencing at hearing the break in Mike's voice. He sounds like a stranger, some broken and scared kid. Not my Mike, my sarcastic rock, the virtual badass who can accomplish anything I desire, the cocky sexual demon who flirts out of one side of his mouth while keeping my ego in check through the other.

His voice hardens, a bit of the man I know coming back. "You aren't taking this seriously. You need to run as far away from your apartment as you can get. This guy is scary. He was not 'fucking' with me. He came here for you, was pissed to find me. I have a hole in my shoulder big enough to kill me. He's got a hard-on for you, he's—"

"Could this be about Ralph?" I interrupt. "You think that's what this is about?"

"Are you listening?!" Mike's voice is at a level I have never heard from him, and I have to smile at the shake in it. No joke, the man is scared. Really scared. Pissing himself, and it's all over the sniffling, droolingalloverhimself wimp that is on my floor.

Honestly, after hearing the tremor in his voice, I'm surprised he didn't hand over my Cayman account funds also. "Can you get my money back?"

"I could, but I'm not touching that shit. That psychopath let me live. Hopefully he will forget my name and move along on his merry way. I'm not doing something to bring him back here. I'm sorry, Dee, but I can't."

"Don't worry," I snap. "He's not coming back. But you're saying you don't need any information from him in order to get the money back?"

"Not if it's been left where I put it." He sighs, his voice dropping off slightly, as if he has moved the phone away from his mouth. "If it's been moved around, if someone did the smart thing, subdivided it and hopscotched it around, sent it offshore, put in a few trans—"

"Check it. Don't take it, but check the account. Make sure it's where you put it. Then call me back. *Soon.*" I pause, waiting for a response. "Can you handle that?"

"I don't think you understand the shape of my body right now. I need some serious care. Like sexy-nurse-outfit-with-no-panties-type care."

"Verify the money." I smile at the tone of his voice.

"Run. Don't try to be a badass. He's not Ralph."

"Which finger was it? The one he nicked?"

"Right index. It's not *nicked.* I can see bone. Well, not right now because they—"

"Thanks. Check the money and text me the verdict." My mouth curves as I drop my voice and use the sexy tone that he loves. "Bye, baby."

I hang up, slide the phone back in my pocket, and pull on the mask, shoving open the door and stepping inside. The floor feels damp beneath my feet as I move closer to him and I prop up a foot on his body, shove with it until he rolls onto his side, his swollen eyes opening enough for me to see that he has calmed and is *pissed.* His face strains beneath the duct tape, a muffled curse sounding. I reach down and run my hand along the jeans, finding the bulge and digging into his back pocket, pulling out and producing his wallet. I straighten, glancing down, his red-rimmed eyes leaking as his pupils make the ridiculous path up my body.

"You like what you see . . ." I flip open the billfold, looking at a driver's license with a surprisingly stern-looking face, a night-and-day difference from the red-eyed pussy before me. My gaze skips over to his name, my brain skittering briefly. "Marcus Renza." FingerCutter has a name. A name that tugs on my memory. This is the dickhead from camming. The one with the rape record. The one who was so insistent on meeting. A name that clears everything up in one moment. God. Men and their pussy. I bark out a laugh as I run a thumb over his photo. Wow. First client who's gone through the steps involved to grace the stoop of my fabulous abode. How neighborly of him. I yank with my foot, rolling him onto his stomach, interrupting his view with one strong motion. "Nice to meet you in person, Marcus. My name, as you now know, is Deanna." I step back till I am in reach of the counter, my hand sweeping out and gripping my pruners, a Home Depot purchase from today. "And that man...the one you tortured to find me?" I move back, stepping over his body and bending over, grabbing the zip-tie chain and lifting it up, pulling his hands to an awkward vertical angle. "He's mine. You, Marcus Renza, don't fuck with what's mine." I yank at his wrist, enjoying the tightening of his face. "Now, I'm just gonna need one of your fingers, if you don't mind." I skip my fingers lightly over his, till I find and hold his right index finger firmly. "And I'm new at this. So I'm sorry if it takes me a few tries."

Screams. I have fantasized about them for so long. It is a shame that, the first time I've really had a chance to savor them, they are muffled by duct tape.

An eye for an eye. A tooth for a tooth. An index finger for an index finger.

CHAPTER 93

"FUCK!"

Jamie almost drops the glass at Mike's yell. Turning off the water, she puts the glass gently into the suds, and hurries to his bedroom, pushing open the door and sneaking a glance inside. His cell is on the bed, his arms pushing at the blanket, any trace of sleepiness gone. "What's wrong?"

"I need my computer."

"Lay down. Will the laptop work?" She hurries to his desk, unplugs the laptop.

"Yeah. Bring it here. God, that girl's stubborn."

"What's wrong?"

"She's up to something. I want to know what."

"What do you need the laptop for?" She perches on the edge of his bed. Watches as he tries to type, the cocoon that dominates his right hand making the task infinitely more difficult.

"Checking her feeds. See this?" He spins the computer around, showing her a ridiculously gorgeous woman, her body spread out on a pink sheet, her face grinning as she blows a kiss into the camera.

Jamie shifts uncomfortably. "Yeah."

"That's Dee. This is showing as a live feed, on her website's cam. But it's not live. I can rewind the feed, and it doesn't show an interruption for the phone call we just had. She's looping an older feed. A normal person wouldn't have any way of knowing." His face winces, and he moves his right hand into his lap, pecks at the laptop keyboard one-handed.

"That's Deanna? The chick who verbally bent me over and raped my ass?" She can't put them together. Not this bright-eyed chick with the Justin Bieber poster taped to the wall above her bed. The one with a body she would chew off her right arm for.

He snorts, his mouth curving into a smile. "She's an acquired taste. But don't judge her too harshly. At the time of that conversation, she was under the impression that I had stolen from her."

Now it was her turn to snort. "You've been stabbed. Are missing half a finger. Plus, you've got the money to cover it. She had to have known you'd pay her back."

He shoots her a look that indicates the intelligence level of the statement. "Not quite. Few people can cover a million-dollar debt."

Her legs move on their own accord, pushing her to her feet and she gawks, physically *gawks* at the man before her. "You took a million dollars...she *has* a million dollars?" She points a shaky finger at the laptop, newfound respect and appreciation for the maybe-not-such-a-bitch.

He doesn't respond, his brow furrowing as his one hand moves. She moves around, climbs upon the bed next to him, watching as he types, the screen opening and closing browser windows.

"What...What are you doing?"

"The webcam feed is fake, so I'm tapping into her cameras. Activating them privately to take a look into her apartment, see if she is there. Or if *he* is there. A normal girl would have taken my advice and got the hell outta Dodge, but she..." He presses a complicated sequence of keys, something that changes the screen and opens a window showing the same angle as before, the pink bed and Justin Bieber poster, but no girl, only empty sheets. He types, and the camera changes. The bare floor, the image grainier than normal, almost as if there is some smoke in the room. Fingers fly over keys. Empty wall. More strokes. The bed. Then another. Then another angle. More strokes.

Jamie gasps, and they both lean forward at the same time, watching the screen as a body lies on the floor, jerking, his head tilted back, his face contorting in a duct-taped scream of agony, a body straddling him, the head in a gas mask, her hands moving in some action that is causing the man inordinate amounts of pain. Jamie swallows, pulling her eyes from the screen and finishes the sentence for him. "Isn't normal."

"Yeah." His voice sounds tired. Defeated. "She isn't normal." He pushes the laptop away from her, blocking her view at the moment that Deanna severs an appendage, shutting the screen on the image, his stomach rolling with sudden nausea, and she leans against his chest, his arm moving to grant her access, her body curving into his as she buries her face into his warmth. Then, with the image of the man's face contorted in pain, branded in her mind, she starts to cry.

CHAPTER 94

IT TURNS OUT my hand strength is that of a small child's. I'd like to say I took his entire finger off—got the whole digit, something with some substance to hold on to. But I don't. Can't. With his squirming and howling, and my puny muscles, I have to move the pruners down. To his knuckle, where I don't have to snip through a bone. Where I just have to cut through the cartilage of a joint. That is easier. I am still covered in blood when I finish.

Accomplishment. I feel like I have run a marathon, my chest heaving, my blood on fire, the still-dripping-blood appendage triumphantly grasped in my hand. He shouldn't have fucked with Mike. Not my hacker, the man who protects my lifestyle and shares the information highway so freely with me. I have no family. I have no friends. Don't fuck with the only acquaintance on my payroll. I set the finger on the counter, ripping off a dedicated paper towel for it to lie on. Then I rinse the cutters under running water, watching the diluted red water run down my white sink before turning the tap closed and setting them down into the sink. I wipe off my hands and turn back to the man.

Marcus Renza. I search my brain. The username had been Freebird-something. It's been a while since I blocked him. A month or so. And we'd had...three chats? Four? He'd wanted to hire me for an in-person session, if I recall correctly. I look at the man before me, a slow, pained wheeze coming from his chest, his back arching off the floor as he squirms. I grin. Guess he got what he wanted. My undivided attention, my hands on his skin.

I crouch, examine him closer, my bare feet moving soundlessly as I stare. I can't believe he came here, hurt Mike, all over being blocked, an act I do to a hundred men a week. It seems so excessive of a reaction. I look at his squirming figure, moans rolling across the space at me, and wonder what took four weeks. Why he hasn't showed up sooner. What he found out about me in that length of time. What his plans for me had involved. I have the bizarre desire to interview him, examine the mind of an evil individual, and compare it to my own. I'm certain that evil was his intent. Otherwise, why condoms? Why zip ties? Why the syringe? He failed to get at me online. Probably felt disrespected by my block. Showed up to fix the situation. Reassert his manhood. But is it really that simple?

I lift my mask, testing the air. Better. Still rancid enough to make me cry like a baby girl, but nothing I can't handle. I pull the mask back down anyway. Tears aren't very intimidating. I stand and step closer.

To kill or not to kill? It'd be so easy. I could open up my safe and test every blade I have on his skin. Listen to his screams. Watch the slow slip of death as it claims his soul.

I need a minute. To think. To be intelligent.

I turn away from my prize and sit, in my desk chair. Roll back and forth, toward the man. Away. Toward the man. Away. He is still. Quiet. The sniffles stopped. The whimpers gone. This is the moment. The moment when the whispers of my insanity are quiet, my hands still, no shudder or shake in their movements. I am in control. So...now what do I do?

CHAPTER 95

"WHAT IS SHE doing?"

Jamie and Mike stare, as one, at the screen, this one from a different cam, one that shows the girl seated, staring at the man as she slowly rotates the desk chair—left, then right, chewing on her lip, a blank look on her face. "I don't know..." Mike responds. "Looks like she's thinking."

"About what?"

He shoots her a perplexed look. "Do you have to ask?"

"Jesus. Should we call the cops?"

"I'm not going to even dignify that with a response."

"We just saw her chop the guy's finger off!"

"Cut. She *cut* his finger off."

"And you think that's the guy who fucked you up?"

He nods, absentmindedly cradling his injured hand. "It's him."

"What do *you* want her to do?"

He doesn't respond. Just pulls the laptop closer and begins typing. Jamie watches as screens change, the process slower than she's seen in the past, due to his injury. Their view into the apartment minimized, different sites popping up in its place. "Text her," he says.

She picks up his phone, pulls up his texts, her cheeks coloring slightly as she scrolls down, their prior text streams primarily focused on one thing. "What do you want me to say?"

"Tell her I can get back the money."

She types, her thumbs flying over the metal nubs. "Can you?"

"I don't know. It's not an easy process to find out. It would normally take me twenty minutes or so. With my hand..." He shrugs, his eyes on the screen. "It'll probably take an hour or two. But I don't want to stand here and watch her scrape off his skin. The news might cause her to step down." He glances up, his blue eyes meeting hers. "Did you send the text?"

She finishes typing. "Yeah."

"Then you should probably go. I'm good here. Thanks for breaking my window." His mouth releases a grin, one that tugs at her.

"Leave now? With your psycho girlfriend about to do who knows what?" She hoists herself onto the bed, leaning her body against him and earning an irritated look for her efforts.

"Go. No need for you to become an accomplice." He shuts the laptop. Fixes her with a look that is heart-tuggingly sexy in its firmness. Sexy and obtuse. A look you don't argue with.

She stands, a twinge of jealousy moving through her. Realizing, as she stares into his eyes, that he, by kicking her out, by closing the laptop, is protecting Deanna more than her.

She shrugs, tries to mask her hurt with a smile. "Need me to do anything before I go?"

He watches her eyes, silent for a moment before leaning forward, reaching out with his good hand and pulling on her hand, pulling her over to him and resting his head on her chest. "I'll be fine." He sighs, keeping her close. "I'm just so...stressed."

She knocks him on the top of his head, the motion causing a wince to come from him.

"What? I am!"

"I am *not* sucking your dick right now."

He scowls in a way that is ridiculously endearing. "I wasn't even thinking of that."

She grins, leans down, presses a kiss on his head, feels his arm wrap around her. "Yeah you were."

"Maybe I was. Can't blame a guy for trying." He pulls away, looks up. "Thanks, babe. Seriously."

Her smile fades, and she perches on the edge of the bed. "This is fucked up, you know that, right? You almost died. I almost lost you." Her voice trembles, his hand reaching out and squeezing her hand.

"I know. I'm sorry you had to deal with it."

She laughs, the reaction a half sob in its composition. "Don't apologize, Mike! Just don't..." She sniffs, picking at the edge of her sleeve and wiping at mascara. "Don't get involved in her shit. She's psychotic. You see that, right? And she almost killed you! So...please stay away from this. Or call the cops and let them handle it."

He nods. Meets her eyes in a way that tells her nothing. "You're the best, you know that?"

She smiles. "Yeah. I know." She waits, her eyes catching the pulse of his fingers against the covers. "Well." She says finally, "I'll call you in the morning and check in. I can come by, change your bandages."

He nods again and she can see the impatience in his eyes, mixed with gratitude but present all the same. And she hates that it makes her mad. That she feels left out of a fucked-up illegal situation that she shouldn't want to be included in. Hates that he is friends with the dark presence that put him in such danger. Hates that the dark bitch is so freaking gorgeous.

CHAPTER 96

I CONTINUE TO sit and stare. Think. I've worked myself into a bit of a corner. This man came to rape me, do whoknows-whatelse with fourteen condoms. Kill me? I'm thinking yes. He'd had enough darkness in his soul that he tortured Mike and drove fifteen hundred miles to my door. I have, no doubt, fueled that anger. Now that his hysteria, the brain fuck that the gas took his head through, has passed, he is furious. I have watched his swollen eyes. Watched as they gained some ability back, enough to look at me with a look that clearly communicates hate. Taking off his finger was the big fucking pile of straw that broke that already-puny camel's back. So now I have an asshole in my apartment with every intent to kill me should he regain the ability. That's grounds for murder, right? My conscience rolls over uneasily. It's debatable. I can't exactly call the cops. And I can't exactly let him go. Cut his zip ties and unhandcuff him, wave a cheery good-bye as he walks off, one finger lighter. And I'm keeping the damn finger. I'll send it to Mike as a response to his next invoice. I smile, excited at the prospect. It's witty, I'll give myself that.

I glance at my watch. Eleven thirty-five p.m. My phone dings and I glance down, read a text, short and sweet, from Mike. "I can get back the $."

Good. One thing off my plate. I text back. "Do it." Then I set my phone down, pull off the mask—fuck the fumes—and step over to my visitor.

I should walk away. I should step into the hall, take the stairs down, enter the night sky and let FtypeBaby take me anywhere but here, in my apartment, at the motherfucking witching hour, with a knife in my hand and a body before me.

This is bad. All the elements of an impossible temptation. I feel the moment my soul loses the decision, my madness starting to flow with greedy inhibition. The dam breaking, power surging through my body, excitement in my veins, my limbs unrestrained, my mind at full iwillkillthismotherfucker strength: All are very, very bad. Not for me, not for my sick heart, which is orgasming at the—I unsheathe my knife—future, but for him. The blood pulses, all sane thought leaving my head in the loud rush of excitement. I fight it, try to curl, try to cover my ears, the action only amplifying the sound. It is useless and the moment that I surrender to it... it is the best moment in the world, a full-body rush of euphoria, one that bursts through me with clear and perfect energy. I am high, able to do anything and everything, but I have only one want on my agenda.

I step forward and lean over, roll his body to its back and straddle him, resting my weight on his stomach, his attempt to buck me off met with a warning look. This is bad. I hear the cry of my soul and ignore it as I finger the knife.

I should walk away.

I have so little control.

I smile.

CHAPTER 97

EVEN THROUGH BLURRED vision, waves of nausea rolling through him, tears pooling in his eyes, and pain—worse than any he has ever encountered, every breath a fresh smack of madness—Marcus wants her. Two years since he's had cunt. He thinks about her naked, the glow of her skin on camera, that impression only slightly dampened by the clothes covering her skin. Gorgeous, her legs on either side of him, the light weight of her body straddled atop him like she is about to give him the ride of his motherfucking life. But her smile worries him. It beams, as if today might just be the best day ever, as if she has just became the fucking prom queen. It doesn't mix with the knife in her hand, *his* knife, the one that she flips with surprising efficiency, as if she was born with it in her grip, as if she has plans in store with it.

And suddenly, her looks don't matter. Because the sudden fact, one that eluded him while he was writhing on the floor, his mind breaking apart at the seams, hits him square. She, this tiny girl with long dark hair and eyes that scream her madness to the world, might be his downfall. And with death, not prison. An even more intolerable sentence, one impossible to return from, one that fills him with fear, his Catholic upbringing suddenly pushing to mind all of his crimes. All of the people he stepped on. Women he damaged. Lives he ruined. He'd thought the devil had come in the form of Katie McLaughlin. But no. It is *Her*.

He blinks hard, the action clearing the tears, his improved clarity taking in the view before him, his chest inhaling as she runs the knife softly across his shirt. Her hand shakes, the knife jiggling slightly in her palm as it makes its path. Nerves? She doesn't look nervous. She looks...excited. Eager.

It is almost, in the final moments of his life, arousing—the knowledge that this beautiful creature could embrace, look forward to, *enjoy* the art of pain, of control. They say that love is finding your soul's match in another. His cock hardens of its own accord, her eyes flickering to his as the consistency beneath her changes. He rolls his shoulders, trying to relieve the pain of lying on handcuffed hands. She shifts, rolling backward, testing his arousal. Then she chuckles, clicking her tongue disapprovingly and reaches up, gripping the knife with both hands and, with one swift move, buries it into the muscles of his chest.

His hard-on withers and dies, right about the time that his chest seizes with incredible pain.

CHAPTER 98

MIKE STILLS, HIS eyes fixing at the upper right corner of the screen, where the video feed is. The video looks jerky, as if it is stuck on repeat, the stick figure on top repeatedly moving, arms up down up down, every other piece of the clip still, frozen. The body beneath her thrashes, her movement becoming that of a bucking bronco for a short moment before the man's upper torso raises, the girl shimmying up his body with greedy movement, before one final downward swipe causes any and all motion beneath her to cease.

He exhales, closing the top of the laptop, not sure if he could take any more, the image branded on his mind, contrasting sharply with the sunny smile he has grown attached to. He knew she had a dark side, had gotten a taste of it when she did the impossible five months ago. But that video, seeing the image of her physically taking a life... it paints over every image of her with a dark brush, adding shadows and depths that scare the hell out of him. He's spent the last days hating that man, cursed him during bouts of clarity during those two days of hell. Hated him more than he'd even known was possible. Still—he feels a reaction to watching him die. A bit of pity, guilt settling into his stomach as if for a long residence. The last few minutes have taught him a lot about her. A lot that he hadn't really known. He shoves the laptop to the side and closes his eyes. Swallows a wave of nausea.

CHAPTER 99

THE FIRST STAB is difficult, both of my hands needed when the blade pierces his chest. His reaction is immediate, his body bucking beneath me, his eyes wide, breath wheezing as he jerks, my knees tight on him, enjoying the ride, my euphoria mounting with each buck.

Again.

I yank the knife out, the effort strong, blood pumping out of the hole in quick rivulets, ones that splatter as he jerks. Again I raise the knife, his eyes following the movement, fear in them, my eyes narrowing down on my next target as I slam down the blade.

Again. I hit his neck, the sensation completely different, a sticky crack of connection.

Again. A stomach hit. His movements are less, his eyes still open, still on me as I smile at him, his blood splatter painting my face, the taste of rust on my lips when I wet them.

Again. The final blow, his chest this time, and I fight to mentally describe the stab, try to cement this moment in my memory and hope that it will last me the rest of my life. The best comparison? The moment when a dental pick sticks in a weak spot of tooth, and the hygienist has to work a bit to get it out. I twist the knife as I yank it out, my chest heaving with exertion, and I watch his chest as it stops. Watch his eyes as the hate leaves them and they close. My nose flares as I roll my neck and lean my head back, wanting to bellow. Wanting to scream my awesomeness to the entire building. I have taken, I have conquered, I have killed. I lean back, my legs loose and rubbery, collapsing until I fall backward, lying flat on the floor, my arms spreading out and flopping to a stop on the wet plastic stretched beneath us on the floor. I close my eyes, my heart pounding out a furious rhythm, one that slows as I take measured breaths, the post-kill high orgasmic in its release of every fantasy I have harbored, every need I have controlled, every want I have denied myself. Then, a smile on my face, my dark soul happy, I fall asleep.

CHAPTER 100

MIKE SHOULDN'T REOPEN the screen. He knows that she is safe from harm, there is no need for further spying. But he does. He lasts fifteen minutes before logging back in, fingers tapping impatiently as the screen loads with maddening pauses for processing. It appears that Deanna, Internet minx who has fake-sucked his dick to countless orgasms, has fallen asleep, her body sprawled out over the man she has just stabbed to death, in a manner that seems wholly unconcerned with his demise. More than unconcerned, she seems blissful, her ear-to-ear grin visible from the webcam's eye more than ten feet away. Mike opens a second window, taking a moment to follow the money trail—for no purpose other than to know if his own life is also in danger. If the money was moved, divvied up and sent out into the world, then his might be the next dead body Dee lays atop of. A pent-up breath whooshes from his chest when he see what he wants to see, $1.3 million, safely in the business money market account of RDC Enterprises. Not a cent touched. His fingers get to work, moving the money back, scattering it over thirty different transfers, to ghost accounts, accounts they barely touch green foot in, skipping it across the world, occasionally joining forces only to separate again, the process long and tedious, any oversight meaning that thousands might be overlooked. When it is all back, settling in and making its home in her account, he relaxes. Turns off the feeds to her cams. Sinks back into a pile of pillows, his shoulder still stiff, an unbandaged hand finding a bottle of painkillers, washing them down with a Bud that is a good half hour away from cold. He swallows the pills and relaxes, leaning his head back, a drug- and exhaustion-fueled sleep seconds away.

He is so confused by her.

CHAPTER 101

I WAKE AT some point. Drag myself off of my mystery guest and stumble to my feet. Give myself a moment to wake up while staring down at his body. Realize, while awakening, that I don't know what to do with his body. A hundred and fifty pounds of pain-in-my-ass.

It was easier with my other kills. I did the deed and walked out. Left their bodies for others to handle. I don't have that choice now. I can't leave him here—he'll smell. Put out an aroma that will raise curiosities until cops show up. Plus, there's Jeremy to consider. I'd have to break up with him just to keep him out of the apartment long enough for FingerCutter to decompose. For all of my planning, this was one big oversight.

I am clueless in how to dispose of a body. I haven't watched television in . . . years. My recreational reading is more of the erotica genre, less true crime. I don't have a tub I can fill with acid, don't have a chainsaw I can use to hack up and bag his body, wouldn't know how to operate it if I did have one.

My houseguest is, in the light of my kitchen light, fairly fucked up. Face swollen, his eyes puffy, like he's had an allergic reaction of the anaphylactic shock variety. His neck is split, the cut unnecessarily deep, the puckered cut hanging open like a stuffed bag's zipper. Decorated with wounds, his chest is eerily reminiscent of my father's, the resemblance causing a shudder to pass through me. But there the comparisons stop. FingerCutter's chest is still wet with blood, each stab of my knife bleeding his body, the thin tarp beneath my feet wet, rivers of red running and collecting in the creases and dips of plastic. My father's wounds were dry, a likely effect from the fact that his heart had already stopped, the shotgun blast to the neck ending his life minutes before a knife ever broke the surface of his skin.

I can't prop this guy up, walk his body down to the elevator, then load him into my car. Even here, where screams in the night and the crash of glass is ignored, a corpse will raise eyebrows. Some do-gooder somewhere will call the cops. And FtypeBaby already gets looks whenever I take her out. Necks crane, her occupants are examined, a dead body would be noted. Plus, her trunk is puny. Big enough for designer luggage, too small for a dead body. I should have thought over these things during my car selection process. I do a slow sweep of the apartment and try to think.

❦

The engine roars in a battle cry that mimics my heart. FtypeBaby opens up, screaming to ninety-four miles per hour before I bring her back, my foot easing off the gas, downshifting into third gear. The navigation screen showed a car rental place three blocks from Mulholland Oaks, but I wanted speed. Highway. The chance to let the wind blow through my hair and wash out any residual death. So I go farther, moving down two exits and pulling into a twenty-four-hour Hertz, parking on the far end of the lot, away from any other car. Get out, shut the door, caress her hood, and arm the locks. Then I step to the front, open the glass door, and wince when a bell dings. Loudly.

A square glass room. Empty, save a cheap counter and displayed brochures advertising GPS and additional insurance.

It takes three minutes for someone to appear, a gum-smacking girl who slides a clipboard across the counter without so much as a "kiss my ass" greeting.

I don't touch the form. "Do you have any trucks?"

"Trucks?"

"Yes."

She leans forward, an action that stretches her shirt tight across a huge chest, and I feel a bit of insecurity as I glance at my much smaller bust. Her weight on the counter, her boobs squashed together and beaming out of the neckline of her polo, she surveys the well-lit parking lot. Left, right, and left. I shift, certain there is a more technical process than this I-hump-the-counter-and-look method.

"Looks like we got a white Chevy. Fifteen hundred. Single-cab, that'll work?"

"Yes."

She nods to the form. "Sign the waiver, I'll need a driver's license." She lifts a butt cheek and makes her way fully onto a stool, then types a few keystrokes.

"Name?"

I give her an alias I rarely use, one that Mike created while bored. The end result was Beverly Jane Norcross, who came complete with a driver's license and prepaid credit card, the items overnighted to me along with an invoice, the words "defile this chick" scribbled in the margin. I paid the five grand, figured it'd come in handy at some point, but have rarely used the alias. Today, the day of moving bodies, seems like a good time to whip it out.

"How many days?"

I glance at my watch. 2:13 a.m. "I'll have it back later today."

"Morning, afternoon, or evening?"

"I don't know. Put me down for evening, just to be safe."

She goes through a halfhearted attempt to rent me a GPS

system, a roadside assistance premium package, and three different levels of insurance. I'm at the stage of stabbing her to death
with her cheap pen when she finally shuts up, returns my credit
card, and looks up with a dry expression that I think is a smile.
"Here are the keys. Bring it back full of gas or you'll have to pay
for us to fill it up."

"Will my car be safe here?"

She blinks slowly, her eyes on mine, and I can't tell if she is
processing the question or has mentally checked out, her ability to
process thought maxed out for the day. I start to repeat the question, but she jerks back to life with one slow gum snap. "The parking lot is fenced. I'm sure it will be fine."

I nod, take the keys, and walk out, casting a wistful look at
FtypeBaby as I walk toward the boring white truck that will be my
accomplice in crime. I can practically hear her growl as I start up
the Chevy and leave her behind.

Driving the truck reminds me of Jeremy's. A similar size, the
same XM options for my listening pleasure. I backtrack, at the
apartment within ten minutes, the drive infinitely less enjoyable
at a paltry sixty-two miles per hour. But the truck gets fewer looks.
And when I back it up to the stairwell door, no one pays attention.
I leave the truck and head upstairs to 6E.

I have never moved a man's body. I used to drag Trent and
Summer across the waxed floors of our home, a firm grip on the
back of their jackets, or their pant legs, their squeals of pleasure
setting a theme song to our play. But they were light, thirty or forty
pounds. This man is heavy.

I move lights, stands, boxes, clearing a space in the middle of
the room. Then I pull my mattress off, lean it against the wall,
and drag my box spring to the middle of the room. Using a hammer, I pry off the staples that hold the fabric covering. Pull the
nails that hold the cross beams. The work is not laborious, but

is time consuming, my smooth hands not accustomed to manual labor, splinters piercing the delicate skin, calluses already forming on my palms by the time I stand, stretch my neck, and look at the finished product.

A box. Shallow. So shallow I stop, use a book as a ruler, and make sure that the depth will be enough. The base planks are strong, strong enough, especially since there shouldn't be too much weight placed at any one point on them.

I take a break, return e-mails and eat—roasted pork, stuffing, and green beans, a new diet plan called Medifast. *Yum.* Then I tie my hair back, pull on gloves, and prepare for heavy lifting.

Dead weight is an appropriate term. I do as I've been taught. Lift with my legs, not with my back. Discover it's easier to move the mattress box close to him rather than drag his heavy ass over. I thank God he isn't Ralph. Ralph was over two hundred pounds. This guy is thin. Thin and short, with a lack of muscle tone that indicates he doesn't have a gym membership. I lift him limb by limb, rolling one leg, then the other, my hands digging into his ass as I heft him over the edge and onto the wooden frame. He is stiff, rigor mortis beginning to kick in, the effect making him cumbersome, uncooperative. I fashion a lever, using a broom handle and a cardboard box of laundry detergent to help, the new synergy lifting him in a way my scrawny muscles couldn't. His upper half is easier. I step into the box spring, grab both wrists and pull, the plastic wrap sticking to his back as I roll him into the hole, the pull of his lower half helping his movement. Then he is in, his body rolling into place, the stiff bend of his arms almost comical in their mannequin-ready form. I grab the hammer, nailing back into place the lateral beams and following their progress with the staple gun, floral fabric soon hiding every view of Marcus's body.

An hour and fourteen minutes after parking the truck, the box spring is reassembled and, by all appearances, completely normal, should someone not try to pick it up. I turn it vertical, leaning it, with a heavy thud, against the wall. Then I clean up, tucking the ends of the bloodied plastic in and then roll it, bit over bit, until the black tarp is in one tight roll. I glance at my trash can, then back at the mattress. *Fuck.* I remove a few staples, enough to peel back the fabric a bit and slide the tarp inside. Then I restaple, cursing myself for the simple oversight. Ten minutes, a handful of used paper towels, and two bottles of bleach later, every surface he might have touched has been sanitized and wiped clean. I throw on a sweatshirt, pull the hood up, and prepare for whoever might be outside my door.

A box spring, on its side, furniture mover disks underneath, slides easily on threadbare carpet. I am almost surprised at the speedy path we make down the hall, beelining for the elevator, my head down, shoulder pushing, hands gripping the sides to keep it upright. I can't feel the body, the framework of the box blocking his body from swinging and face-planting against the thin fabric of its walls. So Marcus and I slide down orange carpet until we come to the elevator I hate, the one I avoid on the rare occasions when I brave the outside world. I press the button and pray for an empty car.

Ding.

Empty. I send a thank-you up to the big guy, struggle with the slides and floor changes, terrified, for a brief moment, that the mattress won't fit, that I'll be stuck here, trying to pull it out, when the elevator moves, splintering the frame with one forceful decline, one that causes a bloodied body to pop out unannounced and get stuck between dinging-its-heart-out doors.

But I am fine. This elevator was built to haul sofas, appliances, and beds. The mattress fits easily, its descent uninterrupted, and I breathe a sigh of relief when we hit the ground level and the door opens.

Five minutes and one sweat-soaked T-shirt later, the mattress is flat in the bed of my rental truck, the tailgate up, wheels turning the vehicle away from Mulholland Oaks. I turn up the radio and head north with no earthly idea of where I am taking him.

CHAPTER 102

SHIVERS RACK JEREMY'S body, bringing him to life, lifting him from the dark hole that his mind has been in. He tries to lift his eyes, tries to open his lids, but they are weighed down, his vision blurred, his tongue too heavy in his mouth to create speech. Shivers. Uncontrollable, his abs cramping with the fight to control limbs, awareness becoming stronger as his mind crawls up the tunnel into life. Enough awareness to realize that his mind is not the only thing restrained. His limbs are also stuck, arms and legs unable to move. *Straitjacket.* That is his first thought. But that is wrong, too many things wrong for that to be possible, and any other thought disappears as he pitches forward, his stomach twisting, retching, wrestling itself as his mind awakens enough to panic. Vomit. It's about to happen, that queasy upheaval of his organs fighting to push any and all stomach contents to the surface. He is about to vomit, unsure if his tongue will even cooperate enough to move out of the way. That detail is of small consequence to his sluggish brain, because his mouth is taped shut. He fights against the tape, trying to force his lips to move, sudden claustrophobia hitting as he struggles to take in enough air through his nose to live.

Another wave hits, the uncurling feeling in his stomach verifying it, the panic only speeding the nausea along and he swallows hard, tries to blink, tries to open his eyes, tries to find his bearings as his vision refuses to come.

CHAPTER 103

A SOFT TOUCH, gentle but incessant against Mike's shoulder, brings him to consciousness, his room coming into focus when he bats away her hand and rubs at his eyes. Dawn, peeking through the open window, his angel of rescue leaning over him in jeans and a tight sweater.

"Fuck." He jerks upright, every muscle in his body screaming in protest. *At least I can feel it.* His blurry vision finds the bedside clock. "You're here early."

"You say that like it's a bad thing. You needed more meds. Here." Jamie holds out a glass of water and a handful of pills, which he takes without argument. "What's going on with your girl?"

Moving weak legs to the side of the bed, he sits fully up. "I don't know. As you're well aware, I just woke up."

"Don't you have the ability to check on her somehow? Hack into her phone or cameras?"

He shifts, gesturing for his chair. "Yes and no. Yes, I can, but no, I won't. I did that last night. Hadn't ever done it before. We, as hackers, most of us are . . . well—we don't get out much. So we have an unwritten rule. No hacking for emotional gratification. You see, if we wanted, we could tap into dressing room cams, personal laptop webcams . . . take a look into any girl we really wanted to see. Somewhere, whether it be a cell phone or an iSight, we'd get eyes on her. But that's invasive, an abuse of our knowledge. I'm not saying all of us adopt this morality stance. There are plenty out there who are jacking off each night to their next-door neighbors, watching housewives changing and coeds fucking. But it shouldn't be done. I'll screw with corporate America all day long, rearrange someone's personal and financial details as I see fit. But spying isn't my thing. I turned on her cams last night to see if she was okay. As it was...I had them on longer than I should have."

She wrinkles her face in disgust, misinterpreting his comment as something sexual in nature. "So. She's cool? You think she's safe from this guy?"

"I think she's safe." He moves to the computer and powers it on.

She follows, pushing at his personal space, the hand she puts on the chair arm invasive in its ownership. "If you don't call her, it will seem odd. Your last conversation you were telling her to get out of there, like you were worried for her life. It'd seem strange to not call her back."

"Give me some room; I can't think with you hovering over me." He closes his eyes and settles back in the chair, the rock of the seat soft and gentle in its movement. "Plus, I returned her money." The thought mumbles out of his lips, his mind liking the idea more as he turns it over. Maybe she still needs help. Maybe she is upset. He does need to tell her about the money. That will make the bloodthirsty beauty happy. He wonders, for a moment, if she is still sound asleep on his dead body.

He reaches with his bad arm, appreciating the movement in the socket, the wound not as debilitating as his mind had envisioned in the handcuffed hours of contemplation he had endured. He picks up his cell, unplugging it from the wall and settling back against the leather, Jamie's hand finally leaving the chair, her stroll into the kitchen watched closely as he tries to think. Initiating the call, he wonders what Deanna will say.

CHAPTER 104

THE LAST TIME I left my town and headed east, it was to save a life. Now, I am trying to hide one. Both times in trucks, my previous drive a fight between fantasy and focus, my dark needs popping up at unexpected times, the freedom and possibilities before me too great to resist. It filled both ditches along the road, a black pool of temptation, my hands fighting to keep the truck straight, not wanting to dip my toe into a place that would grab hold and drag me under. This drive is better, my thoughts more concerned with capture than attack, thoughts of pulling into the closest gas station and murdering the occupants the last thing on my agenda. I want only to get rid of this demon and return to my apartment. My psyche can't take this day, the last twenty-four hours of activity so different from my norm.

My third kill. Each of them so different. I felt no guilt with Ralph. Never thought twice about it. But I don't know enough about this man. Is a man's attempt to rape me valid cause for execution? I have, on my side of the jury, his violence against Mike. But still. A knife wound and finger scraping isn't the same as sending someone into a dark pit of hell for the rest of eternity.

I roll my shoulders and try to relax the tension in my neck. Keep my eyes peeled and try to think, try to find a place to put his body, somewhere it will not be discovered. Somewhere it can drop into oblivion. I wish I were in the South. Where swamps and gators lie in wait, ready for a juicy dead body to rip to shreds, the evidence crunched and slurped down in minutes.

Oklahoma doesn't have swamps. We have open stretches of land, nothing for miles, a guaranteed ability to stand out like a sore thumb if doing anything other than driving. I drive until the sky starts to turn, a hint of pale blue and lighter pink, streaks of yellow beginning to smear across the landscape like a child's finger painting. I turn off the highway, turning my headlights off and scanning, worrying. Once day breaks I will not be able to hide, could be discovered halfway through my drop. I wind down country roads, my eyes taking notice when a recycling sign, drooping and bent, the faded splay of white along its metal bottom indicating that it was, at one point, victim to a paintball gun. I turn, following its arrow, the paved road turning dusty, and move between crop fields, picking up speed until I see chain-link fence and Dumpsters.

A county trash depot. Small towns don't have curbside pickup. My childhood home did, the huff and clang of six a.m. often eliciting a curse from my mother, our cans locked and hidden in the garage, no one remembering to drag them to the curb. But my grandparents' home, the big old two-story, stuck at the north end of a long dirt road, didn't have those city comforts. We bagged our trash, kept it in the barn until the plastic pile rose high, then loaded up the back of the truck. Drove four miles to the county dump and stood, tennis shoes on tailgates, and heaved the bags through the air, out of the bed and into the giant green Dumpsters, praying the bags wouldn't bust, our waste stacking atop others, making the green monster one big rectangular box of nasty.

Our bottles, few that they were, went in a round hole, one of three on an orange trailer, the other two holes dedicated to cans and paper. And in the back, lined up like misbehaving children, were the Dumpsters dedicated to yard waste and large items. Our weak arms and dead hearts tossed the items without thought, piling the bits of our life high, a compactor once a day crushing everything together into one squished-together cube of waste.

I pull up to the gate, an unhinged padlock hanging loosely from the latch. I hop, unlatch, open, then pull through, the layout different but similar to my grandparents'. I'm alone. The night is so quiet that I hear a coyote howl, over the fields, the lonely animal probably a half mile away. I find the bulk waste on the right, the Dumpsters clearly marked, the trash not yet compacted. They probably squash in a few hours, at the start of the workday, a gazillion tons of force crushing toilets, two-by-fours, and fifteen-year-old sofas flat, in one effortless push. That works for me. I jump into the Dumpster, moving carefully around a tire, what looks to be a wrecked lawnmower, and someone's ancient CPU, pushing a few items into place until there is a hole. A gap between abandoned items, one that looks deep enough to submerge at least half of my mattress.

More sweat. It is harder this time, the initial lift of one end until it is high enough to push, the edge of the truck and Dumpster beds acting as fulcrums. I work in the dim light of dawn, the truck off, the gate closed behind me, my vehicle between two Dumpsters, relatively hidden. But I still pray. I pray that no one will also spontaneously decide to embark on an early morning trash run. Hope that kids on four wheelers don't come screaming over the closest hill, their headlights picking up my form, their curiosity bringing them closer. Just a girl, dumping a mattress. No cause for alarm. But later, if something goes wrong and his body is found, that girl, dumping that mattress...it won't take long to put the clues together. I heave, every muscle I barely have working together, the box spring making the slide into the Dumpster, the momentum of my push shoving me over the edge of the bed, and I grip with my fingers and hands, coming back into the truck. The box hovers, one end jutting out over the hole I have created. The good end. The one that contains Marcus's body, the body that, despite the cold temperatures that are fogging my breath and chapping my nose, will start to smell. Need to get it compacted and moved. Put in the dump, alongside festering maggot- and rat-filled heaps of trash, where its odor will mix with a thousand others and be ignored until it decomposes into nothing.

Again, that guilt. It chases me as I lift the light end of the spring, physics behaving as the other end dips, allows itself to be pushed, and falls, three or four feet down, the top, empty half of the box spring sticking up like a flag. Look at me, look at me. But no one will look. Things are jutting and hanging all over these boxes. Toilets don't stack neatly upon bifold doors upon broken treadmills. The guilt nags at me as I brush my gloved hands off on my jeans. No proper burial. Not for this man. No idea, for his wife or family, what had become of him. A trip to Mexico gone wrong? A bullet in a motel room somewhere from an affair gone awry? I almost wish I could write a letter. Explain. But I'm not sure that would help them. Hearing about his death would not give them peace. Maybe ignorance will. Or maybe I am a justifying monster. Yeah. Most likely that.

The guilt follows me, as I open the gate, hop into the truck, start it up, and leave, closing and locking the gate behind me. I was never seen so I was never there. One dead body less, I drive back to the city, the weight of my actions heavy on my shoulders. It was so much easier before. I felt lighter last time. Freer. This time I feel the lift of my killing impulses, but the weight of a different pressure. Guilt. In many ways, a heavier weight. One that I cannot discuss with Dr. Derek. One that I must deal with on my own. I hope he didn't have a family. I hope he really was a monster.

I am wired, my after-kill nap reviving me, the jittery realization of what I've done keeping me awake. I return home, park the truck, and thumb my still-gloved hands through the key ring that I had found in the man's pocket. Keys and a roll of fresh dollar bills, almost a thousand bucks folded neatly and stuffed into jeans that looked brand new and ironed. The key ring holds a Mercedes key, the lock and unlock buttons part of its design, seven or eight house keys, and something that appears to be a mailbox or locker key. No tags to a gym, discount cards, the last item on the ring being a small fob of some sort. I need to deal with his vehicle. It can't sit wherever he parked it. It's like a beacon, a giant "look here for your missing person" sign, especially a Mercedes. I walk to the window, crane my neck until I see it, an S-Class almost out of eyeshot, sitting in a metered spot at the curb. I drum my fingers on the glass and think. Chances are, in this area, it will be, at some point in time, stolen—I could leave the keys on the front seat and wait—but I can't risk that. With my luck a Good Samaritan will do the right thing and call the cops. Better to move it now. Better to cover my tracks and leave bread crumbs at the same time. Something for the man's wife and kids to stew over for the next two decades. *God, I'm a bitch.*

I leave the sweatshirt on, grateful for the cold temperatures that will aid in my disguise. Its hood up, gloves on, the baggy sweatshirt that hides my figure—none of it will be looked at twice. The streets outside my window are empty, most people huddled inside. Few to report or notice anything other than the ache of their joints or the freeze of their toes. I exit the apartment, heading down the stairwell, working through the plan, examining it for flaws, then pause on the third-floor landing. Decide I need more, a prop. I jog up the stairs, my calves aching, my breath running out before I reach the top. I am a weakling. My daily crunches and exercises, designed for cellulite reduction, don't cut it in the "getting rid of dead bodies" role. I huff my way inside and drag my duffel bag out, the insignia-covered tote that used to be a staple of my normal life. Soccer balls shared space with headphones, windbreakers, tennis shoes. Trendy outfits were stuffed alongside heels and makeup bags, DVD cases and face wash. Now, in my new life inside this apartment? It has collected dust. Some paperbacks stuffed in at one point just to clear up some floor space for cardboard box storage, TV dinners or toilet paper. I dump the books out and stuff in some clothes and shoes, a few more items that take up space. I toss in a makeup bag and grab a scarf. Something to wrap around my neck and hide the lower half of my face. I put on a pair of nonprescription glasses, the ones I use on camera when I want to be a disobedient secretary or a straitlaced professor. Or a landing zone for a guy with a cum-on-your-glasses fetish.

I move to the safe and grab cash. A thousand bucks in twenties. Paired with Marcus's money, it's more than enough to cover my needs with some extra for a bribe, should one pop up its head and need to be courted.

Then I use my intelligence. Pile my hair on my head. Wrap it in Saran Wrap like I once saw on a Lifetime movie. Pull a wool hat over it, return my hoodie to the upright position, and step outside, locking my door, the scent of bleach still strong, the duffel bag tossed over a shoulder. In my pocket, my phone rings. I ignore it and step for the elevator. Skip the stairwell entrance and listen to the ache in my legs, the weight of my bag. Swallow my I'm-a-badass pride and get on the elevator.

The key fob works, my guess at his car confirmed, one block down. I move quickly, tossing my bag into the passenger side and moving the seat forward, mentally reminding myself to put it back once finished. Then I drive, keeping the radio where it is, on a sports station, the discussion unfamiliar, my brain listening for a good stretch before I reach out, stab the button with a gloved finger, having had enough of statistics and football chatter to last me this trip. I take the highway, travel a hundred miles west, then exit and follow the signs for the Oklahoma City airport. Pull into long-term parking, pocket the ticket, move the seat back, and grab my bag. Lock the car, keep the keys, and walk into the airport, bag in hand, head down. No one looks, no one cares. I use the restroom, buy a Happy Meal, spend ten minutes reading in a worn seat by the baggage claim, then swing by an automatic trash can. Toss the keys in with my trash and walk out. Get in the first taxi in line.

"Downtown, please."

The driver says nothing, just nods, slouches in his seat, and drives. We ride in silence, '80s rap playing through the speakers until the yellow cab hits the morning streets of downtown. I have the couldn't-care-less-about-my-safety cabbie drop me in front of a Walgreens, then I walk through downtown, flag a new taxi, and give the driver the address of a hotel four blocks from my apartment. He frowns, plugs it in his GPS. "That's a good hour and a half away. You gonna be okay with that fare?"

From the privacy of the backseat I pull a handful of cash out, count out four hundred-dollar bills and push them through the window. "Will this cover it?"

He takes the money. "Buckle up." Then he does what I'd hoped he'd do. Reaches out and turns off the meter. I stretch out in the backseat, put my head on my duffel bag, my face out of sight, and sleep, dragged easily into it by the hum of the road beneath our tires, the city disappearing into the night sky, passing streetlights fading until it is just darkness, the soft sound of radio, and the wheeze of the heat slipping through the back vents. I sleep, guilt fading a little as I leave the last piece of him alone and deserted in the long-term parking lot of the Oklahoma City airport. I saw an article once that described a woman who racked up $105,000 in airport rental fees after her car sat in the long-term parking lot for three years. I wonder, as sleep drugs my mind, how long it will take before the Mercedes is noticed. If it will be impounded and auctioned off or if police will be contacted. If...

I sleep.

❖

The man calls out, his voice dragging me into awareness. "You said the Red Roof Inn, right?"

I sit up, adjusting my hat to make sure I am covered. "Yeah."

"We're here. You sure you want to stay here? This area looks pretty rough."

"I'm good." I crack the door, the burst of cold air making me regret my decision to walk the four blocks home. "Thanks."

"Have a good night."

I don't look back. Blink and try to fully wake, my limbs sluggish, my left leg asleep as I limp from the car, into the cold day. The bright sun should have cast a cheerful light on my street, minimizing the street filth and homeless mounds. It doesn't. I stuff my free hand into my pocket, heft the duffel bag over my shoulder, and walk. Walk and think of my apartment. Warm, clean, and empty. Even my shower, with its puny spray, is tempting at this moment in time.

The guilt problem gets solved an hour later, when I have showered and changed, the truck is back at Hertz, and FtypeBaby and I are having a getting-reacquainted visit to the tune of a hundred and four miles per hour. Open skies, empty highways, a deathly sprint that will one day get me pulled over or smashed into a hundred pieces...but this time, when my phone rings, Marcus finally and completely taken care of, I answer it. Ready to hear Mike's voice. Ready to forgive his weakness. Ready to hear that my money, as unused as it may be, is back where it belongs. Not ready to hear the first words out of his mouth.

"Jeremy's missing."

CHAPTER 105

JEREMY'S FEET ARE numb. He's tried kicking, and ended up doing some horrific version of a mermaid flail. He now moves his toes instead, working his ankles back and forth, trying to find some give in the zip ties that bind them together. If only he'd worn boots today. Then his ankles would have some bit of protection, some room. He might have been able to slide a foot out, kick free. Instead he wore Nikes with barely present socks, leaving his ankles naked and unprotected, the hair there not enough to stop the ties from cutting into his skin, the warm ooze of blood coming when his foot manipulation gets too enthusiastic.

Whatever drug he was given has worn off for the most part. He stills feel light-headed, bits of nausea still sweeping along, increasing every time he remembers that the sour taste in his mouth is vomit. He must have, at some point in time, chugged a gallon of it. That is unknown. Everything is unknown. He'd come home, grabbed mail on his way in...and that's as far back as his memory goes. Nothing else. No explanation of why he'd been tied up on the floor, hands tied behind his back, ankles bound together but knees left free, looking like a police suspect banished to the ground for resisting arrest. Whatever bastard did this also felt the need to tape his eyes, one duct-tape strip running from ear to ear, the sticky side pushed down, into his eyes, pushed hard, like some asshole had wanted to make damn sure that every individual eyelash would adhere to it, to torture his lids into submission while robbing him of his sight. A second piece covers his mouth.

He can move a little. Crawl for a bit before his legs are stopped. They seem to be tied to something, his range of motion restricted to an arc that spans from counter to counter, the point of connection being... the kitchen sink? He tries to arch his back, feel with his hands the chain of zip ties that leads into the cabinet, but can't get far. He can only guess that his feet are chained to a pipe or the garbage disposal. Whatever it is, it is sturdy. He's yanked and only worn his skin raw as a result.

Jeremy catalogs the house in his mind, tries to discover what is of value, what they could have wanted. Was it a team of men? Highly trained or neighborhood thugs? He wonders, when this tape is finally removed, if his entire house will be empty, wiped of all contents, his truck stolen with the keys they probably took from his pocket. He tries to calculate time. It's Thursday night. He doesn't work until Saturday. Should easily survive thirty-six hours. And he doesn't miss work. Someone will worry. Deanna will notice, call someone. Maybe drive over, not that she knows where he lives. Scratch that possibility. Given the tone of their parting, she might think that his silence is intentional.

In Boy Scouts he was taught the Rule of Threes. Death will come from three minutes without air, three hours without shelter, three days without water. Thirty-six hours will be nothing. He will be fine.

It is at that point, that relaxation of his muscles, the mini-release of stress from his body, when his senses relax that he hears the beep. Coming from behind his head. From, best Jeremy can tell, the direction of the oven.

In that one beep, in that tie of his brain that connects the sound to the appliance, he feels his first moment of panic.

CHAPTER 106

"EXPLAIN." I DON'T ask the other questions, the ones that are shooting from all directions out of my mind. How much does he know about Jeremy? What kind of tabs is he keeping on my life? How does he know he's missing? Have I given him too much access? Is there any way to take it back? Jeremy is missing? What have I done? I say nothing, back off the accelerator, move Ftype-Baby into the slow lane and listen to him speak.

"I don't know for sure that he's missing, but I've dug a bit. Things are coming back to me...things I said to the guy who was here. I was playing back our conversation, trying to think if there was anything you might want to know—just in case..."

"Skip to the fucking point."

"You can't be pissed at me anymore. I put your money back and was tortured trying to protect you. Let's not forget that."

His response is tinted with fear and that worries me. Mike has never, in all the emotions I have pulled out of him, sounded scared. And most definitely not scared of me. Aroused by, amused by, smart-assed by, but not scared by. And now he sounds scared and nervous, neither of which I like. "Shut up about the money, tell me about Jeremy. Quickly."

"He hasn't made a phone call since five o'clock yesterday. Or logged onto his computer, or used his cell phone's data—that'd include playing a game or checking his e-mail or sending a text—in at least fourteen, maybe fifteen hours. I called his cell, it went straight to voice mail."

I breathe. Not that bad. *Missing* is a strong fucking word for Mike to be throwing around. "Maybe his battery died during the night."

"He stopped using his phone that early in the day? Plus, he's at home all evening and he doesn't bother to plug it in?"

"What else?"

"Well Marcus found out about him. Knew his address." Any fear in his voice is now at maximum height. *This* is why he is worried.

"Found out what *about* Jeremy?" I try, and fail, to keep my voice level.

I did this.

I pissed off Marcus.

I blocked him.

I pushed every button he had and did it with glee.

I put Mike in this position.

I put Jeremy on this prick's radar.

"I didn't *volunteer* anything. He saw a photo of him...wanted to know more. His name. Address. I told him I didn't know who he was—if he was a brother or your boyfriend."

"How interested did he seem?"

"Interested enough to write down the info."

I speed up, eyeing the center median and wondering if the car has the grit to make it over and through. Probably not. I head for the next exit, needing to end this joyride, turn the hell around, and head back to town. "What else do you know?"

Mike perks up a bit, speaking quickly. "I got into OnStar. His truck is pretty new, and he subscribes to the service. It shows his truck at his house, but I can't tell how long its been there. There's been no activity on his credit cards or bank account since last night."

"So...you think he's missing because his cell phone hasn't had any activity and his truck is at his house." I slow FtypeBaby's roll down a bit, my breath moving at a more normal pace in and out of my chest. I spy an exit sign and prepare to depart.

"Yeah. It's not much. But...I don't know. When it came to me—that I had told him that—I just wanted to check. The cell phone activity is odd. Even a dead phone I should be able to follow. This thing just disappeared, like someone took out the SIM card or dropped it into the toilet. This guy. He's not fucking sane. If he thought you had cared about me, he probably would have brought me with him to use as an intimidation tool."

Something in his voice catches me. Something I have never heard. A vulnerability there. "I care about you, Mike."

He laughs, the sound hollow in tone. "You care about what I do for you."

"I'm not gonna massage your back and gush out compliments. You don't want to believe it, don't believe it."

"I don't need the compliments. Just check on your boyfriend, okay?" He hangs up the phone before I can ask for Jeremy's address, an embarrassing request. Something a real girlfriend should know. A text from Mike, thirty seconds later, provides it without my needing to ask. I send a silent bit of thank-you karma his way and plug the address into my GPS. Eight miles, fourteen minutes away. I'll get there in half that, providing I don't get pulled over on the way. I slow down a bit, just to behave.

I'm coming, baby. I cross my fingers and hope he is fine, asleep on the couch, his sexy ass stretched out, pillow marks deep on his face. I don't stop myself when the speedometer inches higher.

CHAPTER 107

IT IS BREATHING, the oven taking measured sighs as it ticks its way to warmth. It is alarming, the awareness of it near Jeremy's head. He doesn't know why it's alarming, but it is out of place, as out of place as his hands and feet being bound on the kitchen floor. Out of place is worrisome. He hasn't used the oven much, frozen pizzas being the main course entering and exiting its depths. The old oven was faulty, two hundred degrees one moment, four hundred the next. So he replaced it, a few months ago, the stainless steel fixture the only bit of this kitchen younger than him. Six or seven pizzas have made their way through those doors, eggs have been cooked on its surface, grilled cheeses flipped on frying pans. There is no reason why, randomly, the oven would turn on. It shouldn't. Jeremy lies there, mind working, and starts to smell pizza.

CHAPTER 108

JEREMY'S NEIGHBORHOOD IS Beverly Hills compared to my slum, but nothing that my highbrow mother would have approved of. Small cottages built in the '40s or '50s, the trees have taken over, dwarfing everything, casting heavy shade on anything and everything their large arms felt the need to cover, the homes barely visible behind decades of overgrown hedges and small yards. In my haste I miss his house, circle the block again, and examine the numbers again. Recognize his truck and pull in.

Marcus is dead. He can't be waiting behind door number Jeremy, a knife in hand, ready to assault me as I walk through the door. But I am still cautious, my turnoff of the engine heavy and slow. What if he is dead? What if this man killed Jeremy just to hurt me, *then* came to my apartment? I never let Marcus speak, I got too fucking excited and killed him too soon. If Jeremy is dead, I will kill Mike. It doesn't matter that this is my fault. Fuck him for blabbing. He should have lost his fingers like a man. Share my money but don't share details that endanger an innocent person. I open the car door, take a deep breath, and close my eyes. Say a quick prayer that he is alive.

My eyes are still closed when the house explodes.

PART 5

There are no lights. There is no pink.

CHAPTER 109

YOU WOULD THINK that ash would be hot. Floating through the air, coming off of a fire. But it's not. It's like whispers on my cheeks. Like gray snow, slightly damp in its arrival. I open my eyes and try to understand its presence. Try to understand why I am on the ground, a strange ground, looking up at oak trees that flicker in the light of a fire. I take a shaky breath and hear the crackle of wood settling, the crash of something falling.

Fire.

Ash.

I jerk to my feet, the world tilting briefly, and the sound of sirens starts, muted. The sound growing louder. Closer. An ambulance. Cops. I find my bearings, reach a hand out, grab hold of the side of my car and stare at the furnace before me. A kindling square of home, crackling into the night, Jeremy's truck silhouetted before it. I drop to my knees and scream his name.

My scream. It is so familiar that I try to stop it, the sound ripping me back into my childhood kitchen, the howl of anguish and regret so similar in pitch to my mother's that I am sick. Is this how she felt? When she looked around and saw the destruction that she had created? I try to close my mouth, try to stop the sound, try to block out the fire and the blood and my sister's face and the man that I love and all I can think is that I turned him away. Jeremy wanted to come with me and I pushed him away in the parking lot. I pushed him away and now he is dead. He is dead and I can't stop the scream. I repeat his name, screaming it to the fire, to the gods above, to the man that I hope is alive to hear it.

CHAPTER 110

IT IS UNLIKELY that Mike will ever again sit in his empty house and not think of those hours. The hours he was chained to the bed. The hours he waited, unsure of his future.

Now, the emptiness haunts him. Reminds him too clearly of those hours. Of, for the first time in a long time, how alone he feels. Jamie left a few minutes ago, life and work calling, plants somewhere needing to be tended to. Without her, this house feels empty. Like he is not a soul. As if he doesn't, in some way, breathe life into this space.

He doesn't *have* to stay in this house. People in wheelchairs go out—have normal jobs, live normal lives. But truth be told, leaving? Forcing himself to participate in daily interactions with normal, I-walk-around-on-two-legs people? Doesn't interest him. Never has. Everything he needs is here. A job he loves. Freedom, inside these walls. Fuck what society thinks is needed to be happy. He doesn't need the sympathetic looks of the public, their chips and pokes. He can read their looks. One hooker just spat it out, without hesitation, saying what he can see in so many of their eyes. *You'd be so hot*, she drawled, popping her gum and crawling on top of him. *If you weren't in that wheelchair. Does it bother you?*

His dick wouldn't cooperate after that.

Being alone is better than being with someone who is there

despite the handicap. The worst is the constant waiting—expecting that crestfallen look, that moment where the girl will be caught with her guard down, with a look of pity she doesn't hide fast enough. Fuck that.

The outside world doesn't care if he has paraplegia or is paralyzed. It's all the same to them. Wheelchair boy. Wheelchair boy with an "isn't that a shame" pretty face. Crestfallen looks of apology accompanying any introduction or passing greeting. So Mike will keep his life indoors. His world online. There he's a king. There he's popular and beautiful and the captain of the mother-fucking football team.

But right now he's nothing but alone and scared. Scared that he's ripped apart a piece of Deanna's life. A piece that code and firewalls won't put back together. Scared that she, after this act of destruction, won't talk to him anymore. Won't answer his calls or IMs, won't accept his chats when he invites her to private. Scared that he's ripped off a piece of his own life that the false walls of cyberspace won't put back together.

Jeremy is dead. Has to be. No calls or text, no Internet activity? Drove his truck home yesterday afternoon, parked it out front and did NOTHING that evening? Nothing that night? Unlikely. Mike checked his cell phone records for the past three years. Never silent for this long. And he's been power calling him. Routing the calls so they look like they're coming from her. No response, and now his battery is probably dead, 'cause it's going straight to voice mail. So he's dead, or maybe tied up, like Mike was. A gag or tape over his mouth, handcuffs around his wrists. That's the hopeful side of him talking. She'll bust in, rescue him. Be the hero. Kiss the guy. Wrap her legs around him and probably fuck him right there on the living room floor. Or on the bed, if he is tied up where Mike was. Welcome back to life; you only had to suffer for one night and now she's here, naked. Everything you ever wanted. Prick.

There is a moment of guilt for cursing a man who is most likely dead. Mike wonders, for the umpteenth time, if he should call the cops. Send them over to Pacer's place. But she is going there. Was already close by. And she'll be beyond pissed if cops show up. She's probably got Marcus's fucking finger stuffed in her jeans pocket—his dead body in her trunk—his blood on her shirt. A wave of nausea rolls through him and he bends over the trash can, noticing, as his body fails to vomit, that it's empty, a fresh white liner in it. Jamie. Helpful woman. There is something, a background word that catches his attention, the police scanner feed jabbering for the last six hours with absolutely nothing of interest. He turns up the volume and listens.

"...a 911 call regarding an explosion. Fire and medical respond to Twenty-three Prestwick Place."

His heart stops, his hand moving the volume control higher. An explosion. His world suddenly closes a bit, his fingers moving before his mind even catches up, typing furiously and bringing up iCloud. Deanna's cell. Find-A-Phoning its ass until the green dot destroys his world. Prestwick Place. On a square that has got to be his house. Deanna. Wrapping her legs around his body. Fucking him on the bed, celebrating his safe release from capture. *BOOM*. He feels his heart unnaturally quicken, his breath keeping pace.

Holy shit.

Holy shit.

Holy shit.

"Fire and medical, please update me to your status in regards to Twenty-three Prestwick Place."

The crackle and pop of empty air.

"Um…Captain Scott here with Engine Twenty-nine. Looks like a chemical explosion of some sort. Whole house is up right now. We're working on containing the blaze and locating any survivors. One female found, in front of the blaze." His words are cut off by a scream, a scream that—even through the miles, through the distortion and feedback of the radio—is haunting in its anguish. Mike grips the desk, listens to that scream, his heart rising and falling in one quick roller-coaster ride as it vibrates through the room.

CHAPTER III

I AM CARRIED away from Jeremy's house, my legs dragging at the dirt, my body limp, by a man in yellow. He speaks to me, words that I ignore, words I can barely hear through my screams of Jeremy's name. Screams I am not sure are even coming from my mouth; they may just be screaming through my soul, my head, imaginary breaks in my sanity like bright-ass light streaming through a wasntpulledtightenoughclosed curtain.

I am dragged away, and my view of the house disappears as an ambulance door replaces it.

I will kill Mike. I don't care if I brought Marcus to his doorstep. I will kill him and then kill myself. Slowly, in a fashion that will cause as much pain as my body can physically take. Fuck, I may skip Mike, my self-hatred too strong to control. I, killer of good, am not fit to live.

I am lifted, a second face joining the first, and they speak, a light shining into my eyes, useless questions coming forth from their lips. I speak, through the screams, the only thing they need to know.

"Jeremy." I repeat it, just in case they didn't hear it. Repeat it again, louder. And again, my strength dropping. Then I am whispering the name, and I don't know if anyone, other than my soul, can hear it.

"Jeremy."

CHAPTER 112

WHY DOES JEREMY love her? Why love a girl that he doesn't really know? A girl he's afraid to question, afraid he won't like the answers, that his conscience will step in and pry their hands apart, will push his heart into a blender and shut the door to 6E forever. Maybe the damaged are the easiest to fall in love with. She is damaged. Damaged in a strange way that has strength—a silent, don't-open-that-door, watch-your-back-in-the-dark strength. Her eyes sometimes glint in a way that is unnatural; her hands shake from something other than nerves. She has told him that she is dangerous, that she wants to hurt others, to kill. That alone should make him leave, should put distance between them. He should find a girl who is normal, whom he can bring home to the family and not worry about curfews or Mom's knife drawer. But her vulnerability, her fear, her rules, her absolute adherence to isolation…she has good in her. She tries so hard, she worries so much. He wishes he could take that worry. Give her a clean life full of children and carpools and grocery lists and vacations. Wipe the stress from her eyes. It fades a bit, every time they are together. His strength reassures her, his ability to physically restrain her softens the fear that she may hurt him and allows her to drop her guard. Let him touch her. Let him distract her mind in ways that make his cock hard.

He doesn't know why he loves her. But does anyone know why

they love? We don't love people for their traits—traits are common. We love them for their unique ability to tug at our soul, to connect to us in a way that no other person can. Love is unexplainable, unpredictable, and often unreasonable. It doesn't make sense, and doesn't care to explain to us its thought process.

He hears his name, a scream from her lips, and everything else stops. He tries to lift his head, tries to move, but the weight on his back is excruciating, his body pinned beneath something, most likely hundred-year-old chunks of brick and pieces of a house that was never intended to come apart. There is the feel of heat, incredible heat, and he wishes he could call her name. Wishes for something other than to struggle silently, his world dark. He feels the sharp edge of something along his cheek and tries to work it over his eyes. Tries to move in a way that will rip open the tape and give him back his sight in these last moments of life.

He fails, the sharp edge doing nothing but scratching the hell outta his face, his attempts stopping at the first bite of pain.

The heat is incredible, building. Growing. It feels like his skin is cooking, yet he can't move, can only lie still, blind and burning.

And still her screams continue. The sound rips at his heart, and he prays that she is not in pain.

CHAPTER 113

EVERYTHING HAPPENS AT a moment when I want nothing. I want to stand by my car and scream some more. I want to run through the burning debris and find Jeremy. I don't want to be wrapped in blankets and coddled like a victim when I am the one responsible. I don't want valuable personnel helping me when they should be looking for him.

But shock victims are treated with warmth and reassurance, and I am lumped into that prognosis. Warmth and reassurance. I do appreciate the blankets, the ambulance way too cold, no one else seemingly mindful of the frigid air. My teeth chatter, the blanket not enough, the second and third one helping slightly. They get moved, the blankets. They get lifted and adjusted as different parts of my body are examined. I feel the sharp prick of glass being pulled out, the wet flow of blood that is promptly stemmed.

Glass. I now remember the glass. It felt like a blast of desert air, shards instead of sand, a wall of getthehellouttatheway coming too fast, too soon, my shock at the explosion leaving me vulnerable for a moment too long before reflexes kicked in and I ducked, covering my face, turning my body away from the blast. My eyes had been closed, my mouth moving in silent prayer, the sound of the explosion confusing me, a moment of absolute quiet before insanity boomed. In the brief pause of life, I had opened my eyes.

Even though it exposed the most vulnerable piece of my body. But, I had to know, my curiosity sharing space with my fear.

I should have kept them closed. Now I have that image branded in my mind. The second ending of my life.

Warmth and reassurance. My body temperature is finally starting to rise. I blink, looking into the face of the too-calm paramedic, and will her to shut the hell up. I don't want her words. I don't want her words unless they speak the impossible. I want her to shut up, to stop talking before I roll my broken body off of this bed and silence her myself.

"Jeremy," I whisper.

But she doesn't respond. Doesn't look up. Continues moving her mouth and saying words that don't help. Words that don't say what I want to hear.

"Jeremy?" I speak louder, asking it as more of a question, then repeating myself. Louder, because she is raising her brow as if she doesn't understand.

Then the woman yells, her voice too loud, not calm, and I look at her in confusion, the sound piercing through me, the combination between it and my chattering teeth too loud for reasonable thought to occur. Then more faces appear, dotting the landscape, firm hands shoving incessantly on my torso, unnecessary as I am already lying down, and a mask appears, covers my nose and mouth, stale air pushing incessantly, too cold. My entire world is too cold, too dark. I fight my eyes but they close and the last thought I hold on to is one that doesn't make sense. *Jeremy*.

CHAPTER 114

I COME BACK to sanity, or my best form of it, in a hospital. I blink, my lids crusted closed, the action of them slow and painful. My room is empty, no one sitting in the chair, no nurse standing by the ready. I celebrate the silence for a moment—a chance to gather my wits before someone comes in and sees my psychological vulnerability.

I turn my head slightly, testing my range of movement. Move my arms and legs. Everything works. Some bandages, nothing major. A woman in scrubs walks by the open door, pauses, reroutes into my room when she sees me.

"Good. You're awake." She lifts my chart from the door, steps in with a friendly smile. "How're you feeling?"

I shrug, not sure of the correct response. Not sure what I want. Do I want to stay here a few nights? Enjoy the experience, live up my moment in the real world? Then I remember how I got here. Jeremy. My world dulls. "I'm fine."

"We can get you back home as soon as the doctor checks you out. But let's get you some food; you've got to be starved. Are you up for a phone call?"

"A phone call?" I ask slowly.

"Your boyfriend's been calling." She smiles. "A lot." She rolls a tray to my bedside, opens a low refrigerator, and pulls out some generic purple form of Jell-O. Cracks it open with easy efficiency while I stare at her, trying to move my dry lips and get out words. "We can't share anything about your condition without your consent, so he's pretty worried. I know he'd love to hear your voice."

"He's alive?"

She shoots me an odd look. "Oh yes. Would you like me to get him on the phone?"

❧

An impatient four minutes later, my phone rings, the nurse sticking her head in. "That's him, dear." I reach for it with eager hands.

My throat doesn't cooperate, my greeting coming out hushed and scratchy. "Hello?"

"Dee."

Anger surges through me, so strong I almost come off the bed. "You piece of shit." The nurse's smile fades and she flees the doorway, the swing of the door so quick that I feel a breeze.

"Deanna, please." Mike's voice is so strained I barely recognize it.

"You told them I was your *girlfriend*? I will kill you. I will kill you slowly and you will regret every phone call as you bleed a painful death below me." I hiss, meaning seeping through every word. "You made me think he was *alive*, you asshole. When she said—"

"Jeremy's alive, Deanna." His quick words sound so surprised that I hesitate, caught off guard by his words and his tone.

"Go on." I grind the words between clenched teeth, refusing to let the happy part of my heart celebrate without justification.

"I mean—I don't know exact details, but the scanner talk said they pulled him from the house. That he was responsive. They took him to the hospital, he's there somewhere, the same hospital as you. They won't tell me shit about his condition, and all

I can tell from their systems is that he's not critical. Everything statuswise is done on paper charts; they're stuck in the fucking stone age." He blows a hard breath into the phone.

I close my eyes, lean back on the bed. "He's alive?"

"Yes. I *swear* to you he is. If he wasn't, I wouldn't be calling you. I'd be hiding under a rock somewhere drowning my regrets in tequila."

I swallow a lump of weakness, allowing a small bit of hope to enter my heart. "Fuck you, Mike."

"I got your money back. You can't be pissed at me about that anymore."

"I was only mad about the money when I thought you had stolen it. I'm over that." The money isn't why I'm mad. It's the betrayal of everything. "God, I hate you."

"He's alive, Dee."

I snort. "You don't know shit. Alive doesn't tell me if he'll make it through the night or live to be a hundred. You want to give out my personal info? Go ahead. Marcus's issue was with me. I deserve whatever he wanted to bring my way. But you didn't have to mention Jeremy. You shouldn't have fucking known about him to begin with." I lean forward, hiss into the phone with my last bit of energy. "You crossed the line, Mike."

There is only silence. No visual of how his face is or if there is a sag in his shoulders.

"I'm sorry."

I say nothing, and hang up the phone. Press the nurse call button until my finger aches and I hear the patter of white-soled shoes.

"There was another person in the explosion with me. A Jeremy Pacer. I'd like to see him."

CHAPTER 115

MIKE IS RIGHT; Jeremy is alive. I ask the question to two different nurses, certain that someone is wrong, that God is fucking with me and someone will jump out and go *aha!* with a death certificate. But there is a consensus, and they agree to take me to him.

It takes time to get up the three floors to Jeremy's floor. Not travel time, but bullshit time—they won't move me from my bed until the doctor signs off. When the old man finally comes in, my attitude is running at full steam, complete with a small side of cheer at the fact that my man has survived. He made it through the explosion I have no doubt, despite what I said to Mike, he will pull through intensive care. My man is strong and doesn't give up. But I need to see him. Need to apologize. Need to take the blame and explain to him what happened. Need to tell him exactly what he is dealing with when it comes to me.

Maybe I won't tell him exactly. Not while he is hooked up to a breathing machine and hovering on the brink of death. That might be too strong a blow. Maybe I'll put it off a few days. Or weeks. Or just a couple of years. Just to be safe.

Shit. I'm doing it already. Justifying my way into lies. Lies by omission.

"I don't need a wheelchair. I'm perfectly capable of walking."

"Awww... we have to keep you in a wheelchair until you leave the hospital. Will someone be picking you up?" This bitch is way too cheery to be working in a place where people die. No wonder they stick her on the cupcake floor, where bumps and bruises are kissed and covered with Scooby-Doo Band-Aids and imitation Jell-O.

"I'll get a taxi." A taxi. Three taxis in twenty-four hours is definitely a record for me.

I don't think SunshinePusher likes that response. There is a pause, a stumble in her step, and then the wheelchair roll powers on. Silence hangs as she tries to think of an appropriate burst of happiness to respond with. "You are so sweet, not to want to burden your friends."

Not a bad save, though it does nothing but remind me that I have no friends. We approach a set of glass doors and I steel myself for What Is To Come.

❖

What Is To Come ends up being the waiting room. Jeremy, apparently, is already surrounded by family and friends, the two-person limit filled in the four hours that have passed since our admission. I feel like an invalid, still in this ridiculous chair, SunshinePusher fastening a belt around me like I might go popping out. She sits next to me, opens a *Woman's Day* magazine, and settles in.

"I don't need a babysitter."

She grins happily, like a crack baby who has no sense of their affliction. "Oh, this is the best part of my job! I'm happy to help."

You're not helping. You're unhelping. You and your big white smile and questions about my friends. You and your clean mind unbothered by thoughts of pain infliction. I growl under my breath, squeezing the fabric of my gown, and try to distract my mind. I glance down.

"Where are my clothes?"

She glances at me, setting down the magazine. "I think they threw them away. They had to cut them off of you. They were ruined by blood. You wouldn't believe how much those little cuts of yours bled!" She shakes her head in dismay, then reaches over and pats my hand. Like we are friends and she has the right to touch me.

Covered in blood. Thank God I changed after getting rid of Marcus.

"Is that why I was brought to the hospital?"

She shakes her head. "No. Your cuts were all superficial. They could have bandaged you up in the ambulance. But you went into shock pretty quickly. They subdued you, then you woke up. Started screaming about something and thrashing around. Kept arguing with the paramedic, saying she was saying things she wasn't." She blushes. "You got pretty violent. Went after her. They had to sedate you."

I sit back. Try to remember anything after the explosion, but I can't. It is all a blur of madness, probably washed over by sedatives. I can remember the ground shaking, the house swallowing me in its razor-sharp grip of chaos. Can remember screaming for Jeremy, my world ending in that moment when I thought I caused his death. Nothing else. Nothing else but this perky bitch and finding out that Jeremy is still alive.

What is taking so long? I twist in my wheelchair, turn to look at the receptionist, but sit back quickly. I shouldn't rush. And I shouldn't waste time chatting up SunshinePusher. I should think. I should plan. I should organize my words in a way that softens their truth.

CHAPTER 116

I FEEL A push on my shoulder. Soft, like a gentle sway from an ocean wave, rocking me back and then returning me to my upright state. Another push. Back and forth. Then the wave gets rude and I get poked, my eyes popping open.

"Deanna," SunshinePusher coos. "It's time to wake up. We can go in now."

It's time to wake up. Like I am six years old and she is my mother. I blink at her, willing the sleep from my eyes. I can't believe I fell asleep.

"It's the sedatives," she says gently. "You'll be groggy for a few hours."

"I'm not groggy." The room sways before me, her face turning blurry before refocusing. I smile, through the blur, and hope that it passes muster. My vision clears and she rolls me forward.

❖

I watch the door open and pray for strength. Pray that when I see him, that I will be cool. Smile. Isn't that what normal women do? Smile. I watch the door open and strain forward, wishing this infuriating woman would roll me faster.

I can see little of the man I love, but he is made no less handsome by the breathing tube through his nose, bandages on his face, the IV in his arm, and blankets covering his body. Sunshine pushes me to the side of his bed, my hand stealing out and under the blankets, grabbing his carefully, unsure of his level of injuries. His eyes open, green finding me, and his mouth tugs into a smile. "Deanna."

His voice is scratchy, weak. But his hand squeezes mine, and it is strong. I stand, pushing the wheelchair back, and send Sunshine a pointed look. "Could we have some privacy?"

She smiles brightly. "Of course. I'll be in the lobby. The receptionist asks that you limit this visit to thirty minutes." I watch her, wait for the door to close behind her cupcake-covered scrubs, and turn back to him. My hand moves, shaky in its path, up his arm and down his side. "What's hurt?"

He reaches over, pushing a button on the side of the bed that raises him slightly, his face tightening, a white flush of pain passing briefly through it. My heart seizes at the look. *I caused that.* I am the reason he is here.

"Nothing major."

"You're all bandaged up. Something major."

He barely shrugs, the reduced movement my second clue that he is in pain. "Some internal injuries. I was caught—when the house collapsed—under part of it. I have a lot of bruising, some small burns."

I frown. "And internal bleeding."

"I don't even know if I have that anymore. They took me straight into surgery. I haven't talked to the doctor since." He smiles. "Nothing for you to worry about." His eyes sharpen, move to the chair. "Are you hurt?" He pushes himself up, worry making his movements too quick.

I shake my head quickly, push on his shoulders. "Lie back. Relax. I'm fine. The wheelchair is some stupid hospital policy thing."

His eyes travel over my face. "But your face. The cuts..."

"Superficial," I brush off. "Neosporin-worthy, nothing else." I move closer to him, reach out and bend down. Hug his chest as gently as I can. Breathe in the scent that is not Jeremy. It is medicinal and sickly, yet I inhale as much of it as I can gather. I relax, rest my head on his chest. "Does this hurt?"

His hand comes up, brushes gently over my back. "Not in the least."

We stay there, for long moment, and then I straighten. "Tell me what happened. I saw the house explode—you couldn't have..."

His eyes study me. I don't like how they look at me. As if they are fighting a war beneath the green. "First, what happened to your face?" His eyes drop down. "Your hands." He pulls back the sleeve of my gown, flipping over my hands to reveal my shredded palms. "Jesus, Dee."

I push his hands away. "It's nothing. I pulled up to your house right before the explosion. Got scratched up from the blast. *Tell me* what happened." I keep my eyes on his, my face so tight I feel as if my skin will rip.

He looks away. "I don't really know. I came home from work. Walked in the house, don't remember anything happening, but woke up and was tied up."

"Tied up?" My voice is harsh. Harsher than I meant it to be, the anger pushing and pulling my vocal cords without my permission. His eyes return to mine, a bit of wariness in their depths.

"Yeah. My hands behind my back, with zip ties. Feet tied. I had some kind of tape—probably duct tape—across my mouth and eyes."

"For how long?" Fuck. Any compassion, any guilt that may have stuck around, lingered in some traitorous vein in my body, disappears. It's a waste of a question. I know when Marcus arrived at my house. I know the time I spent with him, the time I spent dumping his body. Taking my sweet fucking time while Jeremy lay alone.

He shrugs. "Not sure."

"How'd you escape?"

"I kicked my feet instead of yanking them. Broke half the kitchen before I hit the pipe I was tied to. Rolled my way to the side of the house. Really heroic, manly stuff." He smiles and I try to but I can't.

"So you never saw the guy."

"Nope. Why? You know who he was?" The question changes the dynamic of the room. I try to read his eyes. Try to understand the vibe between us. Not anger, but wariness. Hesitation mixed with curiosity.

"Yes. A client." I don't give him anything more. Wait to see what pawn he slides forward. I don't want to tell him what I did. There is no short way to tell this story, a Pandora's box of outcomes to revealing my soul. Plus, he's got to be tired. Medicated. The responsible thing would be to let him rest. "That was why I was so rude yesterday afternoon. I thought he was coming to my apartment—didn't want you to be in danger."

It is a horribly brief explanation, one that should be followed up with a flurry of questions, but Jeremy stays silent. "Do you want to know more?"

A long silence, then he shakes his head. "I don't want him to hurt you."

I shake my head. "He's not going to."

"I don't want you going back to the apartment. If he came to me he could have gone to you next. He could be waiting there, like he did with me."

I raise my chin, look into his eyes with enough resolve that he stops talking. "He's not going to hurt me. I'm not saying that to reassure you, I'm telling you it as fact."

He says nothing. We hold a long look, then he nods.

I am scared of the question but ask it anyway. "Do you want to know more?"

His head slowly moves. Shakes. "Not right now. The, uh, the nurses said that the police came by. Want to talk to me. Are investigating the explosion. I want to be as truthful as I can when I speak to them. As ignorant as I can." He lowers his voice, as if he has suddenly remembered where we are. "If you want to talk later, once I get out of here, we can talk then." He rests his head against the pillow, turns it to look into my face. "Do you want to tell me?"

I laugh through an exhale of breath and shake my head slightly. "No." I look back at him. "But I think I should. There are things about me that you should know."

His eyes squint a bit as he focuses on me. "Just because we are in love doesn't mean you have to share all your secrets."

"You might not love me if you knew all of them." I smile sadly.

He pulls at my hand, tugs my mouth to his. "I will always love you," he whispers.

I lower my head to his chest to avoid a response. *No,* I think. *You won't.*

I can't do it. I can't ruin this beautiful loyal man's impression of me. I can't destroy the only person in this world who looks at me as if I am not broken. Who knows about my dark desires, yet still loves me. Who might not be able to handle the fact that I have acted on those desires.

I can't do it. My weakness, my lack of courage is dismaying, my own subconscious stepping away with an offended look. But my heart is too strong. It beats too loud and too rebelliously, drowning common sense as it sets up roadblocks and dams, keeping out anything, including morality, in a quest to protect its claim.

I love him.

He loves me.

I can't destroy everything. Not when he doesn't even want, isn't even asking, for my secrets.

I try to think, try to fill our silence with something, some response to his words, some delay tactic that will get me out of this thorn bush and back to safe, non-relationship-ending conversation. I straighten, realizing, as my gaze finds his face, that he, beautiful man, claimant of my heart, is asleep.

CHAPTER 117

One Month Later

THERE ARE NO lights, there is no pink. I don't wear stockings, or a garter, or sexy panties. There is only me, in a tank top and cotton underwear, on hotel sheets, Jeremy's temporary home until he finds a new one. And his body above mine, his shirt off, sweatpants low enough that I can see the V of his hips.

"Are you sure?" he whispers.

I reach a hand up, run it through the short tufts of his hair. Gently trace the line of his strong jaw, stubble beneath my fingers, his lips parting slightly when I reach their edges. The vulnerable look in his eyes giving me courage. I nod. Wrap my hand around the back of his head and pull him down, onto my mouth, his soft kiss gaining strength as my mouth opens, as he tastes my willingness and pushes further. Then his body moves, my legs spreading, wrapping, his weight taking its rightful place atop me, and he pushes forward slightly, into my body, hard pressure against me proving his need. He lifts his head, leaving the kiss, the rough scrape of his jaw moving lower, the soft trail of his mouth moving across my jaw, down my neck, his weight lifting off of me as his hands gather the bottom of my tank top and slide underneath. I close my eyes, relax my head against the pillow, and release a breath. Shudder as fingers slide up my body, hitting the curve of my breasts and sliding outward only to come together. Cup the weight of them in his hands gently as his mouth nudges lower, moves over the fabric of my thin tank, his mouth kissing them each in turn, sucking gently through the fabric, wet and hot, the sensation of the cloth and his mouth, his tongue, his teeth, causing my pelvis to tilt, hot need to shoot through me.

"Jeremy," I beg. "I'm ready."

"Soon."

"Now."

He slides down, between my legs, loops fingers under cotton, and drags my panties off, lifting my legs and dropping a quick kiss on the underside of my thigh, his eyes catching mine, a smile tugging at his lips. "God, you don't know how long I've thought about this."

"How long?"

"Too long to admit it here. It'd ruin the moment."

I smile. "Creepy?"

"Creepy." He throws my panties to the side, running strong fingers slowly down the length of my legs, his breath hot as he takes a small nip of my skin, his teeth causing me to shiver. Then he spreads them, moving back up the length of my body, in between my legs, coming to a stop above me, his eyes on mine. "I love you."

I study the thick lashes, his eyes behind them open and trusting. "You shouldn't."

He lowers his mouth, brushes against my lips, taking his time with the kiss, his tongue soft and suggestive. "I do."

"I love you too."

He sits back, his eyes on mine, loosening the tie of his pants, the green glow of his stare darkening, my breath inhaling in one soft gasp when he pushes down the material and his cock pops out. Hard. Ready. Our soft kisses and sweet words had done nothing to pause his arousal. "You ready?"

"You don't have to be gentle." My body is already broken, penetration an old game my body has played too many times to make this special.

But he ignores me, his fingers testing me, taking a slow swipe down my legs, taking a measured draw over my pussy, swearing at the moisture there. I myself am surprised, still, at my body's reaction to the heat of his touch. How much my cunt responds, body arches, a moan slipping from me when he does the simple action of pushing a finger in. I can't think of anything but how much I want his cock, its hard stiff bob sticking straight out, bumping against my sex occasionally, the dark need in his eyes telling me that he knows. Knows exactly where his cock is. Exactly how far it is from my wet need. I reach a fast hand down, wrapping my fingers around his shaft, his eyes closing at the contact, his hips thrusting forward, the organ shocking in its warmth, unbendable yet alive in my hand. A drop of clear liquid appears at his tip, and I run a hesitant thumb over it, my name dropping from his lips at the movement of my hand, my fingers, his own hands dragging my shirt up, making a slow tour of my skin, his eyes still closed, tightly. "Let me get a condom," he rasps, pulling his hips away, opening his eyes, raw want in their depths.

I resist, holding firm to him, the movement of his body causing my hand to jack his cock. "Keep it like this." I have had enough latex in my life. This is my first moment with a man, the first chance that my body will have to experience a real cock, this incredible beating organ that twitches in my hand at the words.

"No." He shakes his head, his eyes on mine. "I can't. You..."

I move my hand, savor the slide of it over his skin, savor the way his eyelids get heavy, his mouth drops slightly open. "You can." I push his cock down, rolling the swollen head against my sex, the wet slide of me against him causing his hips to rock slightly forward, a groan dropping from his mouth as he lowers himself down, his mouth suddenly on my neck, teasing and tasting the skin there before moving to my ear, the heat and static of speech against my ear. "I don't know if I will be able to control myself…"

I take over, the virgin leading the man, making the decision for him, my legs wrapping around him, my hand pushing his shaft slightly down and I pull with my feet, moving my arms around his neck.

"Fuck me, Jeremy. Right now, I need a loss of control."

And there, my arms wrapped around his neck, his cock taking the first real thrust my body has ever known, I release the final strings of my own control. Let myself fully fall in love with this man. Let every push of him draw a little more of my vulnerability out. He cradles my head in his hands, his breath ragged against my neck and lips, his mouth stealing rough kisses in between breathless words of love, my name a gasp on his lips when he gives a complete thrust, going all the way in, the full connection one that makes my back arch, the feeling greater than any I have ever known, better than my kills, better than my freedom. *This* is all I need. *This* is stronger than my affliction, my dark needs. *This* is what is important. *This* love might be my salvation.

Don't miss the next Deanna Madden novel

If You Dare

COMING FALL 2015

ACKNOWLEDGMENTS

The creation of a book takes an army. I never realized that. I always thought authors sat alone in dignified places and created masterpieces. Now I know.

I know that I couldn't write without my husband. Thank you for stepping in when I didn't have time to breathe. For cooking and bringing me plates of food. For putting together a telescope in the middle of our living room without asking me a single question. For spending evenings alone because I am locked away writing. For dealing with the irritable monster that I become when I haven't slept in two days. For lifting me into your arms and hugging me when a plot hole has brought me to tears. For letting me wake you up at two in the morning because writing my kill scene has caused me to be scared of the dark.

I know that I couldn't turn my jumbled words into a book without Susan Barnes. Thank you for carrying us through six drafts of this book. Thank you for speaking up, for pushing, for asking for more. Thank you for digging through this book and pulling out beauty. Thank you for not shying away from my gore and for daring these pages to be wilder.

I know that this book wouldn't find you, the reader, without the Orbit/Redhook/Hachette team. Thank you to Wendy Chan, for creating a cover that causes the reader to stop and stare. Thank you to Lindsey Hall and Angelina Krahn for finding every typo, error and brain-lapse that my brain tried to hide through these pages. Thank you to Andromeda Macri and Giraud Lorber for formatting this book and for Alex Lencicki, Ellen Wright, Laura Fitzgerald, Andy Swist, and Rachel Hairston for spreading the word and getting it in front of readers. Thank you to the entire Redhook team for believing in Deanna and for giving her a chance to shine.

I know that this book wouldn't have found the Redhook team without my agent, Maura Kye-Casella. You, more than anyone, are why this book is on shelves. Thank you for believing in my work and for letting me publish in any fashion I choose to. Thank you for bringing my work to the next level. Thank you, most importantly, for being my friend.

I know that my talent would not be possible without God. These words are not enough, but thank you for all that you bless me with, in this life and the next. I am not worthy but I am truly grateful.

I know that I wouldn't be able to write full-time if it weren't for the readers. Thank you for picking up this book. For seeking out and enjoying my other works. For recommending my books to others, for leaving reviews, and for loving my words. Thank you, thank you, thank you. Truly. You are what make this career, and these books, possible.

Sincerely,

A. R. (*Alessandra*) Torre

NOTE FROM THE AUTHOR

I honestly didn't know where to start with this book. I didn't know where I wanted Deanna to go, how I wanted her journey to advance and end. I will tell you these two secrets. Secret #1: Jeremy originally was going to die. I'm very glad I saved his life. It gave me a surreal feeling of being in control of something, a feeling I very rarely experience—plus, it gave him and Deanna a more complete journey. Secret #2: I had written in Mike losing his fingers, Marcus cutting them off during the interrogation period. All of them. When my husband found out, he blew his lid. Literally. Pulled over the car, wouldn't drive another step forward, and made me promise to change the scene. Right then. Wouldn't drive to the restaurant for dinner until it was changed. And for me, withholding dinner is cruelty of the nth degree.

He was right. It would have been cruel to take Mike's fingers. Sometimes my mind jumps full force out into darkness and I have to crawl my way back up the cliff to sanity. What's crazy is that I really like Mike. Again, like with Jeremy, I'm glad that I revised the story. Thank you, my wonderful husband, for forcing the issue.

Deanna. I love this chick. I really do. When I first wrote *The Girl in 6E*, I had never planned on it having a sequel. Yet here one is, and honestly? I might love this book more than the first.

And...after having this extra time in her head, I can't let her go again, not just yet. Look for more of Deanna in late 2015—I can't *wait* for you to see what happens next in her world.

Until the next story...

A. R. *Torre*

MEET THE AUTHOR

Romona Robbins Photography

A. R. Torre is an open pseudonym for *New York Times* and *USA Today* bestselling erotica author Alessandra Torre.

Alessandra lives in the southern United States and is married, with one young child. She enjoys reading, spending time with her family, and playing with her dogs. Her favorite authors include Lisa Gardner, Dean Koontz, and Jennifer Crusie.

INTRODUCING

**If you enjoyed
DO NOT DISTURB,
look out for**

THE GIRL IN 6E

A Deanna Madden Novel

by A. R. Torre

I haven't touched another person in three years.

*That seems like it would be a difficult task, but it's not.
Not anymore, thanks to the Internet.*

*My anonymous clients spend thousands of dollars to watch
me take my clothes off for the camera. What they want, I give.
Their secrets, I keep.*

Everything I tell them is a lie.

UNDRESSING IS AN EVERYDAY occurrence. Most women do it mindlessly—automatic motions that accomplish an end result. But, if done correctly, stripping can be the ultimate foreplay, a sexual seduction that can wipe clear any rational thoughts and leave a man totally and utterly at your mercy. I have mastered the art.

I kneel on the bed and trail my fingers over my skin—light, teasing caresses designed to heighten my senses and stimulate my body. I exhale slow, trembling breaths as my hands travel near sensitive areas, the dip in my neckline, the lace over my breasts. I keep my eyes down, subservient to him, and wait for the command. One always comes.

"Take off your top. Slowly." The voice is foreign, English words dipped in culture and dialect. I comply, lifting my eyes and biting my bottom lip gently, my tongue quickly darting out, and hear his gasp in response. I run my hands down my neck, grazing the top of my collarbone and dipping under the silk of my negligee. I slide down one strap, then two, the silk bunching over my breasts, the fabric clinging to my nipples. Then I rise to my knees, crossing my arms, sliding the fabric higher, letting it reveal inch by slow inch of skin until it unveils the curve of breasts, dip of throat, and the pout of pink lips.

"Good," he groans. "Very good. I like you, Jessica."

Jessica. Not my real name. He thinks he knows me. They all think they know me. After all, they've seen my Facebook page, seen the Photoshopped photos that construct my manufactured life. They believe what they see, because they want to believe. Like I want to believe.

I turn to the wall and stand, dragging my expensive thong down over my toned hips, bending over and exposing my most private area to his hungry eyes. The embroidered lace slides the rest of the way down my legs and drops around my ankles, snagging on the Italian stilettos that encase perfectly pedicured feet. I am naked now, and slide down to lay on my side in front of him, propped up on one elbow, his eyes hungrily feasting on my body. The lights, bright and hot, illuminate my bare skin, causing it to glow. He speaks, the arousal present in his voice, in the slight thickening of his accent.

"Touch yourself. Just your fingers. I want to see you come."

He wants my fingers, a seductive performance of gasps, moans, and slick foreplay. Eventually, fingers won't be enough. The next visit he'll want more, something bigger, deeper—my moans to be louder, my orgasm stronger. There will be no secrets anymore, no boundaries, no requests he won't be comfortable giving. At this moment, I am his, to do with as he pleases. And right now, he wants fingers.

I angle my body so that he can see my parted legs, my completely bare sex, wet, opened and closed with experienced movements. I dip one finger, then two, inside of me, moving them in and out with slow, seductive strokes, my eyes closed, head tilted back. I hear his gasp, the rustle of clothing, a zipper, and a moan as his hand finds his cock. Unintelligible words, a brief slip into a foreign tongue, the meaning clear despite the language. I increase the speed of my fingers, then pause, spreading my lips and exposing the sensitive bud that holds the power over my ecstasy. I moan softly, a breathy sigh that speaks of want and need, spreading wetness over my swollen clit, the change in pace causing a groan from him.

"Jessica," he whispers my name, longing and need filling every syllable. "Please. I need to see you come."

I open my eyes, staring forward into the bright lights, with a thin sheen of moisture on my skin. I bite my bottom lip, widening my eyes when my fingers again plunge into my core, quick, fast darts of movement, skin on skin; every thrust placing the heel of my hand over my clit, with a delicious friction that moves me in the general direction of an orgasm.

I won't come. An actual orgasm is an occasional occurrence, one that my tortured body spits out in exhausted exasperation, one of those 'here take it' gifts. But for the most part, I am severely oversexed, and my body, my pussy, has grown immune to stimulation. But he doesn't know that. All he knows is that, ten minutes after my fingers make their first dip into the wet folds of my sanctum, my back arches, eyes close, and I have a full body, toe-curling, best-orgasm-of-my-life. I shudder, I gasp; I own the shit out of that fake orgasm. As I always do.

He groans at my climax, his hand creating slick sounds at an impossible speed, and a strangled sound meets my ears, a shuddering moan that disappears into thick gasps.

Then, pure silence. No breaths, no fabric rustling, no sated sighs.

An electronic beep sounds, a tone that I've heard thousands of times. I stretch, grab my lingerie and roll over, hop off the bed, and walk carefully across soft carpet in four-inch heels until I reach my computer's keyboard. I press a key, ending our session.

The lights go out.

CHAPTER I

I HAVEN'T TOUCHED a human in three years. That seems like it would be a difficult task, but it's not. Not anymore, thanks to the Internet. The Internet that makes my income possible and provides anything I could possibly want in exchange for my credit card number. I've had to go into the underground world for a few things, and once in that world, I decided to stock up on a few fun items, like a new identity. I am now, when necessary, Jessica Beth Reilly. I use my alias to prevent others from finding out my past. Pity is a bitch I'd like to avoid. The underground provides a plethora of temptations, but so far, with one notable exception, I've stayed away from illegal arms and unregistered guns. I know my limits.

The UPS man knows me by now—knows to leave my boxes in the hall and to scrawl my name on his signature pad. His name is Jeremy. About a year ago, he was sick, and a stranger came to my door. He refused to leave the package without seeing me. I almost opened the door and went for his box cutters. They almost always carry box cutters. That's one of the things I love about delivery-men. Jeremy hasn't been sick since then. I don't know what I'll ever do if he quits. I like Jeremy, and from my warped peephole view, there is a lot about him to like.

The first shrink I had said I have anthropophobia, which is fear of human interaction. Anthropophobia, mixed with a healthy dose of cruorimania, which is obsession with murder. He told me that via Skype. In exchange for his psychological opinions, I watched him jack off. He had a little cock.

While I may go out of my way to avoid physical human interaction, virtual human interaction is what I spend all day doing. To the people I cam with, I am JessReilly19, a bubbly nineteen year old college student—a hospitality major—who enjoys pop music, underage drinking, and shopping. None of them really know the true me. I am who they want me to be, and they like it like that. So do I.

Knowing the real me would be a bit of a buzz kill. The real me is Deanna Madden, whose mother killed her entire family, then committed suicide. I inherited a lot from my mother, including delicate features and dark hair, but the biggest genetic inheritance was her homicidal tendencies. That's the reason I stay away from people. Because I want to kill. Constantly. It's almost all I think about.

Over the last three years, I've learned how to optimize my income. From 8 a.m. to 3 p.m. I use a site called Sexnow.com, which has a clientele of mostly Asians, Europeans, and Australians. From 6 p.m. to 11 p.m., I'm on American turf, on Cams. com. In between shifts, I eat, workout, shower, and return emails—always in that order.

Whenever possible, I try to get clients to use my personal website and also make appointments. If they go through my website, I make 96.5% of their payout, plus I can hide the income from Uncle Sam. The camsites only pay me 28%, which officially constitutes as highway robbery. I charge $6.99 a minute. On a good month, I make around $55,000 and on a bad one, about $30,000.

Camming makes up seventy percent of my income; the rest comes from my website, which allows men to watch my live video feed. I broadcast at least four hours a day and charge subscribers twenty bucks a month. I wouldn't pay ten cents to watch me mas-turbate online, but apparently two hundred and fifty subscribers feel differently.

The $6.99 a minute grants clients the ability to bare their sex-ual secrets and fantasize to their heart's content, without fear of exposure or criticism. I don't judge the men and women who chat with me and reveal their secrets and perversions. How can I? My secret, my obsession, is worse than any of theirs. To contain it, I do the only thing I can. I lock myself up. And in doing so, I keep myself, and everyone else, safe.

Sometimes I allow myself to be delusional. To daydream. At those times I tell myself that one day I will be happy—that I am banking all of this money so I can move to the Caribbean and lie on the beach. But I know that if I did that, the sand would be cov-ered in blood soon enough.

I try to sleep at least eight hours a night. Nighttime is when I typically struggle the most. It is when I thirst for blood, for gore. So Simon Evans and me have an agreement. Simon lives three doors down from me in this shithole that we all call an apartment com-plex. He has, over the last three years, developed a strong addic-tion to prescription painkillers. I keep his medicine bottle filled, and he locks me up at night. My door is, without a doubt, the only one in the complex without a deadbolt switch on the inside.

I used to have Marilyn do it. She's a grandmotherly type who struggles by on the pittance that is her social security. She lives across from Simon. But Marilyn stressed out too much; she was always worried that I would have some personal emergency, or fire, or something, and would need to get out. I had to find some-one else. Because I worried over what was coming. At night, my fingers would start to itch, and I would come close to picking up that phone, to asking her to unlock my door. And then I would wait beside it, wait for the tumblers to move and my door to be unlocked. And when I opened it, when I saw Marilyn's lined and tired face, I would kill her. Not immediately. I would stab her a few times, leaving some life in her, and wait for her to run, to scream. I like the sound of screams—real screams, not the pathetic excuse that most movies tried to pass off as the sound of terror. Then I would chase her down and finish the job, as slowly as I could. Dragging out her pain, her agony, her realization that she had caused her own death. I had gotten to the point where I had picked out a knife, started to keep it in the cardboard box that sat by the door and held my outgoing mail and various crap. That was when I knew I was getting too close. That was when I picked Simon instead. Simon's addiction supersedes any concern he has for my well-being.